*Published by* **CIGNUS STUDIO**, *Columbus, OH*

Author photography by Harry Acosta. Cover art created by Roger Cunningham.

E-book ISBN no. 978-0-692-89033-2.

Print ISBN no. 978-1-54391-465-8.

# VEGA'S SANCTUM

CHANNING CHEA

# Contents

4

**Chapter 1**

# Graduate

The table was prepared.

The straps and buckles that were attached to it were unfastened and ready for the next person. It would only be used one time today, so the witnesses would be even more attentive than usual. Only Doctor Nathaniel Jones was in the room. He stood in the corner by the small workstation and prepped the necessary equipment. Only one syringe was needed. It was rather large, holding ten milliliters of a highly concentrated, translucent, yellow liquid. It glowed dimly, reminiscent of a glow stick. Doctor Jones inspected the entire area and made sure that everything was in order. He was ready.

Adjacent to the chamber was the witness room. Jones looked into the window and casually beckoned for the guards on the other side to come in with the prisoner. A moment later, three guards entered the room with a blindfolded and handcuffed man. Doctor Jones stood back and leaned against the workstation as the guards secured the prisoner onto the execution table. He wasn't really paying attention to the process; he had seen it many times before, and it was nothing special. Once they were finished, two guards stood on opposite ends of the window that the witnesses were looking through. The third stood by the door. Jones cleared his throat, picked up the syringe, and checked his watch. The time was 8:43 a.m.

"Okay, then," he said. "Shall we begin?" The young man on the table said nothing. Though the blindfold had been removed, he kept his eyes closed tightly. Jones saw moisture around his eyes and a slight twitch on his face. "Looks like you've done all the crying you were going to do earlier. All right, then."

Jones connected the EKG. He felt for the vein on his right arm, injected the liquid, and quickly wrapped the area so no blood would escape. It was done. Jones walked to the door and allowed the guard to open it for him. Before walking out of the room, he could hear the prisoner. His breaths were getting louder already. He knew the potion was taking effect. In the next room he saw that there would only be the usual four witnesses, including himself.

"Good morning, everyone," Jones said. All acknowledged him with a polite nod of the head. Catherine, a short blonde in her mid-thirties, was the first to respond.

"Good morning, Nathaniel," she said. "Did everything go well?"

"Oh, of course. Just as usual." Jones took a seat beside her. "The visium was very clean. I made sure that there was a fresh batch produced this morning just for the occasion. If anything, the dosage itself won't be the issue. But then again, it rarely ever is."

"That's true, I suppose."

"That's a fancy-looking suit you're wearing. Are you going to this man's funeral later?" Jones let out a sophisticated chuckle.

"Oh, no. I'm heading to a couple of other prisons later today, so I came prepared."

Out of their peripheral, they noticed the movement of the prisoner and both turned to watch. He was lifting his head up as far as it would reach and then dropping it back down, seemingly to fight off nausea. Everyone could see his chest rising and falling as he took deeper breaths. A full minute and a half had passed since the injection. The prisoner began to shake more prominently. Within the course of another minute, the shaking had gone from looking like a small seizure to a violent convulsion. They could hear screams through the window.

The stone-faced guards on the inside of the execution chamber began to wince just a little bit, but they did not lose composure. They knew it would be over soon. The four witnesses sat in the other room analyzing the scene. Hopefully, they would see something new, something that was out of the ordinary and different from what they had seen before. Nothing. The man screamed and screamed. Saliva poured from his mouth as he kept swinging his head around and convulsing. He let out a final shout.

The man's body stopped moving. The EKG showed a flat line. The execution was complete, but the experiment had failed again. Jael Moriz, who had been sitting on the far end of the witness room, let out a disappointed grunt.

"Ugh, damn it. Log it, Jones," He exaggerated with his raspy voice.

"Yes sir, Warden. Time of death: 8:48 a.m." Jones wrote the information down on a document containing the prisoner's information and signed it. "He lasted a full five minutes. That seems to be slightly shorter than the usual duration of the trials, but that can most likely be blamed on the fact that I concentrated quite a bit more visium into this dose. I'll switch the formula back for the next trial and observe from there so I can—"

"The point is to get them to live," Moriz interrupted, "not drag out the execution for longer."

Vasya Negatov sat in the back of the room. He remained silent while they conversed.

"I understand that, Warden. But I'm sure I don't have to remind you that I can only hold trials during a scheduled execution. There isn't very much room for leeway if we intend to keep this confidential, you know."

"Quit making excuses, Jones! We've had nearly a decade to get this right, and we haven't gotten far. I don't think you have *any* excuses for the lack of progress."

"That's not entirely the case. Recently, we've been able to deduce that the visium concentration itself is not the main dilemma. From what we *have* accomplished we can say that factor that determines the success is in the subjects themselves."

"Catherine has been able to draft above exceptional convicts so you can have whatever variety you need to choose from. In fact, doesn't she choose people based on the criteria you give her?"

"I'm not blaming Catherine for anything, sir…" Jones said. He was beginning to lose his cheerfulness. Out of discomfort from hearing her name brought into the conversation, Catherine intervened in an attempt to ease the tension.

"Jael, please relax," she said. "Like Nathaniel mentioned, we have had some pretty compelling and reassuring progress up to this point."

"Not nearly enough if you ask me," Moriz said. "You're wasting all of our time with this—"

"That's enough, gentlemen," called the deep voice from the back of the room. Negatov did not stand nor raise his voice, but the gravity of his words could still be felt. It was difficult not to sound intimidating through his Russian accent. All stopped and turned towards him. "Both Doctor Jones and Catherine are doing their job as asked of them." A feeling of relief waved over the two.

"...Yes. Sorry, sir," Moriz said keeping himself in check.

"Overlooked," Negatov said. He slowly stood to his feet and took a deep breath before speaking again. "This process has been rather frustrating, but you have no reason to be any more impatient than I." Negatov looked over their heads to view the execution chamber again. The guards had just finished putting the body in the cadaver pouch and were locking up the room.

Moriz, Catherine, and Jones were all standing straight up and facing Negatov, as if they were waiting for their next orders.

"We have three more scheduled executions to conduct this week," Negatov announced. "This is just another failure that we will learn from. What is the status on Project Arbo?" Negatov directed the question toward Jones. He was happy to have an answer.

"Arbo is still alive! He has shown a slight decline in his health, but we cannot confirm whether that is from the visium injection, or just from his emotional state."

"Good," Negatov said. He then turned toward Moriz. "More importantly, has he been telling anyone about his experience?" Moriz gave him as clear and convicting of an answer as he could.

"We have been keeping a close watch on his communication

with the other inmates. Fortunately, he's not the social type. The most he's done is brag to those who confront him about how he survived the execution attempt, and how we let him live because of it. It appears that even the girl he spends most of his leisure time with doesn't know anything. It surprises me that he hasn't informed her yet. In any case, that thug only knows that he was given the name 'Arbo', besides that, he doesn't know much of anything. He isn't even aware of what we injected him with."

Negatov nodded in approval.

"There is only one thing that comes to my attention," Moriz continued. "Inmate Lynx frequently speaks with Arbo. The two never spoke before Arbo's execution trial."

Negatov's eyes narrowed. He was silent as he processed the information.

"Wait, you mean…Jack…no, Jason Lynx?" Catherine asked. "That guy creeps me out. I remember hearing that he was some sort of genius when I found him."

"I've noticed him around the prison myself," Jones said. "He seems like the schemer type, but I doubt he's any real problem."

"He can be as suspicious as he wants," Negatov declared. "He is no threat to us. Even if he did begin to do something problematic, we would only need to place him in isolation, but that doesn't seem to be necessary."

"Well, he is here to be executed, if he gets out of hand, couldn't we just—"

"No!" Negatov's voice shook the room and was filled with disgust. "We cannot risk tarnishing Sanctum's reputation by making it known that we killed someone because we couldn't handle him. Lynx will be observed and dealt with accordingly."

"Y-yes sir," Jones responded.

Negatov began to make his way toward the exit.

"Are there any other issues that must be addressed?" No one

responded. "I have an interview later today. I will be on television. I trust you can handle the place while I'm gone, Warden?"

"Of course, sir," Moriz said.

"Good. I'll see you all at the next trial."

It was 9:15 on a Monday morning and Chad Galen did not have school. School was a thing of the past for him now. There were no more buses to catch, no more homework due, and no more teenage drama. Those are all perks of being a high school graduate, and another perk was being able to consider waking up at 9:15 in the morning sleeping in. Chad looked at the clock, partly disappointed that he couldn't sleep until 3:30 in the afternoon or something outlandish like that. But since he was awake, and there was no immediate need to get dressed, he just lied in bed, staring at the ceiling.

It was peaceful outside, and it was peaceful in his home. He wasn't used to this kind of silence in the apartment. He figured both of his parents were gone by now, which was a blessing all on its own. He had the place to himself. That called for a celebration. *I'll nap to that,* he thought. He put his hands behind his head and lied back against the pillow. He began to drift off into snooze mode and felt the essence of what it truly meant to be chillin'.

Four loud beeps from his phone ruined the atmosphere he created in his mind. With a scowl on his face, he leaned over and picked up his phone. It was Ricky.

"Yo, you awake?" Ricky's text message said.

"...No." Chad locked the phone and lied down again. He tried to find his happy place again inside of his eyelids, but he wasn't really tired anymore. Another four beeps pierced the air. Chad checked his phone again.

"Easton. 20 min." Chad winced at his phone, making sure that he wasn't reading it wrong. *Who the hell does he think he is waking me up and talking about going to the mall this early?* he thought. *Lucky for him, I'm awake now.* Chad had nothing planned that day anyway so he supposed it worked out for him. He would just chew Ricky out for texting him so early when he saw him later.

"Alright, come get me," he responded. Chad went through his morning routine of showering, brushing his teeth and picking out clothes. He dressed casually, but nice, as if he were going to a party. That's what life was going to be from now on. A pair of Eddie Bauer jeans and a button shirt from Calvin Klein would do the trick. When Ricky arrived Chad walked out the front door, only this time he wouldn't need a book bag. Knowing that he left his books at home never felt so comforting. Chad got in Ricky's car. It was a newer hybrid coupe that ran on electricity and visium; a special gift from his parents.

"Ehh, whuz good, bro?" Ricky asked.

"Nothin' much." He almost mentioned the early text message, but he wanted to hear Ricky's excuse first. "So, why in the world are we going to Easton now?" he asked with emphasized curiosity.

"The new IHOP is opening down there. Karli and Chris are meeting us down there. They're giving away free pancakes all morning."

All was forgiven. That whole early-text thing was twenty minutes ago anyway. Chad was over it.

"Ah, I see. Well, if that's the case, I'll take the opportunity to reveal my good news to everyone there!"

"What good news? Oh yeah, you never told us what school you're going to yet. Where are you going?"

"No spoilers. I'm not saying a word until those pancakes you say we're getting hit my stomach. Then I'll tell all." On the way to IHOP Chad couldn't stop grinning. Despite being on the passenger's side of his best friend's ride, he felt like more than just a scrub. Nothing was stopping his world from expanding now, and he couldn't wait to deliver the good news. Arriving at the restaurant, they saw customers lined up outside of the entrance waiting to get in.

"Don't worry," Ricky said. "Chris already got us a seat."

"Boss status." Passing a group of hungry and frustrated customers to get to his own seat only added to Chad's self-esteem. Ricky and Chad walked in and were flagged down by Chris and Karli, both of whom had already ordered their food.

"Well, thanks for waiting for us, guys," Chad said sarcastically after sitting. "What polite friends you are."

"Oh, no problem," Karli said. "We couldn't start without our guests of honor."

"Pshh, I wasn't holdin' out on my food any longer," Chris laughed. "If you were as hungry as I am you'd understand. And by the way, we're picking up your bill today as a graduation present, so don't complain."

"Wow, how nice of you to pay for my free pancakes," Chad said. "I don't know what I'd do without you guys." Ricky and Chad ordered their food. Once everyone was finished Chad took a butter knife and loudly tapped it against his empty glass of water, inadvertently grabbing the attention of everyone in that area. "Ahem! Gentlemen… and Karli, I have a formal announcement to make." The other customers turned back in their seats when they realized that they weren't included. "Now, as you know I've been receiving offers to quite a few schools, both in and out of state. And I've finally made my decision."

"Ten bucks says he's staying here in Ohio," Chris said.

"Why would he stay here when he could go anywhere else?" Ricky said.

"'Cause the schools here are amazing! And he's not gonna leave his friends," Chris exclaimed. Chad cleared his throat. He almost didn't want to say anything now.

"Shh, let him finish," Karli said excitedly. "Go ahead, Chad."

"Umm, right. Thank you, Karli." Chad paused for a moment. "Well, I hate to break it to you, but I'm definitely not staying here." There was a short silence at the table.

"Figures," Ricky said. "I had a feeling you were headed off somewhere else."

"That's bull," Chris said with a scowl on his face so pronounced one would think he had just been slapped.

"Chill, Chris," Karli said. "At least hear where he's going instead."

"I don't care, man. There's no good reason at all to be leavin' here." Not at all surprised by Chris's reaction, Chad continued.

"I'm going to USC. I'll be living in the dorms and everything."

"That's freakin' sweet, bro," Ricky said. "When are you gonna leave?"

"Sometime within the next couple months. I have a crap-load of money saved up from both work and graduation. Once I get out there I'll probably get a car off Craigslist or something like that."

"That's awesome man. I'm happy for you," Ricky said. Not everyone felt the same. Chris's eyes pierced over the table, but Chad just avoided them and kept the conversation going with some extra enthusiasm to offset the tension.

"While I'm there I'll go out for a Basketball team or something," he said. "I may not be good enough for Division-1 ball, but I'm sure they must have some mini league so I can keep myself in shape." Chad hoped that Chris would have encouraged him to go out for the team, but he still received no reaction. "There is a Metaphysics club out there, too. I've heard they actually teach people how to move matter with their mind! I'm definitely joining that." Chris finally broke his glare and began to completely ignore Chad altogether. He was the only guy Chad knew who actually used the silent treatment.

"You really think you're gonna learn to do that kind of crap?" Karli asked. "You know that stuff isn't real."

"Yeah, it is," Chad argued. "I know I've told you before that Psychokinesis is real. Either way, it's not like it's my major or anything. It's just going to be my hobby while I'm there. That and a little hiking on the side."

"So I'm guessing you decided your major, too?" Ricky asked.

"Well, not really... I mean, I'll just stick with a Physical Science Major for now, but I really don't know what I wanna do with myself yet."

"Yeah, Physical Science would *so* be your thing," Karli said. "You're pretty good at science and all that stuff anyway."

Chris finally broke his silence.

"You know good and well your parents aren't letting you go anywhere," he said.

Chad's heart felt like it skipped a beat for a moment. He chose not to remember his parents. Just the mentioning of their possible reaction nearly ruined the entire morning. Chad toned his attitude down to something more serious.

"I'm not worried about them," Chad responded.

"What makes you think they're going to let you leave without their permission?" Chris asked.

"It doesn't matter. They won't even know about it."

"And you're just going to run away without them knowing? Your dad will hunt you down and only God knows what he'll do to you then."

"Dude, shut up. It isn't his problem anymore. I've worked hard to get a full-ride at USC and that's where I'm going. My dad will never see the tuition, he'll never need to know where I went, and he'll never be able to touch me again."

Chris took a deep breath and calmed down, realizing he was causing a lot of tension at the table. After seeing Chris's change in energy, everyone at the table was at ease, just for a moment.

"Dude your dad's crazy as hell," Chris continued in a more agreeable tone. "I'm not gonna lie, I don't want you gone, but I don't want anything crazy to happen to you either."

"I see what he's saying," Ricky chimed in. "It might be the best idea to just let your parents know the situation, even if it's just to let them know you're thinking about leaving." Karli and Chris nodded in agreement. Chad was silent for a moment and looked down onto his plate. There was ketchup from the hash browns he ate smeared across it. Thin, runny tomato juice from the condiment flowed from one end of the plate to another. The red coloring looked vaguely familiar.

"Sorry, I'm not going to risk that," Chad said. He remembered the stains on the carpet at home that he was once forced to clean up. The stains that appeared after his mother told his father she wanted a divorce. All he could remember from that day were the red streaks of blood across the carpet. It was more of a reminder than he wanted. "I don't want there to be any unnecessary drama. I love you guys, but I have to do what's right for me. This is likely the safest choice for me."

"Okay... I understand, I guess." Chris said. Chad could hear disappointment in his voice.

"What will happen with your mom when you leave?" Karli asked.

"Ugh, damn... I don't know," Chad said. He hadn't thought about that. But in all truth, he didn't care very much. She had fought with that man for this long; he was just hoping that she would find her way out like he was going to. As far as Chad was concerned, his father was no longer a factor in his life once school started. "I bet she'll work it out," was all he could say. In his opinion, it was all that needed to be said.

"How'd you manage to get out of the house today anyway?" Ricky asked.

"They were both out when I woke up. For once, I didn't hear any yelling going on, so I could actually sleep in. Or at least I would've been able to sleep in if you didn't text me at the crack of dawn like we were on a mission to find pancakes."

"Oh, my bad," Ricky said. "Next time I'll just leave your non-drivin' ass at home, I just thought that pancakes would have been important to a foodie like you."

"Well, thank you for thinking about me," Chad laughed. Finally, there was a chance to laugh again. It was never fun to be serious for so long. Everyone welcomed the opportunity to lighten the mood. "Welp, I officially have all day. Who's up for prank calls using the Apple store iPhones?"

"Chad, it's like ten o'clock," Karli said. "Why would we go to the mall now? There's nothing to do and most of the stores probably haven't even opened yet."

"Let's just head back home," Chris suggested. "We can hang out at my place. Oh, I know what we can do! We need to find Chad a girl to have a fling with before he leaves. I'm sure *some* girl around here is desperate enough to do something with him."

"Funny…" Chad said. "As much as I would love to impregnate some girl and get stuck here having to raise some kid, I'd rather wait until I get to USC before I deal with any baby-mama-drama."

"Dang," Chris said. "He caught on to my plan." Everyone laughed. After the bill had been paid, everyone made their way to the parking lot. "Karli, I'm going to ride with Chad and Ricky," Chris said. "We'll meet you at my house." With the plan set, they drove back to Violet City.

Chad glared outside the window on the ride home. He sat in the backseat, so neither Chris nor Ricky could see the sentimental expression on his face. The ride back home was about twenty minutes from the mall, a moderately long drive for any trip in Ohio. But for the first time, the ride seemed too short to enjoy. He wanted to savor the scenery for longer.

"Things are gettin' real now," Chad said. "It's finally starting to hit me that it'll be a long time before I get to do any of this stuff with you guys again."

"I thought you said you don't leave for another couple months," Ricky said shooting his eyes back and forth between the road and the rear-view mirror.

"I don't, but still, I can't believe it's finally happening. I'm finally leaving this place and starting over."

"That's why we wanted to give you that now," Chris said. He turned over his left shoulder and nodded a gesture toward a box that laid in the backseat beside Chad. The box was white, and it was smaller than the average sized pillow, but it still took up a good amount of space in the seat. Chad couldn't figure out how he had missed its presence before.

"That?" Chad picked up the box with caution. It looked like it could have been a box of cupcakes, but it was too lightweight.

"We all pitched in to get it for you, as your REAL graduation gift," Chris said. "But since you're goin' to California, I don't know if you'll need it."

Chad shook the box firmly, like a boy shaking his wrapped Christmas present to assess its contents. "Haha, what is it, a sweater?" Chad joked. After taking a couple wild guesses, he sat the box on his lap and slid the top cover off of the bottom. Tissue paper concealed the hidden item. Chad removed the paper and revealed the article of clothing that lay beneath.

Chad had been waiting for this. He pulled from the box a black North Face vest. He recognized every detail of the sleeveless jacket to its fullest. The vest was lightweight and soft-shelled. From the smooth texture of its fabric, Chad could tell it was the weatherproof model. It felt like it could be worn in the middle of a hurricane and could still come out of it dry. There were three pockets on the vest; two on either side, in the normal torso areas, and one more over the left side of the chest. The zippers—zippers that were all a deep, but glowing red—were positioned vertically on the vest. It was the one Chad knew as the Apex Bionic, and it was now his.

Ricky and Chris watched as Chad admired his gift, Ricky through the rearview mirror and Chris from over his shoulder. They could feel Chad's gratitude as a series of 'wow's and 'whoa's escaped his mouth.

"You're welcome," Ricky said with a smile.

"Haha! Oh, wow. Thanks!" Chad iterated his words through his excitement. Not wasting any more time looking at it, he slipped the vest on while still in the car and zipped it up. It fit perfectly. Even if it didn't, there was no returning it now. "Trust me, I'll have plenty of chances to use this."

"Just in case we don't get the chance later," Chris added, "I wanted to let you know that I'll be pullin' for ya while you're in Cali... though I really don't want you to leave. But if something happens and things don't work out, you're more than welcome to come back and stay with us here."

"Aww, dude, thanks. But where would I stay?" Chad asked.

"We're all going to move in together during this fall. We were actually going to invite you to move in with us, but it didn't really seem necessary after your big news about USC."

"Yeah, Chris, Chad's definitely not coming back," Ricky said. "Why in the world would he move away from freakin' Cali to stay with our broke asses?"

"I never said he would," Chris retorted. "But shit happens, Ricky. I'm just sayin' if he ends up getting kicked out or things don't go well for him, then coming back can be an option."

"He's too smart to get kicked out of USC," Ricky said. "Quit trying to jinx him."

"I'm not trying to jinx him, idiot. I'm just trying to be a good friend. Why don't you offer him something nice?" Chad sat back in his seat watched the two go back and forth like it was a movie. It was always entertaining to listen to them argue. This was one of the treasures that he wouldn't forget when he was gone.

"I'm gonna miss you dumbasses." Chad laughed. "I really do appreciate the offer, but I'm not going to get in the way of your—"

"We're not letting you go back to your dad," Chris said with a definite conviction. "Once you make this move, there's no going back there and you know it."

"I guess you're right," Chad said. *There's no arguing with that logic.* His father didn't particularly threaten Chad when it came to a comparison of physical condition. Chad was far more athletic. Even when it came to combat, Chad even had a couple years of martial arts training under his belt. What bothered him the most about his father was that his random acts of violence came without any warning, and when they came, it was with a fury.

"Could you, by any chance, warn your neighbors about the crap your dad does," Ricky asked. "Maybe if they knew what was going on they would at least step in." Chad paused for a moment and began to consider it, but only for a moment.

Often times the neighbors would get involved, but the furthest they would ever interject would be coming to the door and asking if everything was okay. They never actually saw what happened behind closed doors. Chad never knew what influenced the neighbors to come over. He supposed the obvious signs of a struggle: the distressed shouts, the sound of furniture being damaged, and the occasional broken window would be more than enough to assume the worst. Despite those seemingly obvious signs, they did nothing to help. Maybe it wasn't their place to save him. Maybe they just wanted him to finally step up and fight back when the time came. Was that their way of helping or were they just too afraid of getting involved? No matter what they thought they were doing, they could have helped… but they didn't. And Chad despised them for that.

"No," Chad answered. "I wouldn't be able to trust them to do that."

That was the world that Chad just wanted to leave behind. Whether he could forgive his neighbors for not being good Samaritans, or his father for being the loony he was, or his mother for creating a family with a man such as his father; soon enough, none of them would be a factor in his life. Chad just kept telling himself that. *Just hold on for two more months.*

"Could you do me a favor," Chad asked. "Drop me by my house."

"Why?" Ricky asked.

"I need a little time to clear my head."

"So I guess that means you're going on a hike then," Ricky concluded.

"You're not comin' over?" Chris asked in a tone that revealed a clear disappointment.

"I'll ride down to the mall with you guys later," Chad said, "but now I just need to take a walk." Ricky agreed, and after they reentered Violet City's limits he drove into Chad's apartment complex. "I'll catch up with you guys later."

Walking back to the apartment door, Chad couldn't ignore the good points Chris brought up. It may not be in his best interest to disregard his parents. Not that they were the smartest people on the planet, but there were many signs that pointed to the fact that Chad was looking for schools that were out-of-state. On top of that, Chad was always able to tell when someone had been in his room, at his desk, or even on his computer. It was like a sixth sense. All teenagers had it. Clearly, someone had been going into his room and looking at the search history.

Searches for apartments, cars, schools, and job postings were all listed in Google's history, but Chad knew which sites he traveled to first. It was suspicious that some sites were out of order. Someone didn't trust him. Someone knew his plans. That in mind, Chad knew that it wouldn't be wisest to pretend that his parents were oblivious to the great exodus that he was planning. He would have to rethink his strategy. It was time for a walk. And it was time to try out his new vest in the field.

## Chapter 2

# Confrontation

Chad unlocked the front door and walked into the apartment. There was no immediate sign of anyone's presence, but the television was on. *I don't remember turning that on.* Chad stood completely still, hoping that whoever was sitting in the family room did not hear his entry. The channel was turned to CNN. Only someone as boring as his mother would be watching the news.

"Chad!" called the voice from around the corner of the hallway. Chad exaggerated a dismaying grunt and closed the open doorway behind him. "Where did you go?" asked the voice.

"With Ricky. To IHOP." There was a silence. Chad took the lack of response as his opportunity to get to his room before more conversation began. The staircase was awkwardly placed adjacent to the front door. Chad never appreciated the placement of the stairs until now. He tip-toed up a few of the stairs before he heard the volume of the TV lower.

"Come here for a sec," The voice called again. Chad swore under his breath and made his way back downstairs and into the family room. He saw his mom sitting on the sofa in her usual attire; a pair of lounging pants, slippers, and a very loose T-shirt. It wasn't much of a wardrobe, but playing the role of the housewife didn't call for anything more. She smiled as Chad came around the corner. "I didn't hear you leave this morning. You didn't say good morning."

"I didn't know you were here," Chad said.

"Remember Miss Vonda next door? She came by earlier to give you a graduation gift but she missed you. I told her to check back later tonight."

"Okay. I'm about to go on a hike, so I gotta go..."

"Can we chat for a bit first?" she asked. The thought made Chad cringe. The last thing he wanted to do was spend quality time with his mother. It was a sentiment he never understood. He thought of a quick excuse as to why he couldn't stay, and then she pleaded again. "Vasya Negatov is about to have a press conference about the next phase of the Renaissance. Isn't he one of your heroes?"

Chad shifted his head to the television. The next image that appeared on the television was a podium. A microphone stood erect on top of it.

"Press conferences bore the crap outta me," he said. "I find it hard to entertain myself with anything old people talk about behind a podium."

"But you *have* to see this one," his mom uttered with an emphasized enthusiasm. "Especially if you're gonna major in Physical Science at USC." The words came out of her mouth in a coy fashion, so coy that Chad felt both exposed and annoyed. "When were you planning on telling us?"

"Why were you going through my stuff?" Chad retorted in defense.

"It was your father," she said. "He wanted to know what you were planning for college."

"Why didn't his crazy ass ask me?"

"I don't know, Chad... you know him."

"I don't care, he doesn't have any business going through my stuff!" Chad raised his voice louder and louder. He knew it was an easy way to get his mother to crumble in confrontations. He had seen it work enough times before.

"You should have told us, and you know this." It wasn't working this time. Chad had no idea of what to say, so he turned his attention to the only logical distraction he could find: the television.

"Vasya Negatov is about to talk," Chad said. To his surprise, his mother welcomed the distraction, also looking for a way out of the immediate conflict.

Standing behind the brown podium was a man that was clearly taller than everyone in the room. At first glance, if nothing else, the first thing that Chad could tell about the man by looking at his face was that he was European. The second thing he could tell from seeing his wardrobe was that he had money. The man didn't wear a normal suit. Instead, he only wore a dark-colored blazer over top of a white, casual, button-less shirt that fit tightly on his chest. It was as if the man was trying to make a statement about how big he was in both physicality and status. Chad even read his body language. He almost seemed too old to have that kind of confidence and energy about himself.

In the lower third section of the television screen, a text read "Dr. Vasya Negatov: Engineer and Entrepreneur". After reading that, Chad realized who the man was. Seeing what he looks like over the television was surprisingly different from how Chad had envisioned him. But still, it would have been a crime not to recognize him. The name had been nearly synonymous with the terms "future" and "energy" and "new era". At some point in high school education, he and all his friends had written a report on something this very man had done. Since they lived in a state that was so relevant to his work, they heard about his achievements more than any other student in the country.

The event was a press conference, but journalists and other spectators still did not hesitate to applaud the man as he stepped to the podium.

"I almost didn't recognize him," Chad said making sure that he successfully changed the subject. "That guy was on the cover of the Forbes Magazine I saw at Barnes & Noble one day. This guy is like Donald Trump rich, or maybe even Bill Gates by now."

"I haven't seen the man in an actual interview before either," his mother added. "Let's see if he has anything cool to say."

"He most likely will," Chad said agreeably. He may not have enjoyed watching news conferences, but Chad did want to be caught up on current events; particularly, big events in the science community. Vasya Negatov was as influential to a tech-enthusiast as Steve Jobs.

Chad knew that whenever Negatov made an announcement, it was always a big deal, and it always takes the Visium Renaissance in a 'whole new direction'.

The studio was surprisingly smaller than Negatov had expected. He had been in conferences with many more people in the audience than this. This stage only had the camera production crew, a few dozen lights, three cameras, and a stained-wood podium that was brightly lit in the middle of the set. It wasn't the most interesting setting for a conference, but he would only be there for a short time. Immediately after taking his place on the podium, the journalists got down to the heart of the matter.

"Doctor Negatov," one man began, "could you please tell us about some of NegaLabs' most recent projects?"

"There are a few newer projects I have been working on," Negatov said. "A few months ago, I began conducting experiments on portable devices in an attempt to replace lithium-ion and other rechargeable batteries with a longer lasting, visium-powered energy source. Recently, I finally signed a contract with multiple cellular phone manufacturers to use the visium-powered solution in all of their portable devices. Phones, tablet notebooks, laptops, and other such devices will now have batteries that last for up to fifty hours at a time between charges." The audience gasped and gave applause. Negatov expected such a reaction. Despite his satisfaction, he couldn't help but become slightly annoyed with the group of journalists. It seemed unprofessional of them to give such a reaction while he was still talking. He spoke casually, without the excitement one would expect to see from a man who is pulling in millions of dollars a year for his contraptions. His accent gave his delivery all the suspense it needed.

"Additionally," he continued, "a contract with General Motors has also been written. The same technology will be used in car batteries in order to reduce the need for gasoline and increase the efficiency of electric cars in the wintertime. I predict that the gasoline will no longer be a necessity for vehicles in another eight years or so." The jaws of everyone in the audience dropped, and there was another applause. He still wasn't finished. How rude of them. "Novadyne, Inc, the Japanese cybernetics and robotics company, has also been one of my main focuses over the last few months. The Nova Limb, which is their most acclaimed technology, is a robotic armor that was designed for assisted living and military purposes. Its main flaw was its inability to maintain power over a long period of time. The same technology that will be used for the new portable electronic devices will also be used for Novadyne's Nova suits, and that will finally prepare it for mass-production around the world."

The audience barely let him finish before they cheered to the top of their lungs. It was as if Oprah Winfrey was giving everyone there a new car. Even so, Negatov was not fazed by the people's reaction. It wasn't the first time he had delivered big news to people. He had done it so much that seeing people's reactions began to bore him. The longer they cheered, the longer he would have to wait before he could finish his speech.

"I know that questions have been raised recently about whether visium can be used on people," commented an older female reporter in the front. "Will it be used in the medical field for any purpose?"

"Unfortunately, not. As of today, there have been no conclusive studies on the effects that visium has on human beings, or any living organism. However, it is safe to assume now that visium has lethal effects on people like you and me." The demeanor changed slightly on Negatov's face. It would be the same woman to ask the seemingly obligatory question.

"I had the honor of meeting your wife before she passed," she said. "Is it true that you believe the overexposure to visium is what caused her illness?" Negatov answered without any hesitation or apparent grieving.

"The autopsy conducted on Celeste revealed that an excessive amount of visium was found in her bloodstream. I think that is more than enough reason to believe that the element should not be used on humans. Now, that maybe bad news to some, but given the direction the Visium Renaissance is headed, I don't think too many people will be disappointed with the progress my company has made."

On that note, the reporters felt it was time to switch gears.

"I keep hearing you say 'I' instead of 'we' when you talk about the new products the company is releasing," a reporter said jokingly. "Do your workers get jealous when you take all the credit like that?"

"They probably would if they existed," Negatov smirked. "I have people that take care of most of my legal work for me, but when it comes to the engineering itself, I'm the only one who experiments using my own facility."

"Is that ever difficult for you?" the reporter asked.

"Not in the least. If I ever need assistance I can rely on my good friend Jael Moriz to lend me a hand. He's always been a great aide."

"How does Moriz find time to help you when he's so busy running a prison?" asked a random voice. "Of all places, Sanctum doesn't seem like the type of prison that can go a day without its Warden. How does he manage?"

"As Jael would tell you, Sanctum is much easier to handle than most prisons. Though the only criminals that go there are on death row, there are only several-hundred inmates there in total. Furthermore, security is state of the art. It's quite impressive. I go there from time to time to visit Jael."

"What is the relationship between Sanctum and your company?" another man asked. Negatov was careful to answer this question.

"NegaLabs and Sanctum have no legal affiliation. Sanctum inmates do collect and mine samples of visium for my company to process and work with, but there is no relationship between the two beyond that." If there was only one thing Negatov wanted to clarify to the people watching this show, the absence of affiliation between him and Sanctum would be it. He could not have his name associated with death. He also could not allow Sanctum's reputation to fall below anything less than an exceptional prison.

"There are many people who think you are monopolizing the distribution of visium," another reporter stated. "What do you have to say to those who think that?" Damn those old reporters. They always asked the tough questions, and that was one of the toughest questions Negatov ever had to answer over the years. However, he was prepared.

"I'm honored that the government trusted me with full authority over the excavation and distribution of the visium, but I'm not in this to make a profit. I'm here doing my job. Taking the visium and finding the best possible application for it. That is my goal, and I plan to make the world a better place." The reporter nodded, and Negatov took that as a sign that his speech made his point. It had held up over the years, so there was no reason to change it. In any case, the most difficult part of the press conference was over. He retained the love from his supporters.

Once the conference ended, the crowd applauded and the program cut to a commercial break. Negatov did not stay at the studio for the remainder of the show. He only said his polite goodbyes and left. Outside of the studio, a black limousine was waiting for him. After pulling off Negatov was quiet. He did not turn on the radio. He did not look out of the window. He only gazed at his hand, to the diamond ring on his finger. It had been a long time since someone had mentioned Celeste in an interview; it took him by surprise. He clenched his fist tightly and slowly neared his hand to his face until the ring touched just between his lips.

"People act like he's the President," Chad said. "Those people love him so much, God forbid he actually runs for office. He may pull a Schwarzenegger and take over a state."

"Yeah. Well, he would be more prepared for it than anyone," his mother said. "The Russian Einstein there has an IQ of like 140 or something ridiculous like that. I saw it on TV a while ago."

"Okay… Well, I'm going for a walk." Chad walked away as

quickly and casually as he could.

"Wait!" Chad halted where he was and grunted. He was so close. "I'm proud of you," his mother said after grabbing his attention. Chad stood where he was but did not turn around. There wasn't much he wanted to hear from his mother, but for some reason, those words struck a nerve. Was it a trick to get him to stay?

"I'm still leaving," he said.

"Good," she responded. "I'm glad that you can get away from here." Chad heard her voice begin to waiver. Tears were surely welling, but Chad wasn't very impressed by her performance. He started for the stairs again, and his mother did not stop him.

Chad closed his bedroom door when he entered. He was used to his mother saying random things to him, but that was weird. He never knew that she really cared about him. But Chad's definition of caring was different from what he saw from his mother. His mother could not protect him from his father, nor could she protect herself. It was hard to take those words seriously. *I'm proud of you.* How dare she pretend to care for him now after all these years? If she truly cared for her son, or for herself, she would have tried to escape the hell she allowed her reality to become. It wasn't that difficult. It couldn't have been that difficult. Chad planned his own escape because he chose to protect what was precious to him: his future. His mother had no excuse to not try the same.

In any case, those were not the thoughts Chad needed to concern himself with now. It was time for his walk. It was time for him to clear his head and protect something else that was precious to him: his sanity. Chad changed out of his dress-casual clothes and into his hiking gear. Timberland hike boots, Eddie Bauer pants, and now his new vest to complete the wardrobe. It may not have been the most stylish of outfits, but Chad was going for functionality more than fashion. If it was any consolation, all of his gear was dark-gray and black in color. So no one could say he wasn't matching.

In reality, Chad knew it was overkill. There weren't any real hiking trails for miles from where he was in Ohio, but the stream behind his apartment was covered in foliage. Just enough to justify wearing nylon and spandex pants. It took true dedication for that.

After he was done suiting up, he stealthily made his way down the steps and out the front door. The hard part was over, but now for the fun part. Chad walked over to the small cliff behind his apartment. He gazed downward. The stream was about a half-mile ahead of him, and below were three small ledges, each a ten-foot drop from the next. To anyone else it was suicide, but to Chad it was a staircase.

He leaped down to the first ledge, and immediately jumped to the second, then to the third. He finished his performance with a parkour roll at the grassy floor underneath the third ledge. He turned back to look at the distance he just jumped from, and with a satisfied smile, he brushed the dirt from his vest and headed for the stream. Walking through the greens of a forest was a sure way to remind him how far away he was from any distractions of the world. The sounds of leaves being blown in the wind, the smell from the leaves that the wind carries onward, the sound of water cascading off rocks, these were the sounds of peace; the same sounds that kept Chad sane throughout his life.

He arrived at the stream and took a seat on a rock. His rock. The rock of decision making. The rock of meditation. All issues of the world were contemplated on this rock, and this is where he would take another look at his life. He closed his eyes and covered himself with the sounds of nature around him. His body was still; his head was calm. It was time to pose the question to himself. *My dad knows about my plan to leave, but does he know when I'm leaving?*

An hour passed.

Two hours passed.

Chad came to only one conclusion: he had to assume the worst; that his father knew everything. That means the night of Chad's exodus would be moved up in date. Rather sooner than later. He had the money for the trip, now he just had to make the trip happen. The next step in the process was figuring out how.

Four piercing beeps from his cell phone broke his train of thought. He pulled the phone out of his chest pocket and read the text message. It was from Ricky again.

"Change of plans. Meet at Steak&Shake in 1 hour."

"Fine," responded Chad. He checked the time. He always surprised himself when it came to how long he could meditate without disturbance. He felt like a master of his mind. But he spent enough time admiring himself. He stood from his rock, wiped the dirt off his butt—which was now numb from sitting—and ventured home. He had to take the longer path home, especially since there was no adventurous way to climb the cliff he jumped down without the possibility of falling backward and landing on his neck. He didn't want to worry about a hospital bill before he left for college.

Chad walked to his apartment and saw his father's car in the driveway. He kept his glance forward and kept walking past the car. He would have showered, but the last thing he wanted to deal with was his father at the moment. He was fine with eating lunch in his hiking gear. Chad walked to the restaurant and waited outside in the parking lot until everyone arrived.

Everyone rode together in Ricky's car. As small as the car was, no one else felt like wasting the gas to get to the restaurant, so by a popular vote Ricky was elected the driver for the remainder of the night. He wasn't very thrilled to be given the job, but it wasn't the first time it happened. He was almost used to it by now. When they arrived at the restaurant, Chad walked to the car and greeted them.

"I just realized that going to the mall on a Monday night probably won't be such a fun idea after all," Chad said. "Good call."

"I figured you'd be up for a burger after a hike anyway," said Ricky.

They were quickly seated after walking in. They were in a booth in the middle of the restaurant, which gave them a fairly good view of the space around them. Chad immediately began to scout the area, turning his head just enough to be able to see everyone in the area out of the corner of his eyes. After five short seconds, Chad spoke.

"Chris, Ricky, check it out," he whispered. "...back, left corner of the restaurant, by the door... two sexy girls sitting with some dude. He has small hands… could be a gay friend." Chris and Ricky tried their best to keep from laughing.

"Oh my goodness, Chad," Karli said. "Can't we just eat without you having to flirt with some girl?"

"No. Shh. Look at the table closest to the kitchen. One more girl… sitting alone, I think she ordered take-out… And three more girls in a group sitting by the window to our right."

"Are you gonna say something to them?" Chris asked.

"Naaw," Chad said, "I'm just considering my options. I'm going for the hot waitress. I guess I deserve a little fun before I leave. Here she comes."

"How are you guys doing today?" asked the blonde. From the quick look Chad took of her, she seemed to be around 5"7', and definitely to Chad's liking. He was the first person to say something at the table.

"We're doing fabulous today!" Chad said. "What about yourself?" Chad's energy was so exaggerated and enthusiastic that it was obvious that his intentions were obvious.

"I'm pretty good," she chuckled. She didn't seem to mind. "My name's Alexa, and I'll be taking care of you guys this evening."

"Wait… Alexa? Haven't I met you before?" Chad asked. Chris, Ricky, and Karli couldn't tell if Chad was being serious or just trying to drag out the conversation. They assumed the latter.

"Uhm… I don't know," she said.

"Aren't you a cheerleader at the high school?"

"Well, yea. I mean, I was. I just graduated last week."

"Oh, I thought I recognized you! I used to play basketball for the school team. I was on Varsity: Chad Galen."

"Oh yeah, I remember you now!" Chris, Ricky, and Karli's heads shot towards the waitress in amazement. "You were pretty good. People love you around here. Didn't you get accepted somewhere to play basketball?"

"Unfortunately, no. But I am headed off to college in a couple months. We're here now havin' a little celebration dinner. Later tonight we're headed to see a movie."

"We are?" Chris asked obliviously. "Ouch!" Chad stomped on Chris' foot underneath the table.

"Yes… we are," Chad confirmed. "That new Taylor Lautner movie came out this weekend."

"Seizure! Oh, that looks so good," the waitress gasped.

"Yep, that's the one," Chad said. "We're going to see it sometime late tonight. Since you seem to be such a big Lautner fan you should come too." Chad turned towards everyone sitting at the table, stalling and waiting for the girl to say something. Karli didn't look as amused by Chad's conversation as Chris and Ricky did, but he continued. He felt he was so close. "We haven't decided what time to go yet…"

"I get off at eleven!" the waitress was quick to respond.

"I think there's a showing at 11:30. You guys okay with that?"

"All right," Chris said.

"Sounds good," Ricky said.

"Whatever," dismissed Karli.

"Umm… okay," said Chad. "We'll go at that time then. Just take my number, Alexa, and text me when you get off."

"Okay!" the girl grinned from ear to ear. "What's your—"

"JUST TAKE OUR DAMN ORDER!" Karli commanded in a voice loud enough to get everyone's attention in the building. "We'll all take waters."

"Yes ma'am…" the waitress squeaked. "Are waters okay for everyone?"

"Y-Yes…" Chris, Chad, and Ricky responded. Their heads were lowered out of embarrassment and fear. Karli was rather unpredictable when she was angry. The girl sped off.

"Chad!" Karli patronized. "This night is supposed to be for the four of us. Quit acting like you can't just pick up a skank once you move. You're hanging with us now."

"Haha, I guess you're right," Chad said. "Sorry, Karli." For the rest of the time at the restaurant, things continued as they normally would, just now, Chad stopped flirting with the waitress. She continued to wait the table, but out of fear of Karli she didn't speak any more about tonight. Chad figured he could come back for her another time, but his friends were the priority for tonight. They ate, talked, and enjoyed their meal together. If nothing else, Chad always enjoyed his time with his friends. He tried to savor the time he had with them, but they could only spend so much time together in a single day.

"All girls aside, is everyone still up for a movie tonight?" Chad asked. They all agreed. "Awesome. We'll meet up later tonight then. I have to go home and finish some chores before my dad gets home and throws a hissy fit. I'll walk home from here, it's not that far."

"Okay then," Ricky said. "We'll see you later."

Chad left money on the table for his bill and left the restaurant. When he arrived home, the apartment was silent. Since his father's car was no longer in the driveway Chad assumed that he went back to work, so he went to his room. Chad made himself comfortable by changing into different clothes. He took a minute to debate with himself. *Should I wear something different or just wear what I wore earlier?* he thought. *It's just the movies, I guess. I'll just wear the same thing.* It was decided. He hung the jeans and button-down shirt up from that morning on his bedroom door so he could easily find them later. Now it was time for the chores.

After going through his long list of domestic responsibilities, all that was left was taking out the trash and doing the laundry. He decided the pile of clothes stacked in the corner of his room was too much laundry to do in one night, so he took the pile and stuffed it underneath his bed so no one would see it. A chore for later. On to the next task. Chad grabbed the trash can in his room and emptied it into a larger bag. Remembering the can in his parent's bedroom, he made his way to the door. He turned the knob of the closed door and loudly barged in. When he walked in, Chad froze. In the bed, his mother lied there, motionless. She was asleep. Chad exhaled in relief that he didn't wake her; he didn't feel like having any small talk conversations about his day again. He continued into the bathroom, emptied the trash can, and left the room.

Once he was finished with his chores Chad went back to his room. He checked the clock and saw that he had plenty of time until the movie. It wasn't often that he had so much time to himself. Another perk of graduation, he supposed. Chad sat on the floor at the foot of his bed. If he was going to prove to Karli that it was possible to move matter with his mind, he had better use his time wisely.

Although he was always one of the popular jocks, Chad never revealed to anyone other than his close friends how much of a nerd he really was. He was a firm believer in metaphysics, and nothing appealed to him more about Physical Science than the possibility of learning telekinesis. It was his favorite superpower. It was the one he knew he could have one day, and on *this* day he would sit there—by his bed— until he made some progress.

But it wasn't completely Chad's fault that he believed in having such a power. He was a victim of academia. Besides Vasya Negatov, Doctor Nathaniel Jones was one of Chad's favorite scientists. Jones' book, *Marvels of the Mind,* was a short compilation of research papers and public experiments that Jones accomplished over the years. He was such a young doctor, too. A brilliant mind. It was a shame that he mysteriously vanished off the face of the planet nearly a decade ago. Chad was only a child at the time, but he still felt as affected as any young person could for his favorite fallen celebrity. Jones was assumed dead, but Chad wanted to believe that Jones' research led him to find a way to fly to the heavens using only the power of his mind. Oh, the imagination of a child.

Chad closed his eyes and crossed his legs. Quickly, he began to slip into a calm state. He took one slow, deep breath after another. The air felt cool entering his lungs, and he felt cleaner with every breath taken. His body was relaxed; he felt rested. Now that he was calm, Chad took it a step further. Time for the first exercise.

He opened his eyes to see a penny on the floor; the same penny that Chad dropped months ago and neglected to pick up until he saw it move on its own. He fixed his eyes on the coin. Unwavering. Unblinking. All focus was on the round piece of copper before him. He began to shift every bit of imaginary energy there was in his body. All chakra, chi, and ki was focused on moving that penny one inch to the right.

Nothing.

Maybe it was the wrong type of energy, perhaps something more tangible would get it to budge. Anything with the word "electro" in it had to be loaded with energy, right? So Chad tried to focus his body's electrolytes. Every ounce of electrolyte power (whatever that was) Chad focused on the penny's movement. And there lied the penny. So shiny, so smooth, so stationary. This wasn't working. He decided to start with something a little easier. It was time for a visualization exercise.

Chad began to picture the world around him in his mind. He looked past his own eyelids to see the room he sat in. He saw the large stripes on his comforter and the pinstripes on his sheets and pillows. From his bed, he moved his focus to his desk. It had been collecting dust for quite some time. Even his Tae Kwon Do sparring trophy on the desk was littered with dust particles. He imagined a wind blowing a cloud of dust off of the desk, revealing the black grain of the wood and the luster of the plastic. But that was enough from his plain desk. He shifted his focus again and began to see the window. He peaked through the open blinds. He remembered that the time was still early evening, but picturing a blue sky would have been boring, so he painted the sky red… no, more of a crimson-orange. Yes, that was much prettier. It was much more peaceful. He added clouds, but only small, creamy wisps here and there. He made the clouds streak lightly upon the horizon. That was a perfect picture for him. He was content.

But it was time to add sound. He added trees, but only around the bottom of the picture frame he created. Now that there was a home for animals, he could place the birds there now, and make them sing.

He listened to them chirp and he was pleased with his own brainchild.

After a while he heard a machine running. He didn't remember creating that sound, but he went ahead and created a visual to match it. The sound would come from a garage. That sounded close enough to what it was. The machine stopped, and started again a moment later. Chad was positive it was a garage. He heard the squeak of an opening door following the garage. His imagination was starting to feel frighteningly real. He heard the squeak again followed by an aggressive SLAM—

Chad opened his eyes with the panic of waking from a nightmare. He heard keys hit a counter top. His father was home.

"Ugh," Chad muttered to himself. "He *would* ruin my meditation. Damn it…" Chad gave his room an examination, checking to see that he was fully conscious again. He looked at his bedroom window from where he was sitting and noticed that it was dark outside. "How long was I out?" The clock on his cable box read 9:17. "Wow, a full couple hours? I must be getting good at this." The room was dark, giving Chad the feeling that he woke up in the middle of the night.

Chad heard his father's footsteps coming up the staircase. Chad just ignored him. He hoped that maybe his father would assume he just wasn't home, and he wouldn't bother him with some kind of drama. *Good thing my door's closed,* he thought. His father's footsteps came closer to Chad's room. They were noticeably slower than they would usually be. His steps were fairly quiet, too. Did he already know that Chad's mother was sleeping? His father's footsteps stopped at the bedroom door. The light was on in the hallway, and Chad could see the shadow of his father's legs at the bottom of the door. Chad remained silent and hoped that the inactivity in the room would hint that no one was in it. His father's shadow disappeared as he turned and walked away at more casual volume. Chad exhaled in relief. *Dodged that bullet.* He looked at the clock again and began to think to himself:

*Okay then, it's 9:20 now. If I leave here at around ten o'clock I'll have plenty of time to get my movie ticket and grab a snack while I wait for everyone. Or maybe I should just wait until my dad takes a shower. That way he won't be able to hear me when I walk—*

A thunderous bang erupted from the other side of his door.

"AAAhh!" Chad shrieked. "What the hell was that?" Chad gave his head a shake, quickly regained composure and shot to his feet. He walked over and put his ear to the door, listening for any other sound that would give it away. *It sounded like a gunshot... it had to have been a gunshot.* He heard his father mutter something as he began to make his way to Chad's room. It almost sounded like he was stomping. When Chad heard his father coming, he instantly realized how much he did not want to find out if the sound was a gun or not. He had to hide, and he began to panic. *Uhh where, WHERE?!* He thought frantically. He saw his bed out of the corner of his eye, and instinctively leaped for it. Just like a baseball player would slide headfirst to a base, Chad leaped on top of the bed and ended up bouncing off of it, crashing to opposite side. After hitting the floor, Chad figured he probably should have thought it through more, but he forgave himself when he realized there wouldn't have been time for anything else. His father charged through the door. Chad didn't even hear the knob turn. Chad heard his father walk into the middle of his room and pace around desperately.

"Where are you?" he said with a fury.

"..."

Chad wanted to slide underneath the bed but knew he couldn't do it without making noise. So he just lied there on his back. His father didn't stop moving. Chad heard the friction of his father's clothes rubbing together as his head shot from one corner of the room to another. Chad's body began to shiver, he tried his hardest to remain in control of his body and mind, but the fear was taking over. He could feel his teeth begin to chatter. Chad sucked his lips into his mouth to act as a cushion between his teeth. He was ultimately immobilized from fear. He could still see, but he couldn't hear what his father was doing anymore. Chad froze in place.

His father looked around, but never left the middle area of the bedroom. If Chad were in his room, surely he would have seen him. There's only one place his father hadn't looked yet: underneath the bed. The man dropped to his knees. He looked briskly underneath the bed but found no one. All that he could see were mounds of clothing from one end of the bed to another. Chad couldn't have been under the bed.

But his father was convinced he heard something. The man shot back to his feet and stormed out of the room, slamming the door behind him.

The sound of the slamming door released Chad from his trepidation paralysis. He began to pant uncontrollably. His father's footsteps moved through the hallway and down the steps. Chad was safe for now.

Chad gave his head a violent shake in an attempt to regain his composure. This was no time to be afraid. What was all the meditation for if he could not keep himself calm in such a situation? He stood up quickly, but careful not to let gravity pull him so far into the floor that it created a sound for anyone below to hear. After a final deep breath, he was ready to come up with a plan.

*Okay… he's downstairs now,* he analyzed. *That means the only time I have is the time it takes for him to realize I'm not down there… He may try my room again afterwards… he knows I'm here.*

Chad wanted to see if his mom was still in her room, but if that was indeed a gun he heard, then of course she was. The confirmation of what kind of weapon his father had on him may have helped him gauge his options, but what better confirmation did he need than a loud bang? Maybe it would be better to avoid his father altogether. The only way out of the apartment was downstairs, but his father was also downstairs. *Stairs are out of the question…* he deduced. But that meant there was only one other way out: the window. He was up on the second story, how would he get down? He figured jumping was the only way. Jumping was possible. He knew parkour after all. Or more accurately, he watched parkour on television. Chad knew if he rolled the right way at the right time he would come out unscathed. On the other hand, land incorrectly and he would break his neck. Dangerous as it might be, it was either jump and possibly die, or stay inside and definitely die… Choices. He chose the former.

Chad took wide tiptoe steps toward the bedroom door to lock it and headed for the window. When he was there, he opened the blinds and opened the window. Only the screen and twelve or so feet of free-fall stood between him and safety. He looked at the sidewalk and noticed an older woman wearing sweats staring at him. Chad recognized the woman; it was his neighbor from next door, Miss Vonda. She was facing Chad and holding a phone to her ear. This was great. As soon as Chad escaped, he would be able to take shelter with his neighbor.

His father was stomping his way up the stairs again. He must have heard Chad. It was now or never. Chad punched through the screen door, stared at the grass below, and hesitated. It was a pretty long drop. His father was at the door and was banging away.

"Open the door!" his father screamed.

"Uh, NO!" Chad didn't know why he responded, but it gave him all the courage he needed to go through with the jump. He sat on the ledge and braced himself for the jump. Another deafening bang came from behind him. The noise shocked Chad so much that he inadvertently jumped out of the window before he was ready.

"Whooa," he yelled during the fall that felt like it lasted for a full five seconds. Right before hitting the ground, Chad leaned forward. As soon as his feet made contact with the ground he tucked his head underneath his chest and rolled over his shoulder, letting the momentum of the fall carry him forward. Before he knew what happened, Chad was on his butt. He pulled off the roll. However, there was a pain in his left thigh. He checked himself quickly to make sure he wasn't shot. He was okay. The landing wasn't perfect, and his hip suffered a bruise. There was a lot of pain, but he couldn't stop to examine himself; there wasn't any time. Chad looked up at the window. No one was there, and there was no sound coming from the room. Chad was overwhelmed with relief. He slowly turned back around, his eyes stayed on his aching thigh and he was slightly disoriented from the fall. He looked up, and his father stood in front of him.

The streetlights behind him cast a shadow over his face. Making the only thing visible on him the white of his eyes. That was more than enough for Chad to see the anger in his eyes. Surprised, Chad shouted in utter terror. His father took the gun in his hand and swung it at Chad, hitting him in the face and knocking him backward. Chad hit the wall of the building. He looked up and saw his father pointing the gun at him, only three feet away from his head. They paused and looked at each other. His father seemed to have been taking the moment in. The expression on his face through the shadow changed ever so slightly, and Chad knew that this was the end.

Out of a final desperate attempt to resist, Chad swung his uninjured leg upward in the form of a kick. His foot hit his father's hand and the gun was knocked from his possession. Although surprised, his father watched the gun fly through the air to see where it would land. Chad took the opportunity to strike. He punched his father in his exposed chin with everything he had, causing his head to swing backward and knocking him to the ground.

Chad stood there, letting his mind finish processing what just happened. As he stood, the gun came crashing to the ground.

Chad heard the smash and began looking around for the gun. It was on the sidewalk. His father was beginning to rise up. They both looked at each other and then darted for the gun. Chad reached it first. He pointed it at his father.

"Stop! Or—" Before Chad could finish his statement, his father was already grabbing his arm. While his father tried to twist Chad's arm, Chad kept the gun pointed at his father's head, hoping that he would have enough sense to stop attacking if a gun was in his face. No such luck. Chad tried his hardest to maintain a tight grip on the gun. The grip was too tight. The trigger was pulled and the gun fired a round.

This thunderous bang was the loudest of them all.

## Chapter 3

# Judgement

Chad stared at the firearm. A white, thin smoke flowed upward from the end of the barrel. He wasn't holding the gun anymore, but it was still in his hand. The pistol merely hung from its trigger guard as it quivered at the same rate as Chad's hand. His agape mouth took in air as he hyperventilated. He knew exactly what just happened, but he hoped with every fiber of his being that it wasn't true; that if he looked down, he wouldn't see the motionless body of a man. But he had to make sure.

Chad slowly lowered his hand. As it descended, the gun that hung unsteadily from his finger slipped and crashed onto the sidewalk. Chad didn't look down yet, but he could see an arm out of the lower peripheral of his vision. His face tightened as he tried to fight off tears, but they welled in his eyes too fast for him to resist. He finally blinked firmly and allowed the initial drops to stream down his face. He felt the weight of the tears as they bombarded his feet. He opened his eyes wide again, waiting until the blur in his sight was gone, and then he gazed downward.

His father lied beneath him. His feet were tucked underneath his body as if he had collapsed to his knees and fell backward. His left arm was flopped to his side, and the other above his head. His face still wore a look of anger on it, but the emotion only had three-quarters of the space it used to have in order to be interpreted. The entire upper-right quadrant of his head was missing. From his eye upward, the skull had taken the shape of a partially devoured apple.

Blood continued to pour from the body as Chad gawked endlessly. He was horrified, but he couldn't look away. The corpse of the man he just killed lied before him. The body seemed to be lying foreground with the streetlights revealing every detail, while everything else was black. Chad's body seemed immobile once again. It was shutting down on him. He had no idea how to handle such an experience, so he stayed silent. He shrieked as loudly as the voice in his head would allow, but he couldn't hear himself. He only heard the hard beating of his own heart pounding in his ears.

"Freeze!" A man's voice woke Chad from his madness. "Stay where you are." He looked up and saw multiple people. There were two police officers with guns in their hands. The red and blue lights from their squad car flickered behind them. Beside the car were more people whom Chad recognized to be his neighbors. The police officers strutted briskly toward Chad with their guns pointed at him.

"Put your hands on your head!" one of them commanded. Chad attempted to formulate a sentence, but his tongue and lips failed to cooperate with each other. He was still in too much shock. "Do it NOW!" the officer yelled again.

"Ya, uhh, okay…" was all Chad could articulate.

"Put your face on the ground!" Chad did as he was told. It was slightly relieving for him. With his eyes so close to the cold pavement, he would not be able to see any evidence of what took place a few moments ago. The officers began speaking to each other. Chad couldn't make out what they were saying, but he could tell they were distraught. After a moment, one of them yanked Chad's hands from his head to behind his back and handcuffed him. He pulled Chad to his feet and walked him to the squad car, shoving him inside.

The shiver in Chad's body had calmed slightly. He rested the weight of his heavy head on the window of the car and looked outside. There were many more spectators now than he had noticed before. Many of them were looking from the windows of their apartments; however, Miss Vonda was out in the yard, crying to one of the officers. Chad couldn't believe his eyes. It appeared like one of his neighbors finally decided to act for a change after hearing a sign of distress, but it didn't look like the action taken benefited Chad. Why did the officers arrest him? How much did Miss Vonda see, and when did she call the police? Chad could not make sense of the situation, so he stopped trying. His mind was wearier from the last five minutes of his life than it had ever been before. His head felt like a bowling ball, and thinking was such a tiring process. All he wanted to do was rest. Chad gave in to the weariness. He let his eyelids fall, and he faded out of consciousness.

"Galen. Galen!" a voice called. Chad pealed open his eyes. A blinding light above him made opening his eyes difficult, but once he could finally see again, he looked around. He was in a small room with only a couple rough-looking people. He also noticed that he was lying on a very hard floor. Chad slowly sat up and felt a slight dizziness. He used both of his hands to support his head until the nausea went away. "You're staying the night here. Get comfortable." Chad looked to his left and noticed a police officer walking away from him; consequently noticing the bars separating him from the officer. *Bars? Am I in... a jail? But how? What happened? When did I fall asleep? I swear I was just home a second ago.*

Chad examined his surroundings. Around him were two older men who seemingly had no immediate interest in him. Chad considered that a good thing. Metal bars substituted for what would be a door, while the walls around him were white—a very dirty white. There was no mistaking it; he was in a jail cell. Clarifying his location helped put Chad at ease for a moment, but then he tried to answer a more important question: *How did I get here?*

He attempted to think back to what happened moments before he lost consciousness. Nothing. Chad stood and a sharp pain shot through his left leg. In that instant, all of the vivid images passed through his head. He saw a smoking gun in his hand, a corpse flopped on a sidewalk as its blood flooded the pavement, and flickering lights that illuminated the street in front of his apartment. After recollection of the events returned, Chad felt his heart beat heavily. The images he saw couldn't have been true; there was no way that something that drastic happened to him. But he *was* in jail, how else could he have ended up there? He limped to the closest corner of the cell and rested his back against the wall so he could see everything around him.

"Galen." Another officer entered the hall and stood in front of the cell. "You have a visitor." The officer beckoned for someone to come over. Ricky strode briskly to the cell. Chad ran to the bars, happy to see a familiar face. The officer walked away from the cell and left the room. "You got ten minutes," he added in a cocky-cop attitude.

"Chad, what the hell did you do?" Ricky asked in a condescending manner.

"Ugh, shit. I don't remember," Chad lied. If the images he saw were real and not just a nightmare, then Ricky should be able to confirm the truth.

"How in the world do you not remember?" Ricky shouted.

"Calm down, maybe I got drunk or something... I guess I got caught." Ricky glared at Chad with a look of anger and confusion.

"Dumbass! We saw your place on the news, rushed there to find you got taken to jail, and now we're here and you can't remember a damn thing? Your parents are freakin' dead! Does that ring a bell?" Chad closed his eyes in dismay. The images must have been true. He felt weak all over and used the bars of the cell to keep him standing.

"Ah, crap. I remember now," he said weakly, letting the weight of his head drop and hit the bars.

"What happened?"

"A lotta shit, dude. Where're Karli and Chris?"

"They're outside. Karli's in the car and Chris is finding out how much bail is gonna be."

"There isn't gonna be a bail..."

"What? Why?" Ricky stood silent, waiting for an explanation. Chad slowly raised his head and made eye contact with Ricky. Not a word was spoken, but Ricky saw shame droop from Chad's face.

"Oh my GOD!" Ricky shouted backing away from the cell. "YOU did that to your parents?"

"No, it wasn't like that," Chad explained. "My dad came at me and it was all I could do to defend myself..."

"And what about your mom?"

"My dad did that to her, NOT ME."

"Then how'd the hell *you* get arrested?"

"It was my next-door neighbor. I saw her on the phone. I guess she must have been calling the cops, and they showed up at the worst possible time."

"Two minutes left," called the officer's voice.

"All right," Ricky answered. "Ugh, okay then. If that's what you say, then I'll believe you. You're definitely telling all of us the whole story later though, but right now, we got your back."

"Of course I will. Thanks." Chad felt a little better. At least he had someone on his side for whatever would come his way in the future. "Schedule a visit tomorrow if you can and I'll tell you guys everything."

"We'll be back here tomorrow morning," Ricky said with assurance. Chad and Ricky gave each other a final nod, confirming the plan that they had just made. Ricky then turned and walked down the hallway filled with metal bars. After he disappeared through the doorway, Chad turned and limped back to his self-appointed corner of the jail cell and took a seat, leaning against the wall and trying to sit as comfortably as he could. It would be a long night, but he had a lot to think about. He wanted to fall asleep again to pass the time until morning, but he knew sleeping wouldn't be easy.

No, sleep was out of the question. There was no way Chad would trust the other people in his cell enough to risk falling unconscious in front of them. He may not have been vain, but Chad knew his innocent, pretty-boy appearance wouldn't do well in jail. After all, there was no telling what his current cellmates did to end up incarcerated. For all Chad knew, they could have raped or robbed a person. But maybe that wouldn't be the most positive way of thinking at the moment. Chad was in jail, too. And killing a person is far worse than either of those example crimes he thought of.

*But it's not like I meant to do it. Maybe if there are sympathetic people out in the world, they'll give me the benefit of the doubt and actually believe me... No, they wouldn't.* If Chad's first impressions of the men around him were rapist and thief, then there would be no way for someone to assume anything other than the worst with him. From what Ricky said, the story of his parents' death was already on the news. He knew it was likely that he was being blamed for everything. He could only hope that people who knew him would think otherwise. In any case, the whole ordeal would surely taint Chad's reputation and put a damper on his future plans.

*My future—Damnit! I may as well kiss that goodbye.* In that instant, he realized the real impact of his broken reputation. Was there any way that a college like USC or any other university worth its salt would even stop to entertain the thought of accepting a potential murderer? Of course not. The news of last night would definitely be played locally, but if nationally as well, then there goes any hopes of a normal life.

All he knew was that he was criminal now, whether it was an intentional crime or not. He had to accept that fact and move on. It took the entire night, but it finally sunk in. He could only hope that the news story wouldn't catch too much attention.

The next morning slowly rolled around. At about 10:10 a.m. Chad was brought into a larger room with many tables and chairs. All the furniture in the room had been bolted to the ground. The walls were the same dirty white as the jail cell walls. There were no other convicts in the room, only police officers. Handcuffs made their presence felt on Chad's wrists with a tight, uncomfortable grip. From those handcuffs, another pair of cuffs seized him to the table where he sat.

After securing Chad to the table, one of the officers allowed Chris, Karli, and Ricky to enter the room. They all looked at Chad with a great relief, seemingly amazed that he made it through the night.

"Chad, are you doing all right?" Karli asked with tears welling in her eyes.

"Yeah," Chad responded. "I guess I'm okay. These cuffs are kinda overkill, though." Chris, Karli, and Ricky all took a seat at the table where Chad sat. It took five minutes for Chad to explain his side of the story. The tale sounded surreal to them. It was a chilling scene from a movie that they didn't want to be a part of. "Ricky, you said you saw it on the news? What all did they say about what happened?"

"We went back to Chris' after you left," Ricky explained, "and when we got there we started watchin' TV for a few hours. We were flippin' through channels 'til we got to the news."

"What channel was it?" Chad asked frantically. "Hopefully not too many people heard about what happened."

"It was local," Ricky said, "but something this big would more than likely be on CNN by now."

"Not really what I wanted to hear…" Chad said.

"When we realized it was your house we saw, we shot over there as fast as we could!" Chris said. "There were people everywhere—both cops and normal people."

"Yeah, I couldn't even park nearby," Ricky noted. Chad attempted to raise his hands so he could bury his face in his palms, but the handcuffs restricted his movement. He grunted out of frustration.

"When I finally got around the crowd I saw a policeman talking to some woman," Karli added. "She was wearing sweatpants and a hoodie, I think I've seen her before taking walks in your neighborhood."

"Wait, it was Miss Vonda!" Chad exclaimed. "She was there for the whole thing. I remember seeing her before I jumped out the window. That's great! Now she can tell the police what happened and they can get me out of here."

"Uh, do you think that's gonna work?" Ricky asked.

"Why not?" Chad said.

"Because," Karli continued, "she didn't see everything that happened, did she?"

"She saw me when me and my dad fought!" Chad jumped to his feet but was immediately yanked back down by the restraints on his wrists. The cuffs irritated him further. "What more does she need to see?"

"I guess that's all she needed to see, right?" Karli asked.

"Okay, that settles it!" Chris said. "We can use her when the trial comes along to prove you're innocent!" Chad took a deep breath. He was glad that Chris was optimistic about the situation, whether it was justifiably so or not. But it was times like this that made him somewhat annoyed with Chris' perpetual enthusiasm.

"You think that's really gonna be enough to clear him?" Ricky asked. Chad took a moment to piece together all the information in his head. His demeanor changed, and he began to calm down as an image of the situation became clearer.

"Hate to say this, but witnesses tend to be pretty unreliable when it came to telling what happened," he explained. "Right before I jumped out the window I saw her on the sidewalk. She was holding a phone. Looking back, she must have been calling the cops then. No, she had already called them much earlier and was only waiting for them to get there. That would explain why they showed up so early."

"Yeah, but still," Chris interrupted. "Why doesn't she just tell the police that you were defending yourself so they can let you go already?" Chad paused again and closed his eyes before he answered.

"'Cause people don't see things to remember them. She probably had no idea what she was seeing when it happened. Besides, assuming that she had already called the police when I saw her. She most likely heard the first gunshot and assumed the worse then." Chad couldn't help but feel responsible for the situation. He always wished for Miss Vonda to intervene when there were signs of trouble.

The conversation paused as the four looked down at the table, formulating a plot. That was the situation as they knew it. Chad was in jail, he was accused of murder, and there would be no bail for a potential murderer. The story had hit the news, or at least Miss Vonda's side of the story. As far as they knew, the news must have been viral at this point on the Internet. It would be the news reporter's word versus theirs, and there's no guarantee that anyone will believe a bunch of minority teenagers on such an issue. It was difficult to take in. Chad lifted his head.

"Okay," he began, "there's only one thing I think we should be focusing on right now." Everyone broke their stare and gave Chad their attention. "We need to clear my name."

Chris, Ricky, and Karli nodded. Of course, it was an obvious statement, but it needed to be declared.

"Yeah, you're right," Karli concurred. She turned toward her right to direct her next statement toward Chris and Ricky. "Thinking about the past isn't going to help us right now." Chris and Ricky wore a face that showed they weren't quite ready to move on to the next topic, but Karli continued. "We need to worry about important things... like finding a lawyer... or something like that."

Chad looked at Karli. The two seemed to be on the same page. Did she have a plan?

"Just what I was thinking," Chad said.

"Okay, but I don't know anyone who could possibly fit the category of a lawyer," Ricky chimed.

"We'll find someone," Chad said. "We really don't have a choice."

"Where the hell are we gonna find money for that?" Chris asked. He shrugged his shoulders and held his hands to his sides as if to further emphasize how clueless he was.

Chad glared at Chris. He felt like reaching over the table and slapping him for being so pessimistic now of all times, but moving his hands was out of the question at the moment. As much as Chad hated to admit it, Chris was right about that point. Finding an attorney for a case as extreme as this one would be pricey.

"Okay then," Ricky began. "I think that we can all agree that getting a lawyer is the next plan of action, right?" Everyone gestured his or her agreement. "Before we go any farther though, I just need to be sure of one thing." Ricky turned to face Chad.

"Yeah?" Chad asked.

"The story you told us... Is everything you said true?"

A scowl overtook Chad's face. Did Ricky think he was lying about something? This was not the time to be second-guessing him. Chad looked at Karli and Chris. Both of them bared an expression that showed equal curiosity to Ricky's.

"We really want to believe you, man." Ricky continued. "But we can't move on until we know for a fact that we're all on the same page." Chad's scowl slowly faded.

"Yes," Chad said as assuringly as possible. "I told you guys everything that happened—the way it happened." Ricky, Chris, and Karli exhaled in relief. It looked like that was all they needed to hear. They even cracked a smile.

"Good," Chris said. "Then know that we got your back!"

"Okay, now back to the lawyer," Ricky started again. "Does anyone know how much money a good one will cost?"

"It depends," Chad said. "What am I bein' charged with?" They turned towards Chris. He stroked his naked chin with his fingers while recalling the information he obtained from the officers the night before.

"Uuh, I think it was double... homogul—no homicide. Double homicide," was Chris's response. Chad grunted to himself.

"I think it can be anywhere between...twenty-five and fifty thousand," Chad said. Everyone's jaw dropped. The reality of a murder didn't set in until they heard what the price of freedom would be. "Any ideas on fundraising?"

"Ah, a fundraiser!" Chris exclaimed. "That's gotta be the best idea!"

"I don't know, dude," Ricky challenged. "I don't think that people who got their information about the situation from the news would really want to contribute to Chad getting released."

"Well, maybe we could—" Chris' words faded out of Chad's head. The three continued to talk, but Chad stopped listening to the conversation for a brief moment. He knew well that there was no way that a few teenagers would be able to produce that much money—no matter how long the time period given. Especially if there wouldn't be anyone outside of that group of four who would be willing to believe Chad's story. Fortunately, Chad had an alternative, although he did not want to resort to that option. Chad tuned back into the conversation at hand. No one seemed to have any good ideas.

"I know what we can do," Chad interrupted.

"What is it?" Karli asked.

"I got a couple thousand bucks. I *was* saving it until I moved but…" Chad trailed off.

"Oh yeah, I forgot about that!" Chris said.

"Only a couple thousand?" Karli questioned. "But are you sure you want to use up that money for this?"

Chad lowered his head and caught a glimpse of the cuffs that bound his wrists. He turned his head to the left and saw another police officer standing by the door. There was a window on the door. Through the window, Chad was able to see the foyer of the jailhouse; and beyond that, he could even see outside. It was beautiful beyond the foyer, and the sun shined bright on the trees and grass in the outside world. It was so much brighter outside than it was in that room.

From the beauty, Chad came to the realization of the obvious choice. Option one was to spend the money. It would be a wise investment to find someone that could keep him out of prison for the rest of his life. Of course, the downside to that would be becoming a broke, homeless, free man after the successful trial.

The second option would be to keep the cash and possibly represent himself in court. Chad knew a good bit about criminal justice. That's what happens after watching a few seasons of CSI. But the obvious downside to that option is the possibility of failure. If he were to lose the trial, he would, without doubt, receive a life sentence. Would two thousand dollars be the price Chad would pay for keeping what was left of his life? After thinking it through, the second option wasn't even worth considering.

Chad turned back to face his friends at the table. They were all waiting for his response.

"You guys, you're really with me no matter what, aren't you?" Chad asked.

"Of course we are," Karli said without hesitation.

"No doubt," Ricky added.

"Would you really want us to just sit back and let this crap happen to you?" Chris asked with a slight chuckle. "We're here to fight with ya, no matter what." Chad tried to fight back a tear. This wasn't the time to get emotional, but he was glad to feel secure for once.

"All right, then. Let's do it." Chad sat straight up with confidence. "We'll look for a lawyer right away. In the meantime, I won't be allowed to leave this place though. So…"

"We'll keep you posted on everything we get figured out, especially the stuff with Vonda," Karli added.

It was agreed. Tentative as it may have been, Chad had a plan and that gave him a certain level of security. In the end, it wasn't much, but it was just enough to keep him sane. After the plan was made, Chad tried to make a transition and have a normal conversation. The attempt wasn't successful. There was nothing normal about being in a jailhouse visitation room. But at least pretending it was made him feel a little better.

When it was time for visitors to leave, Chad felt mentally and emotionally prepared for what would be his first full day in jail; likely to be the first of many. He would see his friends again soon, but for now, Chad had to do his part: survive.

Catherine sat behind the desk in her office. The television on her desk was on and the volume was raised to the maximum. The sound was the only thing keeping her awake. It was a slow news day, as Tuesdays usually were. She continued to drowsily gaze into the screen as she cradled her face in the palm of her right hand, while her elbow rested on the table.

"Watching an execution wouldn't have been this boring," Catherine moaned. She sat back and let the weight of her body recline the large office chair she sat on. Feeling the need to distract herself from the boredom of the television, Catherine looked around her office. The lightly blue painted drywall displayed frames of abstract artwork, and wooden bookshelves covered the wall beneath them. A small television and a larger laptop occupied the space on top of her desk. Behind the electronics were a few neatly stacked piles of paperwork, all of which had been completed. Despite how vibrant she tried to make the room look, she could never figure out why she always felt so drowsy and bored when she was in that office.

She could only assume it had something to do with the fact that the office was in a prison. That could be fairly demoralizing at times. It almost made her feel bad about doing her job. From the opposite side of the office door, Catherine saw a shadowy figure appear through the translucent window.

"Are you in there?" the figure asked following a few hard knocks. Catherine didn't recall having any appointments that day, but she didn't have anything else to do at the moment. She welcomed the break.

"Yes. Come on in," she replied. The door opened and Jones walked into the room.

"How's it going?" he asked as he made his way to Catherine's desk.

"It's going, I guess. Have a seat." Jones sat in the chair on the opposite side of the desk.

"What are you watching?" Jones asked.

"Just the news." She turned the television so that both her and Jones could see it. "I was looking for new candidates, but nothing interesting has been coming up."

"Speaking of which, I wanted to talk to you about that."

"Yeah?" Catherine turned down the volume on the TV.

"Well, I've been thinking about what Moriz said about the trials, and I want to make another small adjustment to the criteria you use to filter out subjects." Catherine prepared herself for a long talk with a yawn and stretched. She reached into her desk and pulled out a pen and small black notebook. She flipped to an empty page and readied herself for the details to come.

"All right, go ahead," she said awaiting a lecture.

"Don't worry," Jones chuckled. "There's not that much I wanted to say." Catherine exhaled in relief and put the notebook down. "When you go search for new candidates, make sure you find younger ones from now on. Can you do that?"

"Younger ones?" Catherine asked. "How young?"

"As young as you can find them, honestly. The age of majority is eighteen, right? Then if you could, start looking for people around that age."

"Eighteen? It's really unlikely to find criminals that young who commit crimes severe enough to get the death penalty."

"I understand that, Catey," Jones said as he ineffectively exercised his nerdy charm, "but I have a hunch that that's going to be the secret to succeeding in these trials."

"And where did you get this from?" Catherine queried further. Jones reached into his large lab coat and pulled multiple manila folders from the inside, seemingly out of hammerspace. "What are those?"

"Profiles," Jones answered. He laid out the folders across Catherine's desk and began pulling files out of each one. He was ready to give a short presentation.

"Come on, Nathaniel, don't start—"

"Just listen, please," Jones pleaded. "Look at all of the subjects here that we've tested." Jones laid down several profiles next to each other across Catherine's desk. Each of the files was of past inmates. Catherine recognized them all. It was because of her that any of them made it to Sanctum. "Of all the different inmates here, only one survived, and that's Project Arbo. What is the one thing everyone except Arbo had in common?"

"They're dead…"

"No, no, no. What particular traits did they share?"

"They shared a lot of traits, Nathaniel. I brought them here because they met the criteria YOU gave me. Quit screwing around and tell me already!"

"They were all old!" Jones exclaimed. "Look, here at their ages. Arbo is twenty-three. Most of the other subjects who we ran the experiments on were all in their thirties or older!"

Catherine picked up the files Jones laid across the desk. She took a moment to read over all of them to make sure he had some idea of what he was talking about.

"I'm only thirty-six, you know," she began, "and I don't feel *that* old. I'm pretty sure that it wouldn't make that much of a difference." There was a slight hint of annoyance in her voice.

"But you cannot deny that all of the younger subjects have lasted longer during the trial." Catherine dismissively dropped the files she held back onto the desk.

"Okay, Nathaniel. If you think that will work then I'll start looking for younger criminals."

"Aah thank you," Jones said graciously. "You'll see results soon enough, I can assure you."

"Whatever you say, but just know that I may only be able to find such a candidate once in a blue moon."

"Don't you worry about that. I already know who you can start with." Jones reached for the television and began flipping through channels. "You may not have heard about this yet because it's local, but this kid meets the requirements." The channel stopped on a local news station. Jones raised the volume and turned the television back towards Catherine.

The current news story that played was of a Violet City High School graduate who was charged with double homicide. The victims: the culprit's parents. The event was apparently new since the crime had just taken place the night before, which meant that this was the perfect time to gather information about the criminal.

"You sure this kid meets all of the criteria you gave me?" Catherine asked.

"Indeed. He was the star on his school's basketball team, which means he's athletic. No major health problems were mentioned on TV. He also received a full-ride scholarship, which tells me the kid is smart."

"Not to mention crazy. The kid killed his parents, he probably isn't too stable."

"That means there is a high chance he'll be receiving the death penalty. Let's keep our fingers crossed and hope he does. What's even better is that this happened in Violet City. That's just an hour away from here. So he may end up being sentenced here anyway."

"It looks like all the hard work has been done for me then," Catherine said, she leaned back once again and allowed her chair to recline. "I'll just keep an eye on this trial, pull a few strings, and wait for the verdict."

"Good deal." Jones reorganized the files that were laid over the desk and placed them back in their respective folders. He turned and headed for the door with the small stack of profiles in hand.

"Oh, and before I go," Jones said as he turned the doorknob. "The last thing I want is to be on your father's bad side, so can you do me a favor and let him know we're making a breakthrough here?"

"Sure I will," she replied, "but there's something I need to tell you anyway. It's about my dad and you." Jones took his hand off the doorknob and looked vacantly at Catherine. "He's requesting that you deliver to my office every file of every subject we've ever tested. Also, he wants any texts or essays you studied or wrote that are relevant to the effect of visium on the human body."

"Al-alright. Do you know why?"

"Honestly, I think he may be letting you go soon. Just hope your idea works." Jones smiled and left the office without a word, closing the door behind him.

Jones knew there was no more room for failure at this point. He did not want to lose his job, but employment was not the only thing he could lose. He knew how secretive his job was. It would be difficult to believe that Negatov would just let him go without the guarantee that he wouldn't say anything about the experiments they performed over the years. The trials weren't very ethical, to say the least, and the one thing they were sworn to over the years was silence.

Jones thought it best to just continue with his research. If there was anything that was important now, it was achieving results. Hopefully, Catherine would be able to obtain the kid from the news for a trial in the near future. It could be his last chance to keep his job, or even his life. Back in her office, Catherine readied her notebook once again and turned up the volume on the television.

Coverage on the story continued over the summer. Violet City was not geographically very large, but there were a lot of people who lived there. It did not take long for the news to spread through the schools by word of mouth. Local news channels also stayed on top of the story. Eventually, the story gained attention from national news channels. Chad Galen was close to a household name within the course of the summer, and with every huge homicide case comes elaborate coverage of the trial.

Catherine paid close attention to every detail of the trial and began tuning in daily. The defense was weak. There were only two people at their table. One young man, seemingly in his mid-twenties, wore a suit. He must have been the kid's attorney. Based on observation alone, Catherine knew that this kid didn't stand a chance. Having an attorney that was so young only meant that the defense didn't have enough money for an attorney with experience. The only other person at the defense desk was the culprit. Chad Galen was his name.

He was wearing the normal jail garment for criminals of his type in that area: a red-striped, two-piece outfit. The description on the profile that Catherine received from Jones seemed to be accurate. This subject was six feet tall, 200 pounds, African American, and had a very athletic build. However, she couldn't tell too much through the baggy uniform he wore. The profile said that he was a star basketball player for his school and practiced martial arts. It didn't take very much to clarify that. All Catherine had to do was Google his name and see what sports websites popped up. It took a while to sift through all of the news articles, but eventually she found videos and pages of him on the school's website. *Distinguished Honor Roll? Martial Arts Club? This kid had a lot going for him,* Catherine thought. *What in the world made him kill his family?*

In all the Internet pictures Catherine found, none of them showed Galen with an angry look on his face. Athletes usually never smiled in pictures, but this kid didn't seem to care. His smile was vibrant, and there was no sign of hostility anywhere on his demeanor. Even his appearance seemed well maintained. His hair was short; only about an inch long, but it was well kept, lying nearly flat against his head. In his profile picture, Galen had no facial hair. But during the trial his face was filled with whiskers. Considering that he probably didn't have access to grooming utensils in jail, Catherine let that slide.

The trial began on July 3, which was only four weeks after the crime took place. The defense didn't seem to have much of a plan. Usually, trials would be delayed months, even years for this sort of thing. But that didn't matter to Catherine. As long as Galen would end up being convicted for his crime, she would be able to enlist him as the next inmate for Sanctum. All she needed to do at this point was show up at the end of the trial.

Unfortunately for the defense, the only thing they had in their favor was an eyewitness. This woman was apparently a neighbor of the defendant. She witnessed the shooting of the father, and could confirm that the bullet was shot accidentally and in self-defense. The defense seemed confident in whatever this Vonda Marshall would say once she was called to the bench. It was unlikely that a witness' statement could be the turning point in a murder trial. Either way, it wouldn't hurt to pull a few strings here and there. It would be a shame for a subject like this one to get away.

After two more weeks the jury was prepared to give the verdict. There was no doubt in Catherine's mind, Galen would be found guilty. But as a formality, she still would need to be present in the courtroom for the verdict. On Monday morning, July 17, Catherine dressed in her usual black suit. It was the only thing she found to be appropriate for occasions like this.

The guy was about to be sentenced to death, after all.

Chad sat quietly in his wooden chair behind the defense desk. He tried not to look around too much; it would only make him more nervous. But he couldn't help but notice how much furniture in that courtroom was made of wood. He noticed it every day. The defense desk, the prosecution desk, all the chairs, and even the judge's bench was made from lumber. Everywhere he looked, dark brown paneling covered the walls and floor. Seeing so much of the same thing surrounding him gave Chad an unshakable feeling of claustrophobia, as if he was already in a prison. It was something he'd never felt before, and he hoped the feeling was not an omen. The only thing that broke the uniform brown theme in the room was the United States flag that hung behind the judge.

The courtroom was crammed with people. It remained full for the entirety of the trial. Chad did not know many of the people there, but he recognized their faces from around town. Many of them were parents of his friends. They all sat in the benches in the audience. None of them looked too supportive of Chad, though. Almost everyone he made eye contact with snarled at him and turned to the jury. Chad couldn't tell if they did that just to avoid looking at him, or if they wanted to signal messages to the jury via dirty looks. The only people that were obviously there to support Chad were Chris, Karli, and Ricky. They sat directly behind Chad, in the front row of the audience.

The trial had only lasted two weeks, but it seemed to go on for an eternity. This was the final day of the trial. Chad was nervous, but he tried his hardest to remain calm. But when a key witness in the case stops showing up to the trial, it doesn't look good for the defense.

Miss Vonda had not turned up. Not during the entire second half of the trial. Chad was undoubtedly upset; once again, his neighbor proved to be absent during his time of need, which was astounding on its own. Chad was pretty sure that someone who witnessed the taking of a life would feel some sort of responsibility for reporting what he or she saw. Wasn't she obliged to attend and state what she saw? How could someone just go missing like that? That just summed up her role in Chad's entire life. She was consistently introuvable.

Chad wanted reassurance on the possibility he could walk out of the courtroom a free man. The only way he could be so sure was if his attorney was confident, but he wasn't. The man was sweating hailstones before the final trial day even began.

Chad knew from the beginning that a two thousand dollar budget would not be enough to buy freedom. It took his friends three full weeks just to find a lawyer they could afford, and they only had a week's worth of preparation time before he would charge them more than they could afford. On the other hand, Chad didn't know that the lawyer would have done such a horrible job representing him. Explaining what happened as 'self-defense' didn't get them very far.

The prosecution's attorney was an older man. He wore a large Rolex wristwatch and a different suit every day. That guy had experience. That guy had confidence. And that guy had Chad's freedom in the palm of his hands. It was a lost cause from the beginning, but in times like these, optimism helped keep Chad sane.

At ten o'clock in the morning, the cameras at every end of the courtroom began to roll. The public attention was the last thing Chad wanted, but it couldn't be helped now. By the order of a policeman, everyone in the room stood and saluted to the flag. The court resumed session for the final time.

The judge began speaking with the formalities of the trial. He turned to the members of the jury and asked if they had reached a verdict. They had. The verdict form was passed to a bailiff and was then given to the judge. As he reviewed them, Chad felt heaviness in his chest. His breaths became deeper and he felt slightly lightheaded. *No, stay strong!* He encouraged himself. *It can't end here. It won't end here.*

Thoughts of his future flashed in his mind again. He saw himself getting onto an airplane and flying away. He saw the dormitories of a university. He saw his roommates and the bed he would sleep in throughout college. He would be in class, taking notes, doing homework, flirting with the cutest girl he could find, everything… He saw his college diploma, the cap and gown he knew he would wear, even the car he would drive. All his visualization practice made his fantasies seem so real. He wanted to stay in that world. He could see it all in that one moment. That was the life he should have. He would have it some day. *It won't end here…*

"You may publish the verdict," the judge said to the clerk on his right. His words woke Chad from his daydream and back into the courtroom. As the clerk took the verdict form and walked to a podium near the side of the courtroom, Chad's attorney turned and gave him a look. There was so much anxiety on the man's face that Chad couldn't tell if he was trying to express confidence or if he was trying to tell Chad how screwed he was. The man seemed to be taking the suspense harder than Chad.

"Superior Court of Ohio: Fairfield County," the clerk began. She stood erect and spoke loudly, as if announcing the news during a town lecture in medieval times. "The People of the State of Ohio; Plaintiff vs. Chad Galen; Defendant. Case number SA 102…" With every word the woman spoke, Chad grew increasingly uneasy. This was the moment that would decide the rest of his life. "We the jury find the defendant, Chad Galen, guilty of the crime of double homicide…"

Chad's eyes widened. His jaw dropped. *This can't be happening. There's no way it can be happening.* He sat motionless in his chair and began to zone out. He heard someone making a fuss behind him. It could have been one of his friends, but he wasn't listening to anything anymore. He only sat in the quietness of his own head as the clerk finished reading the verdict. There was nothing else Chad needed to hear from her.

When the clerk finished speaking, the judge began talking again. He was prepared to give the sentence, but like any judge, he wouldn't say what would be the final ruling until after he gave the defendant an earful. Chad blankly watched the judge's mouth flap open and close. Nothing he said meant a thing. He went on for what felt like a half hour before the sentence was finally given.

"It is the judgment and sentence of this court, for two counts of voluntary manslaughter, that Mister Galen shall be put to death within the walls of the Ohio State Penitentiary at Hocking Hills."

**Chapter 4**

# Sanctum

"To DEATH?" Chad interrupted. He stood from his chair and glared at the judge. "No—There's no way…"

"Mister Galen, have a seat," the judge said as he dismissively waved his gavel.

"You're kidding me. You've got to be kidding me!" Chad raised his hands to the top of his head as a gesture of disbelief. He chuckled nervously in an attempt to laugh off the angst. It was the most expression Chad displayed during the whole trial.

"Mister Galen, please sit down," the judge urged with more agitation. "You may have a word once I'm finished giving the sentence, but as for now—"

"You just put me to death for something I didn't do! How the hell'd you expect me to sit down after that? I'm not sittin' down!" As Chad riled himself up more the audience in the courtroom began to get restless. The policemen that were standing against the walls in the courtroom walked over to Chad. One of them grabbed Chad from his shoulders and forced him back into his seat. Breaths of satisfaction escaped from the audience.

"Unless you want to get transported to the prison right now you'll behave," barked the officer. Chad kept his eyes on the judge, who appeared to be beyond arguing over the issue. He began to speak again, but Chad interrupted once more, turning in his chair towards the audience.

"How can you believe that I did something like that to my parents?" he asked. "You all know me better than that!" The officer barked more orders at Chad. In that moment, Chad did what he was told and calmed himself. The judge resumed the sentencing, but Chad still wasn't listening. He would not go to prison; he would not die. He wouldn't let it happen. Even if no one in that room believed him, if no one in that world believed him, Chad knew he was innocent. He wouldn't let his future escape him.

As the judge kept speaking, Chad examined the room around him. He sat upright in his seat and faced forward, trying to look as if he was listening. There were only two possible exits he could escape from. To his right, he saw a tan, metal door next to the jury box. *The jury walked in and out of that room multiple times during the trial. That must be their deliberation room or something. It probably doesn't lead anywhere.* To his left, there was a wooden door in the back corner of the room. An "exit" sign was illuminated above it. *Unlike that other door, this one has a cop guarding it. He's been there the whole time. That has to be the way out of this building!*

His exit was chosen, but then it was time to create the exit strategy. Chad had been escorted through the hallways of that courthouse many times before the final verdict day. Finding his way out shouldn't be too hard, so that left the final issue: How would he get past the officers? Chad knew many techniques from his martial arts training, but there was an added factor in the mix at this time. Even a month after the time of the accident, Chad's leg still felt pain. He wasn't allowed to see a doctor while in jail so he wasn't able to figure out the true cause of the pain. But the bottom line was that the injury slowed Chad down with a limp. He wouldn't be able to run as fast or perform the necessary techniques for an escape, but that wasn't going to keep him from trying.

The loud crack of the gavel hitting the judge's table shot through the air. The sentence was given. It was over sooner than Chad thought it would be; there was no time to think up a strategy. But it didn't matter now. It was time to escape. *It's now or never!*

An officer took Chad's arms and pulled them behind his back. Chad heard the rattling sound of handcuffs behind him. Now was the time. Chad shot his body around to the right in his chair and faced the officer. He threw off the officer's grip and then grabbed his arm. After grabbing hold, Chad raised his right leg and stomped downward onto the officer's knee, hyperextending it. After he fell to the ground, sudden panic came over the audience.

Chad glanced at the man's belt and saw a holster. There was a gun. Chad immediately picked up the gun and pointed it at the other officers in the room. When pointing the gun, the image of Chad's father's bloody corpse popped into his head. Chad cringed at the thought. He never wanted to hold a gun again, but he had no choice now.

"Don't you move!" Chad ordered. There were only three other officers in the room. Conveniently, they were all standing on the same side of the room. None of them had drawn their weapon yet. As each of them made a motion to their belts, Chad pointed the gun in their direction, halting their movement. Chad started for the door. *As soon as I get to that door, I'm jetting!* His steps were slower than he wanted to go, but his limp wouldn't allow him to move any faster.

"Chad, cut it out," Karli cried. "Don't make this any worse than it already is…"

"Dude, stop it! You're making a scene here," Ricky yelled from behind the wooden wall that separated the audience section and the defense's bench. There were other voices calling to out him, but Chad ignored them.

"I am NOT gonna die! I won't let it happen," he shouted. Chad continued to make his way to the door. It only took about ten seconds. Once he was there Chad took a deep breath. No other officer made his way into the courtroom, so he was still clear. Now he had to make sure no one would follow him. Chad sternly pointed the gun to each officer there, ensuring that they wouldn't move again. He pointed the gun to the ceiling and fired a round. Everyone in the room took cover on the floor and concealed his or her head underneath their arms.

After Chad fired his warning shot, he quickly turned to the exit door, turned the metal, bar-shaped knob and walked into the hallway. He slammed the door behind him. Phase one of his improvised getaway plan was working. Now it was time for phase two, which in that moment Chad decided would be finding a way out of the building. He cocked the gun beside his head and looked down both ends of the hallway.

There was a walkway to the courthouse foyer to his left. More police officers came storming through that end of the hallway. Chad's immediate response was to fire off another warning shot. The officers stopped in their path and began to fire at Chad. Each bullet missed but buzzed past Chad's head. He briskly limped in the opposite direction of the men. Ahead he could see another metal door with an exit sign above it. That had to be the way out of the building.

Chad turned again and fired more rounds at a target past the officers. His bullets hit a fire extinguisher hanging on the wall at the end of the hallway. The tank exploded and white foam covered the area. It was just enough of a distraction for Chad to escape. He was almost to the door.

"I'm pretty sure I know the woods in this area better than the cops," Chad encouraged himself as he ran towards the door. "As soon as I make it through that door I'm so outta here!" Right before reaching the exit, Chad launched a final warning shot in the air and threw the handgun down the hallway. He didn't intend to use one of those ever again.

Chad turned and reached for the push-bar on the door. As soon as he pushed in the bar, two sharp metal probes permeated the skin on his forearm. Chad instantly felt an incredibly high voltage of electricity palpitate through his body. He collapsed to the floor. The electricity continued to shock him with a pain he'd never felt before, he couldn't even focus on how to get out of the predicament. After a few seconds, the shock stopped, but Chad's body kept twitching as residual electricity made its way through his nerves.

"You're not the first person to try this, you know," said a woman's voice. Chad tried to look for the source of the sound. A blonde lady wearing a formal, black suit stood a few feet away in an adjacent hallway. Chad didn't notice that corridor while he ran, nor considered the fact that someone would be waiting to trap him. The woman held a taser gun.

The officers from down the hallway caught up to the action and greeted Chad with handcuffs around his back and a few swings with their batons. After a short and demoralizing beating, the officers yanked Chad to his knees.

"Hold on for a second before you leave guys," the woman said in a casual tone.

"Yes' ma'am, Miss Negatov," responded the officers. They roughly yanked Chad over to face the woman. Chad spit some of the blood from his lip onto the floor and slowly raised his head.

"Miss... Negatov?" he murmured to himself through his heavy panting. He looked at the woman who single-handedly foiled his escape plan. He recognized the face. *Her—Catherine Negatov? What in the world is she doing here?*

Catherine squatted down to Chad's eye level and examined him.

"He fits, I suppose," she whispered to herself. She stood up and took a couple steps back. "Since you're in such a rush to leave this place, you'll be coming with me. Take him to the bus."

Chad was pulled to his feet and escorted to the front of the courthouse. His attempt to escape earned him a total of three police officers whom roughly ushered him to the prison bus. In the courthouse foyer, paparazzi and other journalists were using cameras to immortalize what would be Chad's final moments in freedom. After the mischief that just took place, they were even more eager to do so. Chad walked through the path in the hallway that was created using velvet ropes. He walked out the front door and was escorted onto the bus that would transport him to the prison. Outside of the window, he could hear people. They were cheering. Did they all really hate him now? What happened to the love they all gave him before?

Chad wanted to take a look around him. He wanted to glance one final time at the city he grew up in, but he didn't risk it. He didn't want to be reminded of what he lost; the life he almost had. There were so many possibilities. So many things he could have accomplished, but it now meant nothing. Nothing he did before meant anything now. Who he was before didn't matter. To the public, he was a murderer, and he got what he deserved.

Chad knew he wasn't a murderer. He went over the events of that night again and again and had plenty of time to affirm with himself what truly happened. But even though he knew the truth, why did he feel shame? This overwhelming guilt for something he didn't do, he didn't know where it came from. To fall from such high esteem with the people in Violet City, and then to be hated by them; maybe that had something to do with it. Of course, he wasn't the first person to ride that bus. Maybe it was the shame of other prisoners before him lingering in the air. The spirit of remorse probably stayed in the bus at all times and made itself known to whoever enters its presence.

The bus pulled off from the courthouse parking lot. Chad kept his eyes fixated on the seat in front of him. It was a distraction from everything outside. He was the only prisoner there. Catherine, who rode in the front seat, was the only other person who was not a cop. Everyone else seemed to be watching Chad intently, making sure that he wouldn't try any more tricks. Chad had enough of a beating for one day; he wasn't going to try anything else. Getting tased wasn't fun.

The ride from Violet City to the Hocking Hills prison was about an hour and a half. *That wasn't too long of a drive. Maybe Chris and 'nem wouldn't mind stopping by— I never said goodbye…* In the chaos of his escape attempt, Chad didn't get to let his friends know how much he appreciated them. After realizing that, true shame overwhelmed him.

Hocking Hills was a highly wooded area. After exiting the freeway, the bus drove on a small, two-lane road that led through the forest. The area looked familiar to Chad. He and Ricky had traveled to a nearby tourist attraction before. Old Man's Cave was the name of the site, and although it was a beautiful place to be, the site was so far away from the city that Ricky's GPS lost a signal. It always seemed odd to them: putting a prison so close to a tourist attraction. It was another half hour of driving on the small, windy road before they finally arrived at the penitentiary.

The bus pulled up to a large, secured fence. It stood around ten feet tall with barbed wire garnishing the top. The only way to enter was through the security gate, where there were multiple guards on duty. One came onto the bus to inspect it and apparently to intimidate Chad with a minute-long glare. Chad felt more uncomfortable than intimidated. Once the guard left the bus, the gateway opened and the bus drove inside. There was another long road that led deeper into the woods inside of the gates.

After clearing the trees, a large construction appeared. There were multiple buildings that were spread out over a large open land. If the buildings weren't painted such a depressing shade of gray, Chad would have mistaken the place for a college campus. In the courtyard in front of the main entrance, a statue was erected that read:

SANCTUM

OHIO STATE PRISON OF HOCKING HILLS

Catherine stood up as the bus came to a halt in front of the main building. She walked off the bus as its door opened and disappeared into the front doors of the prison. Chad noticed a difference between these guards and the guards from any prison documentary he had seen before. Sanctum's guards had two firearms. They all seemed to have the normal handgun strapped to their hips, but some of them even had what looked like small shotguns. Chad examined the area. He had been taking in every detail he could for future reference. He didn't care how difficult it would prove to be, he would escape that prison and nothing would deter him. But maybe now wasn't the best time the try. Those *were* shotguns, after all.

Chad was escorted off the bus and into the prison. The processing was done similarly to the jail he attended back in Violet City. That wasn't fun either. After he was issued his number and given his uniform, which was a classic orange jumpsuit, he was escorted to his cell.

Two officers, one on either side of Chad, walked him through a long hallway and into the main facility. There was an armored door at the end with reinforced windows that allowed for people to look through. One of the cops opened the door and walked Chad inside. The area on the opposite side of the door was grotesquely large. The space was wide and open, but it didn't seem any different from television prisons; other than the fact that the inmates were real. None of the other inmates acknowledged Chad. They seemed unaware that he existed. That was a big switch from the courtroom.

Both officers continued to walk Chad through various corridors until they approached a cell. The door was built with metal bars that allowed a space for a tray to slip through. One of the officers unlocked the door with a key that he pulled from his waist and slid the door sideways to open it. The other officer removed Chad's handcuffs, shoved him into the cell, and locked it behind him.

"After that fiasco you pulled at the courthouse, you get to spend your entire first day in your cell," mocked one of the cops. "Have fun with your new butt-buddy." The officers laughed and walked away.

Chad brushed the joke, knowing it would only be the first of many. He started to look around his cell. The walls were the same unattractive, dirty white as the last cell he was kept in. He could live with that. Above him, Chad noticed a conspicuously placed camera in the middle of the ceiling. Through the black, glass dome that protruded from the ceiling, the camera seemed to be facing the toilet that was connected to the wall opposite the door. *They could not have chosen a more awkward place to put that camera…* he thought. He just ignored it.

There was a red stain directly in the middle of the white-tile floor. It was dried and crusted, and Chad knew exactly what it was. A quick chill shivered through his body. The thought of how the stain got there didn't disturb him, but the image of the stains he created returned to mind. It would be a while before the traumatic memory would leave his head.

Chad looked at the beds on the right side of the room. It was then that he noticed a man lying in the bottom bunk. His eyes were closed and his hands were folded behind his head, creating a pillow. The man hadn't moved since Chad walked into the cell, so Chad assumed he was sleeping. He felt relieved to not have to deal with another inmate just yet, but since he would have to interact with this guy eventually, Chad figured he should take the time to examine his new cellmate now.

The man was young but noticeably older than Chad. He was slim, but built like a fighter. He was Caucasian with blonde hair that was somehow spiked upward. There were no toiletries in the room, so maybe his hair naturally did that. He had very little facial hair, but still had a rugged look on his face. He looked tough, but Chad wasn't alarmed by him.

"I could beat his ass if I needed to," he whispered to himself.

"Really?" retorted the man. Embarrassed, Chad tried to keep his composure.

"Er, um... maybe. Just sayin'," Chad stuttered.

"What the hell are you looking at?" The man kept his eyes closed as he continued talking.

"I was just trying to see if you were awake," Chad said.

"Don't get any ideas," the man warned. "I killed the last homo who tried to get friendly."

"Whoa, buddy, I'm not like that," Chad interjected. "Okay, look. We're pretty much gonna be roomies for the next few years or whatever, so how about we start off right?" The man scowled at Chad's words and finally opened his eyes. He turned his head to make eye contact with Chad. Chad extended his arm and offered a handshake. "We cool?" The man dismissed Chad's gesture by turning his head in the other direction. "My name's Chad." There was still no response. "Come on, now, quit being a douchebag. We're gonna be seeing a whole lot of each—"

The man threw his legs off of the bed and jumped to his feet, surprising Chad and making him lose his train of thought. The man kept his eyes fixed on Chad's and walked forward, closing the space between the two. He seemed taller than when he was lying down. He was about the same height as Chad.

*Don't look away, don't look away,* Chad encouraged himself in his head. The two kept their eyes locked on each other. *I bet he's just testing me.* After a minute-long staring contest the man broke his glare and turned back to the bed. Chad considered himself the winner of that battle.

"You're not a pussy like the rest," the man said. Chad thought of something tough to say, but he couldn't come up with anything, so he kept quiet. The man sat back on the bed and went into the same position Chad found him in. "I don't have any intention to be your friend. Remember that, kid."

"Don't call me kid, dude," Chad exclaimed. "I'm eighteen."

"Don't call me dude, kid. My name is Jason." Chad walked over to the bunk and climbed the ladder that led to the vacant, top bed.

"Aah, now we're gettin' somewhere," he said. Chad jumped onto his top bunk and tried to make himself comfortable. He placed a pillow under his left leg to elevate it and laid his head against the mattress. "It's still pretty early, but since I don't think I'm getting out of this cell today I'll just take a nap." Jason didn't respond. "Do you know what we're gonna be doing tomorrow?" Chad asked.

"Shut up," demanded Jason.

"Hey, I'm trying to make the best outta my situation, dude."

"Don't make me kill you," Jason said calmly.

"Like you've actually killed someone before…" Jason didn't respond, but Chad heard a slight chuckle from around the sheets. Chad wanted to say something else, but he had the last word. That was good enough for now.

Chad lay in the uncomfortable bunk and struggled to relax. He had a long morning, and the memory was fresh on his mind. He still had a lot to think about. Whether he wanted to accept it or not, he knew that he was in prison, and he would be there for a while. He would have a long time to make peace with that fact; the rest of his life, to be exact. Or until his death sentence would be carried out. These thoughts cycled through his head repeatedly, for the remainder of the day. Though Jason left the cell, Chad was forced to stay and was given his meals through a tray hole through the bars. After exhausting himself by playing back the day over and over again, he finally went to sleep.

Chad woke not long after falling asleep, still feeling drained. After a few moments of trying to peel open his eyes, he turned to look off the ledge of his bunk. It was dark in the cell, but a light in the corridor shown through the bars of the door and provided just enough light to observe the area. Jason was asleep. He was still in the macho position he was in earlier; lying face up while his head rested on his clasped hands. Chad looked around the rest of the cell and looked out of the window. The sky was dark but it began to turn a shade of blue, with the stars still prominently glowing. He had made it through his first night in prison. It almost felt like an accomplishment.

He took the time he had to himself to mentally prepare for the day ahead, though he wasn't altogether sure how much it would really help. The main thing Chad worried about was his left leg. Eventually, the time would come when he knew he'd have to defend himself. Hopefully, before that happens, the sharp pain that kept throbbing in his thigh with every step he took would cease. But after a month the pain hadn't gone away yet. He only hoped the injury—whatever it was—wasn't permanent.

After an hour, there was activity in the corridors.

"All right, freaks, you know the drill. Time to get up," exclaimed an older man as he and a half dozen others paraded down the hallway. All of them held either a black nightstick or the shotgun-like weapon and banged them against the cell doors as they passed by. The noise in the halls woke Jason from his sleep. Calmly, he opened his eyes and slid his legs over the side of the bed. Chad looked over the edge of his bunk.

"Hey, you're awake," Chad said. Jason didn't respond. He only stood and put on the orange jumpsuit that hung from the foot of his bed, ignoring Chad completely. "Who was that old guy? And what was he talking about?" Jason continued to put on his jumpsuit without any apparent intention of responding. "Douchebag, could you *please* answer my question?!"

"It was Moriz; the warden," Jason responded evenly, keeping his eyes focused on the task at hand.

"Oh... what was he talkin' about then?"

"We're going to the mines. Hurry up and get dressed." Jason finished tying his shoes and made his way to the cell door. He stood behind it and waited for the door to open as he watched other inmates be escorted by officers out of their cell. Chad, still wearing his jumpsuit and shoes from the night before, slowly climbed down from his bunk.

"We mine? Wait, how do we even do that?" As Chad asked, an officer came and opened the door to Chad and Jason's cell. He stepped to the side and allowed Jason to walk by him without restraining him with handcuffs.

"All right, Lynx," the man commanded, "get going." Chad watched Jason walk down the hallway and out of the nearest door. *Do they really trust us to go by ourselves?* he thought. The officer noticed Chad's eye gleam as notions began to grow. "Don't get any ideas, Galen," he added. "If you make a run for it I got a nice cold bullet I'd more than like to put in your back." The man patted the gun on his hip. Chad wanted to respond with a wise remark, but he decided to stay on everyone's good side until his leg felt healthy enough to defend himself with.

The officer pulled out a taser from one of the many utility clips on his belt and pointed it toward Chad.

"All right, come with me," he ordered. The two left the cell and began walking down the corridor. Chad hadn't paid very much attention to the details of the prison the day before, but he began to notice the amenities of the facility. It seemed nicer than what he thought he knew of prisons.

The man led Chad through the main halls of the facility. He entered into the incredibly large cafeteria, which Chad noticed to also be nicer than he expected. The tiles on the floor shone brightly and the paint on the walls almost looked fresh. The room itself was full of people. It looked like the perfect location for a brawl to happen, but none of the inmates were rowdy. They all still seemed tired, but it was still the break of dawn; it seemed appropriate. The officer ordered Chad to get into the line and eat. Chad did as he was told. After limping to the end of the line, the officer disappeared. Chad realized he was on his own from that point on.

There was plenty of time to look around while in line, so Chad examined the area some more. He looked at the inmates. Contrary to what he expected, the room seemed diversely populated. The round tables, which were placed evenly around the cafeteria, were filled with people of many different colors. It wasn't very difficult to tell exactly how many groups of people were present. They all had segregated themselves to different sections of the cafeteria. The officers definitely did not tell the inmates to do that, so Chad figured they must have decided to sit in those places by their own choosing.

Everyone there wore an orange jumpsuit, but it was worn underneath some other article of clothing. Many inmates had on some sort of sweater or jacket over top of their uniforms. It seemed to be the only form of individuality they had. That would explain why the guards let Chad keep and wear his vest.

One table was particularly rowdy. Toward one corner of a cafeteria, a very noisy group dominated the air of the cafeteria, which otherwise would have been silent. That was the only table that was not completely segregated. Chad looked across the way and saw the people sitting at the table. There were only six persons there. From a distance, Chad could only see that a couple were Caucasian, the other three had sun-kissed, brown toned skin, but the man making the majority of the noise was definitely black; a very confident and vocal black man. Chad would do his best to avoid that table.

Before returning his attention to the food line, he glanced back at one of the other persons at the table. The person had long, shiny, and well-kept hair. That much could be seen from a distance. That person didn't have a very masculine look to him at all. He almost looked like a female. Chad simply brushed it off. He turned his attention back to the food and received his share. He didn't want to get caught staring. Breakfast that day would be scrambled eggs and bacon. The eggs looked like they were mixed with water while they were beaten. *So unappetizing,* he thought. *But at least it's not gruel…*

It was time to pick a place to sit. Most of the tables were full, and those that weren't did not look inviting. There were a few individuals sitting on the wall around the room. Until Chad found a friend, that would be the best choice. Chad tried his best to hide his limp by disguising it as swagger. It wouldn't be the best idea to show any sign of weakness.

It was clear that of all the people in the prison, the ones at the rowdy table were the ones who established dominance. It was all over their demeanor. The volume of their conversation surely must have bothered others, but no one in that area had confronted them. Chad had to see why, but he wouldn't confront them. He walked over to the wall near that particular table. Close enough to hear a conversation, but far enough not to be noticed.

Chad ate his food as he listened in on their conversation. It wasn't difficult to hear what was being said. The apparent alpha-male at that table spoke audibly enough. Nothing he said particularly caught Chad's interests. It seemed like normal prison talk; fairly uneducated, but spoken with confidence. But from the nature of the conversation, the black man clearly did something to deserve their respect. Or maybe it was fear. He looked to be the same age as Jason. Maybe they knew each other.

With less distance between him and the table, Chad could more easily examine the five individuals at the table. Two out of the five people there looked to be Chad's size or bigger. However, the girl-looking inmate and the black inmate and the shorter white one were significantly smaller than the others. Chad heard the black one's name being called during the conversation, most of the time by himself. Apparently, his name was Trey, and he enjoyed speaking in third-person. He didn't look very tall, but he was definitely skinny, and he was coughing up a storm. The guy didn't seem too healthy. The others at the table began to seem more like subordinates than friends. *What in the world did that guy do to get their respect?*

The effeminate inmate with the long-silky hair was the only one left to examine. How could a guy that looked so girly survive in prison? From the angle Chad sat, that inmate's back was facing him. The guy was even curvy in the same places he would've appreciated seeing on a girl. He started to feel weird for even looking so much. Chad ignored the table for the remainder of the time and finished eating his food.

Jason sat on the opposite side of the cafeteria as Chad. He was also sitting on the wall, but he wasn't paying attention to the other inmates. Above the main floor of the cafeteria, there was a balcony that overlooked the inmates below. Main offices and guards occupied the space all the way around the large room. Standing on the balcony were Catherine, Moriz, and Jones.

It wasn't often that Jason saw them all together. Ordinarily, only one or two of them may have been spotted walking into one of the offices at a time. But Jason knew that whenever the three of them were together, it was because they were observing—not overseeing. Jason made it his business to find out who they were observing this time.

"Where is he?" Moriz asked, scanning the cafeteria for an unfamiliar face.

"Right over there," Catherine gestured with a nod of her head. "He's the guy eating on the wall. They all peered over to see Chad. Jones smiled with satisfaction.

"Yep, that's the guy," he said. "I'm almost certain that he'll be able to survive the trial. When did he come in, Catherine?"

"Just yesterday," she responded. "He gave the cops hell on the verdict day. Actually, he almost escaped from the cops when he tried to run away. If it wasn't for me he would have gotten away, and you would have lost your next lab rat, Nathaniel."

"Until the time comes for his execution, we'll just make sure we break him like the rest of the swine here," Moriz said. "We can't have him running off on us now, can we?"

Jason watched their eyes closely. There was no mistake about it. The three of them were definitely looking at Chad. *So he's the new guinea pig, huh? I'll just keep an eye on him for now,* he thought.

After a while, an announcement was given over the PA and prison guards entered the room, standing by the doors. All the inmates took their food trays and placed them on the trash cans neatly. Chad did the same. Inmates began to line up at one of the doors and were led out by a guard. Unaware of what to do, Chad scanned the area for Jason. By the time Chad found him, Jason was already walking out of the door, far ahead of him. There was no way Chad could catch up, so he just entered the line and followed everyone else's lead.

It seemed like every inmate in the prison was walking out through that door. They walked through a long hallway that led to the back ends of the prison. Guards galore were present to keep the inmates from raising cain, though that didn't seem to be a problem. No one paid too much attention to each other, or to Chad for that matter.

The group was led through more hallways until they finally exited out of the rear of the building. Sunlight was just beginning to break through the skies as they turned blue. It was going to be a pretty day, but Chad was the only person who noticed that.

Hanging across the walls was a surplus of tools. Particularly, there were a large number of four different options: shovels, picks, sifting tools, and wheelbarrows. Immediately, after leaving the building, all the inmates grabbed the nearest object and returned to a single file line. Chad did the same as he tried not to look like the odd-man out. A normal shovel would suffice until he figured out what he was actually going to do with it. While everyone returned to the line, Chad took the chance to look for Jason. He was only about fifty bodies down the line. Chad would have to keep Jason in his sights until he could get closer and converse. A little explanation would have been nice.

The large line began to move through a large field behind the prison. They reached a gravel trail beyond the field and proceeded through the woodsy area that cloaked the premises. During the hike, Chad looked around. There appeared to be about 500 inmates in that line, and it looked as if all of the occupants of the prison were there.

After taking another look around, Chad noticed that more and more of the other inmates had a feminine look to them. Many of them had long hair that had actually seemed neatly maintained to some degree. Eventually, he caught a glimpse of one of their faces. That's when he realized that those inmates were indeed women. It was confusing at first; he had never heard of such a thing. He was aware that certain mental wards or insane asylums that held both male and female patients, but never in a prison. He didn't let that bother him, however. Although he didn't plan on staying at Sanctum for very long, at least he wouldn't get rusty with women while he was there.

After a mile's hike, the trail came to an end, and the woods opened to reveal a large, cavernous hill. Chad slowed his pace slightly while viewing the site. The hill in front of him was ravaged by industrialism, with grass placed sporadically around. However, considering the appearance of the forested trail the prisoners had just walked through, there was no doubt that the hill before him was once a gorgeous site.

The inmates continued their march until they reached the bottom of the large mound. A stream ran across the entire foot of the hill, also showing evidence of some unnatural interference by man. It was across this stream that the orange uniforms aligned themselves. Every single one of the apparent 500 inmates—male or female—formed a line that ran from one end of the mound to another. Chad quickly found his place in the line.

Not one person had uttered a single word during the whole hike there. Chad didn't quite know why. He understood institutionalization, though he was never a fan of it, but the people around him seemed to have no individuality at all; save for the random jackets and hoodies worn over top of some uniforms. But after stopping to think about it, maybe wearing the jackets weren't a way of expressing individuality after all. It wasn't the reason Chad kept his own vest, no matter how much he tried to convince himself. In the end, it was a way to cling to the world he once held dear. Maybe everyone else there felt the same way about their own special article of clothing. Every textile had its own story.

Shovels, picks, and wheelbarrows in their possession, the inmates stood at attention of the older man who stood before them all. The man was armed, but not with the larger equipment other guards had. Chad recognized the raspy voice to be the same one that bellowed through the corridors of the prison that morning. 'Moriz' Jason said his name was. He spoke and mentioned something of a visium quota. That settled Chad's earlier question; they would definitely be mining visium, but he didn't know anything about that. As soon as Chad realized how inexperienced he would be at the current task, Moriz blew a loud police whistle, and the 500 plus inmates scattered across the mound.

Without any conversation, they began to transition to an apparently predetermined destination. Chad managed to avoid standing out, and he was able to keep a close eye on Jason's location.

Jason may not have been the friendliest of people, but he was the only person Chad cared to speak to at that time. He would get a conversation out of that man one way or another.

As the other inmates picked a spot out in the open and began to dig, Jason walked to the stream and kneeled over. His tool of choice was the pick, and as he cradled the tool by its handle in his right hand he slowly reached into the water with his left. Chad walked nearer to Jason's location, observant of what he was doing but not making it look obvious that he didn't know what to do himself. Jason pulled his hand from the water and he held a lightly colored rock. It was a smaller stone, only slightly bigger than a pebble, but it was smoothened by the friction of the stream it lay in.

Jason tightened his fist around the stone and closed his eyes. For a minute, he stood completely still. He was the only person that dared to appear to be having a leisurely moment. Jason opened his eyes and abruptly turned his head to the left. He gazed up the stream to a section that had not been occupied at the time by any other miners. Paying no attention to anyone else, Jason turned and walked down the stream. Chad looked around for the nearest guards. No one seemed to show offense to Jason's actions, so Chad followed him.

Jason continued to stroll beside the stream. He appeared to be following it, as if to be searching for the source of the water. Chad noticed the area begin to transform as they walked. The gravel and unhealthy dirt that seemed to ravage the land around the mines became less and less apparent as the kept going. After walking a hundred feet down the watercourse, Jason halted. Chad trailed him, staying a good forty feet or so behind. Close enough to not lose sight of him, and far enough to not give away that he was following him. Jason paid no signs of acknowledgment toward anything else in his surroundings but the water by his feet. Both—the large, rocky mound and the stream that flowed by its base—had changed in nature. The environment began to seem more natural as plant life flourished.

However, the natural appearance did not extend for more than a few meters beyond a certain point. There had seemed to be a small, thriving area of abundance, and Jason was standing at the epicenter. He opened his hand to reveal the small stone he picked up earlier. Once again he closed his fists tightly around the rock, but this time, it was only for a brief moment. He dropped the rock and clasped his now free hand around the handle of his pick.

Chad had not made a sound. He only observed and attempted to learn a new skill, though he did not particularly know what he was watching. Before going any further, Jason stopped and shook his head. It was the same motion that one would do when he wanted to show his disapproval on something. It confused Chad. Did he not find what he was looking for? Jason turned his body sideways and looked at Chad from over his shoulder. Jason showed no signs of surprise, but his face displayed a look of disgust.

Chad had been found out.

"Okay, ya caught me," Chad said, trying to jest off his embarrassment. Jason didn't respond, he only dismissively turned his back to the ground and resumed his task. Feeling disrespected, Chad took it upon himself to find out what was so Jason was up to.

Jason rose his pick up into the air and swung it ferociously downward. The metallic end of the pick dug deep into the gravel beneath him, leaving the pick in its place. Chad walked up and stood beside Jason. He placed one hand on his hip while the other held his shovel like it was his own walking stick. His body language demanded the explanation he felt entitled to.

Jason took a step back and kept his eyes fixed on the pick.

"Dig here," was all he cared to say.

"What?" Chad queried, unsatisfied by the response.

"Dig the gravel from beneath the pick, and throw everything you get into the water." His tone was one of annoyance.

"Can you tell me what I'm supposed to be look—"

"Dig before guards come and *force* you to." His tone became more serious. Chad took a look around, but he didn't see any guards. There were only a few other inmates digging in the area. Despite the lack of immediate authority watching them, they still worked industriously, as though they were still constantly being monitored.

Chad didn't want to deal with more authorities just yet. He was still burnt out from the day before. He paused for a moment, and then he got into a shoveling-ready position; in an attempt to pass off Jason's threat. If Chad was going to dig, it wouldn't be because Jason told him to. He placed the head of the shovel underneath the pick and kicked it into the dirt. At that moment, Jason grabbed his pick and removed it from the shovel's path.

Chad took the chance to make conversation. But now that the opportunity was there, he couldn't think of any real question he wanted to ask. Starting a casual conversation with a prisoner seemed a lot harder than flirting with a waitress. Out of all Chad's real concerns, he may as well start with the most relevant one.

"So…" he began, "what exactly are we digging for?"

There was no response. Chad was not pleased. He just ignored the disrespect while he continued to scoop the land from beneath him and throw it into the stream. While he dug, he noticed lightly colored rocks emerge from the ground. The deeper he dug, the more they surfaced. They appeared to be glowing, even in the daylight.

After reaching a couple feet into the ground, Chad stopped to rest. Jason, who observed Chad like he was a guard himself, walked over and kneeled to observe the hole. The glowing stones covered the surface of the bottom of the hole. Jason reached into the hole and grabbed a handful of the stones that were mixed in with dirt. He examined them casually, like they were nothing special. But for a second, the intensity on his face eased.

"What are those things?" Chad asked. He was leaning forward and using his shovel like a crutch. His eyes gleamed with a genuine curiosity.

Jason stood up again and threw the handful of earth into the adjacent-running stream. A cloud of brown dirt formed underneath the ripples of the water's surface. Chad watched with confusion as he also tried to fight off annoyance. He began formulating a smart-aleck remark, which he would surely make if Jason's demonstration didn't lead anywhere. However, right before Chad could speak, he noticed the lightly colored stones rise to the top of the water's surface. Slowly, the stream carried away the clouds of dirt as multiple rocks drifted on top of it like white flower petals.

"It's visium," Jason answered.

As soon as Jason's words left his mouth, the few inmates who were in the vicinity all turned their heads at neck-breaking speeds to face the two. It was conspicuous enough for Chad to notice. After seeing the stones of visium at Jason and Chad's feet, all the inmates in the area rushed over to dig as well. They urgently ran over and claimed the hole that Chad had just started, inadvertently shoving Chad and Jason from the space. The attitude of the prisoners reminded Chad of slaves. They seemed so desperate; but why?

Jason walked several steps away from the point of action and turned to observe the scene. Chad, figuring that Jason was probably aware of something that he wasn't, did the same. Soon, other prisoners from further down the stream, those who were mining the distant corners of the mounded area, swarmed the hole that was quickly growing in size. Jason increased his distance from the crowd, and Chad did the same.

After finding an appropriate distance, Jason picked a small rock from the ground. He rolled it between his thumb and index finger as he scanned the crowd. As he did so, a smirk overcame his face. Without warning, Jason flicked the rock into the crowd of prisoners. A taller man's face was the coincidental landing pad for the stone.

The man, almost instinctively, lashed out on the smaller inmate to his side. A punch to the face felt like the appropriate response. The smaller man fell back into the crowd but was shoved back in the taller man's direction by another. The taller man threw another punch at the smaller one, but he ended up missing his target. His fist connected with a female inmate who was near. The woman responded by swinging her shovel at the taller man's head.

In that instant, the small circle of violence grew until the entire area was rioting. Chad clutched his shovel tightly and chose to quickly escape the drama before he was invited to join against his will. As soon as he cleared himself from the action, a large group of guards arrived and stormed the scene. Several of them carried a musket in hand. When they came into a comfortable range, they all took aim.

Chad noticed the pointed guns. His heart dropped. He wanted to rush over and help, but all he could utter in time were the words, "GET DOWN!"

The guards fired their weapons and Chad flinched dramatically, as if to dodge any stray bullets that would ricochet his way. Screams filled the air. Startled by horror but unable to fight off curiosity, Chad looked up at the crowd. They were all on the ground, and they were covered. A wide web that was weaved with thick, orange cords covered every inmate who was in that area. Each web was connected to the gun it was fired from by a long cable. Once relieved that there was no blood to be seen, Chad realized what the nets were. The large muskets were cannons, and they fired nets as ammunition. Judging by the color of the nets, and the prolonged, agonizing screams, the nets were giant tasers.

Chad recollected himself. He took deep breaths as he watched the guards remove the electrical nets from the prisoners and reassume order. He glanced back over to Jason, who had kept his menacing smirk throughout the entire event.

"Learn to enjoy it," Jason said, satisfied with the chaos. "You'll be seeing a lot of anarchy from now on."

## Chapter 5

# Resource

Chad had never witnessed a situation with rioters get so out of hand so quickly. Those situations were always unpredictable, but the fact that he was so close to being at the center of the conflict made him slightly shaken. More so than he wanted to admit.

Hours had passed since the riot had broken out. The sun was in the middle of the sky, shining and burning with all its intensity. Wanting to stay clear of any more possible outbreaks, Chad chose to keep a safe distance from all the other inmates. That included Jason. If Jason was only going to start more trouble that would require Chad to defend himself, then Chad figured he should at least wait until the pain in his leg went away. Disguising a limp as swag could only fool so many people for so long.

After watching the other inmates, it didn't take long for Chad to figure out what he was supposed to be doing. There were only a few different types of mining that any given prisoner was doing. Those with shovels dug holes in spots that were seemingly random. People who carried picks went to work on the walls of the taverns, either inside or out. Even the stream wasn't safe from excavation. And all of the findings—after being sifted—were taken to the ones with the wheelbarrows. It was a fairly simple setup. The process reminded Chad more of what it may have been like to be a gold miner. Not that that would be any less difficult.

The lightly colored rocks, the ores of visium that were pulled from the earth, didn't seem like anything worth the hype it was given by from the news outlets and other media. Besides the fact that the ore appeared to be glowing, there was not much physically appealing about the stones.

Chad's only personal experience with visium was in high school Chemistry class. The lab project's instructions were simple: With an AA battery and about two ounces of recycled visium in its liquid state, illuminate a large 100-watt, incandescent light bulb. All the materials were provided, plus an extra set of rubber-insulated pliers, but how in the world could someone get it to work?

The lesson of that lab was to demonstrate how visium, the newly discovered element that was "the future of all technological advancements" as Miss Stevenson—Chad's teacher—had so enthusiastically stated, was a natural amplifier of all kinds of energy. She refused to explain what she meant by that until after the class figured out how to accomplish the assigned task. It wasn't very difficult for Chad to figure out.

The experiment was similar to one he had done at home one day as a personal science project. He filled a glass bowl with salted water and sent an electric current through the water with a modified tesla coil. By using that method, he figured that the density of the water would allow it to effectively conduct the electric current. He tested his theory by placing a smaller 40-watt bulb into the water, submerging only the cap of the bulb. The experiment was a success. Right when he placed the bulb into the water it began to glow dimly, flickering slightly with the flow of water in the bowl. But even in that project, the materials he used to accomplish his task were different. The bowl he used at home was much larger than the flask that was provided for the class assignment. At home, it took a couple quarts of water and a lot of salt just to get the 40-watter to glow just a little bit. But two measly ounces of visium? How could that possibly power a light bulb with over twice the wattage?

Without seeing any other method, Chad did the first thing that came to mind. He took the AA battery and carefully dropped it in the small flask of glowing liquid. He picked up the 100 watt light bulb and slowly dipped the cap of the bulb into the flask. He glared deeply into the glass sphere in his hands, determined to find any light that may emerge from it. As soon as the cap touched the visium the bulb lit up to its maximum brightness, immediately blinding Chad.

He grunted as he flinched back, clumsily dropping the bulb entirely into the flask. He blinked hard multiple times as an attempt to regain his vision. When he could see again, he squinted as he reached for the light again, burning himself as the heat from the light nearly melted the latex glove on his hand. Chad painfully withdrew front the light again.

At that point, he had attracted enough attention to himself from the entire class that everyone saw the current situation. Miss Stevenson rushed over with an aggravated look on her face.

"Why didn't you read the directions?" she asked patronizingly. "You were supposed to hold it with the pliers!"

"Oh, my bad," Chad said. *So that's what the pliers were for.*

Miss Stevenson swiftly snatched the pair of rubber-insulated pliers from the work table. A growing anxiety possessed her face as she tried to grasp the bulb and lift it from the flask. She squinted into the light, which glowed brighter and brighter, as she tried to pick up the bulb. She made one rushed attempt after another but failed as a result of being blinded. Chad couldn't help but be curious. This was his first personal experience with visium and it was clearly an interesting one, but Miss Stevenson seemed more afraid than impressed at the display. There must have been a good reason.

Feeling responsible but not wanting anything to do with what was happening, Chad took a few steps back and let the teacher, who showed more agitation with every failed attempt to grasp the bulb, handle the situation. The light glowed brighter than Chad had thought possible, too brightly for him or anyone else to even look in the same direction.

"Shoot, shoot, SHOOT!" Miss Stevenson said with clear frustration in her voice. She snapped her body around to face Chad, and she gave him a look that immediately communicated that she was going to reprimand him, but before she could open her mouth a rattling sound came from the table behind her. She turned back to look while shielding her eyes from the light. The rattling became louder.

Something profane escaped her mouth.

"Everyone out of the room NOW!" she quite anxiously vociferated. "Hurry! Just go, go, go!" She gestured toward the classroom door like a traffic cop on a caffeine high.

Without taking the time to question why, all the students rushed out of the door with almost the same level of angst as the teacher. Chad thought it was a little unsettling, really. Usually, the teacher should have a calm head in such a situation. He was worried too, especially since he had no idea what was happening, but at least he didn't let it show. The students fled the classroom as if a fire engulfed the room. Chad was the last one out, closing the door behind him.

After Miss Stevenson made sure that everyone was accounted for, she gave Chad the reprimanding he was expecting. Only a moment into her lecture, a loud popping sound came from the classroom. Everyone who heard the sound turned to look at the door. Small glowing dots, resembling sparks that fly from a ground piece of hot metal, clung to the window of the door. The students stared with hanging jaws as the glowing dots slowly lost their shine.

Miss Stevenson walked into the classroom ever so cautiously. She checked the ceiling as she walked in, seemingly fearful that the tiles above would fall on her. As everything else she did, her movements were exaggerated. After a moment of examining the room, she welcomed the class back inside.

There was debris from the lightbulb scattered about the room like shrapnel. The bulb had shattered into tiny pieces of hot debris, leaving behind nothing but the burned and blackened cap that sunk into the flask of visium. Still reacting to the battery, the visium that remained in the flask kept a healthy bright glow. It was brighter now than it was before Chad dropped the battery in it, but Miss Stevenson didn't seem worried about another impending explosion. So he kept his cool as he walked over to his lab table. Besides the immediate damage done to the table, the room itself didn't have any signs of a meltdown, but that didn't change the fact that a week of detention would be in order.

The class session continued after the mess was cleaned up,

though there would be no more lab experiments. Chad's episode made sure of that, but Miss Stevenson didn't mind using the incident to assist in her visium lecture. She explained that the visium transferred the electrical energy from the battery, amplified it, and sent the energy into the light bulb. She also explained that very little visium is needed to produce big results. They all learned that the hard way.

So that was it. The element of the future. It was such a revolutionary resource that most large businesses began getting pressured by the government to incorporate it in the manufacturing of their products. The resource was abundant, but only a couple places in the world were known for being visium mining grounds. Particularly, the place where it was discovered, Ohio. The demand for it was huge. That fact alone boosted the hell out of Ohio's economy. And since visium was mined by prisoners, the state grew lucratively off of what was practically slave labor. Needless to say, visium was virtually unattainable to the average citizen. Chad didn't argue with that logic. Anything that turns a lightbulb into a blinding time-bomb obviously belongs in professional care. But if it's that dangerous, why was he the one mining it?

There was plenty of it around. Despite its abundance, inmates would still rile themselves up into what would be a potential riot like the one from earlier if someone found a promising spot for digging. Fortunately, there were plenty of guards and drones that stood watch in prevention of such an event.

At a time that seemed predetermined, the inmates all dropped their tools where they stood. The guards began to walk around the entire cavernous mine. Chad paid close attention. The process looked more like an inspection than anything. The wheelbarrows, loaded with glowing, wet pebbles that glistened in the sunlight, were all examined. They were checked off. A quota had been met. It took about twenty long minutes to check the entire mine, and then the inmates were ordered to pick up their tools and form a line again. Chad went with the flow of things. He also kept an eye on Jason; close enough to observe him, and far enough away to not get involved with him.

The line started moving. The drones and guards took their respective places as they escorted the line back on the trail from where they came. Just like it was that morning, no one said a word, and Chad still couldn't figure out why. Was it some rule that no one had the courage to break? The only thing that looked broken was the expression on their faces. Chad recognized the look. It was the same expression he wore throughout the entirety of his short trial. In that moment, he knew what his fellow inmates were feeling. It was defeat.

A feeling like that, the feeling of having your future taken from you, a face that displayed that there was nothing left inside, and knowing that even more life would be siphoned from you every day; that was the feeling. That was the spirit that dominated the air of the prison. It weighed down everyone's heart. Chad immediately sympathized with all the people in that line.

However, Chad's morale was injured, but not dead. There was something else to consider. If there were innocent ones among the hundreds of prisoners, why was he the only one who seemed to have any kind of willingness to live? The spirit of depression that filled the air was sharing its space with another entity. It was apathy. No one cared. Had they given up all hope of escaping their unjust incarceration? There was no telling how many appeals and trials the inmates here had gone through. Chad hadn't asked anyone else what his or her experience was. But In the end, none of that mattered. If they were innocent, they would fight until they were free. Chad didn't see it any other way.

Granted, he knew he was more spirited than most of the people he ever met in his life. Playing school sports would do that to a person. The constant need to win something, the arousing excitement whenever there's a new challenge, and a little bravado here and there were all traits that he recognized in himself. Even being a jokester was necessary at times. Anything short of the word "fun" was not a priority. It was his way of distracting himself from his life at home. It was his way of distancing himself. He was aware of this a completely fine with it. If he could divert his attention from his abusive father and annoying mother, then surely these inmates could distract themselves from a lousy death sentence.

But everyone's story was different. Chad knew that he did not deserve to be there, and he knew that he was not a murderer. *Maybe,* he thought, *I should give them the benefit of the doubt. Maybe some of them are in here for the same reason I am. Maybe. Not all of them, but still, I got screwed. Who else got screwed by the system? It couldn't be Jason. He just started a fight for shits and giggles.* I bet he actually does deserve to be here. That realization frightened Chad for just a second. His cellmate was sent to prison, sentenced to die, and might have deserved it. Curiosity set it, but then he fought it off. Naturally, Chad wanted to know what his new roomie did to wind up here. But if Jason was a murderer, maybe that's something Chad didn't really NEED to know.

"But what about the other guy? He seemed too thuggish to be innocent."

The man from the cafeteria came to mind; the one man who did not appear to be under the same spell of lugubriousness as everyone else. Trey was his name. What was his story? Chad knew that there was a distinct possibility that all of his bravado—the confidence that surpassed even Chad's—was probably just a ruse. If that was the case, it didn't explain why the people at his table seemed so afraid of him.

The line made its way through the forested trail, and it was another hour before they arrived back at the prison. All the inmates returned their respective tools to the sheds they came from. Once all tools were accounted for, the guards flocked the inmates together and led them back into the doors of the prison. All individuals went back into the cafeteria, which now resembled more of a leisurely area.

When the last inmate made his way into the door it was locked behind him. Everyone, except the guards, relaxed. It was as if a long day's work had just come to an end. It felt like they had been mining for about six hours or so. Chad took note of it.

The remainder of the day was spent inside the walls of the prison. A couple meals, a couple hours of leisure time, and then they went back to the cells for the night. Chad had never felt so exhausted from outdoor labor in his life. It was a workout, to say the least. Sleeping on this night would not be very difficult, but there was something very important that he still needed to know before he would allow himself to retire.

Chad lay in his top bunk. He rolled over to the side and poked his heavy head over the bunk's railing. Jason, who surprisingly did not look very fatigued, laid in his bunk, seemingly in deep thought.

"Yo," Chad called, "quick question. Then I'll leave you alone."

Jason, already annoyed, scowled as if Chad's head was invading his personal space. "What?"

"Would you say that today was a 'normal' day?"

"...Yeah," Jason responded dismissively.

"Okay, cool." Chad turned back over and plopped his head against the thin, caseless pillow. He made a mental note of the day. Tomorrow, he would pay even closer attention to every detail he could. From the type of food they served in the morning, to the sun's position in the sky when the mining ended. Every detail was important, nothing could be overlooked.

There was no need to rush the escape. Preparation was the key.

# Chapter 6

# Companions

Jason was right about the normality of Chad's first day. For the remainder of the week, the days transpired according to the same schedule. In the morning, the inmates were woken for a pre-sunrise breakfast and immediately escorted to the mining grounds. When the sun was in the center of the sky, the mining ended and they were taken back to Sanctum. Another meal was served and then they were given leisure time for the remainder of the day. As expected, the leisure was heavily monitored. Options of what prisoners were allowed to do during this time were limited. The only choices were to go out into the large and empty courtyard, exercise in the fitness facility, relax in the cafeteria, or remain in his or her cell. For his entire first week, Chad chose the final option. The cell provided safety. It wasn't as if he had any friends to go out and talk to, nor would he allow himself to get comfortable with any aspect of prison life.

For the first time that week Chad got a full night's sleep. Instead of being startled awake by the raucous of Moriz in the hallway, he woke on his own; though still fairly early. The carved lines on the wall of his cell indicated that It was six days ago that he was convicted. That was a Monday. Simple math told Chad that today was Sunday. Keeping track of the days was important. There must have been some routine that Sanctum followed throughout the week, and he was determined to find it.

Jason was beneath Chad, sitting up in his bunk with his back against the wall. Chad climbed down and walked over to the toilet in the opposite corner of the room. He lifted the seat and hesitated. Jason was seated in a position that faced the toilet, and Chad's approach to the commode didn't seem to faze him. Still facing the toilet, Chad shifted his eyes towards Jason in a weak plea for privacy. Eye contact. Jason did not move.

"Can you quit bein' weird and let me piss in peace?" Chad

apprehensively asked. Jason said nothing, but he sharpened the look in his eyes, studying Chad. "Wow, dude, you're so cool." Sarcasm was the only possible way for Chad to brush off the tension. He awkwardly turned his back towards Jason and attempted to go about his business on the toilet sideways.

Stage fright. Possibly the most vulnerable moment of his life. Chad stood there as seconds passed urging for the waterfall within to flush its way out like it wanted to… but nothing. He was too afraid that the man behind him would do something, anything. Whatever he did to end up here, maybe he had it in mind.

"Still not used to being watched yet?" Jason asked.

*It's another test,* Chad thought. He took a deep breath, encouraged every inch of himself, and finally released. A weak stream dripped into the toilet. Chad felt accomplished.

A loud motion came from the bunk. In a swift and ungraceful movement, Jason stood up and stomped his feet on the ground. Thinking that Jason was about to tackle him where he stood, Chad jumped to the other side of the toilet while still keeping his stream targeted at the water. His right hand still grasped himself while his left became the wall the separated him and Jason. After turning around, Chad noticed Jason's position. He was still by the bed, nowhere near Chad.

Jason chuckled to himself, almost attempting to hold back his laughter.

"It's not freakin' funny!" Chad exclaimed. He panted as he tried to catch his breath. His heart raced, but at least he was done with the toilet. "You're such a prick." Chad flushed the toilet. He took a moment to regain his composure and then started for the door of the prison cell. He looked through the bars and peered across and down the hall. Many of the inmates weren't in their cells. "Since you seem to be in a social mood today, why don't you tell me where everyone is right now?" Chad asked with an attitude.

"We don't mine on Sundays," Jason said. "The others are out around the prison. And don't get me wrong, I have no intention of making friends with a pussy like you."

"Then what the hell was that a second ago?" Chad asked gesturing to the toilet. He emphasized his curiosity with a scrunched face.

"I'm trying to figure out if you're like the others here."

"So that's it? You are just testing me... And what did you decide about me?"

"You're worse," Jason said as he sat back down on the bed. "I honestly don't see why you're here."

That wasn't the answer Chad was looking for. Surely, Chad had recognized some of the tests that Jason decided to put him through, but what could have possibly made Jason believe that Chad was worse than the other inmates at Sanctum? He revisited the tests in his mind.

*The first one was when we first met. He probably wanted to see if I'd back down from confrontation. But I didn't, so I should get some respect for that. The second could be the riot he started on my first full day. Did he want to see if I'd run? But I didn't, so I should've gotten more respect. I did flip out a minute ago, but I had my junk in my hand... He was just being a prick.*

None of it added up. They never had a real conversation until now, and Chad never started a confrontation with him since he arrived six days ago. So then how was he worse?

"What are you talking about?" Chad asked. "Did you hear about my trial or why I'm in here? Cuz I'm not guilty... not that you'd believe me."

"Don't be ridiculous. You're just as guilty as the rest of us. But that's not what I'm talking about."

"Then what are you talking about?" As Chad asked, someone walked by the cell that the two were in. It was a younger man, an inmate who looked about Chad's age. As he passed, his head turned to look into the cell. He looked around for Jason, and once their eyes connected, his glance shifted forward again. He never slowed the pace of his steps. He simply kept walking. When Jason saw the young inmate, Chad noticed a short sense of urgency in his eyes. Jason stood up and calmly made his way to the cell's door.

"You'll see soon enough," he said as he slid open the barred door.

"That kind of answer isn't gonna fly with me, jackass." Chad reached for Jason's shoulder as he passed the door's threshold, but before his hand made contact, Jason's left hand caught Chad's arm, and with his right fist he delivered a powerful blow to Chad's chest. With his fist still on Chad's chest, Jason pushed him to the wall right next to the door.

Chad gasped for air. The wind was knocked out of him. The punch came so quickly, there wasn't time to react. Jason's eyes pierce into Chad's. His eyes were hungry, as if he wanted more to happen. But he eventually backed away, relieving the pressure that pinned Chad to the wall. Jason turned away from Chad, who fell to the floor in a pant, and walked out of the door.

"Consider that a warning," Jason sternly verbalized. "Don't ever lay your filthy hands on me." Chad quickly rose to his feet and tried to think of a clever and threatening comeback, but before he could say something, Jason spoke again. "If you really want to know what I meant, then maybe you can figure it out on your own. But just to be fair, I should probably warn you that Trey doesn't have the self-control I do." He turned and walked down the hallway.

Chad watched Jason walk away. Any past notions of attempting to befriend his cellmate were now thrown out the window. If anything, they were going to be enemies. That sounded much more appealing at the moment. Chad fought down any urge he had to run after Jason and beat him to the ground. The last thing he needed was extra attention from security. Furthermore, only someone who knew martial arts could have pulled such a maneuver as quickly and smoothly as Jason did. Chad, despite his own Tae Kwon Do training, would not have been able to respond so quickly in that situation. He was on the wall before he realized what happened. Challenging someone with those skill sets would not be wise, no matter how much of a prick he was. Jason would get his share of judgment soon enough. Hopefully, he would be executed before Chad's escape, but until that time, Chad would just ignore him. However, there was one thing Chad couldn't ignore.

Jason was hiding something, and he had no intentions of filling Chad in on the secret. Being left out of a secret never bothered Chad before, but this time the secret involved him, and high school secrets aren't as dangerous as prison secrets. Before Chad planned his big escape, he figured it may be a good idea to find out what information may be circulating about him. All he needed to search for answers was a lead. Trey. The loud, skinny, thuggish guy from the cafeteria. That was the only person Jason mentioned, but it was a start. The guy seemed like a loose cannon, though. Approaching him covertly may not be the easiest of tasks, but it may be necessary.

Kyle never enjoyed being the messenger. He thought it demonstrated a lack of status. And yet, there he was, waiting at the meeting location. It was the same spot that was predetermined months ago by Jason for being an unsuspicious place to exchange information. Every Sunday, exactly at noon, he was to meet with Jason on the far side of the courtyard. That's the way it was, and that's the way it would be from then on. Nothing bothered Kyle more than the routine of it. But he was in prison now, it's not like he had anything better to do with his life.

Jason was a couple of minutes late to the courtyard, but Kyle wasn't too bothered by that. After all, Jason had a new cellmate now. And knowing him, he likely was interested in probing his new buddy for information. Anything that would help him in his goal; a goal which Kyle still did not know after all this time. But that didn't bother him either, he was only the messenger. Surely, by now, Kyle had obtained enough information as the go-between for Jason and Trey to be able to piece together what their true intentions were, but it really wasn't any of his business, nor was it important. Staying on Trey's good side was priority.

When Jason finally arrived onto the courtyard, he gave the area a quick scan. No guards or drones seemed to be paying any particular attention to him or Kyle, so it was safe to proceed. Jason walked over to the far end of the courtyard, Kyle stood by the prison's wall and leaned on it. As Jason made his way over, Kyle slid downward until he was sitting with his back against the wall. Jason casually took a seat next to him. Jason sat with legs extended as his back rested against the wall, while his body language was friendly enough to make others in the area think that the two were friends. He was a good liar.

"He's not doin' too good," Kyle said. Jason acknowledged with a nod. "He's coughing more and more nowadays. Big coughs, too."

It was quiet for a moment. Kyle looked over to Jason from the corner of his eyes, trying not to make it obvious that he was staring. Jason's eyes, however, were moving all around. Left, right, up, and left again. He was thinking. His face displayed a mixture of concern and confusion, but Kyle knew that he wasn't too concerned. Jason never cared for much other than himself, so it wasn't like he was concerned for his friend. Friend clearly was not a word that was a part of Jason's vocabulary, but his face still showed an expression that would at least qualify as "disturbed".

"Did you want me to say anything to him?" Kyle asked. Jason finally turned to make eye contact with Kyle. He stood up.

"No," he said. He walked away, back to the entrance of the prison.

"What the —? So that's it?" Jason didn't respond. He was already out of earshot by the time Kyle realized the conversation was over. Jason was never much of a talker, but walking away like that in the middle of a conversation? That was just plain rude. Kyle had only been in Sanctum for a few months, so the realization that almost all prisoners lacked common manners hadn't quite sunk in yet.

Any way he looked at it, it was just something else he'd have to get used to. Unlike the other inmates he associated himself with, not everyone had completely made peace with the fact that they were all going to die there in the prison. Not that Kyle was happy about being executed, but he chose not to dwell on it too much. In fact, he knew something that only a few inmates in the prison did, and that was what Jason was interested in. It was Trey's huge secret, and the only thing that could possibly liven the spirits of any person who knew that execution was imminent. But he wasn't permitted to speak about the secret to anyone besides Jason or Trey, and that was pretty burdensome. It was hard to keep a secret that big.

Kyle kept asking himself why Trey trusted him with that information. Was it because Trey knew he could beat the living daylights out of him if he uttered a word, or did Trey really trust Kyle as a friend? No, friend wasn't the appropriate word. The only thing that frightened Kyle, even more than death itself, was having to answer to Trey if the secret got out. So it must have been the former. Trey knew he had Kyle in the palm of his hands. In the end, Kyle knew that most people in the prison were just as afraid of Trey as he was. Trey just chose the skinny white boy with the shaggy, surfer hair for his own amusement. It could have been anyone else, but Kyle was the chosen one. He felt so lucky.

Fortunately, Trey didn't seem very healthy anymore, and Kyle would only carry the secret to Trey's grave, not his own. So if he did wish to fill anyone else's curiosity about Trey, he would do it when Trey died, and not a moment before. Even so, no one really expressed a concern towards whatever secrets Jason and Trey spoke about. No one was stupid enough to interfere with their business, not even Trey's convict-ex-girlfriend. Everyone else, especially her, had other things on their mind. Mining, court appeals, death; the list went on. It looked like Trey, Kyle, and Jason would be left to their own devices.

Kyle, now bored of sitting alone in the corner of the courtyard, began to take a walk around the field. He watched as other inmates played basketball, conversed, and conflicted. All the things they usually do in their free time. About a half hour passed by as Kyle paced around the courtyard, trying to distract himself from his boredom, and then a hard, open-palmed hand met his back.

The hand shoved him forward, as if it were meant to a friendly, overemphasized, shoulder pat, but this person clearly didn't know his own strength. Kyle turned to face the culprit and was not surprised to see who it was.

"Whuz good, boyy?" Trey asked. He had a smile on his face, but his eyes still revealed that he was trying to intimidate Kyle just a bit. "Wutchyu got ta tell me?"

Kyle tried to catch the wind that was just knocked out of him. He turned to face Trey, making sure he was just out of arm's reach.

"He didn't say anything," Kyle said.

"Daphuc yu mean 'he ain't say nuttin'?"

"He just walked away, pretty quick, too," Kyle added. "Looked like he had somethin' he wanted to say, but he didn't."

"Dat's sum bull," Trey said while exaggeratedly flinging his arm down in disapproval. The gesture looked like an attempt to strike Kyle, which made him flinch slightly. "Where he at now?"

"I don't know. He went back inside."

"Gitchya ass in ther and find him!"

"What? Man, come on, he didn't have anything for you today. The last thing I wanna do is try to pry info from that guy." Even though Kyle didn't want to say it aloud, Jason was almost as scary as Trey.

Trey's aggravation initiated his coughing. His coughs sounded wet, and as he attempted to suppress each one, his long grunts made it sound like he had acid reflux. Kyle felt a bit of relief; Trey wasn't likely to be so confrontational if he couldn't stop coughing.

"You okay?" Kyle asked sympathetically. "Just relax, Jason'll have something for us next—"

"No," Trey wheezed, finally catching his breath. He held his chest as he regained his composure and gave Kyle a stern look. "his ass kno' whuz wrong wit' me. Go back'n find em." He took a couple steps toward Kyle. In response, Kyle tried to keep his distance by matching the distance of Trey's steps in reverse. People were watching at this point, but they all pretended not to see. No one wanted to get involved.

"Dude, chill out. I told you he doesn't wanna talk now." Kyle's back hit something. He had been backed up all the way to the wall of the prison. Running was suddenly no longer an option.

In an instant, Trey's hands went for Kyle like two snakes striking their prey. One hand grasped his neck while the other went for his collar. Trey lifted Kyle off the ground and slammed him into the wall, pinning Kyle by his neck while his legs dangled.

Trey attempted to hold back more coughs, but the pain in his chest only caused him to tighten his hand's constriction on Kyle's neck. Kyle gasped for air as he pleaded for his release.

"I—told—you... He didn't say—" were the words Kyle managed to speak.

"Den you gon' find 'em an' make 'em say sumtin!"

"Put. The white. Boy. Down!" demanded a voice as if he was giving commands through a megaphone. Still holding Kyle in his position against the wall, Trey looked over his left shoulder to find the source of the voice. About ten feet away stood Chad.

"Who daphuc you be?" Trey said as he locked eyes with Chad. Chad slowly raised his hands in the air to show he had no shanks or other such weapons. It was the only thing he could think of to show that he came in peace.

"Relax," he said, "all I wanna do is talk." From the way the guy spoke, Chad could tell that he was definitely the same man from the cafeteria he'd seen all week. The same guy who made a scene nearly everywhere he went. This was definitely Trey, the man he was looking for. He noticed that Trey's forehead was glistening with moisture. Large drops of sweat clung to his head as if they had been accumulating over the past hour or so. It wasn't very hot outside, so Chad figured that Trey was still ill.

Then there was the guy Trey had pinned to the wall. It didn't take Chad very long to realize who he was. It was one of the people that sat with Trey in the cafeteria. It was his apparent subordinate, and it looked like Trey was not very pleased with him at the moment.

"I'd hate to interrupt your conversation," Chad said while putting on a disarming smile, "but I wanted to ask you a couple questions."

"Gitya ass outta here b'fo run ya head through dis wall!" Trey said with a rather convincing tone. Chad expected such a threat from a death row convict, so it didn't disturb him, but he couldn't help but be amazed at the fact that a man as lanky as him could lift another man into the air. Was this the lack of self-control Jason mentioned? Kyle's face was starting to redden, he didn't have any objections to the idea of Trey being annoyed by someone else. It would give him the chance to run away. Trey coughed profusely once again.

"You know Jason right?" Chad asked. Trey and Kyle's eyes both shot toward Chad. "He told me you might know something about why I'm here. Do you talk to him a lot?"

"Dat mu'fucka snitched?" Trey interrupted. He grunted as he held back another convulsion of coughs. He was clearly about to lose his 'self-control'.

"Ummm, what? He technically didn't say anything, just scared the crap outta me while I was takin' a piss and he said some crap about me being worse than the rest of you, and I disagreed. Not that you're bad people... I just mean that I don't think I should be here when I'm not the one picking fights, ya know?" Chad's rambling aggravated Trey to the point of a rage, which did not seem to take very long to reach.

Trey lifted Kyle from his pinned and choked position on the wall and looked at Chad. Dumbfounded at Trey's strength, Chad didn't know if he should be amazed or alert. With a loud grunt, Trey swung Kyle around and threw him at Chad. Kyle flew the full ten-foot distance before Chad could react to the fact that a person was flying his way. The two collided as Kyle's momentum pushed them to tumble backward on the ground. Trey, who could no longer resist the need, coughed profusely as he quickly made his way to the prison's entrance. He did not say a word to either of the two inmates he forced to the ground, but they both knew that he was not done with them.

Kyle gasped for air as he pushed himself off of Chad. They both did their best to recover from the fall while Chad looked around to see how many people might have been watching that little fiasco. Chad had never had a man thrown at him before, it was kind of embarrassing.

From the ground, he turned his head to see Trey rush for the door.

"Wait!" Chad called, but Trey was already out of earshot. He was a fast runner, but Chad had no idea where he was running to. He looked over to Kyle, who was still panting as he tried to catch his breath. The redness in his face slowly went away.

"Are you..freakin'.... crazy?" Kyle asked between breaths.

Kyle, who began his own small fit of hacks, rolled a few feet away as he tried to catch his breath. He felt as if he had just escaped from a gallow. Nothing was fresher than the air in that moment. Chad sat up. He waited until the human projectile that sat beside him had recovered from his flight. When he looked relaxed, Chad spoke.

"Is that guy always a prick?" Chad asked facetiously. Kyle massaged his throat as he looked over to Chad, unsure on how to respond. "You would think he'd get tired of running that mouth of his after a while."

Kyle wanted to chuckle at that last remark, but he was even more confused. No one jokes around here, he thought. *Is this dude really laughing?* Chad stood up and brushed the dirt off of his uniform. Then he turned to Kyle and extended his hand, offering Kyle assistance in standing up. It was something that came naturally from being an athlete, but it was something taboo to Kyle. Apprehensively, Kyle took Chad's hand and was heaved to his feet. Kyle kept his glance on Chad, bewilderment dominating his expression.

"Why are you looking at me like I just broke a rule?" Chad asked in a tone less comical.

"'Cause you... kinda did." Kyle fixed his expression to something more personable.

"Oh, I see. Was I not supposed to speak to ole' boy?"

"You don't even know the half of it."

"Well, I kinda have to talk to him. Do you have any idea where he's headed?"

"Talk to him?... About what?" Kyle's face scrunched up to

display even more confusion. The sudden change in his expression made Chad hesitate, just slightly, before answering.

"My cellmate said that that guy knows why I'm here. I just wanna ask him why."

Kyle almost gasped aloud. He recognized the person standing in front of him. It was the same person who was in Jason's cell with him. Kyle had not seen him up close yet, but the person before him looked like the same guy. Even his upbeat attitude was the same as the guy from the cell, and there weren't very many people within Sanctum who had that kind of energy. But there was a more significant realization that gave away who he was. Anyone who was curious as to 'why' he was in prison, besides the obvious fact of being convicted of something major, must know that there was another factor involved. But out of all the prisoners, only four had any idea of the real truth—not including this newcomer.

Of the four who knew, Kyle knew that Jason was the only person who could possibly benefit from telling anyone about the truth of Sanctum. But in the end, Kyle never really knew how Jason would benefit. He never cared to ask Jason's intentions before. It never seemed important, but now he was introducing someone else to the truth. Someone who is new to the prison, and as far as anyone knows, he can't be trusted. That seemed, if nothing else, dangerous.

"Just guessing here," Kyle said, "but your cellmate... Is he a guy about your height, blondish hair?"

"Umm yeah, pretty much," Chad said.

"Angry dude? Pretentious, hates being called 'dude'?"

"Hahaha yes, that's him! I was wondering if I was the only one who noticed that."

"What all'd he tell ya?" Kyle probed.

"Just what I said earlier. After putting me through some juvenile mind game, he told me I was worse than everyone here. Personally, I think he's full of it. But he told me Trey would know what he was talking about."

"Oh..." Kyle murmured. The story was familiar. It wasn't unlike Jason to put random inmates through some sort of test, but he never mentioned anything about Trey or why he was testing them.

"You know something, don't you?" Chad suspected.

"What? No," Kyle said suspiciously. Chad looked directly into Kyle's eyes, and Kyle immediately broke eye contact and looked away. In that moment, it was painfully obvious to both of them that Kyle was a horrible liar. Upon that realization, Kyle was the first to speak again. "Okay, look. I'm really not supposed to be talkin' to anyone about this stuff—Obviously."

"But?" Chad probed.

"But Jason said that same thing to me once. Ya know, the thing about being worse than everyone else." There was a short silence. Chad took in the information, and Kyle revisited that interaction with Jason. A hint of sentiment wafted across his face. "It really hurt..."

Chad was flabbergasted at what he heard. It almost couldn't be true. Emotion? Someone in the prison actually had feelings? And from the way the guy appeared, the two of them seemed to have something in common. This guy was young, just like Chad, but there was something that separated this one from all others in the prison. He felt remorse. Chad did not know his story, but he only knew that this guy felt out of place. Almost as if he was not meant to be there. Not like any other inmate would prefer to be behind bars, but this guy had something that felt familiar to Chad. It was innocence. But still, showing vulnerability in a prison was dangerous. Hopefully, no one else in the courtyard was watching them. But they did just make a scene.

"Let's walk around," Chad said. "Maybe you can tell me more about Trey."

"Yeah right," Kyle distressed, "So I can get launched like a shot-put ball again?"

"I promise mister 'Thug Life' won't find out about anything you say."

"It's gonna look suspicious if I talk to anyone, man. It's not like I have any friends here."

"Well, you do now." Chad extended his arm again in Kyle's direction, his palm open. Kyle stared at the hand for a moment. Prison life would make one forget what an invitation to shake hands looked like. After remembering what society called for in such a situation, Kyle accepted Chad's invitation and shook his hand. "My name's Chad."

"I'm Kyle."

A grasp and shake of another's hand and there it was: human connection. It was a refreshing experience. They both knew that they needed a friend, whether they would admit it or not. Chad had gone a full week without any real conversation with a person, not including the encounters with Jason. He did not consider those interactions conversations, nor did he consider Jason a person. He was just a prisoner. And he would be left behind when Chad finally would be ready to execute his great escape. But this guy, this Kyle, this friend; he would be welcome to join on the escape. Apparently, Jason and Trey both trusted him with their dirty secrets, whatever they may be. Maybe he's trustworthy enough to help on Chad's AWOL attempt. But there were still secrets to learn and questions on Chad's mind.

*What secret is Jason hiding, and why in the hell is Trey so strong?*

Another week went by, and as Chad had hoped, nothing was different from the last week. That confirmed that he had, in fact, seen everything about Sanctum. Mining in the morning, leisure in the afternoon, and early turn ins at night. As for the people: the inmates were diverse. They were different from the stereotyped majority of African Americans that even Chad would have assumed would be in prison, but he didn't complain about that. He supposed that was a good thing. Despite how many different races were present, no one had any kind of morale. No extra pride or spirit to show off to others. Well, besides Trey, that is. His bravado was enough to make up for everyone else. Jason didn't look depressed, but he had no intention of being happy. He always was silent, deep in thought. He must have been up to something, but Chad tried not to point fingers at Jason, knowing that the same was true about himself.

As for the guards: they were numerous, but often inattentive. For a prison like Sanctum, one that Chad assumed was considered maximum security, the guards appeared far too lax to be serious about their jobs. They were all over the place when Jason caused that riot, but when Trey causes a raucous, they often don't pay the matter any attention. They couldn't be that oblivious, could they? It would make escaping all too easy if they were. Either way, it wasn't the human guards that concerned Chad the most, it was the robotic ones. Those drones, which were even more numerous than the guards, seemed to do most of the work. But of course, one can never really question the attentiveness of a machine. They covered every corner of the prison's interior, but there was much more room to avoid crossing paths with one outdoors, especially out in the mining grounds.

The drones themselves did not look very intimidating in the least. They were about five feet tall and had a frame that resembled an ATV with smaller dimensions. They were rather bulky machines, having some rounded edges and even a defined curvature. They were colored blue and black with all the bells and whistles that a human police officer would be wearing. They were Vasya Negatov's latest inventions. The word "NegaSentry" was stamped on either side of the robots' frame. If nothing else, the man sure loved to put his name on things. In the end, they looked like giant toy robots. The only threatening trait about them were the firearms that were connected to their short arms. From what Chad remembered, the left arm, with the gun that looked like a small cannon, held the electrical net that was used for the mass tasering he witnessed on his first day. The right arm held what could have been an actual gun. That in itself was threatening enough.

Chad considered his options in the unlikely event that he would actually have to face one of the NegaSentries. Option one: run away. If he was too far from the drone then it would be difficult for it to reach him with its electrical net. But although that may have been the most instinctual option, it wasn't the smartest. Chad heard rumors from Kyle about different uses of a NegaSentry. The more recently developed ones were supposedly used by the state highway patrol in order to catch speeding cars. A driving robot didn't make any sense to Chad, and there was no way one of those drones could fit in a car, so that only meant one thing: the drones themselves were fast enough to catch cars. Running was out of the question.

Option two: knock the robot on its side. Hopefully, by knocking the drone off its wheels and immobilizing it like an upside down turtle would solve the problem, but that would be too easy. Chad couldn't have been the first to think of that. Maybe it was harder than it looked. The drones were five feet of metal after all. But it was something to keep in mind if push literally came to shove.

The next order of business involved the security cameras. Chad would have loved to sneak into the control room and shut down all the cameras in the middle of the night, but he tried to not let his imagination run away from him. He was a prisoner, not a Mission Impossible agent. It would be challenging enough to deal with the single camera in his cell. It was difficult to see where the eye of the camera was actually focusing through the black, transparent sphere that bulged from the ceiling, but Chad knew it was there, and it was watching him. It wasn't that he was worried about anything the camera in his cell would see him do, but the fact that there were so many cameras indoors hinted to the fact that there were more out in the mining grounds. That would be the next item on Chad's checklist: find out where the outdoor cameras are placed. That task may be the most challenging, but its importance could not be overlooked.

Chad felt nearly content with the amount of information he had obtained in only two weeks' time. He almost felt like he was ready to escape, but there was no need to rush. He would make sure he had every detail he could think of covered before he would attempt something so drastic. Besides, he hadn't finished prying out all the information that Kyle was willing to share. The two had a mutual relationship. Chad received answers to almost any prison question he asked, although the topic of Jason and Trey was still off limits. Kyle, on the other hand, received positive attention from someone else. He received a friend, and that was all he could have asked for at that time.

Chad was happy with the friendship he established with Kyle.

Though hesitant about getting attached to any aspect of prison life, Chad couldn't deny that having a friend made dealing with his current situation that much more bearable. Chad noticed similarities in their personalities, and he was happy that someone else in the prison knew how to laugh. Even if it was just a distraction from the painful reality that they were both there for the same reason: to be executed.

But moments like these were some of what made their friendship worthwhile. It was almost noon on the second Sunday of Chad's sentence. Chad could tell the time by looking at the sun's position in the sky. It was a skill he learned from being an ardent hiker. But it was a skill Kyle learned from Jason, for being a menial message boy. Chad knew the agreement. As long as Jason did not catch him, Chad could listen to the conversation. Luckily, because of the scene that took place the previous week with Trey, Jason and Kyle would have to find another spot to talk. Kyle suggested an indoor location, and Jason agreed.

Kyle told Chad where the meeting would ensue. It was in the front section of the prison sanctuary. It could not have been in a better location. The sanctuary had twenty rows of actual church pews, and was generally unattended, even on Sundays. If Kyle and Jason were to sit in the front, then there would be plenty of spaces underneath the pews to hide and listen to the conversation. Finally, Chad would learn Jason's secret. Chad took his spot underneath one of the pews a couple rows back from the front and waited for Jason to enter. There were no guards in the room, only a drone, and it had no apparent, default response to an inmate hiding underneath objects. Chad considered that a good thing, and made a mental note of it. Kyle sat in the front pew patiently, ignoring the fact that he knew someone was listening in on the conversation. It wasn't hard to do. It happened a lot in prison.

"Hey," Chad whispered with a loud breath, "remember to ask him about something broad."

"Why?" Kyle asked while keeping his head straight forward.

"That way I'll be able to catch on to what you guys talk about easier."

"Naw, dude. That's suspicious. He's gonna catch on."

"No, he won't." Chad slipped slightly out of his hiding spot to speak. "Look, just say something like 'Oh, dude, it's been so long since we had a real talk I forgot what we talked about last week.'"

"That ain't gonna work," Kyle said, his head slightly turning to respond. "We didn't talk about anything last week so he'll know something's up."

"Just say something else like that then."

"Dude, I got this," Kyle said turning his head almost completely around. "Trust me, I'm slicker than—"

The door to the sanctuary opened and Jason walked in. Hearing the door open spooked Kyle into swinging his head around at a rather unnatural speed. He was facing forward again until he remembered that any normal person would have turned towards the door when it opened. He turned in Jason's direction and gave him a 'what's up' nod. He looked like a high school nerd trying to be cool.

"So slick..." Chad patronized. Kyle brought his right arm back behind the pew and gave Chad a friendly one-finger wave, and Chad slipped back into his hiding spot.

Jason closed the door behind him. There were no other inmates around to watch the interaction. With that in mind, Jason did not feel the need to hide his distaste for Kyle. With his usual, perpetually-annoyed expression, Jason walked over to the pew where Kyle was sitting. He did not say a word until he was by Kyle.

"I heard about your little scuffle," he said.

"What, with Trey?" Kyle asked. "Who did you hear it from?"

"Who do you think he ran to after he was done with you?"

"You two talked to each other out in the open? He wouldn't have had to do that if you actually told me something like you were supposed to do." Jason's hand rapidly met Kyle's face. The loud sound startled Chad. He couldn't see from underneath the pew, but the sound was unmistakable. Chad's father had made him all too familiar with the sound. He listened for signs of an ensuing fight, but there were no such sounds.

"Never tell me what I'm supposed to do," reprimanded Jason.

"M-My bad," Kyle stuttered. Chad couldn't believe his ears. Was that an apology? "It's just that," he continued, "I thought that we were all supposed to be on the same page... All three of us."

"You are not a part of this," Jason said in a tone that had significantly more aggression. "You clearly can't be trusted."

"What the hell are you talkin' about, dude?" I never told anyone anything about what we talk about."

"Hmm." Jason took a step closer to Kyle. "Is that so?" Before Kyle could utter a response, Jason snatched Kyle by his collar and yanked him off of the pew, immediately following with a hard jab to his face. Kyle was on the floor before he realized he was being attacked.

The NegaSentry took action after a moment of processing the situation by playing its default recording. "Stop!", "Step away!", and "put your hands on your head and freeze!" were the direct orders of the drone. Jason, feeling that his point was proven, did as he was told. The drone rolled to the front of the sanctuary and pointed its right-arm weapon at Jason. A red light rotated on top of its head, indicating that reinforcements were on the way.

"Don't worry," Jason said mockingly. "You know I'm not going to beat you as long as this drone is stopping me." Kyle didn't budge from the floor, although he hadn't been knocked out. Chad could see him clearly lying there from a couple rows away. But in that instant, he seemed so distant. Kyle's open eyes held their gaze on Chad's, and Chad tried his best to read the expression on Kyle's face. He couldn't. His face was blank. In that moment, Kyle's eyes resembled the eyes of every other inmate Chad had seen to that point. In that moment, Kyle was broken.

"Go ahead and get up," Jason said. "Both of you." Jason's words snapped Kyle out of his trance. Chills ran down the spine of both Kyle and Chad. They gave each other a look, almost as if to clarify with one another that they both heard the same thing. After an exchange of confusion, Kyle stood up and turned around to face Jason, still fighting off chills. "I said the both of you," Jason added. Admitting he had been busted, Chad slowly crawled from beneath the pews until he was able to stand up in the second row.

"All right," Chad conceded embarrassingly. "You got me."

"How did you know he was here?" Kyle asked, trying to rub the pain from Jason's punch off of his face.

"Trey told me someone was asking too many questions," Jason responded. "I watched the entrance to the sanctuary from a distance earlier to see if anyone would be 'curious.'" Jason looked at Chad. "You really aren't the sneakiest of people, are you? I guess that's why you're here."

The reinforcements, called by the NegaSentry, finally arrived. Five guards armed with smaller handgun-looking weapons came barging into the sanctuary as if they were stopping a bank robbery. Among the five, Moriz also had his weapon ready, but after assessing the scene he only sighed and put it away.

"You again, Lynx?" Moriz asked bitterly.

"Warden," Jason greeted.

"You just can't go one week without causing trouble, can you?" Moriz asked. Jason smiled smugly. Moriz gave Chad and Kyle a stern glance over. "What were you maggots doing in here?"

"Nothing, sir," Kyle said. "We were just go—"

"Jason was just about to tell us all of his little secrets, weren't you Jason?" Chad asked.

"Secrets?" Moriz queried. "Do tell. I would love to hear the shit that's being spread." Jason looked at Chad, almost daring him to say more. Chad was not intimidated.

"Oh, yeah. He says all kinds of things," Chad said. "Well, everything he says is usually to that guy Trey... Didn't you say that he would know why I was here, Jason?" Apparent terror struck Jason's face. He had just been revealed, yet he still responded evenly to Chad's instigation.

"Yes," Jason replied. "That's right."

"Well, what is the reason Galen is here, Lynx?" Moriz asked. He seemed especially curious to know the answer. Jason took his time responding, but when he spoke, he allowed for another cocky smirk to emerge.

"You remembered his name... Is that because you think he's special?"

"What are you getting at?" Moriz queried further. This question asked more aggressively than the last.

"You know what I mean. He's next."

"Next?" Chad interjected. "What's that mean? I just got here!" Moriz did not say a word, but his face showed how angry he truly was. It was the look of an exposed man. He didn't bother to respond. After a moment of meaningful eye contact between him and Jason, he rounded up the guards and walked out of the sanctuary. "Wait, old man! What does that mean?" There was no answer. The guards swiftly left the room and the drone returned to its assigned location in the corner of the sanctuary. After the last guard left, Jason made his way for the exit as well. Chad sprinted to the door before Jason could make it there, barricading the exit with his body. "You are out of your mind if you think I'm letting you leave without telling me EXACTLY what you meant."

"You seem confident you're able to stop me from leaving," Jason said. "Do you *really* think you can fight me with an injured leg?"

"You finally noticed?"

"Like I said before, you're not very sneaky."

"Doesn't matter. What did you mean when you said I'm 'next'?"

Kyle stepped beside Chad, showing that he was just as interested. Jason took a deep breath. He thought about his options at the moment. He was more than confident that if he really wanted to, he could toss both of the obstacles at the door out of his way, but hiding the truth would only complicate things at this point. Maybe it was easier to just fill them in on the secret, but not too much of it.

"All right," he said. His cooperation put Kyle and Chad somewhat at ease. It looked like there wouldn't be a fight. "As sure as I am that you both are going to see the truth soon enough, I'll humor you for a while." The pretentiousness in Jason's tone began to annoy Chad a little more than usual. "There's not much I can tell you that this punk doesn't already know," Jason gestured to Kyle.

"Well, I ain't said a word to him about anything," Kyle said.

"But you brought him here so he could spy on our conversation?"

"He just didn't want to start any more trouble with you or Trey," Chad said.

"Doesn't matter now." Jason stepped closer to Kyle in order to ensure his words would be heard clearly. "I give you permission to tell your new friend anything and everything that I or Trey have told you." He looked at Chad. "Does that satisfy you?"

"Sure," Chad said. "But why don't you just tell me yourself?"

"That could take a very long time, and frankly, I don't want to waste my breath talking to you."

Chad tried to keep his anger at bay. Punching Jason in his mouth would have made him very happy, but another confrontation with him would not have been wise. Chad had what he wanted. He stepped to the side and allowed Jason to advance to the door.

"I will tell you this, however, since my messenger boy doesn't know this," Jason added as he opened the sanctuary door.

"What is it?" Kyle asked. Jason toned his voice down to almost a whisper so that only Chad and Kyle could hear him.

"Trey," he said right before closing the door, "is about to die."

**Chapter 7**

# Secrets

"Lynx knows about the projects," Moriz grunted to Jones and Catherine in Catherine's office. He didn't know whether he should feel angry or afraid that their secret had been discovered. Raising his voice was the only way he knew to communicate at that point.

"What? How do you know this?" Catherine asked as she sat behind her desk.

"The little prick knows that Galen is the next inmate we intend to use," Moriz said. "That smug maggot. We should have drove the needle through his arm a long time ago."

"But that can't be true," Jones declared. "There's no way any of the inmates could possibly be aware of what takes place in the medical wing. Even Arbo didn't know what was really happening."

"Arbo is a dumbass," Moriz said. More anxious energy began to escape and take him over. "That's it. We're bringing the prick in."

"And what are we going to do with him?" Catherine asked.

"Execute him!" Moriz suggested with conviction. "No one's going to miss that murdering psychopath."

"Jael, We can't just execute him," Catherine said.

"And why the hell not?"

"For that very reason," she continued. "He's a murderer. One that many people in the country have heard about. It would be too high profile of an event, and it's likely that the authorities are going to want confirmation when it happens." Catherine leaned back in her chair and gripped the its arm, using the cushion as a makeshift stress ball. Jones ran his fingers through his neatly combed hair to produce the same effect.

"And besides that, do you remember what Doctor Negatov told us before?" Jones quizzed. "He does not want anyone to be executed just because we couldn't handle them. It looks bad on Sanctum..."

"It looks horrible for Sanctum," Catherine added.

"I'll do whatever I see fit," Moriz proclaimed. "You expect me to just let him spread shit around my prison without there being any consequences? I'm Warden, I'll do what it takes to silence him."

"Do you really think that would be the best idea, Jael?" Catherine asked. "Even if he does know something about us, it would look suspicious if we punish one inmate for speaking what other inmates can only assume are lies... It's not unlikely that prisoners would try to conspire."

"Like I said, I'll do as I see fit. I don't need Doctor Negatov thinking I'm incapable of doing my job."

"But he told us—" Jones reasoned.

"I know what he told us, Jones! Just do your own damn job. If anything's going to happen to any of us for not being successful, it's going to be you. Heaven forbid you fail too many more times... Maybe Negatov will make you drive a needle into your own arm."

"That's enough!" Catherine shouted. "Look, nothing is going to happen to anyone, okay? Jael, I know this is an issue that needs to be taken care of soon, but before you do anything, can you at least give us another month or two?"

"For what?" Moriz asked.

"I just need to make sure that the public doesn't hear about this... whatever it is you decide to do. I need to think of an excuse or something that would justify moving his execution date up."

"And if I might add," Jones said, "we somewhat have something else to worry about when it comes to Arbo." Uninterested in hearing about any more problems, Moriz and Catherine took a moment to sigh before they paid Jones any attention.

"What is it?" Catherine asked.

"His health has been clearly diminishing over time," Jones explained. "His body is rejecting the visium from the trial. He honestly does not have very long at all..."

"That's fantastic," Moriz patronized. "So the one thing you did right is about to end up in the grave like everything else you've done." Jones had no response. "Well, at least we won't have to worry about him saying anything once he's dead." Moriz turned and walked to the door.

"One month," Catherine called out before Moriz left the office. "Can you give me that much time?" Moriz gave her an affirming nod.

"One month," he said.

"And you're sure that's everything?" Chad asked.

"Yeah, dude," Kyle assured. It only took a few minutes for Kyle to explain everything that had been discussed between Jason and Trey. But ultimately, Chad did not find any of the information very useful to advance his cause. The more facts Kyle mentioned, the less interested Chad became in hearing more. The information just seemed like a large conspiracy between prisoners to justify why they were imprisoned, whether it was just or unjust. "To be honest with ya, I'm not even sure Trey knew everything that Jason was really getting at..."

"Okay, then. Let me try to sum this up," Chad said, processing the entire discussion in his head. "Jason truly believes that Trey is the result of some execution attempt that failed?"

"That's not what just *he* thinks, that's just common knowledge around here."

"What do you mean by 'common knowledge'?" Chad questioned.

"Well, everybody knows that Trey's execution date was a while ago. That was before I talked to him. He made a big deal about it. Not that I'd be happy about getting executed either, but he really made a scene when the warden came to get him."

"Yeah, I'm sure he did. Isn't it fairly common for prisoners to resist when someone takes them to get executed?"

"I guess it would be," Kyle's voice lowered in volume slightly, almost unnoticed by Chad. "People around here don't care anymore, man. Usually, people lose all hope of ever having a real life after the first month or two. They're just kinda... broken." Chad had seen first hand exactly what Kyle was talking about. It was a disheartening thought, but there was no denying how true it was. "I hate Trey," Kyle continued. "He's a bum, and he was always causin' problems for me and everybody around him, even before his execution day. But I can't help but respect the dude. Out of all the people here, he's the only one who never changed."

"Never changed? You mean his personality, right?"

"Yeah. He may be a hotheaded lowlife, but at least he's always been that way."

"I guess I can't blame you for that," Chad said. He understood Kyle's sentiment. After all, it was the very fact that Kyle had not been influenced by the same curse as the rest of the prisoners that made Chad like him. Although there was no denying the look of emptiness that was painted all over his face when Jason knocked him to the floor. The punch must have been an unfriendly reminder of the reality Kyle was living in, whether he deserved this reality or not. Kyle wasn't a lowlife like the other prisoners, but then again, there was no way to know with certainty how many of the other prisoners truly were. Chad knew he wasn't, and although he hadn't asked Kyle's reason for being at Sanctum, he knew that Kyle probably did not deserve to be there either.

"But for the record, the things Jason talks about... he probably thinks that Trey was meant to survive the execution. And ya know what's really weird?" Kyle asked. "I get the feelin' that Jason actually *wants* to be here." Chad chuckled, assuming that Kyle was being facetious. But a look at his serious face made Chad reconsider.

"Wait, you really think he wants to be here? You think he has a death wish or something? What's he in here for?"

"Murder is all I know," Kyle said. "I don't know any deets on the guy. I don't even know how long he's been here I just know that whenever new inmates show up, they try to stay away from him. Whatever he did, it was a big deal." Chad knew that communication with Jason about his personal life was not easy. But like many other inmates, one secret to understanding his or her past lied in the jacket they wore over their prison uniform. That and their shoes were the only remnants of the past that were permitted to be brought into prison; remnants that would be taken to the grave. Jason's black and white, tall-collared jacket was without a doubt nice, the cat-shaped emblem on the back of it had a style that even Chad could respect. But there had to be something about that jacket that was significant enough for him to bring it to prison. "He *did* mention a few times that we were 'chosen' for something."

"'Chosen, huh? Jason said that? What was he talking about?"

"I don't know, man. It was all just gibberish to me. I just did what I was told."

"Okay, well that seems pretty important, don't you think?" Kyle didn't answer. He just walked over to the nearest pew and took a seat. He brushed back the bangs on his surfer-styled hair and lied down.

"Yeah, probably is," he finally said.

Chad realized his own fatigue after watching Kyle surrender to his own. Chad joined him on the pew and took a deep breath. It had seemed like Kyle truly revealed all that he knew, but Chad still didn't feel like he was any closer to his goal. There was, however, one more piece of information that seemed important.

"I know you're tired," Chad began, "but there's one more thing I need to know, then I won't bug you anymore about it."

"Yeah?"

"What's your story?"

"What do you mean?"

"You know. How did you end up at Sanctum?" Kyle sat up, completely alert. The question caught him off guard.

"It was because of alcohol," Kyle said. Chad swung his head over with a scowl of disbelief.

"They gave you the death penalty for getting drunk?"

"Naaw, it was nothing like that." Kyle was quiet for a few seconds as he revisited the incident. In the silence, Chad kept his eyes on Kyle. As Chad expected, the story wasn't easy for him to tell, but it was when he noticed the look in Kyle's eyes, he could see just how difficult it was. Kyle stared off into space, and he had the same look from earlier. His eyes were empty, and his spirit was weakened. After another few seconds, he was ready.

"You probably already noticed this about me, but I like surfing and skating. Stuff like that."

"Okay..." Chad said. In his mind, Chad tried to find the connection between drugs, skating and surfing, and the death penalty. He couldn't find one.

"Somethin' you probably didn't know is that it's pretty easy for dudes like me to get into drinkin' in that kinda crowd. Me, my best friend Joey, and his brother Ted all took a trip to Hawaii last summer. There were only three of us. It was supposed to be our 'great surfing getaway'. We took the trip because their pops died. Joey started getting really depressed. He even mentioned to me something about suicide, so we decided to take a vacation so he could get away from things.

On the first day in Honolulu, before we left the hotel, Joey took a full bottle of Jack to the head. I never saw him drink like that before, but he called it 'a hit of liquid courage before we hit the waves' so I just laughed it off and we went to the beach. When we got there, Ted went to find a spot to take a piss. We were far away from any of the public beaches, so Ted had to walk a ways, and there weren't any people around. After a while, the Jack started to really kick in, and Joey was officially drunk off his ass. But instead of makin' him stupid-drunk, he got even more depressed. He started bawlin' like he was at his dad's funeral. Then outta nowhere, he darted for the shore and jumped headfirst in the water. He wasn't coming up for air.

I jumped in and pulled him out of the water and tried to snap him out of it. But he was so far gone at that point, he wouldn't even listen to me. He just coughed up the water, whaled on me a bunch of times, and dunked his head in the water again. I kept trying to pull him up, but he was a lot stronger than me. Dude hit me in my solar plexus so hard that I couldn't breathe. It halfway paralyzed me. So I let go, and by the time I could move again... he was already gone.

When Ted came back, I tried to explain what happened, but he ain't believe me. Me and him never really got along that well, so I couldn't get him to listen to me. He called the cops, and when the report came through and the medical examiner saw that there were signs of a struggle, I was charged for murder."

Chad was almost at a loss for words. In a way, this was good— and bad. The good news, from what he could gather, was that Kyle was definitely not a bad person. In fact, it had been a full year since his friend committed suicide, and he was still shaken up from the incident. The look of emptiness, the brokenness of his spirit, it was all derived from that single event. That was the emotional scar that Kyle kept hidden: being blamed for the murder of a loved one. It was similar to Chad's own personal hell.

The bad news was that Kyle's trial was fair. Given the circumstances of the alleged crime, and the fact that there was no one around to witness what happened, the average prosecutor would call Kyle on his ostensible bullshit and say that he murdered the man he called his friend. The story that Chad heard, assuming that it was all true, would not have held up in court. Sadly, any other jury that may have had the same facts brought before them in court would have thought Kyle was guilty. If Chad wasn't so sure of himself that Kyle was a good person then he would have come to the same conclusion, too.

But if Jason, Kyle, Trey and all of the other prisoners were justly convicted, or at least had a fair trial, it would go against Chad's theory that he had been set up. Beyond everything that happened with his parents, what truly bothered him was the fact that the only witness for the case would just disappear in the middle of a trial. It was beyond suspicious, and it almost gave Jason's theory about being "chosen" some sort of validity, but in the end, it was irrelevant. No matter what the circumstances of Chad's incarceration were, he knew the only thing of importance now was finding the best way to escape from Sanctum. Everything else came second.

Chad gave Kyle a hard, but comforting, pat on his back. Chad did not know what the best words were for the moment, but he had a pretty good idea that he should start with the truth.

"I believe you," he said. Kyle froze in place with his eyes wide open, almost to keep himself from crying. His face tensed while his eyes gained an unmistakable gloss to them. Only one year older than Chad, imprisoned for several months, and the guy could still tear up at the thought of someone understanding him. What a softy he was.

"So what about you?" Kyle asked as he quickly wiped any sign of moisture from his face. "How'd you get here? You don't seem like the murdering type." Chad realized then that he had not told anyone within the prison walls his story yet, but if anyone deserved to hear it, it would be Kyle.

"Well, in a nutshell,"Chad began, "I was accused of killing both of my parents." Chad watched Kyle's expression to see if it would change. Amazingly, Kyle didn't seem fazed by his words. Chad couldn't tell if Kyle was that desensitized or if it was just a common story. "My dad shot my mom and then came after me, but I managed to take the gun from him before he could shoot me. We fought over the gun for a few seconds and I accidentally pulled the trigger. He died instantly."

Kyle sniffled and nodded. "At least you're tellin' the truth," he said in a relieved tone. He exhaled and smiled shyly.

"What do you mean?"

"It's just somethin' I can do. For some reason, I can tell if someone's lyin' to me just from lookin' at 'em. I can see the really small details in their body movements. Fidgets and all that ish. It's almost like a superpower," Kyle chuckled.

"Now *that* is something I would love to be able to do. I bet it comes in pretty handy in a place like this."

"It does... but can I ask ya another question?" Kyle asked.

"Sure. It can't be any more personal than the question about how I got here."

"How do you deal wit' it when people say you killed your parents?"

Chad didn't see that question coming—not from Kyle, not from anyone. But he couldn't reject the question. It was honestly a good one. Surely, Chad had some way of dealing with such a catastrophic blow to his reality, but he never took the time to think about what that was.

"Well, to tell the truth," he explained, "I never had the best relationship with my mom or dad."

"How come?"

"My dad was pretty abusive... towards my mom and me. And I kinda hated my mom because she never left him. I guess I wasn't too surprised that all this happened, but I never thought I'd be the one to blame for it."

"But still, ya don't look too shaken up about the whole thing now."

"I just don't think about it. I'm pretty good at ignoring things. I think about other stuff instead."

"Like what?" Kyle queried further.

"Uhhh..." Chad stopped before he answered that one. Chad knew that the only thing that really stayed on his mind was the possibility of escaping, but he couldn't risk Kyle knowing his idea. That could jeopardize Chad's AWOL plan—a plan that had yet to be created. Maybe it was time for a white lie. "Stuff like finding out what Jason keeps conspiring about. You know..."

Kyle gave Chad a cursory glance. "What else ya think about?"

"That's pretty much it," Chad said. Kyle gave Chad another glance then looked around the room to see if the NegaSentry was anywhere nearby. It was in its assigned corner. He lowered his voice.

"You're thinkin' 'bout runnin' away, aren't ya?" Kyle assumed. Chad felt exposed for a moment, then he realized that it must have been Kyle's little superpower at work. "It's okay, I won't tell anyone. I don't really care. It would suck to see you go, though."

"If you don't care, then why would you ask about something like that?"

"I just think it's crazy how you guys can live with bein' accused of stuff like that. It's even worse than bein' accused of killin' your best friend."

"What do you mean 'you guys'?" Chad asked.

"I meant you an—" Kyle cut himself off.

"Me and who? Jason? Trey?"

"Naw. I meant someone else. The girl who eats with me and Trey."

"Oh, that pretty girl! And why haven't you introduced me to her yet?"

"Bro, back off," Kyle warned. "As far as anyone at Sanctum goes, she's Trey's girl."

"I've had competition before," Chad said smugly. "But why in the world would she be here? She seems too pretty to end up in a place like this." Kyle could tell that Chad was joking around, so he didn't answer that last question. On a more serious note, Chad continued. "Is there any way she'd be able to help me?"

"Escape? Naw. She probably ain't even interested in that. But I don't talk to her much, so I wouldn't know what she's interested in."

"You eat with her every day and you don't talk to her?"

"She honestly scares the crap outta me. But if you do talk to her, I had nothin' to do with hookin' you up. I don't need Trey around my throat again."

"Don't worry," Chad chuckled, "I'll just treat her like a she's a new friend. If you do have any trouble with Trey, though, know I got your back. In the meantime, keep me posted about anything that develops between him and Jason."

"I haven't seen him recently, but I will." If there was anyone Kyle trusted, it was Chad. And despite how dangerous the idea of escaping the prison might have been, Kyle found no reason to stand in his way. He almost felt obliged to help. *This* friend, Kyle would make sure he would not fail.

"I haven't seen your boyfriend around," Jason said in a quizzical tone. "Where has he been?"

"I don't know where he is... and he's NOT my boyfriend," responded the girl. She sat with her back to the wall of the cafeteria. She was not in the corner of the room, but she was very close to it. It was her favorite spot. From there, she could see the two main entrances into the cafeteria where all the inmates would come and go from either side of the room, and she could also see the many "hidden" doors that the guards and NegaSentries would disperse from if there was ever an emergency situation. Directly in front of her, and across the room, was the food line. At some point in the day, every inmate would have to walk through that line when they wanted to eat.

It was a good spot for her. She never felt comfortable when she wasn't there. There was safety in that spot. She could see every prisoner, every guard, every drone, everybody—except this guy, of course. Despite being in the best location for being able to see everything that comes in her direction, Jason still found a way to sneak up on her without being seen. It pissed her off.

"Why don't you just go ask Kyle?" she asked. "It's not like I talk to him."

"Maybe not," Jason said, "but he does talk to you." The girl rolled her eyes and dismissively turned her head away from Jason, who was standing right in front of her, demanding all attention. "Andreas," he called.

"What?" she answered.

"I'm sure you know Trey hasn't been the healthiest of people as of late. You may want to spend some time with him before something happens." Andreas took a moment to think about what Jason was trying to hint to her. It shocked her. It was startling to think that someone like Trey, known to be a powerhouse and the only survivor of an execution, would have fatal health issues. Not that Andreas ever cared for Trey as an individual, but he gladly demonstrated his strength to her multiple times. He was like a peacock showing off his feathers. He had so much showmanship. "He never mentioned this to you?" Jason asked.

"I don't care," she said. "Not my problem."

"Looks like you're not in the mood to be helpful, but then again, I guess you never are. I already know where Trey is, I was curious whether or not he told you."

"Where is he then?"

"The medical wing. Just let me know the next time you see him." Jason walked away. Andreas had no idea where he was headed, but she really did not care. She always hated Jason. The way he would show up out of the blue and quiz her with some useless information that the average person would probably assume is gossip and would treat the information as such. But if there was anyone in Sanctum that Jason had difficulty getting through to, it was Andreas. She wanted absolutely nothing to do with Jason, or anyone else for that matter.

It was not that she didn't trust other prisoners around her, she didn't trust herself around them. Unlike some inmates, Andreas was not in denial about the crime she committed to end up on death row. She was well aware of what she did, and she would agree that the only worthy punishment is death. The world would be a better place without her. The prison would be a better place without her. And until that day comes when she'll be wiped from the face of existence, she'll stay in her special corner of the world. The corner she can use to stay away from everyone who would make the mistake of trying to be her friend. Or trying to be her enemy. She would be better off by herself.

As for Jason, Andreas would just keep ignoring him. Maybe he would go away like he just did. Although she could never figure out what Jason wanted from her, he definitely wasn't trying to be a friend—it would surprise her if he could define the word. But she had witnessed what Jason did to those he considered his enemy. It wasn't very pretty. Jason just seemed to be observing Andreas; watching her and Trey from a distance and intervening briefly when he felt it appropriate. What a creeper he was.

Andreas never knew that Jason ever cared for Trey's well being. As annoying as Trey was, Andreas would hate to see him go. Without him around, it's likely that other prisoners who think they have 'game' would try to get in her pants. There hadn't been any cases of rape in Sanctum as far as she knew, but with the Alpha Male erased from the picture, there was no telling what ideas would pop into people's heads. Ultimately, it didn't worry her too much. If anyone tried to attack her, she knew that she would be safe. It would not be the first time someone tried it, but she still hoped that no one would try it again. The last thing Andreas wanted was another reminder of why she was in prison.

Chad's third week of prison life began just as the others did. The early morning wake up calls became much easier to deal with, although the hard labor on the mining grounds only seemed to get more difficult. Every day the load of work just became bigger and bigger. It seemed like there was always more to do, but it made sense why they would be expected to do so much. The city of Hocking Hills was the only place in the nation known to have visium in its land. The only way to truly preserve the forests and keep them from becoming a huge demolition site was to make sure the supply met the demand without the use of bulldozers and dynamite. And the demand for visium wasn't getting any lower.

Despite how challenging the labor was, Chad still adapted to his new job fairly quickly. He was steadily becoming a more efficient worker. And although he was working hard at his new tentative occupation, he made sure he wasn't too busy to find a way out of Sanctum. There were multiple caves in the area. Each one was naturally deep, but they were hollowed even further from the inmates digging for visium. As long as Chad's quota of visium for the day was met, it didn't matter where in the mine he excavated the visium from. This gave him the freedom to explore the vast mines for himself. As long as he found visium, no guard could say that he was up to something.

Chad remained patient. There was no need to run for freedom every time he saw an opening. Looking for every possible route of escape, hiding place, and method of distracting the guards on duty was priority for now. The escape plan would be drawn up after all possibilities were considered.

For his own sake, Chad kept a good distance from Jason as often as he could. The last thing he wanted was to be in the middle of another raucous. It would go against his idea of staying inconspicuous. Unfortunately, Jason was still Chad's cellmate, so they could only be distanced during the daytime. When night came around, they would be trapped inside of the cell with each other. But of course, Jason didn't see it as being trapped. He seemed to enjoy the tension of being locked in the same room as someone he did not like. Chad was no longer interested in trying to befriend him, so there were no more strained conversations between the two. Only tension-filled silences that lasted throughout the night, until they both fell asleep.

But Kyle was a different story. Chad had no problem spending time with Kyle while they were in the mines. He was a good source of information, but Chad knew everything Kyle did at this point. There was no point in probing him for any more information, but there was plenty to benefit from by having another sane person to talk to. The two often worked together on the mines; digging holes, picking rocks off cave walls, whatever was necessary. There was something else very respectable about Kyle's work ethic: it existed. Chad noticed, once again, this appealing difference between his friend and the rest of the prisoners.

Despite knowing that the very reason he was sent to Sanctum was to die, it didn't affect Kyle's attitude towards life in the now. Chad knew that the same trait was in himself, but Kyle did a much better job displaying it.

Chad had, however, become much more interested in particular people at the prison—inmate or not. The first was Trey. Chad hadn't seen him since the day he met Kyle, and that was over a week ago. But of course, the guy was feeling sick, maybe he was sent over to the medical wing until he was feeling better. It was interesting how a man so strong could still fall ill to a disease, but maybe he just had bad allergies. All Chad ever saw him do was cough. The guy would need one hell of a Benadryl.

The second person who came to mind often was the warden, Moriz. As far as Chad saw, Moriz never paid very much attention to any particular inmate. But ever since Jason incurred the wrath of the Sanctum SWAT inside the sanctuary, Moriz seemed on edge. Specifically when it came to keeping tabs on whatever Jason was doing. As long as Chad wasn't at the center of attention, he had no issue with Jason taking the heat. Besides, all the extra attention would keep Jason from being so confrontational, and it would give Chad all the freedom he wanted when it came to exploring the prison grounds.

The one person that Chad thought about most was the one he hadn't even met yet. The female inmate. The Latina bombshell. Chad's next 'friend'. He saw her around the mines every now and then, but never went out of his way to speak to her. Kyle was right about one thing, she was slightly frightening. She had somewhat of a Gothic style, which in itself was intriguing. She was able to maintain that look by wearing only a somewhat fitted black hoodie over her orange uniform. Nail polish was not permitted in the prison, but if it was, Chad was sure a fresh layer of black would have been coated on her fingernails every morning.

Her head always had sort of a downward tilt to it. Not because she had a back problem, but it looked like a self-confidence issue. Her dark brown hair was tied into a ponytail all the time, except for the patch of hair she allowed to hang over her face to shield her eyes (eyes that Chad still had not come close enough to see). Chad never noticed her utter a single word to anyone. Not to Kyle, not to Trey, not to the guys at her table during meals. She was the classic definition of antisocial.

Despite her unattractive personality, Chad would argue point after point about how beautiful the girl actually was. She did not wear makeup, but her face still had a natural blush to it. She did not go out into the yard, yet her skin maintained a natural caramel complexion. She was in shape, curved in all the right places, though she didn't appear to be very athletic. Everything about her was exceptional, seemingly natural from birth. She was everything Chad could ask for in a girl, but of course packages like her come with a little extra crazy. There must have been a reason she was one of the only fifty or so female inmates at Sanctum.

Kyle suggested that Chad and the girl had a similar story. That could be a conversation starter, or a conversation killer. Either way, it was the only topic Chad could think of. Maybe it would be best to just try to have a natural conversation. It worked with Kyle, after all. But whatever Chad would say to her, he had to keep in mind his goal. He needed to make sure he found out any important information about Trey, and determine if that info would help him escape.

It was Wednesday afternoon. Soon the inmates would be wrapping up the last of the visium excavation for that day. Instead of selecting his normal tool, the shovel, Chad took a wheelbarrow. He spent most of his time hauling barrow-fulls of visium from the mine all the way down to the processing center back at the prison. Nearly an hour's hike, traveled multiple times with around a few score pounds of glowing white rock hidden within dark dirt. It would be the last time Chad would ever make the mistake of choosing a wheelbarrow again.

But he didn't choose the wheelbarrow just to break the monotony of shovels and digging. Chad wheeled around all that dirt and visium to raise the chance of bumping into someone. It didn't take him very long to find her again. He kept an eye on her from that morning at breakfast, and he made sure he didn't lose track of her. Inconveniently, Chad had to leave her for an hour at a time when he wheeled his barrel of glowing white gold to the prison and back, but she never left that one spot in the mine.

It was an awkward spot, to say the least. It wasn't close to any type of landmark. Not a cave, not the stream, not even one of the trees held a notable position in relation to that girl's location. It was like she was trying to distance herself from everyone else.

The end of the labor period came to an end, and as usual, Moriz and his company of men and mechanical guards rounded up the inmates. They were arranged in a straight line and then marched back to the prison. This made things difficult for Chad. The girl was certainly shorter than five and a half feet, so Chad could not see her as she walked between two other inmates. Being the clever lad he thought himself to be, Chad simply stepped out of line to look ahead of him every five minutes or so. By stepping only a few feet out of the line, he could look forward to making sure that the girl's brown wavy hair was still in the same position in line as it was five minutes ago. After confirmation, he casually stepped back inline.

It was time for the day's second meal. Chad would make his move after she ate. He noticed himself become more and more excited, which confused him slightly. He had never gotten so excited to talk to any girl before. What made her so different? She was in prison... on death row. She couldn't have been anything worth drooling over, no matter how well her uniform fit her. Either way, it wouldn't be right to approach her while still sweating from the hard labor of the live long work day. A shower was in order.

Bathing around other men was never comforting, but at least this prison did not have bar soap. Not that Chad was afraid of the unspeakable, he was more than confident he'd be able to defend his rear end in such situations. He just was not comfortable with the idea of having to fight another naked man. It wasn't a good look. But after a quick bathe Chad went back into the cafeteria. Leisure and yard time had begun.

This happened to be the one time of the day where Chad had no idea where she was, but he did know the table where she usually sat. It was empty now, so Chad went over and sat in her normal spot. He scanned the room and found about twenty female inmates, more than he saw the entire time he was at Sanctum. He could see why Trey, Kyle, and the girl enjoyed that spot so much: One could see the entire cafeteria from that table. But Chad still did not see the girl.

He sat at the table for a while... no one came to the table. Chad did, however, catch many unwelcoming stares being thrown his direction. He wasn't used to that kind of attention from the prisoners, but he realized soon what it was about. For the three weeks Chad had been at Sanctum, no one besides Kyle, Trey, the girl, and the other two subordinates of Trey — subordinates who were nowhere to be seen after Trey's absence—have not been seen eating anywhere except for that table. Chad was in marked territory. Not wanting to cause any more trouble with the loud and lanky Trey upon his return, Chad left the table and strolled around the cafeteria.

It was possible Kyle knew where to find the girl at this time of the day, but he made it very clear that he wanted nothing to do with her. He even went out of his way to make sure he wasn't around when Chad started a conversation with her, which explained why Chad couldn't find his lunch buddy that day. Chad had no idea where Kyle was now, but he did know that Kyle made a point to stay out of the cafeteria. Therefore, Kyle was pretty sure that the girl would be spending her free time in the dining hall area at the same time he normally would be. How clever Chad truly felt.

But if that was true, then where was she, and why wasn't she sitting at her normal table? Chad continued to walk around the dining area, which consequently became a commons area after the food was put away. Walking through the tables and scanning each one for the girl would doubtlessly have been strange, so he did his best to avoid it. There was only one option he could think of if he was going to find her. He would need to find the best possible spot within that commons area to observe all the people in that room at once.

So he started from the entrance. Chad walked to the corner of the room and turned toward the crowd. There were many heads and faces of people, but his vision was obscured. The food line, which extended inconveniently from the wall by one entrance to the middle of the room, blocked Chad's view. This wasn't the right place to look.

Chad kept his hand on the wall and walked alongside it, making sure he maintained a clear sight of the cafeteria. He approached the opposite corner of the room, where another entrance (the exit mainly used to get to the mines and yard) provided another perspective. The food line was no longer directly in front of him, but it still blocked the view of a good amount of inmates. This wasn't the spot either, so he moved on.

He continued on to the third corner of the large room. His hand kept its position on the wall as he walked to make sure he didn't stray away from the wall accidentally while he looked at the sporadic groups of orange uniforms. Chad knew how eccentric he must have looked; stalkerishly gliding across the floor and glaring into a crowd of people as his fingertips traced the molding on the wall. The type of people who did that in the free world would normally end up in prison anyway, which made Chad look like he was where he belonged. But then again, this was Sanctum. No one in that prison had the right to point fingers as far as he was concerned.

He reached the third corner. This spot was clearly the best when it came to observing everything else in the room. That side of the room was even slightly elevated due to an inclined plane that one had to scale in order to reach that location. This is where Chad's search began.

He casually leaned his back against the wall and pretended to mind his own business while he checked every single table in that room. Every table, seat, and walkway between the seats was given a thorough inspection by Chad, who felt like a camp counselor trying to find the one naughty kid who always went astray. After giving the cafeteria a second go-around, he realized that she was not in that room. Nevertheless, it wouldn't hurt to try a different perspective in the fourth corner. Once again placing his right hand on the wall, Chad locked his gaze on the prisoners in the room as he started for the final corner. After a good six steps into his stride, his march was interrupted as both of his legs tripped over some very large object, and Chad had just enough time to wonder how he hadn't noticed an object so obtrusive before his face met the tile floor.

"Watch where you're walking, asshole," said the object. Chad flipped onto his back and dragged himself off of the unhappy speed bump. After tending to the pain in his forehead, which was his means of breaking his fall, he turned to apologize, and that's when he realized that the person he tripped over was none other than the girl he was looking for.

"Oh... Oh, wow. My bad," Chad stuttered. He seemed more apologetic than the average person would be. "Are you all right?"

"I'm fine," she answered dismissively. She rolled her eyes away from Chad and went back to doing what she was before Chad bumped into her, which was apparently nothing. She pulled her legs in and crossed them underneath her. It was now or never for Chad. He realized if he was ever going to talk to her, now would be the best time. She was prettier up close, though. Far prettier. It was almost distracting.

"Hey, you look familiar," Chad said. The girl did not acknowledge Chad's words. He'd admit it wasn't his best line, but did openers always have to be so artful? He took it a step further. "Yeah, I remember you now. You sit with Trey and Kyle."

The girl looked at Chad with slight surprise, but she kept quiet and looked forward again. Chad, who was still sitting a few feet away from her, took a more casual position beside her, still not coming within five feet of her.

"I talk with Kyle a lot," he continued. "He even mentioned you." The girl's face showed a little more botheration, but she still did not respond. "I wanted him to introduce us, but he was too busy now." Chad kept a friendly vibe, while the girl's was more towards indifference. She was good at ignoring people. Chad knew he should have seen this coming. She wanted nothing to do with any of the men there. Understandably so, since all the men were captives. Despite this, Chad knew what he could do to get her attention. He could mention the real reason he wanted to talk to her. He sighed.

"Okay," he said. "I see you don't wanna talk. But I wanted to talk to you because of something Kyle said." Still no reaction from her. Chad sat with his back against the wall as well and only turned his head slightly to speak. "He said that we're alike."

The girl's head shot toward Chad and space opened between her teeth. Chad had struck a nerve, but he didn't quite know how.

"What did he tell you?" she asked.

"Well, basically, he just mentioned that our stories were similar."

"Doubt it," she said as she turned forward again.

"Why is that?" Chad asked.

"There's no one like me."

"There's always someone out there who is going through the same thing as us," he said, wincing at his own cliche.

"You wouldn't understand."

Chad was convinced at this point that the girl was a bit of a melodrama queen, but he did not give up on her yet. He knew that Sanctum was where the worst of the killers go in the United States. If all this girl was imprisoned for was the alleged murder of her parents, then it wouldn't make sense that she wouldn't think that others in that prison may have done the same thing. That is, unless she considered herself different because she felt a great amount of guilt. But Chad was almost convinced there was something else bothering this her. It was time for the next step.

"I'd like to understand," Chad said extending his right arm over to the girl. She nearly flinched at his advancement. Never before had Chad seen so many people get threatened by a handshake. "My name's Chad, by the way." The girl narrowed her eyes to give Chad a suspicious look. There was no hidden agenda that could be seen in his eyes. That was something new to her. So new that it was almost frightening. But she couldn't trust him just yet.

"I don't shake hands," she said.

"Fair enough." Chad pulled his hand back and laid it on his lap, feeling rejected. "Do you have a name at least?"

"Andreas."

"Andrea," he repeated. "Don't wanna sound corny, but I always liked that name."

"There's an 'S' on the end, idiot."

"Andreas? Well, that's pretty unique," he chuckled. "So... why are you sitting all the way over here?" he asked.

"I like being here."

"How come?"

"Cuz I don't have to talk to anyone," she hinted.

"Ah, I see. You like the peace and quiet."

"Sure." Once again, Chad felt it time to ask the obligatory question.

"So, what are you here for?" Andreas closed her eyes and her head dropped. The part of her hair that wasn't tied back drooped over her eyes.

"Doesn't matter."

"I promise I won't judge you," Chad assured. He put on his most comforting smile. "Not that you'd believe my story. You never know who really deserves to be in a place like this or not. I just wanted to see if Kyle was right about if we're alike." There was that word again. Alike. Andreas would never think that anyone else on the planet shared the same burden she did, but the possibility of it did intrigue her.

"Even if we did the same thing, you still wouldn't be anything like me," she said.

"Is that a good thing?"

"I don't wanna talk about it, okay?" Andreas stopped talking momentarily. Chad had seen this before. Many people did it. This girl separated herself from the rest of the people in the prison, with the exception of a chosen few. She seemed to have a reason for doing this, and whatever she did to wind up at Sanctum, she loathed herself because of it. But alas, humans are a social species. And even though Andreas tried to not let anyone else into her personal life, she was a person, and persons need to vent to someone whether they want to or not. It wouldn't be fair to ask something so personal without revealing the same. So Chad told his story first.

Surprisingly, she listened to the whole story. She did not look like she wanted to walk away, she actually cared about what happened to Chad. She was a good listener. Chad noticed Andreas' eyes and mannerisms as he told his story. They were similar to Kyle's and his own. She did not walk around the prison with a chip on her shoulders. She had nothing to prove to anyone. But unlike Kyle and himself, Andreas definitely had a broken spirit. And it was time to find out why.

"So you know my story, what about yours?" Chad asked. Andreas took a few moments to decide if she wanted to tell him. A sigh and a small shake of her head sent a clear message that said 'oh, what the hell.'

"Long story short," she began, "I killed people."

"How... many?" Chad wasn't too sure if he wanted to hear the answer to that one.

"Several."

"Oh, okay." Chad paused before he spoke again. "Uhm, why'd you do it?"

"I couldn't help it." Her voice trailed off. Andreas still had never told anyone the truth about herself. No one at Sanctum could have known what she was unless they knew about her trial. People had asked before now, but none of them seemed to truly care, but this guy was different. There was something about Chad that made her feel safe. There was something oddly likable about him. More importantly, she could tell he wasn't a threat to her. That was something she knew. He wasn't trying to hurt her, or else she would have had another episode.

"What do you mean?" Chad asked.

"You really wanna know?"

"Yes, I can handle it. And I promise I won't judge you."

Andreas had heard those words before. She'd heard many things that were meant to lower her guard. But for a reason she could not figure out, this guy's words were actually comforting. She believed him. Andreas took a deep breath.

"I'm not the only one who uses this body," she said. She grasped her knees and pulled them closer to her chest. There was a slight tremor in her voice, and an obvious hint of shame in her tone. Chad was quite impressed at her statement. Never before had he heard a woman so creatively reveal the fact that she was promiscuous. Bravo. Her words almost made him chuckle, but he did his best to not sound disrespectful. After all, he said he wouldn't judge her.

"Wait, what?" he said, not quite seeing the connection between whoring it up and murder.

Andreas sighed. "When I was thirteen someone kidnapped me. I was at the pool with my parents one day and I had to go to the bathroom, so I walked away and found the closest public restroom in the apartment complex I was living in. Before I went inside, an old man snatched me and put a rag to my face. When I woke up, I was in the man's basement." Chad noticed Andreas' demeanor change. She was reliving that day, just as Kyle did when he told his story.

"I was so afraid," she said. "He was in front of me when I woke up, and he was naked. I knew what he was going to do, but I couldn't stop him. He grabbed me and I screamed as loud as I could, and I tried to fight him off but I couldn't. He ripped off my swimsuit and that's when... I fainted."

"How did you faint the second time? Was it from the stress?"

Andreas shook her head. "I thought so, but no." She hesitated again. "When I woke up, the man was dead."

"Wait, what happened?" Chad asked thinking that he missed part of the story. Andreas squinted her eyes until they shut as she tried to recreate the image.

"The guy was... on the ground. He was lying in a lot of blood." The image of Chad's father's corpse lying on the sidewalk flashed through his mind. He was reminded of his own attempt to defend himself, but he didn't faint until after he killed his father. Andreas' story seemed slightly off.

"How did you escape?"

"I called the police as soon as I woke up, and they took me to my parents. The authorities were willing to believe that I was defending myself from getting raped, but because the man's body was so battered, they thought I did more than I needed to stay alive; so they put me in juvenile detention for a few years."

"Battered?"

"You sure you want to know?" Andreas said, smiling timidly. The smile was clearly faked.

"Of course," Chad answered. He wanted to look confident, but at the same time, he was slightly fearful of what she might say. He braced himself for the rest of her story. Around this time Chad noticed Kyle walking into the room, and Kyle also noticed them. Not wanting to interrupt the conversation, he took a seat at a distant table, but he still watched Chad and Andreas interact.

Andreas shrugged, dropped her smile, and closed her eyes again. "He was lying face-down when I woke up," she said. "I never saw the front of his body until the pictures of the crime scene were taken. There were deep claw marks all over his body, and the man died from bleeding out."

"Sounds bloody," Chad commented, "but wasn't that to be expected in that kind of scenario? Why did you get in trouble?" Andreas' eyes became emptier as she stared at the floor in front of her. She exhaled, and Chad almost thought he saw the chilliness of her breath as it escaped her mouth.

"His thoraci—his chest cavity... was ripped open." Chad's expression changed to simulate what watching the gory scene of a horror movie was like. He was so distracted by the vision Andreas gave him, that he forgot to think of a clever response to show that he was still listening. Not hearing anything from Chad, Andreas turned her head slightly to see his reaction. It was exactly what she expected. "I won't blame you if you wanna leave now," she said as she buried her face in her knees. It seemed like her attempt at humor, but it only made her feel worse. Chad snapped out of his trance and asked what felt like the most compelling question.

"What in the hell made them think you did that?" he asked with a hint of horror still on his face.

"Uh, well, my hands were—" she regained her composure and clenched her fists. "The forensics came to examine the blood on my hand, and when they went through it they found bone shavings and skin cells under my nails."

Chad was in utter disbelief, looking at Andreas' hands as if there would still be evidence of such an event now. He then looked at Kyle in the distance, almost hoping that he would tell Chad what to say next. Kyle was watching, but did not show any type of reaction; he kept the same cursory glance.

"That's pretty interesting," he said.

"Stop pretending like you're not bothered by me," Andreas demanded with an empty but stern voice. "I already know you think I'm a monster."

"You're no more a monster than anyone else in here. It's just that your case is a little unique, that's all."

"Unique, huh?"

"One more question, though," Chad said. "And be honest." He paused thinking it will help get his point across. "Did you do it?"

"I don't remember," she said, once again trying to hint at something.

"Are you sure you don't remember any of it? Are you saying you were sleep-killing or something?"

"That's not what I'm saying at all, smart ass."

"Then what are saying? You may have noticed this already but I'm not the best at picking up on hints and hidden messages. Whatever you wanna say, just come out and tell me."

"Fine, then," Andreas said. She stopped talking again and licked her lips, seemingly in preparation to deliver a big speech. Out of the corner of his eye, Chad noticed something moving around. Chad turned to see Kyle waving his arms animatedly as if he were trying to taxi in an airplane. Once he got Chad's attention, he continued waving one arm as his other pointed to his left, Chad's right. Silently and dramatically, Chad mouthed the word "WHAT?", but Kyle kept flailing until he suddenly froze and buried his face in the palm of his hand while shaking his head.

"Are you listening?" Andreas questioned. Chad snapped his head back towards Andreas.

"Yeah," he responded.

"I'm only saying this once."

"Got it." Chad put on another consoling smile.

"I have—"

Something swatted Chad on his chest and knocked the air out of him. When Chad looked down, he saw that the force came from a hand, and that the hand was attached to Trey. Trey squeezed roughly—as if he was trying to grip Chad's chest—lifted Chad into the air, and pinned him to the wall while holding him by his collar.

"Whatcha doin' maccin' on ma girl, bruh?" Trey interrogated. He was seemingly back to his old self. A NegaSentry that had been posted in the corner began making its way over.

"Hey, we were just talking about you," Chad jested.

"Trey, put him down," Andreas demanded in an apathetic voice. "We've been over this. I'm not your girl."

"Shutya mouf, girl. You an' errybody in her' know I own you." He grunted to hold back a cough again, revealing that he wasn't as healthy as he looked. "Dis mofo 'bout ta learn betta." He slowly cocked his fist and pulled it back, making it painfully obvious what he was about to do next. Thinking quickly, Chad swiftly punched Trey in his throat, a move that sparked another fit of coughs. Trey released Chad, who managed to gain his footing and take a few steps away from Trey before he was able to catch his breath again.

The NegaSentry took its position between the two inmates.

"Freeze!" was the only prerecorded statement this one decided to repeat over and over. Trey recovered from coughing again and glared into Chad's eyes like a snake eyeing its prey. It was the most threatening stare Chad could ever remember receiving.

"Both inmates, report back to cell," was the next line the robot played. Chad was surprised to hear it say something different, but he was even more surprised when he saw Trey obey the commands. He kept his eyes on Chad, however.

"Dis ain't ova', boy," he proclaimed as he walked away, pointing a finger at Chad. He turned and exaggerated a gesture for Andreas to follow him, but she only shook her head. He gestured again but she did not pay him any attention, which only angered him further. Trey marched out of the commons area and into the cell hallways to the right. Another drone met him at the door and escorted him the rest of the way. Immediately after he disappeared, Andreas walked away too.

"I thought we were having a conversation," Chad said. She looked back at him but said nothing. She kept walking, took a turn, and went into the yard.

"Inmate: Galen, report to your cell," commanded the drone. Unaware that he was on a last name basis with the robot, Chad looked at it with amusement then turned and walked to his cell. The NegaSentry followed him there. Kyle stood by the commons' door as Chad passed.

"I tried to warn you," he said.

# Chapter 8

# Trey

Chad never knew what it was about Trey that intimidated people. Chad never knew what it was about Trey that intimidated people. He assumed it had something to do with the monstrous strength Trey demonstrated from time to time, usually when his anger got the better of him. It could also be the fact that Trey was the only inmate, as far as Chad had been told, to survive an execution by lethal injection. Another reason was possibly that Trey was not solemn and dispirited, unlike the rest of the Sanctum populous. Chad had to admit that any of the items on that list were pretty impressive, but being the stubborn young man that he knew himself to be, he would never admit to being intimidated by Trey. The main thing that bothered him about their previous altercation was the fact that it interrupted him from finishing his conversation with Andreas.

Although Chad felt that he made a new friend, he couldn't help but think that Andreas still had more to say. Chad was literally pulled away before she could make her big reveal, whatever it was about, and there was no telling how willing she was to resume their talk another time. This may not have looked like such a big deal before, but now Trey was back in the picture, and he didn't seem too thrilled at the fact that Chad was talking with—who he refers to as—his girl. But in the end, even that was not what upset Chad most about the situation.

After a somewhat heartfelt talk with Andreas, Chad still felt no closer to accomplishing his big goal. Perhaps it was his own fault for letting himself be sidetracked, but now there was nothing else poking at his curiosity that would distract him. He already scoped out every corner of the prison's internal layout, or at least every corner that was accessible to inmates. The only remaining factor now was finding the best locations outdoors to hide and run when the time came.

Jason knew nothing that could benefit Chad's cause, and neither did Kyle or Andreas. Conversation with Trey was out of the question and didn't even strike Chad's fancy. It wouldn't be wise to mention to anyone else what his intentions were, so Chad would act on the information he already obtained. He gave himself another few days before the appointed time would arrive. The one month anniversary of his arrival seemed like the appropriate time. At that point, he would have faded enough into the background to no longer be such a conspicuous individual. All Chad would have to do until then was avoid any more encounters with the infamous Trey like the one that took place yesterday.

Warden Moriz's morning march woke the inhabitants of the cells and Thursday was underway. Chad got dressed; a process that took less than five minutes considering his entire wardrobe consisted of hiking boots, his prison uniform, and a North Face vest. When he arrived in the cafeteria he grabbed his meal from the food line and took a spot against the wall as usual, but this time he chose to sit slightly farther away from Andreas and Trey's table. Instead of following the normal routine, Kyle decided to join Chad on the wall that morning.

"So I'm guessin' you ain't get her *cell* number, did ya?" Kyle jested as he took a seat to Chad's right.

"Maybe I would have if Trey-Songz over there didn't cock block me," Chad replied.

"Oh, I so agree, dude. A dick move on his part." Kyle took a bite of his food, an egg scramble that was of considerably high quality. "So whad di Anreas tehl you?" he asked between chews.

"Nothing that would've helped me out. But I guess it was pretty interesting stuff nonetheless."

"Did she tell you how she ended up here?" Kyle asked. Chad thought for a few seconds before replying.

"Actually, no. She didn't. She told me how she ended up going to Juvie for attacking some guy when she was thirteen, but she never mentioned how she got here. I guess she never got to it."

"Attacked a guy? She never mentioned that to me before."

"Maybe you should talk to your lunch buddy more often," Chad teased as he also took a bite of his meal. He pondered as he chewed and swallowed before he spoke again. "So wait, if she never told you about the guy she killed when she was young then what did she tell you?"

"She killed a guy that young?"

"Quite gruesomely, actually. Or so she says. I don't really believe her. But answer my question first."

"It was a while ago. Back when I first met her." Instead of staring blankly, Kyle looked up and to the side to remember this story. Apparently, it didn't have a scarring effect on his soul like the other one did. "It was when Trey kinda chose me to be his personal, uhm, assistant, I guess. When he wanted me to start sittin' at that table with them. I asked her what she did to get here, ya know, small talk. And she told me that she killed her parents. She wasn't lyin' either. I could tell." Chad wasn't shocked to hear that he and Andreas had similar stories for being in prison, however, he was put off by the fact that Kyle could clarify that she told the truth.

"What's weird to me," Kyle continued, "is that she ain't tell me what she told you."

"I was thinking the same thing. Should I be mad that she lied to me about what happened to her, or is that a common thing around here?"

"Bro, she wasn't lyin'."

"Are you sure about that?" Chad pressed.

"Yep. Well, depends when she told ya," Kyle said rather matter-of-factly. "If I was in the room when she told you that story, then I know she was tellin' the truth." Chad squinted his eyes slightly to emphasize his skepticism.

"But you were way too far away to actually hear anything she said. How are you so sure what she was saying then?"

"I don't know what she said," Kyle noted, "I just know that whatever she said to you when I was there watchin' ya was true."

Chad paused for a moment to make sense of what he just heard. He thought back to when Kyle showed up in the commons area. It was right in the middle of Andreas' story about the man who tried to rape her. Kyle happened to show up right when her story became questionably bloody, and as much as Chad trusted in Kyle's ability to pick out falsehoods, he couldn't help but challenge the fact that what Andreas said to him yesterday was true.

From a logical standpoint, there was no way that it was physically possible for a thirteen-year-old girl to rip open a man's chest and gouge out his organs. Not only that, but Andreas also claimed to have no memory of the event that transpired after the man tried to deflower her. That in itself seemed to be the kind of thing a person would remember, yet she knew nothing of what happened to the man until the crime scene photos were revealed. The whole story lacked validity, in hindsight.

"Whatever she told ya," Kyle started again, "there's one thing I can tell about her." Chad came out of his thought bubble.

"What's that?"

"She likes you, dude." It wasn't exactly the news Chad wanted to hear.

"And what in the world makes you think that?"

"Few reasons. One; when I asked her for her story all she told me was she killed her parents, but naaw, not with you. She told you a long story that I ain't never heard about."

"Which I still think is a lie," Chad interrupted. "But what else?"

"The second reason; I could tell by how she talked to you. She was open. All she ever gives me or anybody else at the table is poker-faced looks. She really wants nothin' to do with us. I really don't even know why she sits with us." Kyle had a good point. If there was anything Chad *did* know about Andreas was that she was distant from other people. Even Chad was slightly surprised when she told him the story about the would-be rapist. That was something personal, and she still wasn't quite comfortable telling that story yet, which said a lot if she was willing to tell someone like Chad. In all fairness, since Chad did reveal his own story first, it was possible that Andreas told her story because she felt obligated to. But that still did not mean she *had* to.

"Third reason," Kyle said. "Look behind me."

Chad shifted his eyes slightly to the left, where he could see Trey, Andreas, and two other finishing their breakfast at their special table. Chad looked at Andreas, who always sat with her back turned to Chad, but this time she was sitting sideways and away from Trey. That would not have meant anything on any other occasion. But this time, Andreas happened to be looking at Chad, and he noticed her looking at him as inconspicuously as she could before they locked eyes. After being caught she turned away as if she was never looking.

"Ya see that?" Kyle asked. Chad was not used to that kind of look. Of course, he had received looks and stares from classmates before. They were often more lewd, or provocative looks, but looks nonetheless. However, this expression was different. Andreas did not want to be noticed while she was noticing Chad. If she had a sluttish agenda, she surely would not have gone out of her way to hide her interest in the man she was after. Not unless there was emotion involved. "Bro," Kyle said to call Chad's attention back to himself. "I noticed she kept lookin' at the door before you got here. When you walked in the room she fixed her eyes on you. Coincidence? I think not."

"Sure notice a lot, don't you?"

"It's a curse," Kyle chuckled.

As much as Chad appreciated the notion that someone with as much perceivable beauty as Andreas had a crush on him, he wasn't in the best place in his life to start a relationship. Relationship was a sentiment by itself that was nearly foreign. Chad had girlfriends in the past, but the concept of falling in love was alien. There was no room for googly-eyes in the Galen family. Or at least, that's what he learned from watching his father. The last thing in the world Chad would ever do was allow himself to be anything like his father. That said, could he really trust himself to have a romantic relationship with anyone? Chad could only hope the apple fell fairly far from the tree, but with cases of domestic violence, often times the men who committed the crimes were victims of such treatment themselves. It was all they knew.

It was a frightening realization, but Chad refused to allow himself to harm someone that he loved. But then again, he had never experienced love before. He really didn't know what he would do if he happened to fall in love with some girl, but he could only imagine it would not result in his partner's pain and suffering.

Chad halted all thought. These were insipid and irrelevant thoughts for a prisoner. Now wasn't the time to be caught up in the rapture of love, whatever that felt like. It didn't matter how positively pulchritudinous her face was, or how caramel her complexion was, or how dazzlingly dark her brown hair was, or how astonishingly auburn her eyes were. It didn't matter. He had to stay focused on his goal, and there was no room for distraction. It was nice to know he hadn't lost any of his charm from spending so much time around so many rough and unkempt men, though.

Kyle watched Chad's eyes as they displayed the inner conflict that was taking place in his mind, and a smile broke across Kyle's face. Chad came out of his state of deep thought and noticed Kyle beaming at him.

"What's your problem?" Chad questioned.

"Nothin'," Kyle replied. His childlike innocence gleamed through his smile. Aware that Kyle knew what he was thinking about, Chad changed the subject.

"Anyway, who are those other two guys over there?" he asked. Without looking, Kyle knew who Chad was talking about.

"Those guys are Trey's homies. They all knew each other before they came here, and they're probly here for the same crime. I honestly don't know their real names, but they call themselves Skull and Bones. Skull's the bald one."

"Anyone I need to worry about?"

"Naw. They're tools." Chad found Kyle's choice of words ironic, but out of respect, he chose not to say anything to hurt his friend's feelings. He already knew Kyle was a softy. "But I gotta go. I don't want

Trey on my ass about talkin' to you."

"Does he think I'm the enemy now or something?"

"I think so. I'll keep ya up to date, bro." And on that note, Kyle walked back over to his special table. It was like the popular table of prison. The five of them together reminded Chad of a stereotypical group of friends as Disney would perceive, but Trey's vocabulary was nothing that Disney would ever air on television, unfortunately.

Kyle placed his tray of food on the table and then took his seat. To the left of him at the roundtable were Skull and Bones, who had long finished their meals, and had nothing better to do at the moment than give Kyle an antagonizing stare. To Kyle's right, Andreas, who kept her eyes on the plate of food that had barely been touched. And directly across the table was Trey who joined Skull and Bones in trying to leer the brows off of Kyle's face. Trey cracked an openly sinister smile before he spoke.

"You git anythang good fo' me?" he asked.

"Whaddya mean?" Kyle replied.

"Ah bin gawn fo' a week now, boy. You betta have some new infamation fo' me!" Kyle hesitated before he could respond.

"Uhh, Oh. You mean from Jason? I talked to him the other—"

"Ah already tahk to'em."

"Oh, uh, when? I thought you guys weren't supposed to be doin' that in public..."

"Well we ain't doin' dat no mo'," Trey announced. Kyle didn't know what to say. He was well aware of the fact that if he was no longer the go-between for Trey and Jason's private chats, then his purpose had been served, and there was no more reason to stick around a table full of people he didn't even like. Hesitantly, he picked up his tray of food and slowly turned to leave his seat.

"I'll just go then," he said, not sure if that was what Trey was hinting to. Bones, who sat just to Kyle's left, reached for Kyle's arm and pulled him back to his chair with convincing force. His message was well interpreted. Kyle knew he wasn't going anywhere.

"Nah, nah, you still got bidness wit me," Trey continued. Kyle sighed softly as he put his food back on the table. "You needta tell me who ya new friend is. I heard he bin askin' people 'bout me." Kyle noticed Andreas' eyes move. They went from facing forward with the rest of her body to looking at the plate in front of Kyle. She listened for the answer but didn't want anyone to notice.

"Who, him?" Kyle asked nodding towards Chad. "He's just some new guy. He only got here a week before you got sick."

"What he ask you?" Kyle thought it was quite presumptuous of Trey to think that Chad would have asked him anything, despite how true it was.

"Nothin', dude. He just asked how you got so strong."

"An' what you say?"

"Uhh, nothin'..."

"Mhmm, yeah. Well, how 'bout dis." Trey leaned forward, putting one hand on the edge of the table while the other made gestures in front of his face. The current gesture was a finger pointed at Kyle. It almost looked like something an old man would do. "Jason tol'me all 'bout all da shit y'all bin plannin', an' y'all crayz if ya think I'ma let y'all jump me!"

"Whoa, dude, what are you talkin' about?"

"Don' gimme dat' SHIT!" Trey raised his voice to something more aggressive. "I don' believe in dat sapprise attack bull so I'ma let you know exactly wha' I'm 'boutta do. Befo' lights-out tonight I'ma make sure you anyaboy ova there find out how strong I really is."

"What the heck makes you think we were gonna do somethin' like that?" Kyle asked with an exaggerated vexed look on his face.

"Jason gotma back," Trey replied. "he tol' me y'all been plannin' sumtin'. Now getya ass outta here, I'ma see you tanight!"

"What? Dude! We don't even talk to Jason! He's makin' it up."

"He said get outta here," Skull repeated. Bones continued his work at being the physical presence at the table by shoving Kyle backward and out of his seat. Guards entered the room as the transition to the mines began. Kyle stood and looked around to make sure he wasn't grabbing too much attention.

"We don't want trouble," he pleaded a final time, but Trey didn't listen.

"Jus'wait 'til tanight," he assured as he nodded. Skull and Bones laughed together, prompting Kyle to walk away. As all the inmates in the cafeteria began to line up for the exit, Kyle searched for Chad, but he was nowhere to be seen. Kyle tried to keep himself calm. He knew that he had until the end of the day to prepare for a confrontation with Trey, and had until then to inform Chad. He did, however, find it in his best interest to find Chad as soon as he could so they could create a plan together. But until Chad turned up, he would try to find out where Jason was.

Kyle was well aware that Jason had a knack for starting trouble while keeping himself out of the crossfire. Usually, he would create a riot or start some kind of fight if he was up to something, but Kyle had no idea what Jason's intentions were this time.

It was possible that Jason was trying to prove a point to Kyle and Chad. He could be telling them to stay out of his business and don't get in his way, or else. Jason was more than capable of beating someone up himself, so it didn't quite make sense why he would lie to Trey and convince him that he was the target of an attack just to accomplish the same goal, especially since Trey was already so sick. It was definitely a new low, but Kyle wouldn't put it past Jason to exercise his ability to manipulate people just to stay sharp.

All the inmates formed their lines and were escorted to the tools outside the prison. Kyle continued his search for Jason and Chad, but he could not find either. Chad was not seen by his normal tools of choice—the shovels—which was odd, since Kyle was aware that Chad loathed all the other tools. Kyle went to grab a pick and returned to the line. There was never any time to converse with others, so there was no way to ask if anyone had seen Chad. Not that anyone really knew who Chad was, but under the rather dire circumstances, it wouldn't hurt to try his luck at asking around.

The daily hour hike to the mines was nerve-racking, and it was difficult for Kyle to maintain his cheery attitude. It was an emotion he hadn't felt since childhood. It was the feeling of awaiting a spanking from his parents after knowing that he did something that would get him added to Santa's naughty list. He knew a storm was coming that night, and the only person who could help him was nowhere to be seen. Trey was enough of a problem, but now that he enlisted the help of his mindless lackeys it was three against two, which meant Skull and Bones would most likely be the ones to hold Kyle and Chad down while Trey went to town on them.

The prisoners arrived at the mines and Kyle quickly went to his normal digging area, hoping that Chad would join him as he usually would, but after the first hour there was still no sign of him. Kyle surveyed the area. Jason was also nowhere to be seen, and Trey's mouth was still nowhere to be heard. It was a very inconvenient day for people to explore new areas of the mine. Bones was doing what he did best and was hauling visium back to the prison's processing center. Skull was also at his normal station inside of one of the taverns nearby. The last person who could help Kyle save his skin was Andreas.

It was always arduous to have to find Andreas when she was out in the mines. She did a good job of making sure no one could find her, which at this moment was fairly irritating. Kyle took his pick and smashed away at the large boulders in his normal section. Once he made a large enough mess for one to assume he was actually working, he moved on to the next area where he thought Andreas may be. He continued this charade multiple times until he finally found her. She was digging a hole in a spot between a couple average-looking trees. The location she chose didn't appear to be very rewarding since there were no other inmates in her vicinity. Kyle briskly walked over to the opposite side of the hole Andreas dug and joined her.

"Hey," he said, "have you seen Chad?" Andreas gave him a confused look before responding.

"No," she said as she kept digging. Not quite satisfied with her answer, Kyle pried for more.

"Well, have you seen Jason?" he asked more frantically.

"I don't talk to him. What do you—"

"Why does Trey wanna fight me?!" Kyle's desperateness became more visible as his swings got harder. Andreas sighed before answering, not wanting to be involved in Kyle's drama.

"You shouldn't have plotted to jump him."

"But I didn't! Jason lied to him!" Andreas paused from shoveling and her eyes flickered in Kyle's direction, as if she was taking in new information, then she continued again without speaking. "Can ya tell him to NOT attack us please?"

"Leave me out of it," she said. Kyle groaned with anxiety and frustration. It was time to up the ante.

"The least ya could do is help out ya boyfriend."

"Stop. Calling. Trey. My boyfriend," Andreas demanded.

"I wasn't talkin' about Trey." Andreas glared at Kyle and she gripped the shovel in her hand like she was preparing to use it for something other than digging.

"I hope Trey bashes your head in, idiot."

"So does that mean you're not gonna help?" Before Andreas could formulate a proper insulting response, a voice called from over a nearby hill.

"There you guys are!" the voice yelled. Kyle and Andreas looked at the hill and saw Chad wobbling down the declining terrain with a half-full wheelbarrow of dirt and visium. He pulled up beside the hole Andreas and Kyle were digging in and idly began sifting through dirt. "I'm guessing you guys didn't find anything useful, did you?"

"I've been lookin' freakin' everywhere for you," Kyle exclaimed. "Why the heck do you have a wheelbarrow?"

"Uh, no reason... What's up?"

"Dude, Trey is trynna fight us." In his squatted position, Chad looked up at Kyle with a raised brow and semi-smile on his face, unsure whether or not Kyle was joking. "Jason told Trey we were gonna jump him, now he wants to jump us first." Chad's smile quickly went away as he stood straight up. He turned to Andreas in search of confirmation, but she kept her eyes at the hole in the ground as she repositioned her hands on the shovel to do something more appropriate with it. She took another scoop into the land and pretended not to listen.

"Does this have to do with yesterday?" Chad asked her.

"Kinda, but not entirely," she said shyly.

"Bro, he's not playin' around," Kyle added. "He said tonight before lights-out he's gonna do it! Skull and Bones are gonna help him..."

"Are you sure about this?" Chad asked, realizing that it probably wasn't the most helpful of questions.

"Yes, dude. He told me this mornin' right after I went back to the table. I woulda told you then but you disappeared." Finally thinking of a more appropriate question, Chad queried again.

"Have you talked to or seen Jason all day?"

"He's been gone, too. I got no clue where he is."

Chad nodded to assure Kyle that he understood the situation, but he still was not at ease. Kyle was staring intently at Chad, and Andreas cocked her head slightly to the side and leaned on her shovel as she also gave Chad an attentive look. She didn't seem as worried about the situation as Kyle did, which Chad assumed was because she wasn't the one at risk of being beaten to a pulp.

Chad realized that he was apparently the one responsible for conjuring up a plan to escape the situation, but so far nothing was coming to mind. The only thing that pried into his mind was the fact that Jason was stirring up trouble and someone else, namely Chad, was having to deal with the consequences. The fact that Jason hadn't been seen since early that morning didn't bother him as much either. He chose to solve the immediate problem one step at a time. It would be more important to locate the person threatening him at this point.

"Okay then, have either of you seen Trey since the mining started?" he asked.

"Naw," Kyle said.

Andreas only shook her head. "He's not out here today," she mentioned. "He's been exempt from mining because he's still sick."

"I see," Chad said. Andreas smiled bashfully, seemingly happy to help. And when she turned to return to her digging Chad realized that it was the first time since he arrived at Sanctum that he had seen her smile.

"I guess that's good, right?" Kyle asked. Chad didn't hear the question. He became suddenly distracted by the unorthodox appeal of the shoveling taking place beside him. He didn't understand what it was. Something about the sound of Andreas' shovel was smoother when it dug into the ground, much smoother than any other he heard. Even the sound of the dirt she threw into a pile beside her stood out as being above-average grade. Maybe she found visium in that land.

Whatever it was, something became captivating about the simple motions of scooping dirt and throwing it to the side. There was almost a grace involved in Andreas' motions.

"Dude, FOCUS!" Kyle slapped Chad on the side of his shoulder and immediately reminded him of the problem at hand.

"Uh, yeah. It is good," Chad finally replied. He peaked over to Andreas to check if she noticed him watching her shovel. She hadn't, which spared Chad certain embarrassment.

"So what're we gonna do?" Kyle asked, vesting all decision making power to Chad. Not too happy about his new responsibility, Chad spoke as he assessed the situation.

"All right. Well, I do think it's pretty important that we find Jason and see why he's being a dick once again by spreading rumors about us. I honestly wouldn't have minded it as much if we weren't in danger of an ass-kicking at the moment. But either way, we just need to stay clear of Trey, Tweedledee, and Tweedledum."

"Ain't really as easy as it sounds, ya know."

"I'm sure. That's why we should probably stay fairly close to one of those guys." Chad pointed to the robot that stood not too far away. "I don't think it's that likely they'll try to jump us with one of those things around. They can't be that stupid."

"Maybe we should tell a guard to watch our backs."

"Can't. I wish, but if I'm gonna do that *thing*," Chad winked with the eye Andreas couldn't see from her angle, "I can't afford a high profile." The drone posted not too far from three beeped repeatedly. It was similar to a siren, but only lasting for a second at a time. "Crap, did it hear me?" Chad asked as his heart dropped.

"Naw, it does that when it sees people not working for so long," Kyle said.

"Better start digging," Andreas suggested. Another shy smile crossed her face. Kyle grabbed his pick and started walking back toward the main taverns. Chad hesitantly reached for his wheelbarrow, quickly glanced at Andreas, and let it go as he walked to the pile of dirt and sifted through it carefully. The drone's alarm disengaged.

"You coming?" Kyle asked.

"In a bit," Chad replied, "gotta pick up the visium from here."

"Don't ya think we should be stickin' together?"

"Don't worry. Just make sure you stay in plain sight and you'll be okay." Kyle was clearly not satisfied with that response, and he knew what Chad really wanted to do. He then surveyed the area. His posture resembled a child looking into the darkness for the nearest lit landmark to run to. "I'll come find you after I take this pile back to the prison, all right?" Kyle still wasn't satisfied, but he realized that was the best he was getting. Timidly, he walked back to the taverns, being sure not to come too close to any tree or large rock that may harbor any hidden attacker.

Chad took a deep breath and returned to his dirt, which Andreas continued to pile on. There was a short pause, then Chad finally broke the silence.

"So, um, hey," he began. Her eyes flickered to Chad and back to the shovel.

"Hey," she said.

".." And there it was. For the first time Chad could not think of a single word to say to a girl. There were no funny jokes he could throw out in the open, no clever remarks to put a smile on her face, and definitely no way to sneak tension-building physical contact into the interaction without looking like he was going to capitalize on it in a violating way.

This had never happened before, and the lack of conversation was almost discomforting. The pace of Andreas' scoops began to slow, and it was clear she was waiting for Chad to say something. As Chad saw it, she was listening to him as he pretended to be somebody with an idea of how to speak to someone he was interested in. And then there was the clarification. Chad was indeed interested in this girl. It took longer to realize this than it normally would. Chad knew that she was attractive long before he had any intention of talking to her, but that wasn't the dealmaker when he finally decided to approach her.

Chad recalled his original excuse: Find out if she knew anything useful. Anything at all that could serve him well as meaningful information in his plot to break out of prison. In hindsight, it was a bit of a stretch. What could she have known that would benefit him in the long run? Chad questioned himself. Did he lie to himself? It became increasingly likely that he only used his future goal—a completely irrelevant event—for an excuse to talk to this girl whom he had never met before, simply because he wasn't creative enough to think of something legitimate.

It didn't make any sense. What made her so different from all the other girls? Why did talking to her feel absolutely necessary? Why was it so damn hard to think of something to say? Chad wasn't used to making such decisions when emotions were involved. But what emotions could cause such an embarrassing lapse of mental performance? It couldn't be fear; fear doesn't feel warm. The warmth, however, was coming from the middle of his chest. It didn't feel like heartburn, but it was coming from the heart. It wasn't hate, but happiness comes from the heart. Was it pleasure? Joy? Or maybe even—

It couldn't be.

"Yeah?" Andreas chimed, reminding Chad that she was still waiting for him to speak. He still had no ideas for topics.

"Um, what were we talking about yesterday?" he asked. Andreas formed her mouth to answer, but she realized that she did not want to resume chatting on the topic. "Oh yeah, your story."

"Let's not talk about that."

"But, you were about to say something important right before—"

"No," she shot down Chad's attempt. Chad did not want to push his luck, but reaching for another subject would be far too difficult now. After all, he made notable progress yesterday before he was interrupted. It would be a shame to let it all go to waste.

"I'm not backing down so easily," he said, trying his best to muster enough confidence to at least look the part. Andreas kept shoveling, moving to the opposite side of the hole. "Besides, you were ready to tell me yesterday, weren't you?" Her rate of digging increased again, and she was seemingly drowning out Chad's words with loud, hard scoops into the dirt. "It can't be that bad. Just tell me what it is."

Andreas aggressively drove her shovel straight down into the loose dirt. She gripped the edge of the handle and gave Chad a hard glare.

"Why do you care?" she asked, speaking with a stern tone but a soft voice. Taken aback by the sudden aggression, Chad was slow to respond.

"Is that a trick question?"

"You have no idea what I've done... none at all." Her voice wavered and cracked slightly. "People called me a monster. They still do. All the time..."

"I'm pretty sure everyone in this place was called a monster at some point. Except me. Not yet, anyway."

"Well, they're right about me." She brought her dust-caked hands to her face and softly wiped her eyes with the back of her wrists. Chad saw the moisture around her eyes and then noticed how her eyes seemed to glisten an even brighter tone of auburn when they welled with tears. He then wondered if that was a weird thing to notice.

"What makes you say that? A monster would never show remorse for what they did. And all I see from you is remorse."

"Is that supposed to make me feel better?"

"I was just sayin'. No need to be ashamed." Chad wanted to press for more, and he wanted to keep talking to her, but there was something highly unappealing about seeing tears fall from this girl's face. Not that it made her any less attractive, but seeing her upset also made him feel less than okay. There would be plenty of time to get to know Andreas, so there was no need to rush into learning about her. She would tell him when she was ready, and Chad was fine with remaining ignorant for the time being. He beckoned for Andreas' shovel. "Can I borrow that?"

Chad threw the nearly waist-high pile of dirt onto his wheelbarrow and returned the shovel. Afterwards, he grabbed the handles of the wheelbarrow and made his way around the hole and back onto the path from where he came.

"Tell you what," he said. "I know it's not the easiest thing to talk about, so I'll stop asking. But if you ever do wanna talk about it, I'll be here to listen, okay?" Andreas said nothing, but she responded with a nod. Before he walked away, he smiled at Andreas. She smiled back. It was small, but it was there, and it was genuine. Chad turned and started for the prison's processing center.

There it was again. That warmth.

After the daily mines were completed, Chad and Kyle went into the yard and spent the remainder of the day there. Both of their minds were preoccupied.

Kyle spent most of his time pondering the inevitable night that awaited him. He contemplated a myriad of random excuses to escape the situation. *Maybe I should say I'm sick, and I'd get put over to the medic-wing. That'll give me at least one more day or two.* Even the thought of starting a fight with another inmate (who wasn't Trey) and getting thrown into solitary confinement seemed like an exceptional alternative. That would be about a week's worth of refuge by itself, and it would give him plenty of time to think up another way to avoid Trey.

Kyle was also still bothered by Jason's absence throughout the entire day. He was always good at turning up when he wanted something and then disappearing again when he didn't want to be seen, but this was just cruel. He may have been the reason that Chad and Kyle were in their current scenario, but Kyle thought it polite to at least explain why he instigated such a fight. Jason's random acts of shadiness were becoming quite bothersome.

Chad had something else on his mind, and for the first time in weeks, it was not escaping. He became curious how long it would take until Andreas was finally ready to reveal her full story. It wasn't the story itself that was captivating, but it made Chad feel nice to know that she trusted him enough to share even a little. Even the thought of having another conversation with her was enjoyable. It made the warmth feel stronger, and finding out what that warmth was became deathly important. But in order to investigate the cause of that feeling, he would have to remain in the prison for a while longer. Making sure that he didn't jump too far from reality, he posed the question to himself early. Was the warmth more important than freedom? Of course not. It wasn't a question worth considering. But the warmth was worth staying at Sanctum for at least a little longer, wasn't it?

Kyle leaned his head to the right and looked up at Chad who took a place beside him sitting on the wall. He gave his friend a quick once-over, sizing up his new tag-teammate.

"How's that legga yours?" he asked.

"Still hurts, but I could still fight I, guess." Kyle drooped his head as if it gained fifty pounds instantaneous and moaned. "Any sign of Jason?" Chad asked.

"Nope. And I'm outta ideas."

"Guess that means we'll be fighting then, won't we?"

Kyle brought a hand to his forehead and slowly and thoroughly wiped down to his chin, in hopes of wiping off the stress from his face. He looked at the sky and noticed that it was almost time for lights-out. On the outside, he almost looked prepared for a fight, but he felt his insides quiver as the time approached. Then after an agreeable nod to each other, they both stood up and walked towards the door of the prison.

"I got a question for you," Chad stated as they entered the doorway.

"Yeah?"

"Can you fight at all?" Chad knew the likely response was going to be a no, but he figured that small talk wouldn't hurt. And the question at least seemed relevant to the situation. Kyle took a deep breath.

"Yeah."

"Wait, you can?"

"Me and my friends used to watch a lotta UFC. Pretty easy to pick up on stuff."

"Then why are you so worried? You look like a chicken that knows a butcher knife is coming."

"Never said I liked to fight, though." Kyle trailed off, apparently losing interest in the topic. They walked into the commons area and took a seat at a nearby table.

"Okay... but you know how to fight. So tonight shouldn't be too much of an issue, right?" Kyle said nothing. He put his elbow on the table and rested his chin in his palm. "Uhm, hello? This seems to be the best time to use your little UFC skills, don't you think?"

"I'm not goin' to."

"But why not?"

"Because..." Kyle trailed off again hoping that Chad wouldn't push any further. Unfortunately, Chad kept a hard gaze on Kyle; a gaze that clearly stated that Chad would not let the subject go until he had a satisfactory answer. Giving up on avoiding the subject, Kyle continued. "It's cuz of Joey."

"Your friend? Go on..."

"We used to have lil sparring matches all the time."

"So what does that have to do with now?" Chad asked with growing impatience.

"I just don't like fightin' people. It reminds me too much of that day." Chad noticed Kyle's eyes change slightly. It resembled the look that he had when he told the story of why he was in prison. More importantly, the look was even more similar to the one Kyle had when he was hit by Jason. It was the look of brokenness.

Chad finally realized what triggered the depression in Kyle. Unlike the other prisoners, Kyle wasn't broken by the fact that he was condemned to death. The only thing that broke his spirit was remembering the event that changed his life. The fact that he witnessed his friend drown and could do nothing about it. Chad couldn't imagine how much the idea of surfing or skating may have affected him, but when it came to sparring, something else that he and his friend enjoyed doing for fun, it was the definite reminder of the friend he lost.

"Okay, listen," Chad said in a compassionately masculine way, "I know you're still shaken by your friend's death, but you gotta move on from it."

"Ya think I haven't tried that?"

"I'm sure, but it's getting in the way of your, and my, safety. I bet the only reason Trey chose you was because you refuse to fight back. He probably knew you weren't going to resist." Kyle's head dropped slowly. He was either trying to comprehend Chad's words or sulking again. "I know it's not easy to move on, but you gotta forgive yourself for what happened to your friend. You can't be afraid to fight back."

"Fighting back is only gonna remind me how I screwed up," Kyle said, wiping more stress from his face.

"I know, but running from your problem isn't going to solve it."

Kyle chuckled nervously. "Runnin', huh? It's funny you say that." He raised his head and was wearing a fairly pronounced scowl. "I guess we both got a problem with that."

"What that hell's that supposed to mean?" Chad asked combating Kyle's scowl with one of his own.

Kyle raised a brow. "Why did your dad come after you?"

"Uhm, obviously because he was a psycho," Chad retorted.

"So you really don't know what I'm talking 'bout?"

"I seriously have no idea what you're getting at."

"Naw? Why didn't you tell your parents where you were goin' to college?"

"Cause' they didn't need to know."

"Bullshit. You were runnin' away."

"That was different." Chad leaned forward at the table and assumed a more argumentative tone. "I needed to get out of there because it wasn't a good place to be."

"Ya coulda confronted your dad long ago and handled the situation, I bet. But naaw, you just ran away cause you were scared of him, weren't ya?"

"Screw you! I'm in here now 'cause he attacked me and my mom, and I got blamed for it."

"Oh yeah, and now you're in here, what's your goal again?" Kyle asked.

Chad stopped to think for a moment. He knew exactly what Kyle meant, but there had to be another way to phrase it. Chad considered the word 'escape', but that would only strengthen Kyle's argument.

"Breakin' out this place sure as hell don't count as facin' your problems," Kyle added.

"What in the world makes you think you can talk to me about my problem?"

"Probly the same self-righteousness that made you say something to me."

Chad banged on the table and stood up. "You know what?" he said. "Forget it. When Trey comes around and tries to make you his bitch again, I'm not going to help you! Handle it yourself." Before Kyle could respond he stormed off and left the commons. Chad was appalled. How could someone like Kyle, someone who couldn't even defend himself from fear of remembering the past, dare criticize how he solved his problems? The guy had no right.

Chad did not return to his cell, but instead, he tried to clear his head by taking a short walk around the prison. There was no doubt in his mind that the decisions he made were for the best. His parents didn't deserve to be in his life. He knew no one could truly judge him for wanting to start fresh, especially if he was pursuing his dreams in college. And as for Sanctum, he knew with every fiber of his being that he did not murder his parents. He was not to blame for their deaths, he merely did as anyone else would do in that situation and... run?

Of course they would run. The man had a gun, after all. There was no true way you could combat that with hands and fists, at least not from a distance. The logical thing was to jump out of the window. The logical thing was to kick the gun out of his hand. And after retrieving the gun, the logical thing would have been to threaten the person who was attacking someone to stop while using the very weapon he had just used on someone else.

Of course, it was Chad's father who was at fault. He killed Chad's mother. He tried to kill Chad. More importantly, he tried to attack the person who held a gun to his face. Who would do something like that? If he hadn't tried to take the gun from Chad, maybe there wouldn't have been the need for Chad to grip the gun as tightly as he did. There would not have been a bloodstained sidewalk, nor would there be a by-standing neighbor who would become the pivotal witness for a murder trial. A witness who somehow vanished during the trial.

Chad sat down in a secluded wing in the prison. Not many prisoners were in that area, but there was a single NegaSentry guarding the hall. Confirming his protection from any immediate threat, Chad went back to his thoughts.

The vanishing witness. Someone who knew Chad, who knew his family. It made no sense that she would not be taken into consideration for the trial. She disappeared, and no one thought it was suspicious? It had to be some kind of misdemeanor, infraction, or something to not show up to court.

Chosen.

Jason's conspiracy was beginning to make more sense. Or at least, Chad wanted it to. Not everything Jason said could be trusted. If it could, Chad and Kyle wouldn't be in the predicament they were in. But despite the possible lies Jason could be telling, there was no denying the fact that Chad knew he was innocent. Involuntary manslaughter was one thing, but sentenced to death because one woman wanted to relive her high school days and went truant? It didn't make sense. Chad did not belong at Sanctum, and he would do whatever it took to clear his name. And as of now, that meant escaping.

An announcement came on over the P.A. system. It was finally time to return to the cells for the night. Chad felt somewhat accomplished. He made the day without dealing with Trey and his goons. All he had to do now was safely make his way back to his cell. Kyle wasn't around, not that Chad wanted him to be, but without him, Chad would have to find someone else to escort him to the other wing of the hallway. He turned towards the NegaSentry and briefly examined it. It hadn't ceased to surprise him so far, it was time to try something new.

"Uhm, hello," Chad said. The drone turned its head toward Chad. It was intimidating, but cool at the same time. "Ehh, can you please escort me to my cell?"

"State inmate name," commanded the drone in a very robotic voice. Chad tried to keep his amusement at bay.

"Chad Galen," he said with a grin. The sentry was silent and then turned to the opposite end of the hallway.

"Acknowledged," it stated and rolled down the hall. Chad chuckled out loud.

"That's so boss," he said. Further ahead of him, Chad heard a voice.

"*I'm* the boss," it said. From around the corner walked Trey and Skull. Behind them, Bones stood—reprising his role as the physical one—and he was holding someone in his arms. It was Kyle. He was in a headlock and seemingly unable to escape. He was struggling to breathe. Slightly startled, Chad clenched his teeth and fists. He pretended to be unfazed as he and the NegaSentry walked closer to them.

"I heard you guys were gonna come looking for us eventually," Chad stated in a playful and unnerving tone. "I'd honestly love to play, but I don't think we're allowed to with daddy right here." Chad pointed to the robot. "I also don't think it likes the way you're playing with my buddy there."

"Inmate Taylor, release the Inmate Lyons," the drone commanded with an artificially more aggressive voice.

"Told ya," Chad said. Bones looked at Trey and waited for his orders.

"Drop 'is ass," Trey said. Bones let go of Kyle and kicked him over to where Chad stood behind the drone. Kyle gasped for air as he regained his footing.

"Good boy," Chad said. "Now unless you guys wanna get a face-full of taser from the robot, you'll leave us alone."

Bones and Skull took Chad's threat to heart, but Trey did not pay any attention to the remark. The drone proceeded to pass the three and Chad and Kyle stayed close behind it.

"Watch out," Trey said as he clenched his fist. Heeding the warning, Skull and Bones took a few steps behind Trey and seemingly braced themselves. Chad and Kyle got closer to the drone as Trey raised his fist. With a loud grunt, Trey thrust his fist forward right into the face of the drone. The speaker, which was right where the mouth of drone used to be, was smashed in, so it became difficult to hear what it was trying to electronically mutter.

Kyle and Chad jumped back and both let out a moderately manly scream. They maintained a good six-foot distance away from the drone and Trey. The robot began moving its arm upward and took aim. Trey took hold of both of its arms, and with another loud grunt, he pushed the arms outward, ripping them out of their sockets. The taser-net failed to deploy as Trey took its arm, and with one final and victorious shout, swung the robot's arm at its head, knocking it clear off of its intended place and onto the floor.

"Good shit, Boss," Skull praised as he and Bones clapped in a sophisticated manner.

"Yeah, you alrea'y know," Trey replied. He threw the arms of the drone onto the ground, and it stood in place, motionless and apparently offline.

"Ho-o-oh shit," was the only thing Chad could articulate. Kyle was able to do even less.

Trey took a couple steps toward Chad and Kyle and then stopped. He wavered in place and looked like he was holding something back. Chad wanted to ask what was the matter, but he decided to use the time to think of a plan instead. He put his hand on his left leg and gritted his teeth. After all this time his leg hadn't healed. It was either fight or flight, and this time flight wasn't an option.

Trey rolled his eyes to the back of his head like he was about to sneeze. And then he shot his head forward, coughing as violently as he ever did before. The cough was so loud that Chad flinched. Skull ran to Trey to help him, but with each pat on his back, Trey's hacking kept getting worse. Trey swung his arm and pushed Skull away so hard that he fell over. Trey held his chest as he fell to his knees. Blood sprayed from his mouth with each cough until Trey finally managed to control himself once again. After the coughing halted, his body fell to the side and his back hit the wall. His chest almost seemed to be convulsing as he fought to suppress each cough while blood dripped from his mouth.

Trying to see if this was at all normal with him, Chad looked at Skull and Bones, who seemed to be more terrified of the situation than Chad and Kyle.

"Trey, Trey!" Skull called, "You a'ight, bruh?" Trey dared not to speak and start any more coughing fits, but with eyes that were as red and strained as the blood that sprayed from his mouth, he leered at Skull. Carefully he raised his right hand as his left remained on his chest, and pointed as menacingly as one could at Chad and Kyle. The message was understood.

Skull picked up the taser-arm of the drone and gripped it like a bat. Bones did likewise with the other arm. Trey gurgled a word or two through his blood-filled mouth. It sounded like "GET'EM".

Skull made the first advancement as he went for Chad. Kyle jumped back and out of the way, but Chad, who wasn't quite as mobile, simply braced himself for the attack. Skull swung down at Chad's head, but Chad grabbed Skull's arm with one hand and the robot's arm with the other. He was able to match Skull's strength. Unable to move his weapon, Skull kicked Chad in his left leg, causing him to immediately collapse from the pain. Chad let go of the robot's arm and fell on his back.

Skull raised his weapon as far as he could. Chad knew all he could do now was block. Skull's weapon began its descent, but was interrupted mid-swing by Kyle.

Kyle held on to Skull in a similar way that Chad did, and as hard as he could he headbutted Skull in his nose. Skull dropped the robot's limb and stumbled backward on top of Trey, who started coughing again as a result of the added weight. Bones jumped to the aid of his friend's bloody nose and his boss' violent coughs.

Kyle rubbed his forehead and kneeled in front of Chad, who was doing the same with his thigh.

"There's no runnin' for either of us now," he said. "How 'bout we just help each other out?" He extended his hand.

"Deal," Chad responded. He took Kyle's hand and was pulled to his feet. "They use headbutts in UFC?"

"I just wanted to try it," Kyle said.

Skull held his face as he got off of Trey and tried to keep the blood from pouring from his nose. After insisting he was fine, Skull told Bones to finish the job. Keeping the left hand of the robot held high, he made a hesitant advancement at Kyle and Chad.

"Split up," Chad yelled. "Make him choose."

Kyle jumped to the right side of the hall while Chad stayed on the left. Bones went for Chad. He swung the arm sideways at Chad's head, but missed after Chad ducked and rolled over to the right side of the hall. After Chad was clear of the area, Kyle threw the robot arm that Skull dropped at Bones and it connected with his face. He collapsed like a dead monkey.

Chad stood up and looked at Bones' fainted body.

"Good lookin' out," he said. They both turned as Skull stood up and began charging toward them with a football tackle. Chad shoved Kyle out of the way, swung his limp leg up above his head and stomped downward onto Skull's head in the form of an ax-kick. Skull fell on his face, and Chad kneeled down to punch the back of his head to knock him out.

"You know how to fight, too?" Kyle asked.

"Tae Kwon Do club, no biggie."

Chad stepped over Skull and sat down across from Trey, who was in a state that looked beyond weakened. It was almost like he was afraid to move, thinking it would spark another fit of coughs.

"I figured you guys weren't that tough," Chad teased. Trey's bloodshot eyes screamed with an apparent rage that he was too afraid to express. Watching his frustration almost made Chad laugh. Kyle walked over to Bones, picked up both limbs of the drone, then dropped them beside Trey.

"Souvenirs," he said.

Chad noticed the blood that was on the floor around Trey. Some of it was definitely Skull's, but the other blood there was Trey's. Chad squinted to look closely at the liquid. There was something weird about it. It was off in color, in fact, being very bright in appearance.

"You see that?" he asked Kyle.

"What?" Chad pointed to the red droplets on Trey's chest and clothing.

"His blood, look at it." They both moved in closer to observe. The closer they got, the more apparent it was. Trey's blood was far different from Skull's, or anyone else for that matter.

Trey's blood was glowing.

## Chapter 9

# Blood

Blood never daunted Chad before. Whenever he saw some, it almost made him feel more like a man, like whatever he was doing was something so brutal only a true warrior could accomplish it. But seeing blood that shined like the gel in a glowstick did not count as normal by any means. Especially when the blood flowed directly from a person's body.

Chad stared at the red liquid on the ground. He blinked heavily multiple times to make sure his eyes weren't playing tricks on him. Then he looked up at Kyle, who expressed his confusion through a heavy squint and an agape mouth. He knew they were both witnessing the same thing. Trey slowly and feebly, like an elder standing from a wheelchair, leaned to his right arm and tried to push off from the ground. His arm trembled, and as he scooted his legs underneath himself, his left arm held his chest as if to control his breathing manually. Once completely risen, Trey gunned Chad down and made what looked like an advancement toward him before another long grunt halted him mid-step. Another painful grunt rumbled in his chest as he finally gave in to the pain and fell back down to the floor on his hands and knees.

Chad and Kyle wordlessly discussed what their next move should be. It would seem obvious to go get help had it been anyone else, but this was the same guy who tried to accost them both without a good reason. Trey coughed a couple more times. With another silent look, they both agreed to get help. Trey had learned his lesson, whether they were the ones to deliver the message or not.

"Maximum security, my ass," said a voice that startled Chad and Kyle. They searched for the source of the voice, and down the hall, they saw Jason. He was walking towards the group without paying any particular attention to them. He seemed to be more concerned with the ceiling and walls.

"There you are, you PRICK," Chad exclaimed, rising to his feet. Jason continued to observe the walls as Chad approached him. "You're starting rumors about us now? Huh?" Still no response. Chad walked within arms reach of Jason and cut him off. "What the heck did you say to Trey?" Without acknowledging Chad, Jason swiftly punched Chad's weak leg, which again caused him to fall sideways in pain.

"You punks *would* just happen to find the one hall without cameras," Jason said. He stepped over Chad and took a look at the scene. Bones was collapsed on the floor with a bruise on his head, and Skull was face-down on the floor with a small puddle of blood underneath him, and big drops made a trail that led to where Trey was. Jason was most fascinated with the NegaSentry that had been manually and rather amateurishly disassembled. He stepped in front of Trey and began speaking in a condescending tone. "You let them beat you?" He lifted Trey's weight with the top of his foot until he was standing straight up on his knees, and then kicked Trey so that his back slammed against the wall.

Trey started coughing profusely and more violently than before. Blood sprayed from his mouth and landed on Jason's shoes. He stepped back to escape the path of the flying fluid, and when he looked down to observe the mess that was made on his shoes, he noticed the uniqueness of the blood. He lifted one foot off the ground, standing perfectly balanced as he observed the blood that stained the dirty white on his low-top shoes. His ever-stern face slowly crept to a smirk, and then to a small chuckle which turned into a laugh that was almost maniacal.

"Yes... Yes, I knew it!" he declared as he brought his leg back and then thrust it forward to kick Trey's head to the wall.

From the ground, Chad noticed the form of Jason's kick. It was similar in appearance and execution to any kick Chad knew. There was only one martial art that performed kicks by aiming with the knee and then snapping the foot forward. Jason knew Tae Kwon Do, and he was good at it. After being flung into the wall, Chad was almost certain that Jason had some kind of combat training. Being able to recognize it as being the same one he practiced made Chad feel slightly more confident when it came to fighting him, but then again, Jason was incredibly fluent at what he did, which meant he was probably a much higher belt ranking than Chad. That wasn't very reassuring.

Kyle stepped forth, close enough to intervene but not to completely block Jason's path to Trey.

"Dude, back off," he pleaded. "He's hurt enough." After having both feet planted again, Jason lifted his left leg and pushed Kyle back with a side kick. It was another move Chad recognized.

"Not yet he hasn't," Jason noted. He kneeled before Trey, who seemed to be in so much pain that it was difficult to determine if he was actually listening. "I had a feeling you'd crumble if someone pushed you beyond your fragile little limit. Good to see it paid off in the end." Jason rose and walked over to the broken robot. "But you've outlived your usefulness." He searched inside of its body, looking in from where the head used to be, and then ventured around the body of the drone with his hands. He found the object he was looking for. "You two may want to leave before Moriz shows up. He'll be here any minute."

Jason grabbed hold of a lever-like switch and pulled it, sounding a loud siren that echoed through all the hallways. Immediately after its activation, the right arm of the drone, which was still sitting right next to Trey, began to move. Suddenly, it deployed its electric net, and Trey was sitting right in front of the mouth of the weapon. The net swallowed Trey, and the electrical pulses began surging through it.

What were once compressed grunts and coughs became distressed screams and hacks as Trey felt every shock that pulsed through the net. His body twitched uncontrollably and his pain could be felt through the air. Kyle rushed over to the arm of the drone and attempted to pull the net from over Trey, but he only was forced back after being shocked by the electricity that flowed through the arm itself. There was nothing they could do. What was only ten seconds of screaming felt like a whole ten minutes, but after several seconds, the screaming and all signs of motion beneath the net stopped.

Trey was motionless. His eyes were still open, displaying the same look of intense pain that possessed his face while screams were still vociferating. Steam rose from openings in his body, orifices and other slits on his skin that weren't present before the net covered him.

After the electricity stopped, the slits oozed blood at a much slower rate, but the blood itself still glowed at a tone that made itself visible over Trey's dark and now damaged skin.

Jason, Chad, and Kyle all stood frozen where they were. Different emotions were invoked in each of them, but they ultimately were unable to speak after watching Trey's electrocution.

Footsteps stomped around the corridor corner. Led by Moriz, a team of human guards rushed the hallway, and without any intelligence of the situation, they promptly threw Jason, Chad, and Kyle to the ground. Handcuffs bound their hands behind their back as they lay face down on the cold tile floor. Moriz observed the area. He was no stranger to corpses, but he couldn't help but be disgusted at the burned and bloodied body that lay before him; the remains of what used to be an inmate. The three conscious prisoners were yanked to their feet and lined up side by side. Moriz approached them with the normal enmity in his raspy voice.

"Who did this?" he questioned while pointing to the NegaSentry. The query seemed almost silly. It was obvious that only Trey had the strength to achieve the forceful dismemberment of a robot, but Jason was still happy to oblige an answer.

"It was the guinea pig over there," he nodded at Trey. Moriz and Jason exchanged glances. It was brief, but meaningful. Chad and Kyle noticed the exchange and realized something very important. Moriz and Jason were on the same page. They both understood something deeper about what was going on, but Moriz was not very pleased about that.

"Take the maggots back to their cells," Moriz ordered. Without a word, the three were rapidly escorted to the opposite wing of the prison and roughly pushed into their respective cells. The door was locked and the guards walked out of the hallway. Within another hour, the lights in the corridor were dimmed, and the halls and cells were quiet. Many of the inmates were fast asleep, but Jason and Chad sat silently in their cell, still in disbelief.

Chad was facing the doorway, but he did not dare let his eyes venture outside the cell. He kept a sharp glance downward, toward the floor. Although the red stain that resembled blood was still there, it didn't bother him anymore. Chad didn't even see it. He tried to fight back the images that were still fresh in his mind. Hauntingly, they kept playing again and again. His back was pressed tightly against the wall.

Jason sat on his bottom bunk. He leaned over and rested the weight of his upper body on his knees and watched his hands hang in front of his face as the blood on his shoe began to lose its luminance. The same images played in his head repeatedly, but they did not bother him. He watched them, only to reconfirm if what he saw was the truth or just some trick. After much analysis, he confirmed the former.

Jason slowly lifted his head to see his cellmate. Chad's facial expression showed vacancy. Jason knew that Chad wasn't responding the same way he was. Jason was the first to break the silence by snapping a finger. He lifted his body slowly until he was sitting up straight again. Expression returned to Chad's face, as if he had just returned to reality. He turned toward Jason.

"We gotta get out of here," Chad urgently whispered. Jason said nothing. His face was calm, and he continued to look at Chad. Not getting the reaction he was looking for, Chad repeated himself. "We need to get out! Look, Kyle told me everything. About why Trey was allowed to live when he survived, about why you think we're here, all of it. And... I think you're right." Jason scooted back in the bunk until his back hit the wall. He began to relax even more. It wasn't easy admitting to Jason that he was right, especially since Chad still hated him, and Jason wasn't making it any easier. "Do you hear me?"

"Yes," Jason finally responded. The short breath of a chuckle escaped him.

"Wha-what is it? Didn't you see what happened in there?" Chad's whisper became more distressed.

"Be calm," Jason said. "It's not as bad as it looks."

"What the hell are you talking about?"

"Stop whispering so loud. Talk softly or they'll think we're hiding something." Jason shot his eyes up at the ceiling to remind Chad that there were cameras watching. "Come sit over here."

Although somewhat disturbed by Jason's level of calmness and by the fact that he invited Chad to sit with him, he realized Jason was right about how suspicious he was acting. Chad gathered himself on the floor with a few deep breaths. He was calm again. Chad moved over to the bed and joined Jason on the bottom bunk. He crossed his legs and turned to face Jason, thinking this would make the conversation look more casual. The top bunk covered both of their heads so that the camera couldn't see their lips moving.

"Jason, we need to start looking for a way out of this damn prison."

"I figured you would say that. I knew you were dull, but I didn't think you were actually trying to escape."

"Well… don't you agree? Weren't you a little bothered by that at all?" Jason smiled and readjusted his posture. 'Bothered' didn't seem to be the appropriate word. "Why are you acting like you don't care?" Chad allowed annoyance to show on his face. Jason closed his eyes, revisiting the incident.

"Did you see what happened to Trey?" Jason said. Chad felt like punching him for asking such an obvious question.

"Uhh, hell yeah I saw it. I was there, remember?"

"Then you saw what Trey looked like when he died, right?"

"Yeah, yeah, when his skin damn near melted?"

"It wasn't melting. It was more or less withering. Notice anything else?" Chad couldn't tell if Jason was being a smart-alek or being serious, but either way, it was becoming irritating. Jason opened his eyes again but didn't look at Chad. He stared off into space. "I don't remember the Project name he was given…"

"Wait, what?" Chad's irritation turned into confusion.

"Trey was normal once, I'm not getting into details now—"

"You think they are going to do that to us?"

"I know they are," Jason said with a disturbing conviction.

"All of us are expendable to them. You only become important if you survive."

"Okay then, so you should know why it's so important to get out of here then!"

"Shh. Not necessarily. I'm very confident I can survive."

"And do you get a prize for staying alive?"

"Hmph, yes…" Jason brushed off Chad's sarcasm with a chuckle.

"And the prize is?" Chad said.

Jason finally turned and made solid eye contact with Chad. "Power."

The two looked at each other in silence. Chad hoped that the silence would hint that he would like a little elaboration, but Jason didn't comply. Smiling, Jason turned and lay down on the bed and closed his eyes, hinting to Chad that he was finished talking about the subject.

Chad stood from the bed and climbed up to the top bunk.

"Whatever, dude. When you're done being stupid you're welcome to join me. In the meantime, I'll be planning a way out."

Jason chuckled again. "You won't last much longer with that kind of ignorance," he said.

"Oh, shut up." Chad ended the conversation by loudly throwing the blanket over himself. He knew it was immature but he didn't care. The conversation had somewhat taken the image of Trey out of his mind, but that didn't help him sleep.

Jason soon dozed off, but Chad kept thinking about what Jason said.

*Power.*

*What did he mean?*

The next morning there was very little interaction between either of the three. Jason simply disappeared after the breakfast hour, while Kyle and Chad went to the mines on their own, separate from each other. Andreas was in her usual, estranged location, but Chad was not as interested in talking to her today. Skull and Bones also continued their week as normal, but after the events of the prior night, they saw no reason in starting any more fights.

There were no discussions about Trey until later that day. During the second meal, Kyle and Andreas were sitting at their table unaccompanied. Kyle felt like apologies were in order for what he said to Chad before the fight with Trey, but saying sorry was still too hard. So as a way to clear the tension, Kyle invited Chad to sit with him and Andreas. They ate their meals without any unnecessary conversation, but after the transition to the yard began Chad and Kyle were finally comfortable discussing yesterday. Andreas remained in the commons while they went to their favorite corner of the yard.

"I didn't believe you at first, but it was all true...wasn't it?" Chad asked.

"Looks like it. Did you and the prick talk about it?"

"A little bit. He basically just affirmed to me the same stuff he told Trey through you." Chad gave the area a quick scan. There were no more guards out today than there were any day before, but there did seem to be much more attention paid to the two of them. "All these guards around here keep eying us now. Not gonna lie, I didn't know that they were allowed to use tasers that strong in prison."

"Whaddya mean?"

"That taser-net. It was strong enough to freakin' electrocute Trey. I didn't know the robots were packing that kind of heat."

"They're not. The nets are only to stun dudes. You didn't notice it, did ya?"

"Notice what?" Chad asked. Jason had apparently noticed something too that Chad had not. He wondered what it was that only Jason and someone with observational skills as sharp as Kyle would be able to pick out.

"Did ya notice Trey's veins when he got shocked?" Kyle shuddered to shake the image out of his own mind.

"I don't know. I wasn't really looking too hard at his body..."

"They were glowin'. Just like his blood."

Chad didn't say a word while he tried to make the connection. In Jason and Kyle's eyes, there was some clear logic that made Trey's death make sense in some way, but there was no explaining it. How could an electric net that's only tuned to stun a target instead kill it so thoroughly? Trey's body was seared so much that it looked like lightning had struck him. Even the electric chair doesn't do that kind of damage. It was possible that his skin was penetrated and his nervous system was fried, but that wouldn't make his veins glow. There must have been another reason Trey's body was so effective at conducting the electricity, and it was incredibly likely that it had something to do with his glowing blood.

That was it.

It was completely obvious, and Chad felt dunce for not realizing it sooner. The big secret that Jason and Trey shared, all the conspiracy about the executions—or more accurately, the experiments—all held a definite validity now. Trey's body wasn't just conducting the electricity, it was amplifying it. And the reason he was able to survive the lethal injection was because he wasn't being injected with Sodium Pentathol, Pavulon, or Potassium Chloride. Sanctum wasn't using the normal concoction of chemicals to perform executions. They were using something else.

There was visium in Trey's blood.

After nearly a month of trying to figure out the significance of the conversations between Jason and Trey, things were becoming much clearer. Jason was suspicious of the activity of those running the medical wing of the prison—Warden Moriz not excluded. Jason must have been trying to figure out what was going on for a long time. Chad had no idea exactly how long, but it was safe to assume it happened sometime after Trey's execution. Considering what Kyle mentioned, it wasn't until that time that Jason showed any interest in talking to Trey. And since executing inmates by any means different from the legally approved method of lethal injection was most likely frowned upon in Ohio, it went without saying that whatever was happening in the dark, unmentioned corners of Sanctum would be kept quiet.

Assuming that the Warden was involved, he probably told Trey not to mention anything about the execution to anyone inside or outside the prison walls. But then again, trusting someone like Trey to keep quiet was like trying to silence a neighbor's barking dog in the middle of the night by bribing it with more time in the kennel. It was probably safer not to tell him anything. Trey boasted to many other inmates that he was allowed to live because he survived the execution. Chad knew only a fool would believe something like that. If the higher-ups wanted Trey dead, he would have been dead long ago. Besides giving Trey a reason to believe he was a god among men, they succeeded in preventing him from spreading the truth about what happens behind Sanctum's closed doors. The only people who could possibly discover the truth was someone who actively pursued it from within, and no one in this prison filled with broken convicts cared to know the truth.

No one except for Jason. He must have been suspicious after Trey's triumphant return to his cell on the day of his execution. But openly discussing the events of that day was too difficult since surveillance of Trey was likely to increase, so Trey and Jason elected Kyle the messenger, the middleman for the two of them to communicate while in public.

"How come you never told me that they tried to execute Trey with visium?" Chad asked.

"Never told me before. I was just as surprised as you were. I don't even think Trey knew. They never even mentioned it before when they were tellin' me stuff to say to each other."

"So do you think Jason knew about the visium then?"

"Mhmm."

"How do you know?"

"Remember when Jason looked at his shoe last night?" Chad thought back to right before Jason showed off his impressive kicking skills. When he lifted up his shoe to look at the blood, there was a very familiar expression on his face. "'Yes, I knew it!' is what he said," Kyle repeated Jason's words mockingly. "That was kind of a giveaway for me."

"He recognized that glow from the mines," Chad concluded. "I guess it makes sense that he knew what it was when he saw it."

"That's what I thought. Jason was always good at findin' good spots for visium anyway. He knows it when he sees it."

There was something else Chad noticed about Jason from the night before. The fact that he did not seem bothered by watching a man die only hinted that Jason probably did or saw some pretty rough things in the past, but that wasn't important. It was that not only did Jason have an absence of inner perturbation, he was acting strangely. When they returned to the cell, Jason felt no need to test Chad. He did not have any more unbecoming hostility. Instead, he looked fulfilled, like there was something he wanted for a very long time, and he finally received it. It couldn't have been Trey's death. Jason was the only person who ever wanted to associate with him.

No. It had nothing to do with Trey's death, but it had everything to do with his blood. Jason wanted to make sure that everything he talked about, schemed for, snooped for, and hoped for all this time was true, and when he saw the blood, he knew he was right about everything. After last night, Jason finally confirmed his suspicions about Sanctum. But the only question at that point was: what was he planning to do now?

"How ya holdin' up?" Kyle asked.

"Huh?"

"Ya know, 'bout the whole Trey's-dead-now thing."

"I was doing just fine until you brought it up again." Chad shuddered and blinked heavily, his usual approach when trying to un-see an incident. Just like before, it didn't work, "It was a bit... freaky, but I guess I'm pretty good at distracting myself nowadays."

"I see."

"What about you?"

"Hmm? Oh yeah... I'm good," Kyle said, brushing off the question.

"So how did it feel?"

"Watchin' him die?"

"No," Chad laughed, "fighting again." Kyle took a brief moment to think about it.

"I guess it was pretty good," he finally responded with a surprised tone that made his voice raise an octave. "Probly just 'cuz I got to put Bones to sleep with a robot's arm, but it was actually... fun." Chad smiled and looked away. "And, uuh, I'm sorry 'bout—"

"It's cool," Chad said. He chose not to push the conversation any further. As far as he was concerned they were friends again, and Chad was over their quarrel from the day before. Watching a man die would do that to a person.

Chad took a casual look around the yard. From the entrance of the prison, he saw Andreas looking intently around the yard. Chad squinted to see if his eyes were deceiving him, but another long look confirmed it.

"So she *does* like the sun," Chad jested. Andreas found Chad and marched toward him as if she heard his remark and took offense to it. Kyle turned to see who was coming their way and immediately burst into laughter.

"What's so funny?" Chad asked.

"Did ya tell her?" Knowing what Kyle was speaking of, Chad looked at him with offense and smacked his lips.

"Did *you* tell her?"

"I don't talk to her, remember?" Kyle tried to keep his laughter at bay.

"You sit at her lunch table!" Before Kyle could defend himself, Andreas stomped into a planted position in front of Chad and Kyle. Her hands found themselves a mounted point on her hips and she glared right at Chad. It was a look like he hadn't seen from anyone before. It was slightly frightening, and the fact that the sun behind her cast a heavy shadow over her face did not make her any less intimidating.

"Why. Didn't. You. Tell me?" She interrogated, not taking an eye off of Chad.

"Eh, umm, I thought he already did?" Chad said pointing to Kyle, who only scratched his head, looked away and tried to stay out of the conversation. Andreas' eyes burned a hole through Chad's, and he had never felt so helpless in his life. If it had been a few months ago, Chad would have compared Andreas' stare to death, but now he knew better. He had seen death, and whatever Andreas was attempting to visually instill into Chad was much, much worse.

Although it wasn't in the ideal of situations, Chad couldn't help but welcome the warmth. It wasn't too often that he was able to make contact with her for so long. If Chad didn't feel so uncannily ashamed of himself for neglecting to mention to Andreas that her long-time lunch buddy was deceased, he may have enjoyed the moment a bit more.

"How'd ya find out?" Chad asked.

"Some old guy started flirting with me," she said, disgusted. "They don't do that when Trey's around. People are saying he was rolled to the medical wing on a stretcher, then I saw Jason get taken to ISO by the guards this morning."

*ISO?* Chad thought. *Is that his punishment for last night?*

"So ya up and assumed Trey died?" Kyle chimed. Andreas shifted her angry eyes to Kyle.

"His face was covered by a blanket," she spurned.

"Oh." Kyle nodded and turned his eyes to the furthest possible point in the opposite direction of where Andreas was. He kept looking until he felt the heat of Andreas' glare leave his face.

"You believe everything you hear?" Chad asked.

"When people keep saying the same things around here, it tends to be true."

"Not true," Chad said pushing for conversation. "What do people say about me?"

"That you're annoying and nosey. And I can already vouch for the annoying part..."

"Oh really..." Chad looked for a way to recover, but he was distracted by Kyle's chuckles, who was still facing the other direction. Andreas' face softened slightly, and Chad couldn't tell if the insult was just a way to lighten the mood or not. "Well, what do people say about you?"

Andreas face blanked. Her eyes were empty and almost colorless for a moment and a cold, trembling breath left her lungs. Anger then came and occupied her vacant expression and she turned and stomped away saying nothing but what Chad assumed was a muttered curse.

"Wh-Wait! I didn't mean it like that!" Chad shouted as he went after her. He cut her off and held out his arm, motioning her to stop. To his surprise, she did. She planted her steps firmly on the ground with her arms folded in front of her. "I didn't mean to upset you but... you never really told me your story, you know." Andreas paused before she said anything.

"It hurts..." Another pause. Chad chose not to interrupt it. "You know what it's like to hurt every day?"

"More or less." Chad clicked the heel of his left leg on the ground a couple times. "Not really the same kind of pain, but it's a reminder." Andreas took a deep breath. She was calming down, but Chad knew it wasn't because he was forgiven. For the sake of diplomacy, he decided to push further. "I'm really interested in knowing more about you. You and Kyle don't really look like you belong here. Not like Jason and Trey do. I already know his story, I wanna know yours now."

Another pause. Chad questioned if she was thinking or just trying to make him nervous. She raised her head and looked him in the eye. "Fine," she said. "But you're gonna do something for me first."

"Like?"

"You're gonna come take Trey's place as my scarecrow. You're gonna sit with me to keep these other pervs away. Then if I think you're doing a good job, I'll tell you." She passed Chad and kept going for the prison's entrance.

"You're acting like I don't have a choice," Chad chuckled.

"You don't." Andreas walked away without another word and headed for the commons. Chad felt a victory. It may be a small one, and although he was aware that he may be getting used, he had guaranteed alone time with Andreas now. And there was no one to interrupt him this time. He walked back over to Kyle and sat with him again.

"I *really* don't know what ya see in her," Kyle said shaking his head. "She scares the CRAP outta me!"

"I *really* didn't ask you..." Chad retorted.

"What're ya gonna talk to her about? Gonna ask 'er out?" Chad shook his head.

"Couple things. One, she's gonna tell me how she ended up here. And two..." He allowed a quick silence to pass so that Kyle understood the topic would be shifting to something serious. "My plan." Kyle scanned the four corners of the yard. No one was near enough to hear the conversation, but it still seemed risky to talk about it out in the open. And talking to someone else about such a huge secret wasn't the best idea either. Before Kyle could form the question in his mouth, Chad spoke again. "I'm not waiting any longer. You saw what happened yesterday."

"Doesn't mean it's gonna happen to us," Kyle reasoned.

"Jason is fairly sure it will. And though he's still a prick, I kinda trust him. I think he knows a lot more than he's telling us."

"Bro, runnin' away now is a really bad idea! They're gonna catchya." Kyle held strong eye-contact with Chad, who seemed unfazed by Kyle's words. He was much more serious now than he usually was when speaking with Kyle. "Why're you gonna tell Andreas anything about it?"

"Just giving her an invitation," Chad said. "I'm giving you yours now."

Kyle's reaction wasn't exactly what Chad imagined it would be. He was only partly surprised by the invitation, and it looked like the only thing that caught him off guard was its timing. He was more disappointed than supportive.

"Just let it go, dude," he finally said.

"This isn't where I need to be."

"Why can't you just accept it?"

"Cause I know I don't deserve this, Kyle." Chad turned and fully faced Kyle, even firmly grabbing his shoulders. "I know that I'm never going to live with myself if I just accept this as my life now. It isn't what I planned for my life, and it isn't what I deserve in my life." Chad gave Kyle a quick jerk. "And I know it isn't what you deserve."

"When're you gonna do it?" Kyle asked discouragingly. Chad took another casual and cursory glance around to see if anyone was listening.

"Soon."

"Like?"

"A few weeks..." This time Kyle's reaction was more of what Chad thought it would be. He shook his head in disapproval and started walking away. Chad rushed to catch him. "Hey, I know it's a lot to spring on you like that, but can you at least think about it?"

"Naw," Kyle responded without even stopping or turning his head. Chad thought of another method of pleading without sounding too desperate.

"I could REALLY use some help here..." Kyle kept walking. He made his way to the prison's entrance. Before he could enter, Chad managed to jump in front of him and block his way. The extra activity sparked a bit of pain in Chad's leg, and he held his thigh as he spoke again. "Okay, fine. Can you at least tell me why you're not going to?"

"It's not gonna work," Kyle expressed with suppressed agitation. He gestured to Chad's leg. "Look at yaself. Ya can't even run at full speed if ya need to."

"I get it, it's risky. But still—"

"I'm not doin' it." Kyle blasted past Chad, who followed him through the hallways. Chad couldn't tell where Kyle was headed, but it didn't take him long to realize that Kyle was moving through the halls quickly because he was trying to prove a point. Chad struggled to keep up with him due to the simple fact that his leg's pain was too distracting. As much as Chad hated to admit it, moving agilely was a challenge nowadays.

Kyle weaved through the halls until Chad eventually lost sight of him while entering the commons. Chad searched the commons, knowing he could not have gotten far. Chad's first idea was to find the table where he always sat, but he was not there. It was already being occupied by someone else. It was clear that Andreas wasn't the only person who knew about Trey's passing like she said, and the other inmates were quick to take advantage of it. Chad continued his search until he found Kyle sitting at a different table alone. He sat with his back to the table and facing Chad with crossed arms to make it look like he was waiting. Chad walked over to the table slowly.

"You really think you're gonna get away movin' like that?" Kyle criticized.

"I'll find a way around that," Chad said. He took deeper breaths as he sat at the table, hiding that he was actually panting. "But is that what it's really about?"

"This is what I deserve!" With a sudden feeling of skepticism arising, Chad said the first thing that came to mind. He spoke slowly and carefully.

"I thought you said you didn't kill your friend."

"I didn't."

"Then what's your issue?"

"I shoulda been able to save him." Kyle's eyes faded. They went from Chad to drifting down to the floor. It was the familiar brokenness. "I let him do that to himself... but I couldn't save him." Chad wasn't in the mood to sympathize.

"He was going to kill himself anyway. You know that, right?"

"I shoulda been able to help stop him—to save my friend, but I couldn't."

"So you're just gonna sit here and sulk for the rest of your life?" Chad asked. "Is that what he would have wanted?"

"Don't matter. This is my punishment."

Chad knew better than to argue, but he wanted to anyway. He wanted to convince Kyle that he would be wasting his life, but that seemed to be his intention. Another short lecture on how to move on from the past wasn't appropriate now; there was no changing Kyle's mind. That much was clear. Chad took a deep breath and sighed disappointment in a wave of warm air.

"You sure?" he asked. Kyle nodded. "Okay then. One more question and I'll let it go."

"Yeah?"

"I always noticed something different about you. Andreas doesn't have it, Jason doesn't, and none of these other people here have it either."

"Whaddya mean?"

"How in the world are you able to stay so positive? You're always upbeat, and you have a good attitude most of the time, and I really have no idea why."

Kyle unbuttoned the top of his jumpsuit. From behind his undershirt, he pulled a necklace out and let it dangle on one of his fingers while it was still around his neck. Taking it off was out of the question. The necklace didn't look like anything special to Chad. It had a rather unoriginal design. A small leather lace, which was tied into a knot, looped through a tiny hole in a shark tooth with a few black lines on it. It seemed fitting for someone who liked water-sports as much as Kyle.

"What's that for?" Chad asked.

"Me and Joey both had one. The day he died, we both picked one up from a surf shop on the way to the beach. Mine's a shark tooth. He got one that looked like a goldfish. This is all I got to remind me of that day, and what I shoulda done."

"I'm surprised they let you in here with that," Chad said.

"It took some smuggling. Hid it places I rather not say, but I'm not givin' it up."

"And how does that thing keep you happy again?"

"It reminds how me lucky I am."

"You think that you're lucky?"

"Yep. I had good friends back then," Kyle said as he tucked his necklace back under his shirt, "and I got at least one good friend now. I'm happy just cuz of that, but I know that my friend Joey died cuz I couldn't save him. It's my fault he's gone. I couldn't take care of him so this is where I deserve to be."

Kyle's innocence seemed almost juvenile, to give such a cheap necklace so much sentimental meaning, but it wasn't so bad in comparison to Chad's own vest, Andreas' black hoodie, and Jason's cat-symbol jacket. The necklace was much smaller, and it made more sense to wear something that wasn't quite as flashy in prison. Especially if he didn't want it to get stolen. If anything, the hardest thing to believe was that some memory of the past was able to keep Kyle in a good mood all the time.

Chad thought it criminal for a guy to be so emotionally invested in anything. Kyle was like a character straight out of a kids movie. If nothing else, Chad had to respect him for so having such a strong resolve. He was the only person Chad had ever met that was truly willing to die for something he believed. In the end, what Kyle believed didn't necessarily make much sense, but there didn't seem to be any changing his mind.

"So that's it... You're staying then?" Chad asked. Kyle nodded slowly. They both realized that each of their minds had been made, and although Chad wasn't leaving just yet, they both couldn't help but feel like they were saying goodbye. The feeling was saddening, but familiar. Chad related it to the conversation he had at IHOP. Chris, Karli, and Ricky were a little more welcoming of the fact that Chad was leaving then, which made departure slightly easier. This was a different story.

Kyle stood and took a few steps past Chad.

"Welp," he said, not knowing how to end the conversation, "tell me how your talk with ya girl goes."

"All right," Chad replied. Kyle slowly left the commons, not quite as cheerful as he usually would be. Chad wanted to hang out a while longer, but there was one more important meeting he needed to have.

**Chapter 10**

# Preparation

"We can do one more today. Let's make this one a winner!" Jones' words sounded like they were to motivate himself rather than the people around him. Nevertheless, the guards apathetically took the still-warm body off of the table and placed it into the handy body-bag stretched out on the floor. A custodian walked in afterward and scrubbed up the several drops of blood and saliva that still lay wet on the tile floor.

Jones stroked his chin and stared deeply into the clipboard he held just above his lap. He pretended to be calm, but his heartbeat was loud. He hoped that he was the only person who could hear it. Out of his peripheral, he could see Moriz gunning him down, but Jones simply ignored him as he continued to write random notes in the profile on his clipboard. To the average person, it would've looked like he was learning something.

Negatov stood and cleared his throat from the back of the room. It was an understood signal to Moriz and Catherine, who were also in the room, to walk out. Wordlessly, they exited the area while Jones pretended to not notice their absence. He realized what questions were coming, and he tried to think of an answer before he was expected to give one.

"Doctor," Negatov began in a surprisingly calm voice. Jones turned in his seat, wearing an overstated look of attention on his face. "I must be honest with you, I haven't been satisfied with your work as of late." Jones nodded slowly. "Is there something I should know about why our little projects haven't been turning out the way we want?"

"Trial and error, sir," Jones said, trying to sound confident in his work. He flipped through the pages in his clipboard as if he were looking for evidence to prove his case. "We've been getting pretty close with the last few subjects that've been brought in. But I'm sure the most recent inmate will prove successful."

"The younger one. Chad Galen?"

"Y-yes, sir. I didn't know you were aware of him."

"I read through all the documents you compiled. You believe that his youth will be the factor that changes the outcomes of the trials."

*He already read them?* Jones thought. "That's right. Catherine brought him in not long after I gave her the most recent criteria. He meets everything we dis—"

"What makes you think he will truly do differently than the rest?" Negatov asked with the slightest hint of a challenge.

"Well, the success from Arbo leads me to believe the younger ones will have greater survival chances."

"Arbo was not the only young prisoner to be executed. He just happened to be the one to survive. You're missing something, Doctor. I shouldn't have to remind you what your own data indicates." Jones wanted to ask if Negatov had indeed read the few hundred documents that had been compiled over the past ten years, but at the same time, he did not want to question his boss' intelligence—or at least not his reading speed. Even for someone with as much globally recognized intellect as he, Jones found it a bit hard to believe that so many files could be processed in anyone's head in a year, much less a couple weeks.

Jones flipped through random pages of his clipboard again, hoping to find some sort of evidence to rebuttal with.

"Galen also shares other traits with Arbo," he said.

"You have until he enters that chamber to prove that you are qualified for your job," Negatov announced.

"Sir, we're getting so close," Jones pleaded.

"I'm glad you feel that way, but let Galen's trial be your last chance. If he dies like the rest, then your employment here shall be ended. The contract we agreed on will be terminated, and you shall be too." Jones' lip quivered as he tried to think up a way to change his boss' mind, but no sound left his mouth. "I don't think I have to explain why we would resort to such drastic measures. I think it was clear when you were brought on board that you would not be allowed to just walk away, especially considering the things we've allowed you to do here under our supervision."

Another inmate, blindfolded and handcuffed, was escorted into the adjacent execution chamber. Jones saw the guards securing the woman to the table. She cried loudly, as some of them tended to do. Jones heard her wails, and for the first time, he saw himself on the table in place of the inmate. He snapped himself out of his nightmare and promptly returned to the conversation. Negatov noticed Jones' attention lapse.

"Don't worry," he said. "Despite the irony of it all, I would not allow you to die using this method. After all, there isn't a guarantee that this would kill you, is there?" Jones assumed the question was rhetorical, but still nodded awkwardly. "I give you until Galen's trial to prove your worth. On that note, I'll leave you to your work."

"Yes," Jones replied in a voice that stressfully cracked. Negatov left the room, closing the door behind him as he met Catherine and Moriz, who stood patiently in the hallway.

"If you don't mind, sir, a minute," Moriz requested.

"What is it?"

"We have reason to believe that Lynx has discovered a good deal about the trials. With your permission, I'd like to silence him." A clear wave of anger slowly rose in Negatov's face.

"You don't remember what I told you?"

"I do. We just won't kill the maggot right away. We're giving him another month until we decide how to terminate him. I placed him in isolation this morning, as you suggested."

"Good," Negatov approved. He took a few seconds to think before speaking again. "There is something we need to do now regarding him. First, we need to learn how much information he may know about us, and how much he has shared with the other inmates. You've been keeping tabs on his interactions with others, yes?"

"We have," Moriz responded. "He does not associate with anyone during excavation. When within the prison, he only communicates with inmate Lyons, who would spend the dining hours with Arbo before he died. Lynx doesn't communicate with anyone else. He barely even speaks to inmate Galen..."

"Why would he need to speak to Galen?

"Galen and Lynx share a cell."

"Do they, now?" Negatov casually looked into the execution table where Jones was administering the illuminating drug. "That brings me to my second item. Make sure that Galen is executed next, even before Lynx." Moriz and Catherine hesitated heavily.

"But why would you want to do that?" Catherine asked.

"A couple reasons: I'm afraid that Doctor Jones has run out of time to impress me. If his current hypothesis is incorrect, then I'll begin taking the brunt of the research myself. Jones has already given me a compilation of his documents.

Additionally, if Jones is correct and Galen ends up surviving the trial, then I want to make sure that Lynx is the next person that we experiment on. If he survives, he'd be more useful to us than Galen or any other inmate in the prison."

"What makes you think that?" Moriz asked with a hint of annoyance.

"Perhaps you should have read his profile, Jael. In any case, it's clear that he's not by any means ordinary. Considering what he did to be sent to Sanctum, and what he's been able to figure out since he arrived, I'd say he's certainly someone we can utilize.

Now, I have a big conference that I'll be scheduling this winter. I'd like to make as much progress as I can here before that time comes. That said, I want you to bring in Galen the instant he screws up. The public won't question the haste of his execution and I'd like to get things moving along."

"Galen was present at the time of Arbo's death," Moriz said.

"He has a knack for being in the wrong place at the wrong time," Catherine noted. "Plus he tried to run away the day he was sentenced. I don't think it will be very long before he tries something rash like that again."

"Good," Negatov said as he headed for the exit. "When he does, I'll be back."

"Your scarecrow has arrived. Here and reporting for duty," Chad stood in front of Andreas while saluting like a soldier beneath a flagpole. Unmoved by Chad's push for a laugh, Andreas raised her head in her seated position against the wall and threw Chad a look that conveyed that she was both embarrassed and annoyed. Giving up on the joke, Chad sighed heavily and plopped down beside her on the floor. "Well, I thought it was funny."

"I don't need you to be funny," she said.

"Then what do you need me to be, huh? Big? Scary? Mean-looking so I can scare off—"

"Quiet," she interrupted, "that's all I need."

"So my presence by itself is powerful enough to keep all the evil away' is basically what you're saying, right? I feel like such a boss now."

"I hate to break it to you, but that's not the reason you're here."

"Well, obviously," Chad jested. "You need me here 'cause you *really* hate being alone. And what better person to spend your time with than the guy you have a secret crush on?" Andreas glanced over to see if Chad was serious, and after seeing a large grin on his face she rolled her eyes in the opposite direction.

"Look around, moron," she said. Still with a grin, Chad observed the commons. As he raised his head to see the tables around him, he noticed the heads of almost half of the people in the area turn in another direction. It was quick, but Chad was able to see the white of their eyes before they turned away, even though no one was looking at him now.

"So either we're really popular or there are a lot of guys trynna get at you," Chad said. "I mean, you're pretty and all, but I didn't realize how many guys were interested in you. And I'm the lucky one who got picked," he chuckled some more.

"Shut up. Skull told some people about the other night. How you and Kyle knocked out him and Bones, and now Trey's gone... Do you really think these people are thinking about me?"

"They think I beat up Trey, too?" He let his back plop against the wall and sighed, thinking. *No, it's more than that.* "They think I killed him, don't they?" Chad wasn't sure how to react. At first, he figured the rumor that he wiped out the most notorious prisoner in Sanctum would only add to his reputation around the prison. It was no mystery that Trey was feared. If Chad truly silenced him, then no one around would want to challenge him, and fortunately for Kyle, him either. On the other hand, his reputation outside of Sanctum would only plummet further, if that was even possible.

"You have a big kill list for someone who's supposedly innocent."

"So that's why you want me here, to scare off everyone else because they think I killed Trey?"

"I already told you that."

"But you failed to mention that you think I'm the one who killed him. I told you what happened to me. What makes you think I'm gonna be cool with having people think even worse of me just so you can benefit from it?" Chad made a slow motion to stand.

"I don't think you killed anyone," Andreas said. "If I did, I wouldn't want you around me at all."

"Then why do you want me around?" Andreas' eyes followed

Chad as he rose to his feet. Chad could tell that she had something to say, but she was hesitant. He wasn't used to her displaying any type of emotion other than botheration or a clear case of apathy, so despite his own aggravation, he was curious to know what was on her mind without making it look like he forgave her too quickly. "If you're going to say something then say it."

"I just... wanted to... chill," she struggled to utter.

"Chill? And talk about what?"

"I don't know."

Chad couldn't tell if she truly wanted to have a conversation or if she was just trying to get him to stay. Since Kyle wasn't around to show off his evil eyes again there was no way for Chad to be sure if she was lying or not.

"Fine. But if we're gonna talk then it's gonna be about what I wanna talk about," Chad said as he took a seat on the wall again. "You know, you never finished your story about how you ended up here. And I think you were just getting to the good part."

"I told you everything."

"I don't think so. It sounded to me like there was a pretty big piece of information you were about to tell me, or at you least something you left out. If you ask me I think there's a little more to it then blacking out—"

"No. I told you the whole story." Andreas abruptly brushed off the subject. For once, Chad knew how smart Kyle must have felt to know when someone was lying. "We're not talking about it anymore."

"Fine. Then I have another question for you. Kyle says you never even talked to him. How come I'm the more attractive option for you to talk to?"

Andreas started to squirm slightly in place. She was clearly getting ready to say something that made her uncomfortable again. It didn't appear to Chad that she was preparing for a lie. Was telling the truth what made her feel uneasy?

"I don't think... I relate to him," she said.

"Why?"

"He doesn't seem bothered by being here. He looks like he likes it here."

"He tries to make the best of everything," Chad laughed. "Why does that bother you? And what makes me so different? I'm sure I'm not the only prisoner who doesn't want to be here."

"It's what you said about your parents. How you just wanted to escape from them. I feel the same way... I just want to be alone."

*Interesting choice of words,* Chad thought. *Escape...* "You're a bit of a loner, aren't you?"

"I don't trust myself around other people—because of what happened." Chad gave Andreas a skeptical look, one which she didn't see. She was wrapped in her own thoughts, clutching her thighs as if she was reliving her past. Chad knew he wasn't going to get her to reveal any more about herself, so he didn't bother with it. What he really wanted from the conversation he was close to achieving. Like any method of building trust, he felt it necessary to expose himself just a little more.

"You're right about one thing," he began casually, "I did want to escape. And to this day I still remember why. I was so unhappy living with my parents. Granted, the situation with them was bad enough as it was, but I wanted to leave there for more than just trying to avoid my parents." He paused to make sure Andreas was listening. She seemed very attentive. "I just wanted to start fresh, somewhere new."

"Yeah," she agreed. Her response sounded breathy.

"But now too many people know who I am, and they think they know the story about what happened with me and my parents. They think I'm a murderer, and when I get out of here through an appeal or whatever, people all over the country are gonna recognize me for something I'm not. I just want to live without having to worry about being misjudged... without having to—"

"Worry about people..." She was taking the bait. "You really think you're getting out of here?"

"I know I am," Chad answered with conviction. "One way or another."

Andreas shook her head with a slight amusement. "I know what you're thinking, and that's suicide."

"Suicide?" Chad echoed.

"Do you really think you're going to be able to do that by yourself?"

"I wasn't counting on going by myself." Chad's eyes locked with Andreas', and he stood up once more with a genuine smile on his face. "I'm exhausted, and if Jason is in ISO then I think I'll make the most of this time and get some sleep in my cell. Good talk." After examining Andreas' expression, he broke his gaze with her and walked away. She didn't smile. Instead, she was fairly deadpan. Chad could tell that she clearly understood what he was hinting to, and since she didn't immediately reject the offer, there could be hope for him having an escape-buddy after all. However, she didn't say anything at all, which made Chad nervous. Either way he knew there was nothing to do at this point but wait for her response.

With his cell vacated of all possible disturbances, Chad now had all the peace he needed to rest for his big day. Of course, the most important thing to do now was to create the plan. For the first time since he arrived, there was no tension that filled the air from the moment he walked into the cell. There was no one to be suspicious of, and no pranks or tests to beware of. That cell was his and his alone—as far as he knew, indefinitely. It felt a lot homier to have his own space. He even likened the idea of having a private cell to renting a private dorm. He was sure it would be a similar experience to say the least, minus the unbecoming bars and lack of windows. But at least he had his own toilet.

He climbed to his bunk and lay there, using the ceiling as a makeshift canvas. It was about time to create some sort of mental map of the facility. He was familiar with the inside of the prison. There were the commons—where most people spent most of their time—and there were the other less important but notable rooms: the exercise room, the television lounge, the showers, the chapel, and even the empty, wide hallways that didn't seem to lead anywhere. As for the outer areas, they weren't as clear.

The yard was easy enough to map out. It was just a large, square plot of land on the back side of the building. But there wouldn't have been any running from there, anyway. Not with a ten-foot, barbed-wire fence barricading the place. If he was going to run, he would do it during the mining periods. The only problem with that idea was Chad's unfamiliarity with anything outside the building that wasn't a part of the excavation site. The daily walk was an hour from the prison, which equaled out to be about two miles. Chad hadn't had the chance to explore that large stretch of land between the mining grounds and the building, and that was a problem. The wooded areas would prove to be effective places to hide if one were being pursued, but there were a few questions that needed to be answered.

First, what did the forest within Sanctum's gates consist of? Chad knew better than to assume the land outside of the facility would be without security. He was in a prison, after all. The thought of it wasn't completely far-fetched, though. The hallway where Trey died happened to be one of the few in the prison that was not equipped with security cameras. If they thought it was excusable to leave some halls without surveillance, then maybe they wouldn't think to equip the trees with any special type of gear either.

Second, how far does the forest go before one reaches Sanctum's gate? It would be a shame to get lost and have the prison guards find him and bring him back. But if he did make it to the gate without being caught, he knew exactly where he could go. Old Man's Cave was not far away, and because it was still summer, it would not be uncommon to see people walking around the hiking area without much clothing. This gives him the freedom to take off his orange uniform without looking like a complete fool. It would be a stretch, but if he made it to the waterfall, he'd be able to pretend he was swimming with the other tourists, thus justifying his near-nudity.

So there it was. All Chad had to do was find out how much

security the forest had, and how far away the outer gates were. The challenge came in acquiring the information without looking suspicious. Fortunately, he had a plan for that.

The next morning Chad finished his breakfast quickly and unaccompanied. He stood near the commons' entrance, waiting for Warden Moriz to enter after he finished his morning parade. Shortly before the transition to the mines, Moriz walked into the commons. As he passed Chad, he acknowledged his presence with an antagonizing scowl but did not stop walking.

"Excuse me, sir!" Chad called. Moriz turned and gave him more negative acknowledgment. "It's Warden, ehh, Moriz, right?"

"You should know your authority by now," Moriz hissed.

"Yeah, sorry about that. I just don't talk to that many people around here, so I'm not really in-the-know, you know? I share a cell with Jason, but I think you knew that already..."

"I think you're wasting my time, maggot." Moriz continued walking, and not giving up on his plan, Chad followed.

"No, wait, I had a question for you. I was wondering if there was any more, uhm, prison work that could be done around here."

"What the hell are you talking about?"

"The walking to the mines every day is gettin' more and more difficult for me to do," Chad patted his leg. "I wanted to do something else instead of mining every day, just up until my leg heals from whatever it's hurt from. I was thinkin'... like, maybe the kitchen... or maybe even the watchtower."

"What in the world do you want to get into the watchtower for?"

"It should be fairly simple, right? I can just hold down the fort for you guys when you need to go on a break or whatever. It can be just like work-study, except I wouldn't be studying."

"You wouldn't be working either," Moriz said as he finally stopped before a door that was only to be opened by 'authorized personnel.' "Only guards and I get into the tower. If you're too damn lazy to do the mining like everyone else then you're just going to have to suck it up, Galen."

"Can I at least help you guys out with the whole guarding thing?" Chad prodded further. "I mean, that's a lot of forest and trees out there. I can help you guys keep track of the other inmates on the mines or maybe in the area right outside the building."

"That's what robots are for."

"What, they watch all of that stuff?"

"It'd be a waste of manpower and time to have people posted out there, even if they're thugs like you. We're better off letting NegaSentries patrol the areas." Moriz opened the door that led to a staircase. He proceeded to climb the steps, but not before brushing off Chad's request. "We don't need any of you dirtying up any more of the facility. Stick with what you're good at: sifting through dirt. If you behave, we might let you clean the shitters. I hope that answers your question." The door's hydraulic pump closed it behind Moriz as he walked away.

*It definitely does,* Chad thought.

Chad made his mining tool of choice for the day a shovel and spent the first half of the workday fulfilling his visium quota. When he finished, he found Kyle, who was well into meeting his own requirement. Chad beckoned for him to follow and led Kyle to the highest point of the tall mound that towered over the excavation site. Feeling certain that whatever Chad wanted had to do with his escape, Kyle didn't say anything until they reached their destination, out of earshot of everyone in the vicinity.

"Why're we here?" Kyle asked.

"I need you to do me a favor." Chad pushed his shovel into the ground and made a token effort at digging. As he pretended to move dirt from one area to the next, he looked as far into the distance as he could. "Can you look around and count how many of those bots are around here?"

Kyle sighed, "Sure. I've actually counted it before though, just for kicks."

"How many are there then?"

"Twenty-five. That's how many I always see that come from the prison with us every mornin'. Well, twenty-four since the other day..."

"Are you sure about that? Can you count again just to be safe? That'd be really helpful."

"Uhmm, I guess. I'd have to walk around just to count, though. Why you wanna know?"

"I need to know about how many people or robots these guys have on patrol at any given time if I'm gonna do this. If you could give me a clear count of the bots and guards, and maybe a rough estimate of where they're placed around the vicinity, that would be great! I'll just stay here until you get back."

"Oh, great. More errands to run for people," Kyle said wiping the sweat from his forehead. "Is there a reason I gotta do this?"

"You're the super observant guy, remember? Besides, you've been here longer than I have. You'd know where to look, and that's not something I can do without looking suspicious."

Kyle took a moment to think it over. "Aiight, then. I guess I'll do it."

"Thanks, bro. 'Preciate it. See ya when you get back." After a refreshing breath filled his lungs Kyle swung his pick over his shoulder and walked off. Chad, still pretending to dig, looked into the distance again. He stared into the foliage underneath the trees and waited until he saw some sort of movement. After about one minute, he finally saw something moving. It was a NegaSentry.

It was far away and hard to see, but there was no mistaking the rounded edges of the drone as it rolled across the dirt. Chad tried his best to keep an eye on its movements. It wasn't sitting still as he expected the patrollers to. Instead, it seemed to be going somewhere. Moving at a fair pace, it stayed on a path that seemed predetermined. It kept going and going until it eventually vanished beyond the trees. Chad made a note of the sentry and its location and kept looking for more.

Shortly after, he spotted another NegaSentry. It appeared in the same area as the first one he saw. It was headed in the same direction, traveling on the same path, moving at the same speed, and vanished from sight at the same spot. Chad immediately realized what was happening and started to count. *One, two, three, four...* He stared into the same area until he saw another sign of movement. *Seventy-five, seventy-six, seventy-seven...* With every other number, he took a token scoop of dirt and threw it to the side in a pile, oblivious to any visium that may have been hiding in the gravel. He kept his eyes on the trees. *Hundred-eighteen, hundred-nineteen, hundred—there!* Chad spotted in the distance another drone. It was traveling at the same speed, path, and direction as the previous two. *Hundred-twenty. One hundred and twenty seconds. Two minutes! That's about how long it takes them to pass the same point. I'll wait for the next one just in case...*

Once again Chad counted the seconds, and after the two-minute mark, another drone passed by. Chad wasn't familiar with the area that far away, but he did know that the path the drones were traveling on seemed to be a long one. It would take more than a couple minutes for the same drone to loop around the entire vicinity, which left a clear explanation.

After a while, Kyle finally returned to the mound, seemingly exhausted. "You owe me, dude," he panted. "That took a lot longer than I thought it would."

"What did you find out?"

Kyle took a few seconds to catch his breath before responding. "Only saw nineteen, man. I checked twice too. I dunno why they'd havva odd number of Sentries like that around here. I know I saw twenty-four earlier today, too."

"I know why." Chad gestured toward the trees he was observing earlier. "I think the other five are circling this area."

"How do ya know?"

"What did you think I was doing the whole time, actually digging? I was checking out the surroundings when I noticed a NegaSentry pass by over there. When it left, I noticed another pass by not long after that. It turns out that there are multiple bots around here that survey the area, and they're all about two minutes apart from each other in distance. Pretty useful information, right? How many live guards did you count?"

"Thirty, but they're all huddled up in the same spot just chillin'."

"Sounds like an easy enough bunch to get around. I'll keep that in mind."

"Easy? Whatever you say, dude. Oh, and by the way, ya girl wanted me to give you a message."

Chad perked up. "She said: 'tell your friend that he needs to report for duty later'. She even made a whipping sound to go with it. It weirded me out. I ain't know she had a sense of humor."

Chad wiped the sweat from his forehead and scratched his brow. "Neither did I."

Despite being his first time there, Jason wasn't too impressed with the setup of solitary confinement. The cell wasn't too much smaller than the one he was forced to share with his annoying cellmate. It wasn't very dark, and in fact, it even had a small window that allowed him to see the forested area of and beyond Sanctum's campus. The darkly tinted window was probably only there to tease the prisoner who longed for freedom, but such didn't bother Jason. The peace and quiet of the cell provided all the time in the world to think, to reflect, and to analyze.

The results of Sanctum's experiments showed a clear improvement through Trey—or Arbo's—existence, and with the exception of the next prospect, the messenger, and maybe even the girl, no other prisoner knew anything about what was planned for them. They would all be executed eventually, but Jason would be ready. He would try his best to be ready. Dying from the execution was not an option by any means, but he knew that there was a direly important piece of information that he needed to know if he was going to live through it.

How did Trey survive?

There was something unique about Trey that allowed him to live after the execution. But finding what this factor is would not be simple. This much was clear. Had it been easy, some of the experiments following the success of "Arbo" would have been successful as well. Yet, there were still many deaths, and after months of withering health, the only known success perished along with the rest. Jason knew he was partly to blame for that, but it didn't change the fact that Trey was on the verge of death anyway.

Jason knew much about the prison he was in—more than many ever cared to know—and one thing stood out about it above all others: the diversity of its inhabitants. There seemed to be an equal representation of minorities within Sanctum. Other prisons around the nation were mainly populated by Blacks and Whites. Additionally, Sanctum was overpopulated. There were a few hundred criminals that were sent there to await their lawful execution, but before Sanctum's founding, there weren't enough criminals on death row to justify the erection of a new facility for the sole purpose of killing the nation's scum. This reaffirmed Jason's assumption that the unlucky few were being selected through some sort of screening process, and whatever this process was, it was to ensure that they would be able to survive an otherwise very lethal injection of visium.

But despite this screening, prisoners were still dying, even the miracle man that somehow lived. Since Warden Moriz and whomever he was working with hadn't been able to duplicate the results of Trey's experiment, Jason thought it safe to assume that they hadn't figured out what was the special trait Trey had that allowed him to live. Jason knew that finding this information was pivotal for his own survival, especially considering Moriz's growing impatience with him. He needed to find the answer soon.

A click from a door down the hall. Someone was entering the isolation chamber. Jason remained on his bed as the loud click and clack sound of heels on a tile floor increased in volume as the person approached. Familiar with the sound, Jason knew only one person in the prison who consistently wore dress shoes.

"I got some good news for you, bastard," Moriz said as he stood in front of the exaggeratedly bared door. "We finally have an official date set for your execution." Jason was silent. "It'll be in about three weeks, right after we take care of your trouble-making friend."

"I was wondering when you were taking him out," Jason said. "So anyway, I'm curious, what advice do you have to give me so I can walk away from this like your pet, Trey?"

"That is something I'm sure not going to miss; that smart-ass mouth of yours. Don't worry, unlike everyone else here, I'll personally make sure that you won't be able to walk away from it. Who knows, maybe some impurity may turn up in the chemical, or maybe I'll drive the needle in myself. It would be such a shame to miss your vein one or four times. It might be painful, don't you think?"

"The last time I checked, lethal injection was executed by a machine, not by a deranged prison warden. You aren't very good at keeping this whole program you have going on under wraps. How the public hasn't uncovered all this by now is beyond me."

"Once you're dead, we'll make sure you're covered up really well... by dirt. About six or so feet of it." Jason didn't respond. He only turned and lay on his bed with his arms behind his head. "If you really want, I'll tell you how Galen does in his execution. Hell, I might even let you watch. I want you to know exactly how painful it's going to be when your time comes around."

"Why him before me?" Jason asked expressionlessly.

"We were tol—not your concern, smart-ass." Moriz twirled a set of keys around his finger and cleared his throat. Another man standing in the back stepped forward and slid a tray of food through a narrow slot on the door. "I made sure that you had cheap, plastic forks and knives to keep you from accidentally killing yourself when I'm not around. I'll see you again in a few weeks." Moriz and the man left the chamber, signaled by the locking of the door.

Jason sat up and stared at the food on the door as he thought. *If he's being executed before me, they must be confident he will survive.* He went to grab the tray and sat back on his bed, staring at his food. *That guy isn't anything special compared to some of the others here. It'd be nice to have him out of my way, but it'd be even nicer if he helped me figure out how to survive.*

## Chapter 11

# Exodus

Everything was in order.

Chad looked around to find a seat in the white-tiled cafeteria that had not been taken. He found one, sat in it, and peacefully ate his breakfast. The food was filling. Since he may not have been eating again for quite a while, that was a good thing. Jason was still in isolation, so he didn't have to worry about an extra set of eyes watching him. Kyle knew not to bring too much attention to Chad today by talking to him, and Andreas... was being Andreas. There would be no distractions today.

Chad walked in line on the way to the mines with less of a limp than usual. Not that he was experiencing less pain, but just so he wouldn't stand out quite as much. He observed the forest as he made his way to the mine. Even though it was still summer, there were multiple trees that were already showing signs of discoloration. A few orange leaves could be spotted through the blanket of green that each tree proudly wore on its branches. They were preparing for a new season to arrive.

The sun began pouring rays of sunlight onto the path that led to the mines. It was going to be a hot day, but the heavy, thick clouds that commonly polluted the Ohio sky provided temporary shade from the heat as they eclipsed the sun. The shade could be useful in a time like this. Fortunately, it hadn't rained in quite a while, and though the clouds made their presence prominently known as they always did, there was no sign of rain anywhere. That meant there would be no chance of leaving a trail.

Chad took his shovel and walked to the furthest part of the mine. If the rumors were true, then the end of the summer was usually the hardest time to find visium. Luckily, Chad had learned enough from watching Jason pick where the promising spots would be, and conveniently, there was one not far from the edge of the mine. The other prisoners were far too involved in their own work to worry about what Chad was doing. Thanks to the warden, people were a little on edge about not finding enough visium to meet their quota. Plenty of ISO cells were available to the ones who failed to pan out the goods.

There was only one NegaSentry nearby, watching intently. Its eyes never leaving Chad, its tranquilizer and electric-net blaster pointed and ready to fire at any moment. There was only one thing Chad could think of to get it to turn it's back, let alone leave him alone.

"Excuse me," Chad said. The drone rolled forward to gain some ground on Chad. It didn't respond, but it was still listening. *How does this work again? Umm, oh yeah!* "Hey I need to be escorted so that I can find a certain inmate. Can you do that for me?"

The drone spoke. "Whom do you wish to find?"

"Inmate... Uhh, Taylor. Yeah, inmate Taylor. I would like his assistance so that I can pick up this visium I found here." The drone stood silent for a few seconds. Chad looked deeply into its soulless camera-shaped eyes, hoping that was the key to getting it to see his authenticity. After a moment it spoke again.

"Understood. Follow." The sentry immediately turned toward the center of the mine and proceeded to roll forward at a rather quick pace. Chad took a few steps with it, but this Sentry didn't turn around. It didn't even check to see if he was following. *Sanctum's got some nice robots, but the AI clearly needs some work.* He covered his mouth to keep himself from chuckling aloud and making noise. Chad scanned the area once more, took a few steps backward as he watched the drone roll further into the distance, and when he felt it safe he turned and ran. He had done it. He escaped the mine. But now there were two more obstacles in his way.

Chad stopped and hid behind a bush that bordered a path. The path had clearly been used recently. In fact, the wheeled tracks left on it were fresh.

A sound to the right. Chad ducked down behind the bush and

waited for the movement to pass. The sound of wheels pushing off into the dirt approached, as did the sound of a small motor that powered the wheels. The sound was familiar. Chad peeked through the small opening in the bush's leaves and watched as a NegaSentry strolled by on its usual path. Chad waited twenty seconds after it passed until it was clearly gone again. The motor sound was gone and no other motor was in earshot from the other direction. It was time to move again.

Chad shot to his feet and quietly sprinted across the path and beyond. Now there was only one obstacle left. He approached the final hazard; a ten-foot tall barbed-wire fence that barricaded what could only be the edge of the Sanctum campus.

"Wa... u. wing?" A voice from the distance. Chad ignored it. He was so close, he had to keep going. He walked up and tapped the metal fence to test if any electric current passed through it. There was no sensation of pain, so it was safe to continue. He grabbed the fence with both hands, weaving his fingers through the rectangular openings, and the toes of his hiking boots followed suit. He was off the ground. *So close now.*

"Wha... r—u ing?" The voice again. He had to hurry. He pulled his body weight up, reminding himself of his lack of conditioning with every breath he took. It was getting tiring. He had never climbed a fence this high, but he had never broken out of prison before either. Oh, the places life can take you after high school. He was at the top of the fence; all that was left was the barbed wire. He grasped the top of the fence and pulled his legs underneath him. It was time for another jump. Another heroic jump. This time, he would land correctly. He had to, or else he may be stuck there for a very long time. Chad took a deep breath and began to count down.

"Three..." He bounced on the top of the fence, making sure his knees were loose. "Two..." He looked down to try to gauge the distance and time the roll for his landing. Why did it seem so much higher than his bedroom window? He leaned as far back as he could, and then. "ONE!" Chad thrust himself into the air and felt alive, but only for a split-second. As the weight of his body kept moving forward he felt something tug at his leg.

Before he could figure out what it was, his face smashed

against the opposite side of the fence after the momentum of the jump swung him by his feet. Chad looked at his feet and realized that his pants leg was hooked onto the barbed wire, suspending him upside down. He reached for his feet and heard a loud tear. He paused and tried to stop the rip, but the seams could not hold the weight. His pants gave in and ripped completely. Chad had just enough time to take a look at the ground before gravity fulfilled its purpose and introduced Chad's skull to the ground beneath him. The sound of human skull and hardened dirt meeting each other produced the sound of a loud—

SMACK!

"WHAT ARE YOU DOING?" Kyle said after popping Chad on his forehead. Startled, Chad fell back on the bunk he sat in. He opened his eyes and checked out his surroundings. He was back in his cell, and Kyle was standing before him with a puzzled look on his face. Chad sighed in relief and sat up on the bed again, rubbing his forehead.

"The hell'd you hit me for?" he barked.

"Cuz ya didn't answer me when I called you. What were ya doin'?"

"Meditating, genius," Chad said.

"Looked like you were takin' a nap ta me."

"I was planning my day. It's called visualization..."

"Then why didn't ya hear me when I was right in front of you?"

"Because I was focused. That's what focused people do when they're zoned in. What are you doing in here anyway?"

"Second meal's endin' in a bit. You eat yet?" Chad shook his head. "Then c'mon already!"

Chad picked himself up from Jason's bunk. There was no rule saying he couldn't use it while Jason was away, so he made good use of his new private cell and enjoyed it while he could.

He and Kyle made their way to the cafeteria, ate their lunch, and then headed out to the yard again. Choosing not to break a routine now, they walked to the further corner and sat.

"So how'd your 'visualization' go?" Kyle asked."What were ya even tryin' to imagine? It's not like things change up that much around here."

"I was imagining the day I'm getting out of here, which I decided is going to be tomorrow. I've pretty much considered every factor, and it went almost perfectly in my head. Up until the time you came and distracted me, that is." Kyle skeptically nodded, as if he were in favor of the idea. "Anyway," Chad continued, "if all goes well, this will be the last time that we officially get to chill."

"Yeah, yeah. What's your plan once ya get out anyway? I don' think there's a lot a convicted murderer in an orange jumpsuit can do around here before people see 'em and call the cops again."

"I'll find shelter as far from Sanctum as I can. Then I'll try to get back to my friends and see if they can help me clear my name. Once I get all that taken care of, I'll be coming back to visit ya."

"And if ya get caught, I'll probly be seeyin' ya sooner than that," Kyle chuckled. "Either way, I gotta wish ya luck, dude."

"Thanks. Oh, and one more thing I gotta ask you. Do you know what happens to people who get caught trying to escape?"

"Naw, not really," Kyle responded after taking a moment to think. "No one's ever tried it before. Or I haven't seen it, at least. Why?"

"Andreas called it 'suicide'. I'm just trying to figure out what she meant. I'm just going to assume that she's overdramatizing things, but they couldn't legally do anything to me besides put me in isolation, right?"

"Probly... Jus' don't get caught," he said while shrugging.

"I don't plan to. Now, if you'd excuse me, I'm gonna go talk to Andreas. I need to know if she's made a decision on whether or not she's gonna come, though I bet her answer's gonna be no." Chad walked away and started for the door that led back into the prison. It would be smart to just get this conversation out of the way. Someone as boring and overwhelmingly depressing as Andreas wouldn't ever consider doing something rash like going AWOL, but either way, it would be rude to not hear what her decision was if he was the one who invited her. In the end, she was probably satisfied with the way her life was going.

Kyle may have felt like he deserved his punishment, and in all truth, Andreas probably *did* deserve it. Not all of her story added up, and Chad was sure that whatever caused her to eviscerate the man who attacked her that day was most likely the reason that she wanted to stay locked up. From a logical standpoint, Chad accidentally killed a man, and Kyle was blamed when his friend committed suicide; but ripping a man's chest open? That was no accident. Someone who disembowels another did that by choice and was clearly psychotic.

But at the same time, Chad couldn't ignore the evidence to the contrary. Whoever attacked the man, did so with his or her bare hands, and there was no way a little teenage girl had the strength to do that all by herself, or even with help. She *was* unconscious during the whole ordeal. It's possible that somebody set her up... for whatever reason. If that was true, he did a good job of it. Even Andreas believes she did it, and although Chad was still skeptical, as of now he had no reason to assume she was a murderer. She believed he was innocent, he could at least return the favor.

Before reaching the prison entrance, Chad heard Kyle call for him. He looked back to see Kyle waving him down and pointing in another direction.

"Over there!" he shouted. Chad looked where Kyle was pointing, and standing alone, right next to the fence, was Andreas. Chad squinted to confirm that it was definitely her, but he was familiar enough with her shape at this point to be able to tell what she looked like, even from a distance. Chad walked over to her as he tried to figure out what she was looking at. She was staring through the fence at something on the other side, apparently far beyond.

Chad stood beside her and waited to be noticed. After an awkward and silent ten seconds, he decided to be the first to speak.

"Uhh... Hey," he said. Andreas' eyes widened, as if waking from a trance, and she finally acknowledged Chad.

"Oh, hi," she said apprehensively.

"So, you remember what we were talking about last time, right? About my whole idea for the future and whatnot..." Andreas nodded and returned her gazed to the trees beyond the fence. Chad took that as a sign that she was listening. "Well, umm, I'm officially doing it— tomorrow. And I could sure use some company." Chad was quiet as he watched for some reaction from Andreas, but she didn't say a word. Chad noticed her lip quiver just slightly, and growing impatient of her melodrama, he pushed for an answer. "Look, are you coming are not? Just tell me so I can—"

"Yes," she whispered.

"All right, then I'll just go... Wait, what?" Andreas looked Chad in the eye and gave him as definite as an answer as she could.

"I'll go, too." She wiped beads of moisture from her cheek, but Chad couldn't tell if they were tears or just sweat from the hot day. "I'm coming."

"May I ask what made you decide to go through with it?"

"No. I'll tell you why once we make it out. *IF* we make it out. But first, you need to tell me your plan for this whole thing. You have one, right?"

"I, um, actually wasn't expecting there to be anyone else, but it shouldn't take me very long to come up with a new plan. I'll fill you in as soon as I get it together."

"Well, that's reassuring," Andreas patronized. "When will that be?"

"Tomorrow morning. If I can't tell you the plan by then, just stick by me the entire time while we're out in the mines. That's when we'll be breaking out."

"In the middle of the daytime?"

"Trust me. I've already considered everything that could go wrong. As long as you follow my lead *exactly* we'll be able to get out with no problem." Andreas sighed, but it was more like the sigh of a lethargic person than that of someone who actually cared about getting out. Chad took her lack of objection as a sign of cooperation. Instead of being her dramatic and solemn self, she was being sterner. When it came to a situation as dire as this one, Chad would prefer this attitude over a fickle mindset any day. "All right, so are we in this together?" Chad extended his hand for a shake, and Andreas accepted it. "Cool, I'll meet you tomorrow morning during breakfast. Sleep well tonight!"

The two shook hands then parted ways. Chad walked toward the entrance to the prison again while giving Kyle a big thumbs-up. The look of utter disbelief on Kyle's face meant that he knew exactly what just happened, but there was no more time for socialization now. The team had been assembled, the goal was in sight, and now only a plan had to be made to attain it. Chad returned to his cell, closed the door behind him, and sat in Jason's bed. He closed his eyes and began to meditate once again, but this time he envisioned the life he was soon to be a part of.

Fall hadn't begun just yet, which meant there was still time for Chad to try to clear his name after escaping before the next school semester started. USC may be out of the question now, but there were still some colleges that he had time to apply for. The only thing that stood between him and his future now was the mine, a few robots, a fence, and an aging, grumpy warden.

The next morning came, and Chad was fully awake by the time Moriz passed through the corridor. He was used to getting up so early, but he never felt the rush of excitement that he did then. It was time to move forward, and that would be done by leaving the prison behind. He looked around his cell to make sure he didn't forget any of his personal belongings, but the only thing that belonged to him over the last couple months was his vest. It made for simple packing, so he grabbed it, slipped it on, and left his cell. He was ready for his field trip.

Chad was one of the first to enter the cafeteria, and one of the first to get his breakfast. He ate quickly and went back for a second helping before Kyle or Andreas even made it into the room. When they arrived, they grabbed their breakfast and sat at the table that Chad had selected for that day. It was directly in the center of the cafeteria, where he thought no one would notice them. Conversation was kept to a minimum.

"Today, right?" Kyle asked.

"Yep," Chad answered. "Last chance..."

"I'm good," Kyle said. Chad looked at Andreas, who was being quiet but eating less than usual.

"You ready?" Chad asked her. She nodded and continued to poke through her meal, eating only about half of it. "Having second thoughts?"

"No," she said.

"Okay then. Remember: follow my lead the entire time, and stay close by me."

"Fine," she said as she rolled her eyes dismissively. She kept looking down at her plate, poking through some of the food, but not eating very much of it. Chad noticed her behavior, but since he never really ate with Andreas before, there was no telling if she always ate so sparingly or if she was nervous. The lines began forming for the transition to the tool shed outside. Chad got up, gave Kyle a casual goodbye head nod, and beckoned for Andreas to follow him to the line. It was time to begin.

Chad walked as upright and steady as he could. When they reached the tools, he grabbed a shovel and gestured that Andreas pick up a wheelbarrow. She did as requested, and the two returned to the line and stood together. So far so good. Once all the prisoners had their chosen tool and returned to their formation, Moriz and some of the guards took their places in the front and back of the lines. When all were ready, they began the march toward the mines.

For some reason, Chad noticed there wasn't nearly as much sunlight as there usually was around that time. He looked up and saw the problem; thick and dark clouds blanketed what looked like the entire sky. Chad was no stranger to morning overcast, but there was no mistaking the type of clouds that were overhead. It was going to rain. There was no telling when, or how much, but it was going to happen, and it was going to make things difficult.

The convoy arrived on the mines. As the daily routine went, the guards—man and machine alike—took their positions around different corners of the mine, and the inmates went to work. Chad walked toward the south end of the main mining area, listening for the squeaking wheelbarrow behind him to make sure Andreas stayed close. Their first stop was at the bottom of the fields. It was an area that was fairly barren, but Chad halted with conviction and plunged his shovel into the ground.

"Why are you digging here?" Andreas asked. "There's nothing around here."

"I know."

"Then why—"

"Relax, we'll move again in a few minutes." Chad dug up a small pile of empty dirt. He picked through it with his shovel, then sighed exaggeratedly. "I guess there's nothing over here, huh? Let's check the area a little farther down."

"I just told you there's nothing here..."

"Shh," Chad winked, "come on." Andreas followed Chad into the adjacent trees.

"You're not fooling anyone with that horrible acting," she said once they were out of sight.    "Would you chill? I had to fill you in somehow without telling you upfront."

"Did you want to fill in everyone else, too?"

"No one caught on, did they? Besides, I wanted to get moving toward the edge of the campus as soon as possible. I want to get ahead start before—" A drop of water bombarded Chad on the nose. The pressure was so strong it made him flinch. The sky was nearly filled with heavy, blackened clouds that were ready to burst open. "...Before that. If we got out of here before the rain then the water could cover our tracks. But at this rate, it looks like we'll have to walk through mud... I swear I hate Ohio weather!"

"Calling it off?"

"Hell no. We keep going."

They walked further down into another area that was more populated with people. Again, Chad took his shovel, dug another small hole as convincingly as he could, and gave another line explaining why they should move on. Andreas cringed at what appeared to her as a subpar performance, but no one around seemed to pay the two any attention. They moved on and the routine continued.

Finally, they came to a thick brush of trees. The only thing separating the foliage from the rest of the mines was a path of flattened grass and hardened dirt. Either no one had tried to dig there before, or they reached the edge of the mine. Chad assumed the latter.

"I think this is it," he said. "No going back at this point. You sure you're ready?" Andreas shifted her demeanor from one of lethargy to one of focus within the span of a long breath. She nodded. Several heavy raindrops fell at a more noticeable rate. Chad observed the sky once more as he listened to the water droplets smacking the leaves of trees. He took a deep breath himself. It was finally time. "Okay then. Let's g—"

"Inmate Galen. Inmate Lazara." A loud, synthetic voice disrupted the sounds of nature. Chad frantically searched for the source. Approaching him at a steady—but intimidating pace—was a NegaSentry. Its electric net arm was in the ready position. "You are outside of the designated mining vicinity. Please relocate immediately."

"Now what?" Andreas said in a loud whisper.

"Don't worry. Check this out." Chad confidently turned to the robot and spoke again. "Excuse me, I'm lookin' for another inmate for assistance on something... Can you help me find him?"

"Whom do you wish to find?" The robot responded swiftly.

"Inmate Taylor. I need him to help carry some heavy stuff. Can you escort me to him?"

"Understood. Follow." The NegaSentry turned and left its original path. It began riding on the grassy field Chad and Andreas traversed to get to that vicinity. As the robot gained several feet of distance Andreas took a few steps with it. Gently, Chad grabbed her and held a finger to his lips.

"What are you doing?" she asked.

"Watch this," he said smugly. The robot continued along its path without acknowledging who was behind it. "Pretty smart, right? I figured that trick would work after seeing how they operate around here. Even *these* guys don't have eyes on the back of their heads!" The two watched the robot continue on its path. Twenty feet. twenty-five feet. But at thirty feet, it suddenly stopped. Chad felt his heart drop, but before he could react in any constructive way, the shovel in his handmade two loud beeping sounds. The same sounds also echoed from Andreas wheelbarrow. "Oh crap" The Sentry spun one-hundred-eighty degrees and rolled back towards Chad and Andreas.

"Remain within range," it sternly commanded. Saying nothing more, it turned once more and started for the mine. With a wave of embarrassment wafting over him, Chad buried his face in the palm of his free hand. *Of course,* he thought. *The tools are chipped. I should've figured...*

"Brilliant idea..." Chad heard Andreas behind him as she pushed the still-empty wheelbarrow.

"Really don't have time for your sarcasm right now," he said. "Just give me a sec to think." Each step Chad took back in the direction of the mine increased his frustration. He was getting further from where he wanted to be. But he was able to find a rather small silver lining. The trail the NegaSentry found them on was the same one he saw just the other day—the ones that circled the premises. It was the very end of the mine, which was confirmed by the robot. *Once this thing takes us back we'll just try again. If we watch out for these patrol bots on that trail...* "Okay, I've got one more plan. And this time— OUCH!"

Chad ran straight into a now stationary NegaSentry. "Halt," it said.

"Now what?" Andreas said. "We've been right behind it the whole time." They both examined their tools. Neither of them was making any beeping sounds to suggest they were violating some other rule, so they waited for the drone to speak again.

"Halt. Rendezvous point established. Assistance is coming."

"I hope you have a plan for this, too," Andreas added.

"Well, you're sure talkative today, aren't ya?" Chad said with a hint of agitation. "I don't know what the issue is. Just chill, okay?" Within moments another NegaSentry rolled over to the group that was now standing in the middle of a field. It spoke.

"Inmate Lazara. Available wheelbarrow required in east vicinity, immediately. I will escort. Follow." The robot then turned in another direction and continued to ride towards the east of the mines. Andreas looked at Chad, flustered, and started walking behind the second NegaSentry as if being yanked by imaginary handcuffs. Chad returned the look as the first drone spoke to him again.

"Inmate Taylor still remains the destination. I will escort. Follow." The NegaSentry resumed rolling toward the main mine, and Chad stood still until he could think of a plan. He was beginning to lose sight of Andreas as she and her new escort navigated through the trees and brush. Eventually, his thoughts were interrupted by the sound of more repetitive beeps from his shovel.

"Inmate Galen. Remain within range."

Chad and the robot made their way closer to the main mine. Every several steps, Chad couldn't help but peer behind him to see how much farther away from the edge of the campus he was getting. If nothing else, he had to make sure he knew what path he was traveling on so he could make his way back. Ordinarily, he knew it wouldn't be an issue, but the rain was falling harder and harder. If it continued at its current rate, Chad feared that all the landmarks he used to navigate would be submerged beneath the rainfall. Thus drowning his predetermined escape route.

Before long he was back in the midst of the other inmates in what felt like the very center of the entire mine. The NegaSentry halted one final time.

"Inmate Taylor," was all it said. Chad looked in front of the robot to see Skull standing with a shovel of his own in hand. His face was riddled with apparent terror, but Chad couldn't tell if he was afraid of the drone or something else. As the NegaSentry turned and rolled away Chad watched with dissatisfaction.

"Great," he muttered. "Now what?"

"The hell you want?!" Skull frantically said.

"Nothing with you." Chad gave Skull a quick once-over from head to toe and chuckled. "Oh yeah, I heard you were terrified of me because of what happened to... or... because of what I did to Trey."

"I ain't trynna have no trouble, man. Just leave me alone."

Chad felt something that resembled an actual light bulb turning on in his head. "On second thought, I think there is something I want from you." Skull raised his arms as if to brace himself for a fist coming his way. "How do I get to the east mine from here? Tell me."

"I—I don't know..." Skull shrugged.

"Well, you're useless." Without another moment Chad ran over to catch up with the departing NegaSentry. "Excuse me! Can you escort me to Inmate Andreas, er, Lazara?" The drone stopped and gave an immediate reply.

"Inmate Lazara is busy with an assignment. Unavailable. Continue your work." The drone continued on its path. "Wait! I really need you to take me there! She has the wheelbarrow I n—"

"Continue your work," said the drone with a louder volume and more finality. Not pushing his luck any further, Chad considered his next move. The rain was officially pouring at a bothersome rate. Falling to the point where Chad was squinting to keep too much water from getting in his eyes. Not being able to see very far in front of him aggravated him almost as much as his current situation.

Chad didn't expect to encounter multiple speed bumps. The rain was one issue, but it was summer in the Midwest. *It was bound to happen, I guess. I can deal with it. But proximity sensors inside of the tools? Sneaky...* Chad walked back toward Skull, who at this point was back to his previous task. After hearing Chad's footsteps, he was alerted and almost standing at attention. A response he most likely learned from being Trey's Yes-Man. He reached into his pocket and pulled something out.

"What're you doing now?" Chad sighed.

"You want this, don't you?" Glistening in Skull's wet hands were multiple pebbles that glowed dimly through the falling raindrops.

"Ugh, let me guess, Trey made you give him your visium when he was around?"

"You don't wan' it?"

"Isn't it hard as hell to find visium in the rain? Put that crap away before people see you and..." The tug of another light switch clicked in Chad's head. "Ya know what? I think I will take those after all." He snatched the pebbles from Skull's hand and promptly stuffed them in his own pocket. "I'm assuming you have a bit more?" Skull nodded and with a defeated sighed he complied with Chad's request. He led Chad over to a small pile of what was once dirt but was now a muddy hill that was getting eroded by the downpour. With the head of his shovel, Skull pushed the top of the hill over and revealed a bigger collection of visium stones that glistened even brighter than his earlier pocket pebbles. Chad's eyes widened as he smiled nefariously. "Ya know, I'm usually not one for bullying, but I'm gonna have to take your stash this time. Hope ya don't mind."

"Go ahead…"

"Good deal!" Chad grabbed about half of what he saw and allowed Skull to keep the rest. "Don't worry, technically I'm just borrowing this for the moment."

"You're givin' it back?"

"Oh yeah, kind of. Just not now." He took a few steps away as he stuffed his new treasure in his pocket. "For the record, you might want to stay nearby." On that note, Chad picked up his shovel, brushed off all the water that was accumulating on his brows, and walked to the closest pathway. *East, east… which way…* Chad attempted to find the sun's position in the sky, but the thick rain clouds covered it so completely it was like trying to find out what flavor of cake was hidden beneath its frosting. Without spending too much time in one spot, he picked a direction and started walking. Simply asking a guard would be the easiest route, but it may raise suspicion. The best thing to do would just be to rely on his own experience.

Chad thought back to all of his hiking adventures. Surely there was some huge lesson he learned during all of his escapades that would help him in a situation like this one. Unfortunately, Chad was a fan of routine when it came to hiking. Always sticking with the easiest method of navigation made the most sense. Since he always made sure there was no major precipitation during the days that he hiked, he was always just able to use the sun as a reference. And when the day was done, picking out the North Star was never a difficult task.

Chad veered off the path and took a shortcut through the brush, hoping it would lead him to a new area.

Of course, there had to be other conventional ways of navigating, couldn't there? It would just require a little extra ingenuity. Chad fancied himself to be a clever guy, so if anyone could figure it out, it was him. He thought back to all his classes from high school, and even before. *Could Physical Science work here?… Naw, all we ever did there was play with magnets and fun experiments.*

*Magnets! If only I had that. I could make a compass.*

*A compass… Did I ever carry one of those?*

*No. Just my sling bag. And food.*

*Food. What if I get hungry once I bust out? There's nothing edible around here. Just a bunch of grass. And trees. And bushes. Ugh, horrible excuses for vegetat—*

"VEGETATION!" he shouted. He immediately checked to see who heard his outburst, but no one could see him through the foliage. Chad stood under a tree for temporary shelter from the rain, and he looked around for the closest budding plants. In the not too far distance, he saw a small patch of flowers, untouched by any human hands. Chad ran over to it and inspected them thoroughly. "It's still pretty early, and it just started raining a bit ago, so these flowers should be facing the same direction as the sun…" Never before was he so satisfied with Violet City education. After taking a look, he noticed about half of the purple, lily-looking flowers had even bloomed. But the ones that had bloomed were clearly facing a certain direction. Chad stared off into the direction the flowers were pointing, and far, far away, through the trees that seemed to form a wall specifically for the purpose of blocking his vision, he could see movement. He analyzed the flowers once more then turned his gaze beyond the trees. There was definitely a mine over there.

Chad gave a celebratory fist pump and made his way over. After a while of walking, he reached another path and followed it to what was ultimately his destination. Once he got to the mine, he scanned the area, looking for Andreas. What he found was a group of moderately armed guards overlooking the area. His heart dropped, and he quickly made his way down to put his shovel to use.

The mine itself was about fifteen feet lower than the land around it. As Chad walked down the hill he continued his search for Andreas, but her black hoodie, dark hair, and the falling rain did not make the process easy. Fortunately, Chad had that much figured out. He picked a random area in the middle of the mine and started digging, scanning the area in the process. After a few unsuccessful scoops, he picked up the shovel and started again in another section. Before long he found his girl.

Andreas did not appear to be doing very much work, as was the case with wheelbarrow workers. But hers was filling up with dirt, and she would soon be making a round back to the prison's processing center. That could be an issue. Chad approached Andreas from behind and playfully cover her eyes with his wet hands while saying:

"Guess who!" His greeting was promptly met with a short squeal as Andreas' elbow was introduced to Chad's solar plexus. Trying not to draw any attention to himself, he fell to the ground and held his breath to keep himself from screaming from the pain.

"What are you doing, idiot?!" she said with frantic annoyance.

"It was a joke…"

"Not funny…at all." Chad picked himself up after a moment of recovery.

"Yo, I'll take over from here, buddy," he said to the inmate currently filling Andreas' wheelbarrow with dirt. Without any resistance, the inmate, who happened to be another female, threw her current scoop of dirt into the wheelbarrow and walked away. "So sorry," Chad said again to Andreas. "You've caught me talking to another girl," he chuckled.

"Please, stop."

"You jealous?"

"You're so not funny."

"I think I am. Anyway, you ready?"

"Ready for what?"

"Ahem, the *plan*!"

"You can't be serious," Andreas said as she gestured to their surroundings. "Look. There're guards everywhere."

"I see that. I was wondering where they all usually went. I guess this is the new hangout spot for the day." Chad observed the human guards at their post. Only a few of them were attentive of the inmates while the rest were lounging about in their sheltered post. Alternatively, there were only two NegaSentries, one on either side of that area. Chad patted his pocket to feel how much visium ore he stored up and thought back to his recently formulated plan. He was ready. "Okay, there's a new plan, and it involves running like hell."

"You're not serious. When?"

"You'll know when. Just stay close." Chad started walking away from the mounds of dirt and onto a new path. This one led back to the prison Andreas followed him with her wheelbarrow, though she struggled to carry its weight up the hill. Once she got to the top, she continued behind Chad until they reached the beginning of the prison return path. Adjacent to the path was one of the NegaSentries, and Chad tried talking to it one more time. "I need to be escorted somewhere. Can you help?"

"What is the destination?" asked the robot? Chad pointed across the mine toward the shelter of guards. "Understood. Follow."

"What are you doing now?" Andreas asked.

"Keep on the path. I'll catch up in a few." Chad followed the drone as it rolled down the hill, right through the busy inmates. Chad paced himself for the right moment. As he approached the center of the area, he removed some of the visium out of his pocket and held it tight. He would only need a bit. They strolled deeper and deeper until finally, it was time. When Chad reached the middle of the east mine he took the visium he kept in hand and threw it in the air.

There were only a few stones, but they glowed strong enough to be seen flying through the air, even through the rain. Heads turned all across the area, and before Chad saw what happened he heard what sounded like small fights and dog piles behind him. The NegaSentry didn't seem to notice, but the guards definitely did. The majority of the guards dispatched from their dry posts and rushed out to meet the action. That's when Chad dropped his shovel where he was and quickly fled back to the return path.

Once he returned to the top of the hill, he took one more look at the mine. The fights were subsiding but the area was still in disarray. The robots were now on the side opposite of Chad and turned toward the center. But more importantly, the guards were all preoccupied with establishing order. Chad grabbed the rest of the visium from his pocket. It was a sizable handful. It was now or never.

"And for my final trick," Chad said as he cupped the stones in his hand. He tossed the glowing rocks in the air as high as he could and watched them pour onto the inmates below. Chad brushed the dirt off his hands as he watched the ensuing chaos with satisfaction. Every inmate, desperate for a piece of the treasure, began battling for the little pebbles that were now somewhere on the ground while the guards fought to retain order. The NegaSentries were trying to help, but there were too many guards in the way for them to fire any type of tranquilizer or electric net. After scanning the area a final time to make sure he wasn't noticed, Chad darted to meet Andreas.

She hadn't gotten very far, and by the time Chad caught up with her she had stopped and turned, curious about the sounds of pandemonium erupting from the distant trees. She fixed her lips to say something, but Chad got a statement out first.

"Run like hell!" he said. Without a word, Andreas ran with Chad as they took a sharp turn off the path and headed as far away as possible. After a few moments they reached another path. They stopped briefly as Chad decided which way to take.

"What did you do?" Andreas finally got around to asking.

"Riot," Chad managed to say through panting. He realized that the two paths they passed were parallel to each other. He had never been on this path before, and it looked very similar to the previous one. Which meant, "NegaSentries could be close. Let's be careful and get down when I tell you." Before hearing the confirmation from Andreas, Chad took off again. They stayed on their route—perpendicular to the paths they crossed. They both kept a sharp eye out for signs of movement anywhere. Before long they saw something else. "Down. Now!"

They both found the nearest bush and crouched behind it. After a moment, a NegaSentry rushed by them, going the same direction they came from. Farther away, another one followed suit. Chad thought back to the day he scouted the mine from the top of a hill. *These must be the bots patrolling the perimeter. We have to be close to the edge!* He turned to Andreas and signaled her to stay down for a moment longer. Once the coast was clear, they resumed their escape.

Andreas appeared to be fairly even about the whole event, but Chad knew his heart was pounding harder than it should during a jog. His nerves were shaky, but he tried to keep his excitement at bay for the sake of the mission. He could feel it. He was getting closer to freedom. He was getting closer to a new life. Getting closer to—

"The gate!" Chad exclaimed. The two emerged from the foliage to a semi-open area. Chad checked the area on either direction of the fence. There didn't appear to be any cameras in the trees or the fence itself, and there were no indications that NegaSentries patrolled the gate as a perimeter, though the rainfall was making it difficult to know for sure. The fence was exactly how Chad envisioned it, but just a little taller. It had the rectangular wire pattern that made it easy for climbing, and it was even garnished with three spiraling barbed wires on top.

"That's pretty high," Andreas said apprehensively. "I don't know if—"

"It's fine. You can do it! Just go, go." Chad's words were teetering between sounding encouraging and pushy, but they *were* in a hurry. "I'll give you a boost. Let's go." Chad put his back to the fence and cupped both hands together, signaling Andreas to step on. There was hesitation.

She didn't speak, but her eyes suddenly displayed apathy. Of all the emotions to be feeling in this moment, Chad found it flabbergasting that apathy be one of them.

"Hey!" Chad yelled. Andreas snapped out of her mental lapse. She took a breath and stepped onto Chad's hands. With all the strength he could muster, Chad hoisted her high on the fence. He then turned to watch her as she gracefully scaled the top of the fence and climbed back down on the other side. "Not bad…" he said, wiping the mud from her shoes off his hands.

"You coming?"

Suddenly feeling like the one being rushed, Chad followed suit and grabbed onto the fence. The climb was slower than he expected, and the height of the fence and the pain of his thigh was also a surprise, but he kept going. He was unbearably close. The drones couldn't stop him, the guards couldn't stop him, Jason sure as hell wasn't stopping him, and he wasn't going to let anything else slow him down. He got to the top, and with a victorious heave he swung his body over the barbed wired. His arms were getting scratched as he held onto the top, but it wasn't too much pain. He counted to three in his mind. When the count ended, he let go.

Chad tried his best to land on his feet, but his legs couldn't fully support the force of his ten-foot drop. The rest of his momentum caused him to fall back on his butt. It hurt, but at least it wasn't his head. Chad quickly got back up to check if he was still in one piece.

He patted down his body, glanced at Andreas, and then to the opposite side of the fence. He stood motionless for a moment and took it in.

"What is it?" Andreas asked.

"Nothing," he said. A breath escaped him that sounded like a sharp chuckle. "We made it... We're free."

**Chapter 12**

# Execution

"That was absolutely PATHETIC!" Warden Moriz screamed. It had been hours since the eruption of the massive riot on the east mine, and the outbreak resulted in many inmates not meeting their quota for the day.

Even though only several guards were responsible for surveying that area, almost half of the prison's staff was packed into the commons area, receiving an earful from their unsatisfied boss. Moriz was in a state of rage that not many of them had ever seen. Of course, it was rare that he was ever in a good mood, but this level of vocal reprimanding was unheard of. Moriz stood on the second level balcony that overlooked the commons as his subordinates listened to him from below.

"What was that?" Moriz continued. "What are you paid to do? Your job description is frighteningly short because of all these damn robots around here, and you STILL can't maintain order over a bunch of damn orange-suited maggots?!" Murmurs softly floated around, mainly from disapproval of being lambasted so thoroughly. The lecturing continued for what seemed like a half hour. "You should be grateful I waited until 'lights out' before I tore your asses new holes. Only reason I didn't is because we can't have them thinking you actually can't handle them." Moriz spent another moment staring at the guards in silence. There were no words, just a dirty look of overwhelming disgust written all over his face. When he decided he'd made them uncomfortable enough, he said, "Get out of my sight."

The guards immediately dispersed with the sound of footsteps and unintelligible words spoken under breaths. Moriz maintained his disgusted face as he walked down the balcony corridor and entered a room that was visible from the lower level. When he aggressively shut the door behind him, his focus was broken by chuckles from the other side of the room. Catherine Negatov, who tried to hide her smile by covering her mouth, sat in her chair behind her desk.

"I'm sorry, but I think that was the best one yet!" she said.

"I'm glad this is so damn entertaining to you, Catherine," Moriz said.

"Good."

"Where is Jones?" Moriz said, scanning the office. "Why can't he be anywhere on time?"

"I just spoke with him a moment ago. He'll be in soon."

"I don't have time to wait for him. What did you need to talk about?"

"It's my dad," Catherine said, straightening up and clearing her throat. "He said he's back in the state, and he wanted to know when would be a good time to come down for the next execution. I told him that's more of a question for Nathaniel, but he insisted you would know better." Moriz stroked his forehead to remove sweat and calm himself back down.

"Yes, yeah I know," he grunted.

"Would you like to tell me?"

"It has to do with Galen. Doctor Negatov seems to think that Galen's likely to do something dumb in the coming months."

"That sounds completely possible. Did I ever tell you how I gave him a good tasing?"

"Yes, you did," Moriz said. He moved his hand from his forehead down to his chin and began to stroke it. "This is the second riot to happen since he's arrived here. And that troublemaker Lynx has been in isolation for over a week now." Catherine blinked heavily as she tried to process Moriz's logic. After giving up, she made a motion to ask a question but was interrupted by Moriz's fairly abrupt march out of the office.

"Wait," she raised her voice, "don't go yet. Nathaniel should be here any second now."

"He's right here," Moriz said as he swung the door open. Nathaniel Jones stood on the opposite side reaching for the door handle with a look on his face that suggested he was caught stealing from a cookie jar.

"Ahh. Evening, Warden." Jones said, but Moriz was already past him and marching purposefully down the hall. Treating it as a normal occurrence, Jones just closed the door behind him and gave Catherine his normal warm greeting.

"I think my dad wants you to be ready for another trial soon," she said. "Do you feel ready for it?"

"I'm glad you asked! I made some fine tuning to the dosage over the last few days." Jones made gestures of turning the dial on a car radio to illustrate his point. "I've decided not to hold back! If we increase the strength of what we give the subject next time, I really feel like we're going to do it. Seriously, I feel it this time. I feel like we're getting—"

"Closer?" Catherine interrupted. "Is that how you feel?"

"How'd you know? You're good."

"Damnit, Nathaniel, this isn't a game. I'm sure you know exactly how important this is to my father... and for you to be joking around like this...I really don't know why you aren't taking this seriously after all these years."

"Catey," Jones pleaded, "I am taking this seriously. It's just as important to me that we succeed soon. This is what I've been striving toward even before this place came to being..." Catherine gave an exasperated sigh. Jones couldn't tell if this was from frustration with him or from pressure from some other source. Either way, he knew that she knew his time for producing successful results were running short. After a moment Jones spoke again. "Okay, here's my promise."

"Yes?"

"This guy: Galen. When it's time for his trial, I will make sure it succeeds. I'll be ready then."

"Galen?" Catherine asked as she reclined in her chair. "Are you sure about that?"

"Yes, I promise." As Jones finished his sentence, they both heard heavy footsteps down the hall as they made their way closer to Catherine's office. Moriz burst through the door and slammed it behind him.

"Galen did it," Moriz announced sternly. "He fled the prison. He's nowhere to be found. Not in his cell, not in the commons." Jones swallowed big. He glared at Moriz as he took in the information.

"You're sure about this, Jael?" Catherine asked.

"The maggot's gone! The riot was probably his doing! I'll give him credit, though. I didn't expect him to try it so soon."

"You knew he would try to escape?" Catherine asked incredulously.

"Your father did," Moriz said. "Our job was to watch him and be ready, and my men can't even do *that* much."

Catherine shifted her gaze from the livid warden to the petrified scientist. Jones did not move as he continued to process the moment. An inmate just tried to escape from the prison, and everyone in the room knew exactly what that meant.

"Nathaniel," Catherine called softly. "Do you still stand by what you said?" There was a hesitation. A long hesitation. He answered.

"I do... I'll prepare my equipment."


It wasn't often that Chad felt both exhausted and energized simultaneously. But there he was, feeling the events of the day wearing on his body and the liberation of being released from a prison. Of course, 'released' may not have been the proper word to describe what actually happened, but that wasn't important. All Chad knew was that he had accomplished his goal. He escaped bondage, and now he was ready to begin the second phase of his grand scheme to achieve true freedom: clear his name. Unfortunately, that would have to wait for just a bit. There was a slightly more important issue to be dealt with. He had no idea where he was.

Not long after escaping Sanctum's gate, Chad had no problem admitting to himself that he was lost. That wasn't necessarily a bad thing, though. He had been on many hikes in the past while exploring new lands and paths he had never traveled, and he always managed to find his way back home. He found no reason to believe that now would be any different. However, this time it's not just his own livelihood that is at stake. He had precious cargo, and the cargo was losing her patience.

Andreas kept a few paces behind Chad almost the entire time. This was her way of electing Chad the leader, which he had no problem taking the helm on.

"Do you have a plan now?" Andreas asked.

"No," Chad said. "Stop asking me."

"Don't you think you should have one by now?"

"You're welcome to pitch in ideas anytime, you know." Chad looked at the sky and held out his palm, attempting to catch potential raindrops. "At least it stopped raining. I just hope we're going the right way."

"Right way for what?"

"There's a tourist attraction nearby... Don't know where, though. I just want to find shelter somewhere soon before mountain lions show up."

"Mountain lions?!" Andreas halted. It was the first time either of them had stopped in hours, so Chad welcomed the rest. "You knew they were out here."

"Haha, relax," Chad reassured her. "They're pretty rare around here. Besides, we'll be fine as long as we find a place to stay. It's getting pretty dark." Andreas didn't appear any more at ease. However, the lack of movement gave Chad the sudden urge to take care of important business. "Can you stay here for just a sec? I need to use the bathroom real quick."

"Fine."

Chad took a stroll down the hill they currently stood at the top of. As one would expect, there are were many hills in Hocking Hills, Ohio. Fortunately, there was also plenty of forests out there as well. That provided plenty of cover for Chad to do his business without being seen. He liked Andreas, but not that much. Not yet, anyway.

He strolled down to a tree that was only several meters away from where Andreas was posted, but it supplied plenty of coverage. He stood on the opposite side of the tree and unzipped his pants. Sometimes there was nothing more peaceful than the sound of a stream in the woods.

After he began his release, he felt something tickle his forehead. Chad passed it off as a drop of rain that fell from a leaf above. With his hands occupied, he shook his head to fling off the drop and continued his business. The tickle moved. It went from the middle of his forehead to the side of his nose, right by his nostril. He responded again with another shake of the head and a deliberate exhalation through his nose. Certainly, the drop was gone this time.

The tickle moved once more. This time the sensation traveled to the side of his face and upwards to his hair. It was now clear this was no raindrop. *It's a freaking—*

"SPIDER!!!" Chad squealed as manly as he could. With his stream still in progress, he took both hands and frantically swatted his face from all directions. In the midst of his spazzing, he lost his footing, causing him to fall backward and tumble all the way down the wet and muddy hill. His involuntary somersaults ended with him on his back. It was at this point that his stream finally ended.

Andreas rushed down the hill as quickly as she could. Though Chad heard her call his name, he was in too far a state of embarrassment to answer.

"What happened?" Andreas asked.

"There was a spider," Chad said very matter-of-factly.

"Are you freaking serious?"

"I'm very freaking serious…"

"Oh my god," Andreas raised her hands above her scalp and collapsed from distress onto the grassy area beside Chad. "You literally almost scared me half to death."

"Imagine how I felt."

There was a short silence, and then it was broken by laughter. But it wasn't Chad laughing. Andreas' bellows filled the air, and the sounds of her voice echoed off the trees that were nearby and faded into the distance, absorbed by the humid air. Chad remained on his back while he listened to her in awe. This phenomenon he was witnessing was unheard of.

"R-really?" he said. "This is what it takes? I can try all the jokes and witty one-liners, but the thing that cracks you up is the sight of me freaking out and falling down a small mountain. You're a piece of work, you know that?" Andreas regained a bit of composure.

"I thought you wanted to make me laugh," she giggled. "Aren't you happy?" Chad loosened his tone.

"Yeah, maybe I am." He smiled at her, and they both dwelled in the moment. The damp breeze flowed through the air, and as it coursed through the trees, small beads of water came crashing to the ground below. Neither Chad nor Andreas bothered shielding themselves from a bombardment of water. They were both too soaked from the earlier rainfall to care. The moment was also peaceful, and it was the closest either of them came to peace in a very long time. Chad looked around while still lying on his back. Eventually, he looked just above his head. "I'm happy about something else, too." Chad pointed directly above his head.

"Hmm?" Andreas followed Chad's finger and noticed what he

was pointing at. It was a cave.

"I guess we solved that shelter problem, huh?" Chad rolled over and pushed himself off of the ground. He took a solid minute to brush off the dirt that accumulated during his tumble. By the time he finished, Andreas was already inside the cave. Unable to see her from a distance, Chad walked closer to the cave's mouth. "You in there?" he called. Andreas emerged from the darkness.

"Good news," she said, smirking. "No spiders."

"Har-dee-har," Chad said with emphasized sarcasm. "What's inside there, anyway?"

"Can't really tell, but it's dry."

"And that is the important part! I'm going to find a spot." Chad walked into the cave slowly, waiting for his eyes to adjust to the darkness. The process took longer than expected, though, and Chad only managed a few steps before stumbling over what he could only assume was a large rock. "I'm okay! Don't worry!" Chad peered outside of the cave to see if Andreas was looking. She was looking into the cave, but in the wrong direction, showing that her eyes hadn't adjusted yet either.

"I have to go to the bathroom now," she said. "Don't hurt yourself while I'm gone."

"No promises, there."

Andreas walked off to the side of the cave and disappeared from sight. Chad took the opportunity to get a bearing for his surroundings. He got down on his knees and felt around for anything useful. A few feet to the right: rocks. He kept searching. A few feet further: sticks. He wandered a bit to the left: more rocks. He thought of his previous backpacking adventures once more. What can I do with rocks and dry wood? The answer became obvious.

Chad picked up many of the rocks he found and placed them in a circle. In the center, he cleared out most of the dirt and put in its place all the dry wood he could find. His eyes were almost completely adjusted now, so he searched for two dry and coarse rocks. After fiddling with the stones for what felt like entirely too long, Chad finally managed to produce a spark that caught on the wood. He quickly and carefully nursed the spark to a sustainable ember, and then eventually it became a flourishing flame. Chad took a whiff of the smoke and admired the fruit of his hard work.

Feeling that whatever Andreas was doing was taking too long, Chad walked to the entrance of the cave. There was no sign of her. He took a few steps farther out, and he saw her on top of the hill he fell from just earlier. He went up to meet her.

"Hey," he said. "What are you doing?"

"I can't remember the last time I saw the moon at night," she whispered as she gazed at the sky. "We're never allowed to go outside at night, not even to the yard. I just wanted to take it in."

*How sentimental of you*, Chad thought. "Well, I actually got a bit of a surprise for you," he said. "Come check this out." He walked her back down to the mouth of the cave, where only the occasional flicker of Chad's flame could be seen. Andreas apparently failed to notice it, though, since she could not figure out what Chad was so excited to show her as they climbed down the hill. They turned the corner at the cave's entrance and there was the flame, burning in all its glory. The heat could be felt from a distance. Andreas froze. "Tah-Daaah! Awesome, right? It took me forever to get it up, but now—"

"Put it out!"

"Wh-what?"

"Put it out, now!" she screamed even louder. Andreas ran over to the fire pit can kicked the rocks in on the wood. Chad ran over and grabbed her by the arm.

"Relax, already. Tell me what's wrong!" Chad's plea was met with a stern shove from Andreas. He stumbled over another rock and fell over. Not wanting to instigate a confrontation he simply watched from the ground as a panicking Andreas stomped out and covered up the campfire with all she could find. She did a thorough job, since in just a minute later the flame was reduced to nothing but orange, smoking ashes. Andreas' breaths were deep and exaggerated as she promptly walked out of the darkened cave, passing Chad.

Chad noticed Andreas' breathing as she extinguished the fire and stormed by him. Those weren't the breaths of a person fatigue by a difficult task. Not at all. Those were the breaths of person who was emotionally distressed; someone who was just placed in a position that he or she didn't know how to handle. It was something Chad recognized. They were the same breaths he took the very same moment a motionless body dropped before him.

Chad stood up and calmly brushed himself off. He took a final look at the fire he spent so much time on and then walked out of the cave. He scanned the hills for Andreas. After a few seconds, he found her once again on top of the hill he fell from earlier, but this time she wasn't standing. She was sitting with her knees snugged against her chest; the same position she was so comfortable in at her favorite spot back in the commons. Chad approached her slowly. As he got closer, he heard what sounded like sniffling.

"Hey," he said softly once he was within arm's reach.

"What were you thinking?" she snapped. "You really think it's a good idea to make a fire when we're fugitives? What's wrong with you?"

"Well," Chad sighed, "that's a reasonable point, I guess, but I think we both know that's not what this is about."

Andreas glared at Chad's face. Written all over it was a look of understanding, which confused her. Why did he think there was something to understand? She buried her face into her hands and whimpered aloud. Chad said nothing as he let her emote on her own. When she finally calmed down, he spoke again.

"Did something happen? Ya know, before you came to Sanctum…" Chad kneeled down to her level. Andreas nodded. "What?"

"It reminds me of why I'm in this situation in the first place," she whimpered. "It's a long story."

"It's gonna be a long night," Chad grinned and nudged her with his elbow.

"Not long enough." Andreas wiped the tears from her face and regained her composure. She stood up and seemingly reverted back to her old, stern self. "Look, I appreciate it. I appreciate you. Seriously. But it's not something I want to talk about… ever. Okay?"

"Fine," he relented.

"No more fires," Andreas commanded.

"Deal." Chad extended his hand toward the cave. Andreas took the hint and walked back down the hill. When they got to the entrance they observed what was left of the fire, which remains resembled burning coal with smoke softly rising. Andreas timidly walked inside and sat down on the wall furthest from the ashes. Chad took off his vest, which was already dry due to its water repellant features, and took off the orange shirt he wore underneath. Although it felt fairly dry, there was still some moist area. He took the shirt and wrung what was left of the moisture over the ashes. The sizzling sound signaled the definitive quench of the flame.

He left his shirt off and threw it on a larger rock by the wall. Afterwards, he put his vest on again and sat beside Andreas. They sat in silence, neither of them uttering a word. However, the silence was surprisingly comfortable. There were no inmates to harass them. There were no NegaSentries to shepherd them into their cells. There was only stillness. There was peace.

Chad reached out his open hand to Andreas, and she accepted the invitation. She gently took his hand and they slowly locked fingers before resting their joined hands on the ground below. It was then that Chad felt his chest churn one more time. It was the warmth.

Before long Chad heard Andreas' breathing turn from something controlled to a deeper and automatic flow. She was asleep. He thought of all kinds of important topics that they probably should have discussed before the night was over. A topic of chief significance was what the plan would be for the morning and where they would go. But the day was a long one, and so far the night was peaceful. There was no rush to figure those factors out now. All that was important was taking in this moment.

All that was important was rest.

When Chad woke up he was momentarily stunned with confusion. He had never woken up in a cave before, but it didn't take long for him to remember where he was. He looked outside the cave and noticed it was still dark outside. *Why did I wake up?* A quick glance to his side revealed that Andreas was still there with him, and their hands were still connected. He considered getting up, but remaining inside the cave was suddenly much more appealing. He closed his eyes again and tried to doze off.

Not long after, Chad heard a small rustle outside the cave. He opened his eyes again and looked outside. There didn't appear to be any movement. *Must've been the wind.* Chad's response was to shut his eyes again and ignore it. There was another rustle, this one loud enough to slightly startle Chad. He held his gaze outside the cave and looked for anything out of the ordinary. The rustle continued, and it got louder and louder, but there was something odd about it. Whatever was creating the sound was not moving in a rhythmic fashion. There were no signs of footsteps or even a varied pathway. The rustle was steady, consistent, and there was no wind to blow the leaves into producing a similar effect. Whatever was outside wasn't walking. It was rolling.

"Psst, Andreas," Chad whispered in a semi-panic. He shook her awake by tugging on the hand he was holding on to. "You gotta wake up. I think someone's coming!"

"What?" Andrea said groggily.

"Get up. Hurry!" Chad jumped to a stand and quickly helped Andreas get to her feet. He turned his eyes back outside the cave to see if anyone was coming. The rustle was moving farther away, but there was something else even more frightening now in plain view of the cave: a searchlight. "Shoot! Andreas, they're here; we need to get ready to run."

Andreas groaned as she tried to rub the sleepiness out of her eyes. Chad couldn't make sense of what she was saying, but only because whatever or whomever outside deserved much more attention. Chad tiptoed to the opening of the cave and kept his back close to one side. Peering out, he could not see any person in particular, but he did notice multiple smaller searchlights slowly tracing a path on the ground.

Chad studied the lights closely. There were only two of them, and they had noticeably inorganic movements. It was as if the lights were programmed to travel the same path continuously until it found something unique. Both lights started down, floated up, panned to the left, then to the right, continued searching farther up and then repeated the whole cycle again. Not too many things were that predictable, except, of course, the NegaSentries.

"We've gotta go, those robots are here looking for us," Chad silently announced. Andreas quickly snapped out of her grogginess and was ready to move. "When I give you the signal, get ready to run, okay?" Andreas nodded. Chad motioned for her to come stand by him, and she did what she was asked.

"What's the plan?" she asked.

"Those robots are looping the same search pattern with those lights. As soon as they start looking somewhere opposite of where we are, we go! Got it?" Andreas nodded fiercely.

Chad watched the NegaSentries closely as they searched. He poked his head out just far enough that he could see both drones without being too conspicuous. There was one on either side of the cave, but they were much farther down, and fortunately, their lights clearly gave away their position. They continued to search their assigned path when one suddenly stopped in its tracks. Its searchlight clearly stopped the set cycle it was programmed to do, and then as convincingly as Chad had ever watched a robot do, it suddenly gave up. The robot on the left side shifted its light so that it was pointed straight ahead, turned around, and left. Chad kept watching it as long as he could, but he eventually lost sight of it as it went around a hill—the same hill Chad was very familiar with at this point.

Considering the departed robot a non-threat, he shifted his eyes back to the one on the right, which was still doing its diligent hunting. With its light still cycling, it moved further and further to the left, as if going to search where the other had left. But along its path, it halted right within eyeshot of the cave's opening. Then just like the other drone, its light cycle stopped. The searchlight pointed forward just like the other, but instead of rolling away, it began to turn. Its frame stayed perfectly in place as the top half of the machine spun on a 360-degree axis. The searchlight lit all the trees in the opposite direction, but Chad quickly realized that the light would soon be pointed directly into the cave.

"Get down! Now!" Chad said as he grabbed Andreas and dove to the ground. "Don't move…"

Within seconds, the slow moving light reached the cave's mouth, but instead of just swiping across the opening, the light halted completely and held its position inside the cave. Chad held Andreas tightly as he tried to keep them both still. In the meantime, the robot's spotlight was hovering inside the cave, just above them. The light did not move at all, but it illuminated the very back end of the cave, which to this point Chad had never seen because it was so dark. The light hovered for an uncomfortably long time, but after about twelve seconds, the drone seemed satisfied with whatever it did or did not see. The light finished its 360-degree rotation. Chad turned his head over to see the NegaSentry while still hiding on the ground. Without further adieu, it promptly followed its partner's lead and rolled beyond the hill.

Chad rolled over and took deep breaths of relief. Andreas, who was having trouble hiding her disapproval of what equated to being tackled, quickly got back to her feet and brushed off her clothes.

"So now what?" she asked. This time with a genuine curiosity.

"We gotta keep going and find a new spot," Chad said. After regaining a bit of composure he straightened up his clothing as well. "Okay, when I give you the signal I need you to follow me. We're going to head as far away from the prison as possible. It looks like the robots went back toward Sanctum so we should be safe." Andreas nodded. Chad went to the opening of the cave and checked every direction imaginable. There was no sign of any person, and the rustling of the drones rolling through the grass was gone. "All right. Let's go."

Chad took the first steps into the open and Andreas followed him closely. So far so good. Chad took five paces out, looked both ways like he was crossing a street, and took a few more steps. Everything appeared fine, but when Chad reached his tenth step Andreas let out a huge scream.

Chad spun around to find Andreas caught in an orange net. Before he could completely process the scenario, another net deployed and bound him completely like the hand of a giant. Chad fell over and saw multiple human guards standing on top of the cave's entrance, the one place he did not think to check. From behind the guards, Warden Moriz stepped forth with what appeared to be a shotgun in his hands. Andreas, who was still screaming was the first person he visited.

"Shut up!" he yelled. He kicked her over on her belly and lifted his gun into the air. The gun came down in an impaling motion, and all of Andreas movement stopped. She was knocked out.

"No, no, no," Chad said to himself as he tried to free himself from the net. Despite his best efforts, the net was wrapped too tightly to his body, and he could only wiggle a few feet in either direction.

"I hope you enjoyed your time in your suite," Moriz said as he walked over to Chad. He lifted his gun in the same manner as before, and Chad braced himself for the impact as best he could. "Vacation is over." The gun came down.

"You dn't quilize them d you?"

"No. no eson dn't work."

Chad slowly woke to a broken conversation. Someone was talking around him, but he had no idea whom. It did not take very long before he regained consciousness completely. When he did, the first thing he noticed was the unrelenting pain in the back of his head. That was a good start. The second thing he noticed was that he was strapped to a table. Although that information was useful, it was also incredibly discomforting. After a quick and frantic glance of his surroundings, he also noticed there were two large guards by what looked like the door, two other men who were bickering back and forth, and a second table that held Andreas, bound in a similar fashion that he was.

"He's on his way in now, Jones. For your sake, this works."

Chad recognized that raspy and angry voice to be Warden Moriz's, who was currently on his way out of the well-guarded door. The only other person in the room was a nerdy looking, middle-aged man wearing a lab coat and glasses. Not the type of person Chad would trust to be around while he was strapped to a table.

"Andreas, wake up!" Chad yelled. She was lying on her table, but she did not answer. "Andreas, ANDREAS!"

"I didn't realize you were awake," Jones said. He walked over to Chad and stood by his table. "I hope you're feeling well. I could really use you at your best today," he said nervously.

"The hell does that mean?" Chad said. "What am I doing here? Freakin' let me go!"

"Well, you're a spirited one, aren't you? That's good, I suppose. Maybe that will help, too." Jones ran his fingers through his hair and rested his hand on the back of his neck as he went to take inventory of his tools again.

"What the hell are you talking about?" Chad stared at the man in the lab coat with confusion. "Do I know you?" Jones turned to look at Chad. *He... he looks familiar. Like someone I've seen in... was it school?*

"Perhaps you've seen me around Sanctum," Jones said.

"Nate Jones. Nathaniel Jones! That's who you are! Why are you... you're alive?"

"How do you know me?"

"I've looked you up before. You're the guy. The biochemist who's into metaphysics. Yeah, that's you!"

Jones had no idea how to respond in this moment. It was rare that people knew who he was even before he began working for his current employer. But for the last decade, his existence was supposed to be kept secret from the world. How could this teenager possibly know anything about who he was, let alone his name?

"Buddy," Jones began, "I don't think—"

"Get me out of here!" Chad demanded.

"I don't think you understand."

"Understand what? That I don't want to be here? I understand that pretty well."

"You just tried to escape from Sanctum. Don't you know what that means?"

"What're you talking about?"

"It means suicide," Andreas interrupted. Her voice was soft, but her words held enough weight to be heard.

"Andreas? What do you mean?" Chad asked.

Three loud knocks interrupted the conversation. It wasn't until that point that Chad noticed the one-way mirror, which from his current perspective was below his feet. He noticed what sounded like a deep gulp coming from Jones.

"I'll let you two discuss this on your own," Jones said. He walked over to Chad's table, reached underneath it and pressed a button. The table shifted until it became perpendicular to the floor, and within half a minute Chad went from being strapped to a table to what felt like being strapped to a dart board. Jones did the same thing for Andreas' table before promptly leaving the room.

"Andreas..." Chad said. "What do you mean?" Chad waited patiently for a response, and Andreas took her time formulating an answer.

"I remember when you first told me your story," she began. "...about how you killed your parents. About how it was an accident. And how you're actually innocent." Her voice began to crack as tears rapidly welled in her eyes. "I never judged you for that. How could I ever judge you... when I'm so much worse than you in every way?" Chad wanted to speak, but he couldn't find the words at the time, so he just listened. "I knew I couldn't judge you, because I killed my parents, too. But it wasn't an accident, how could it have been an accident?" Tears began streaming down her face.

"Okay, slow down, buddy," Chad tried his best to make sense of the situation, but Andreas' story was not helping at all. "What does this have to do with suicide?"

"There's something I always liked about you. It's the fact that you can be sent to death row from an accident and still keep your hope. It's the way you can do something unforgivable, but still find a way to forgive yourself. I wish I had that inside me... You're even in the face of death now, and you're still fighting."

"Andreas, please focus! Suicide! What does this—"

And just like that, Chad finally understood everything that was going on. In a flash, so many ideas and possibilities made perfect sense in a single, demoralizing swoop. The reason Sanctum's security always appeared more lackadaisical than it should have been. The reason it was so easy to escape this maximum security prison. The reason Jason was so suspicious of the prison's administration. The reason the renown scientist Nathaniel Jones currently had him bound to a platform. And the reason Andreas ultimately agreed to go on this folly of an adventure with him. She kept rambling on.

"The way you always acted like there was nothing wrong with life, like you were the one who was truly innocent. Like you were oblivious to your own life situation... That's what I like about you. I like you because you are a fool. I could never live with myself for doing what I've done."

"Andreas, answer this one question for me." Chad stared at Andreas, but he could barely see through his own filter of tears that became heavier by the second. "Why did they execute Trey when they did?" Andreas blinked away her own tears so she could return his eye contact.

"He tried to escape."

Jones finally returned to the chamber, but instead of making small talk, he went straight to the table with all his equipment laid out. He grabbed the necessary supplies and walked over to meet Chad at his new propped up position. He went through his normal routine of finding the vein and prepping the needle, but he had a seriousness that he never had before.

"Looks like you're up first," Jones said. "I've never said this to anyone before, but good luck."

"No," Chad sobbed. "This isn't what I planned. It wasn't supposed to happen this way."

"I know," Jones said. "It never is." Jones held Chad's arm as he positioned the needle in place. It was then that Chad saw the glowing syringe. The liquid inside was unmistakably liquid visium. After all that, Jason was right all along.

"No, don't!" Chad pleaded. Jones paused, but not because of Chad's words.

"Look at me," he insisted. "I need you to survive this." His words were incredibly stern as he looked Chad in the eyes with unrelenting intensity. "Do you hear me? I need you to survive. Survive!"

He impaled the needle into Chad's vein and emptied the syringe full of the glowing substance. He then swiftly removed the needle, bandaged the entry hole, and stepped back to watch the most important trial of his life.

Chad felt the cold visium flow through his vein and fill his heart. Once it was there, the chill dispersed throughout his body, and the temperature of the visium began to warm up as it mixed with the already heated blood. Almost immediately, Chad's entire body was overwhelmed with pain. It was a pain he had never felt in his life, and one he never could have imagined.

Within moments Chad went from fighting pain to battling death. As the visium circulated through his bloodstream, every part of his body felt like he was being roasted over an open fire. Every piece of his anatomy, every cell in his blood, and every molecule within an atom felt like it was being attacked by an intruder and being forcibly dragged closer to oblivion. It was almost impossible to think of anything but the pain.

Almost.

*Will Andreas feel this same thing? I don't want that for her. It doesn't matter what she's done; she doesn't deserve this. Nobody deserves this. I don't deserve this.*

Deserve. All of a sudden that became the most questionable word in Chad's entire vocabulary. To merit. To be qualified for. *Is that what this is?* Everything in Chad's life—all the events of that eighteen-year span—had led up to this very moment. It has led to the ultimate punishment for a crime that only the worst people on the face of the planet commit. But Chad didn't actually commit any crime… he was just in the wrong place at the wrong time. Or was he in the wrong family at the wrong time? Whatever the case was, this was the path the Universe decided was ultimately the most logical. This is what he deserved.

But what about schooling? What was all that self-hype about attending university for the sake of betterment? Did it benefit Chad to truly believe there was ever a point in building a relationship with his friends—or even with Andreas? What was the logic in the Universe deceiving him into believing there would be an opportunity for a better day just so he could discover his life would be cut short by a series of orchestrated events that were ultimately beyond any his control? This was the flawed logic of the Universe.

The Universe had made its decision. But as far as Chad was concerned, it made the wrong decision.

Once Chad returned to reality from his personal world of thought, he took account of what was going on with his body. It was convulsing severely and in a state of unparalleled agony. But the convulsions began to subside, if just slightly. Chad screamed as he fought to keep himself from slipping under. *I will not die!*

"I will not die!" he shouted. As saliva dripped from his mouth, it was difficult to tell what he was saying, but he continued to speak. "I will not die! I won't die I won't die I won't die!" As Chad managed to secure enough control of his eyes and head to focus in on Jones, who stood just several feet away. He appeared to be in awe, or very concerned. Chad could not tell which, but he didn't care. Jones wasn't who he was looking for.

Chad threw his head to the right and saw Andreas. She was whimpering quietly, and despite all the raucous Chad caused, she seemed more concerned with her own misfortune to pay Chad any attention.

"An-Andreeyaas," Chad called over. She lifted her head but did not turn it to see Chad. He tried to speak again, but when he realized his words were becoming too unintelligible, he stopped. Thinking of what he wanted to say had to suffice as he held his gaze on her.

*Why did you give up? You, Kyle, Trey, everyone else at this damn prison... You all gave up. You all are quitters! But I'm not going to be like you; I'm not going to just quit life!*

Chad's vision began to blur, and the blur thickened until he could only see darkness. The pain all over slowly began to subside, and soon the only thing Chad could feel was the totality of his own weight as numbness flooded his body. He wanted to stay awake, but his body wanted to sleep more. Never before had he felt this type of drowsiness. It was as if his mind was winding down without any intention of coming back. He resisted the slumber to no avail. All he could do now was recycle the words in his mind.

*I won't die... I'm not. A quitter... I. Won't...*

*Die.*

## Chapter 13

# Power

"We gave you one job! ONE JOB! And you couldn't even do that!" Shouts erupted from the small law offices of Schone & Park. It wasn't often that citizens of Violet City required litigation services, which at this moment was a good thing. No one else was inside the tiny house that doubled as an office space except for the young Jonny Schone and his extremely discontented clients. The most vociferous of these clients was currently Karli. "It's like you didn't even try then, and you're SURE not trying now!"

Ricky and Chris sat on one side of Schone's desk. Karli was beside them, but she felt more comfortable standing as she delivered her thoughts in the way she felt most appropriate. On the opposite side of the desk, and on the receiving end of Karli's words was Schone. Schone was a Caucasian man who appeared to be in his mid-twenties, clearly fresh out of law school, and with a demeanor of a professional who just wanted to make work fun. This was displayed with hair that was neatly spiked up and a suit that was worn without a tie. Fun, however, was not on the agenda today.

"Ma'am, please," he said, trying to calm Karli down, "your friend is already convicted at this point, and the jury felt that there was more than enough evidence against him back then. Without any new developments, there's not much we can do."

"That's what appeals are for, genius," Karli said. Schone discreetly peered over to Chris, who showed no signs of wanting to calm his girlfriend down.

"What about the witnesses?" Ricky interjected with a concerned, but much more approachable demeanor. "Can't we find some of them and get them to report what they saw?"

"Possibly," Schone said, "but most were not present until after the incident already occurred."

"And the one lady never turned up during the trial," Chris chimed.

"Still hasn't," Ricky added. "Can't you try to see what happened to her? I know it's gotta be somethin' you guys do."

Schone paused to look through the glass wall of his makeshift office. On the other side, his partner Bobby Park was listening intently to the conversation, though not wanting to get involved. Park shrugged his shoulders as the two exchanged glances. "It's a service we may consider."

"Then do it!" Karli demanded.

"I apologize, but even if we find her there's not much of an argument we have to go off of at this point. In addition, it would take far too much time and money, and I'm not sure you guys have the funds to pay for that service."

"That is NOT your call to make, jackass!" The bickering continued for a while longer. Karli and Chris forcefully pleaded their case for why Schone & Park should consider going through with an appeal, and Schone made his case why that would be ill-advised. In the meantime, Ricky cycled both sides of the argument through his head. After a brief but powerful deliberation, Ricky made up his mind.

"Come on," he said as he stood from his chair. "We're leaving."

Though surprised, everyone in the room seemed to unanimously agree that leaving was the best idea. Schone delivered his most sincere salutation, and Chris, Ricky, and Karli promptly left the makeshift work site. Once they were all back in Ricky's car, Chris had a new proposition.

"We can find someone else, right?" he began. "I mean, I'm sure there are a lot of great lawyers around here who would love to take this case for free."

"There are so many holes in the prosecution," Karli added. "There're plenty of people competent enough to help us."

"No, guys," Ricky said. "I don't think there are."

"Are you serious?" Karli said. "You really think there's nothing we can do to get help? Screw the money, we can represent him ourselves if we need to."

"I guess, but I think there's somethin' we're missing… and it has to do with that woman."

"Yeah, Miss Vonda!" Chris added

"I think Chad knows more about her than we do," Ricky continued. "We should ask him about her ourselves. I think you know what that means…" Karli and Chris smiled as they exchanged a glance. They were all on the same page.

"Road trip!" They all yelled in unison.

"Let's go home and change first," Ricky suggested. "It's like noon now, so if we head up there right away we could be up at Sanctum in an hour or so." It was agreed. Within another few minutes, they pulled into their new apartment. They had only been there for about a week's time, but they were still having trouble making the place feel at home. And they all knew why.

They pulled into the attached garage and hastily entered the apartment. As Chris and Karli went into their bedroom to change, Ricky made his way to the front door.

One fortunate thing about being in that particular housing unit was that the mailbox was right outside the door. The extra convenience was well worth the extra fifty or so dollars on the rent, even if Chad wasn't there to help pay it. Ricky opened the mailbox, took the pile inside and started flipping through the envelopes. As usual, nearly every envelope was sent from a different company; a bill for a service he never remembered signing up for. But one letter caught his eye. It was from the State of Ohio and addressed to "The Family of Chad Galen."

"Hey, somethin' came from the state," he said.

"What is it?" asked Karli. Her voice echoed from around multiple hallway corners.

"I don't know, hold up." Ricky opened the envelope and unfolded the paper. There were only two documents inside of it. And one looked like "A certificate?" Ricky's eyes skimmed the entire paper as quickly as he could. He slammed it on the table, audibly enough so that everyone in the apartment could hear.

"I'm guessing it was a bill?" Chris said from around the corner. He walked into the living room to find Ricky leaning all of his weight against the dining table. In front of him lay a square-shaped, blue piece of paper and a letter. "What is that thing?" he said, pointing at the document.

"It's Chad's… His death certificate."

A Figure woke within darkness to hear nothing but the sound of its own gasps. The sound was accompanied by what felt like a fire in its lungs, but as the Figure persisted to fight for its breath, the burning was quenched by the cool air that was inhaled. Though the air was cool, the smell of it was anything but refreshing. It was a horrendous odor that seemed to fill this entire area—whatever this area was. Whatever the source of this smell was, the Figure had to escape it. It looked all over for something that could cause such a horrible smell, but no matter where it looked there was nothing. There was only darkness. That was all that could be seen in any direction. A darkness that was uniform, and one that stripped everything within it of any type of visual perception. It was difficult for the Figure to tell if its eyes were even open.

As it lifted itself off the ground, the Figure noticed that sensation was returning to its limbs. Feeling the blood circulate throughout its arms and legs brought a comfortable warmth to its previously numb and cold body. But this only brought about more confusion. Why couldn't it see, why was it so cold, and why was its entire body numb just moments ago?

The Figure brought its hands to feel its face, then began to frisk

itself for clues as to what was happening. Before too long it discovered
a strap on its right arm. Finally, there was some clue, but where did the
strap come from? The Figure thought back to the last thing it could
remember: Before there was darkness there was... pain? Agony? There
was a table, too. There was a man with a needle, a needle that found its
way into the Figure's arm. And after the needle was withdrawn there
was a bandage placed over the hole to prevent leakage. That explained
the strap. But what about the man?

The man stood before and watched the agony proceed, but there
was someone else in the room. There was a girl. And her name... it
was:

"Andreas!" Chad shouted, finally remembering the events
of what preceded his current state. "Andreas, are you here? Can you
hear me?!" There was no response. It seemed that even the sound
was muffled by the heavy darkness. Trying his best not to panic, he
searched his immediate area by feeling around with his hands. Beside
him, he felt something familiar: It was an arm. Or at least, it used to be
an arm. The limb was cold and hard, but it was unmistakably attached
to something heavy. Chad tugged on the arm as an attempt to wake
the entity, but the figure did not move in the slightest. Chad squeezed
harder as if a more forceful jerk would have a better chance of waking
the slumbering person, but as he gripped the arm the surface of the
skin broke, and Chad's fingers sank deep into what was now clearly a
corpse.

Now was an acceptable time for panic.

Chad jumped to his feet and frantically brushed his hands
off on his pants. Maintaining equilibrium was difficult since the only
reference he had for discerning up from down was gravity, but as
his eyes finally adjusted to the dark he saw a small, white dot in the
distance.

No, it wasn't very far, possibly only several feet away. From the
dot flowed an outpouring of light that flooded a small path of the air
up to a few feet away from it. Chad didn't know how he didn't notice
the light before, but he was happy to just find something that at least
resembled an escape route. Chad made his way for the light source as
quickly as he could, stomping over objects that made crunching sounds

at varying volumes. Not wanting to risk freaking himself out further, he chose not to think about whatever it was he was stepping on. Finally, he made it to the dot. From up close, it was a hole that led to the outside, but it was far too small to squeeze through. Chad punched the eye-level hole as hard as he could, and dust crumbled from all around the hole and eventually covered it completely.

Chad had never experienced claustrophobia before, but if there was ever a time to feel trapped within a closed-in space, now seemed like an appropriate time. Chad began to hyperventilate as he desperately scraped the wall where the hole once was. It took several seconds before there was any progress, but eventually the light began to pour through the dirt wall and flooded the dark chamber more completely. Chad scraped and dug as the hole became larger, and as he was blinded more and more by the incoming light he only felt more relieved. Eventually, the hole became big enough to fit the width of his shoulders, and Chad climbed through it. With a final heave, he slipped through the opening he fashioned himself, and he tumbled down a mound until he came crashing to the bottom.

He was out, but he didn't know where he was. Chad caught his breath as he attempted to soothe himself. He turned and peered up at the hole he emerged from. It looked like an oversized gopher hole on the side of an otherwise normal-looking hill. The hill was covered in a lush greenness. The grass was so green it almost looked like someone intentionally planted the patches to disguise weeds that grew underneath. Chad figured that the landscapers must've had an interesting definition of "weeds".

Chad gazed at his surroundings as he tried to figure things out. The ground appeared natural, as if no one had ever tried to dig for any hidden resources. That must've meant that he was nowhere near the mining grounds. But if not, then where was he? Clearly he must have been far away from Sanctum, otherwise the environment wouldn't look so natural and untouched. Without any answer making themselves apparent where he stood, he decided the best course of action was to start walking. He heard water flowing nearby.

"I'm freakin' thirsty," he said to himself. "Might as well find some water around here. Don't wanna die of thirst." And with that, he went to go look for the water source.

*Die...* he thought. *Didn't I get executed? How am I...* Chad gave his body a close inspection. There wasn't much that was different; he essentially felt the same. With the exception of a ruthless headache, there wasn't any difference in the way he felt.

Giving himself a quick physical, he stopped to check himself out. He held out his arms and raised them in a stretching motion. So far so good. He made motions like he was punching a target, and though he felt fine then too, his punches were moving a little faster than he remembered ever being able to throw them. *I must've loosened up.*

The next test would involve his legs. Chad touched the ground and then lightly hopped up, doing a simple jump squat. He repeated the motion a few times and stopped when he was satisfied with the results. *Nothing hurting there either.* Everything seemed fine. Chad proceeded with his trek to the stream, but after a few steps he came to an abrupt halt.

*Wait, what?!* He looked down at his thigh and gave it a few pats. *Nothing's hurting... but how?* Chad revisited his previous test and hopped into the air several times. Each time, there was no pain from his thigh. Everything was fine and working properly. *My limp is gone!*

It didn't take very long for Chad's confusion to turn into excitement. Chad kept hopping over and over like a child who just received a new trampoline for Christmas. Suddenly overwhelmed with more glee than he'd felt in months, he tested his jumping ability. He started with a normal jump and imagined himself swatting a shot while playing basketball. Still no pain. He tried again, jumping even higher, and this time imagining dunking a basketball over someone. He was successful once again, and still no pain. With one final attempt, he lunged into the air as high as he possibly could. As it turned out, it was higher than he expected. Suddenly, a large pain struck Chad, but it didn't come from his leg. Chad felt something dense clock him on the back of his head, and he came crashing down, unable to catch himself before he hit the ground.

Chad plopped face-forward onto the dirt. He patted the back

his head with his hand while rolling over on his back. He immediately made it his goal to find out what he bumped his head on, but when he looked up there was only one thing above him. It was a tree.

After a brief but thorough examination of the tree's canopy, Chad was back in a state of confusion. There was nothing nearby that he could have bumped his head on. There were no poles sticking out of the ground, and no shorter trees anywhere in the vicinity. Furthermore, the lowest branch of the tree Chad jumped underneath was no less than thirty feet in the air, and jumping high enough to hit that would have been impossible...

*Wouldn't it?*

Chad kept his eyes on the tree while getting back to his feet.

*Power.*

Chad heard Jason's words whisper in the back of his mind: The prize one gets for surviving execution. *Is this what he meant the whole time? And I got it now?* Finally looking away from the tree, he took the hand that was nursing his head and pulled debris from whatever it was he collided with out of his hair. He studied what appeared to be small pieces of bark. *Power,* he thought again as his eyes went back and forth between the branch above him and the crumbs of bark in his palms. A smile crept onto his face.

"Only one way to clear this up!" Chad squatted low and pushed off of the ground as hard as he possibly could. The resulting leap shot him far into the air, and as he approached the branch he saw before, he reached for it and successfully grabbed onto it. Chad broke out in laughter as his body dangled from the branch. In his hysteria, he lost his grip on the branch and fell thirty feet again. He tried to catch himself, but he hit the ground and tumbled once again. "Okay, note-to-self," he said through chuckles, "learn how to land better."

Thoroughly enjoying the moment, Chad decided to keep on his original path. He turned and started for the stream, but instead of walking, he decided to keep experimenting with his newfound hops. Every few steps Chad took, he bound into the air, frolicking like an excited rabbit on steroids. But despite all the fun he was having, he noticed something else that was odd. He could clearly hear the stream. Without a doubt, there was plenty of water rushing over a coarse collection of eroded stones in the area. And as he approached said stream, the sounds of nature were getting louder and louder. Be that the case, why was it taking so long to get to it?

After a few minutes Chad arrived at the stream, and he had his answer: The stream was a full twenty or so bounds away from the mound he emerged from. Taking the trees and other obstacles that were in his path into account, he concluded that the water must have been a full football field or so away from where he first heard it. *I guess jumping isn't the only thing I'm better at now.* There was no one around in either direction, so he figured it was safe to indulge. Chad dunked his head completely in the stream, feeling utter relaxation as water flowed through his hair, around his ears, and over his neck. He pulled his head from the stream, and with cupped hands, he drank as much water as he could until the thirst finally subsided.

Chad walked to the closest tree and sat underneath it. He took a moment to enjoy the peacefulness of his surroundings, even though he was still fairly lost. On the bright side, the sun was out and on the verge of a beautiful, orange sunset, and most of the rain from the previous day had dried up. Or at least, he could only assume his recent escapade was on the previous day. *What day it is anyway, and how long was I out for?* Chad's peace quickly turned to frustration after realizing there were questions he needed to answer. And even though his newfound "skills" were a pleasant surprise, they made comprehending the entire situation all the more difficult.

Underneath his tree, Chad collected his thoughts. *Okay, so I was caught somewhere in the forest, and then Andreas and I were taken to… was it the prison? We were both there, and they picked me first… and now I'm here. Is Andreas alive, too? If she is, I have no idea where she would've gone.* Even though it was the last thing Chad wanted to do, he knew there was only one way to figure out if Andreas had survived the execution, and the answer was back in that cave.

A thunderous crack ripped through the air. The sound startled Chad, but he could tell it came from far away. Though the sun was setting, the skies were clear, which means that there definitely wasn't a storm. The only thing that sound could have been was a gunshot. Almost immediately, two more loud pops pierced the air. Those weren't shots from hunting rifles, but something was surely being hunted. *Could've been a NegaSentry. I wonder who they're shooting at. Who else is crazy enough to try to run away?* Chad dismissively laughed, choosing to leave the escapee to his own plan. But then his heart dropped, and he suddenly had an answer.

"Andreas!" he shouted. More gunshots banged, and Chad was able to tell which direction the conflict was. Wasting no time, he bolted as fast as he could to go find the shooters. Chad noticed that he was running faster than he ever could before—by a large margin—but he had no time to be impressed with himself. He ran through the forest while listening for more gunshots to help him find his way. The shots were getting louder, and in what Chad determined to be a good sign, the shots kept firing, which meant the shooters likely hadn't hit their target. Or the target was very resilient.

The sun was set just as Chad found the scene of the action. As he suspected, someone was running away, but the pursuers were not far behind with their weapons drawn. Chad was not able to see through the trees, and being on eye level with everyone involved only made him stand out as a possible target. Putting his new abilities to use, he leaped up into a tree with surprising ease. As the thrilling chase beneath him continued, he followed them by hopping from branch to branch until he assessed the situation.

To Chad's deep disappointment, the person running was not Andreas. Nor was it a female, but it appeared to be some man running for his life. He sprinted from one tree to the next in order to take cover from the bullets that whipped past him. The pursuers were, in fact, NegaSentries, as Chad guessed before. There were a total of three, and from Chad's perspective they rolled along the grass like diminutive and angry tanks. Chad wasn't sure whether or not to intervene. Since the man didn't wear an orange jumpsuit he clearly wasn't a prisoner, but leaving him to get shot by terminators on wheels didn't seem ethical.

Eventually, the man being chased came to a small stream. He tried to cross it as quickly as he could, but he was swiftly greeted by multiple bullets to the back as soon as he hit the midway point. He fell into the water. The man screamed in pain as the NegaSentries rolled closer to him, placing themselves in a triangular formation. The closest one spoke.

"Lift your hands in the air and stand," it commanded in a highly synthetic, but uneasily sincere voice. The man continued to scream in pain, apparently unaware that he was given an order. Meanwhile, Chad hopped to the closest branch he could find, which put him right above the three robots. The Sentry spoke again: "You have five seconds to comply or we will fire." This voice was just as synthetic, but it was wildly more convincing. "Five."

The man was screaming less, but he was clearly unable to raise his hands, let alone stand.

"Four."

Chad's head went from the Sentries to the man and back again. *Do those freaking robots know he can't get up? They're just gonna—*

"Three."

The robots took aim. Chad knew he was going to have to do something, but he didn't know what. Fortunately, he wasn't good at landing from high places just yet.

"Two."

Without another hesitation, Chad hopped off the branch. *Stick the landing, stick the landing!* was the last thing in his head before his foot stomped right through the head of the talking NegaSentry. The robot immediately stopped its countdown and tried to roll forward, but Chad, whose leg was stuck inside the robot's head, forced the drone backward with his weight. The robot fell on its back and after a few seconds stopped moving altogether. Chad struggled to free himself as the drones on either side of him decided that he was the next appropriate target. With his free leg, Chad kicked the body of the broken robot, effectively freeing himself just before the others opened fire.

Chad ran and took cover at the closest tree. The NegaSentries were now firing at a much more lethal rate than before, but Chad was safe behind the girth of the tree's trunk. Hearing one of the robots roll closer, he leaped up and over to the next closest tree. He had a moment to consider his options as the robots corrected their firing direction. *That robot close to me is being covered by the one in the back. That must've been what that formation was for. But I took out that third one, so the farthest one from me is defenseless.* By the time the bullets were chipping away at his tree again, he was ready to enact his plan.

Chad hopped from behind the tree and ran to the robot farther away from him. He sprinted as fast as he could, and just before it was able to correct its aim Chad punched its head clear off. *If Trey can do it so can I!*

Forgetting to find another tree to hide behind, Chad felt a bullet whiz right by his ear. The body of the headless robot was still standing, so Chad took refuge behind it. The third Sentry quickly gained ground on its target, but Chad just used the broken robot in front of him as an inhuman shield. The robot got closer and closer, firing away, until it suddenly stopped shooting. Chad peaked over the headless robot's shoulder to see what looked like an elaborate reloading process. Taking his chance, he darted from behind his shelter and went for the robot's head. The Sentry finished its reload, however, and again started firing indiscriminately. Chad felt something graze his shoulder, but he continued his charge, ultimately ramming into the body of the drone. The NegaSentry fell on its back and continued to fire at the sky, but Chad promptly kicked off its arm and immediately stomped its head, crushing it like a tin can. Finally, the Sentry stopped moving.

"How's that for being *disarmed*, huh?!" Chad tried to catch his breath while a wave pride overtook him. He looked at the three broken robots with overwhelming satisfaction. After a moment, coughs erupted from over Chad's shoulder. "Oh, crap! Hey yo, are you okay?" The man managed to get to his knees, but not much else. Chad ran out to meet him in the stream. "Hang in there. Can you walk?" Chad asked helping the man to his feet.

"Coming. More coming. Have to go," the man uttered in a wheezy voice that revealed how much he was fighting pain.

"If you know a place around here, I'm down." Chad was distracted by all the blood, and though he didn't want to stain his vest, it was clear he was going to have to carry the man to safety. "Can you tell me where to go?"

"Y-yeass," the man squealed.

"All right, then." Chad carefully put the man on his back. "Lead the way. Just don't bleed out on me."

"Through—the back," the bleeding man said. With a wobbly point, the man directed Chad to the back of a small log cabin after a twenty-minute piggyback ride. It was very dark, and there weren't any streetlights in the areas away from the main routes, so Chad was able to proceed without being seen. He walked up a short flight of steps and approached the back door. "Keys are under the mat." Chad lifted the welcome mat to find a single key on a ring. He grabbed it, unlocked the door, and entered as quickly as he could.

"Where'd you get shot?" Chad asked as he laid the man on the floor.

"In the back," the man cringed. "A few spots."

"Shit." Chad turned the man on his stomach and gawked at the blood. He was able to fight off unwelcome flashbacks of his father, but he was still at a loss for words. A nightlight lit the area well enough that he didn't feel compelled to find an overhead light.

"Bleeding out!" the man announced.

"Ahh, shit! Okay, we need to get the bullets out, right?"

"Yes! Pliers are in the drawer by the sink." Chad looked around and realized they were currently in the kitchen. He ran over to the sink and opened all the drawers until he found the needlenose pliers. He grabbed them and ran back over to the man. Chad swallowed deeply.

"All right, better bite the bullet, dude," Chad said. He found the first of three entry points for the bullets. He took the pliers and held them over the first hole that steadily leaked blood. He paused. "Wait, no pun intended on that…"

"Hurry!"

Chad plunged the pliers into the first hole. He felt his own stomach churn, but it wasn't long before the nose of the pliers tapped something metallic. Chad, rather ungracefully, yanked the bullet from the man's back, and he tried his hardest to ignore the man's screams. He sat the bullet onto an adjacent table and continued to the second hole. After several seconds of digging the second bullet tapped the pliers. Chad promptly snatched it out and went on to the final one.

"How ya holdin' up?" Chad asked. The man only cringed and pounded the tile floor repeatedly to cope with the discomfort of the unprofessional surgery currently being performed on him. Chad took the screams as a good sign. "Well, it sounds like you're still alive; let's keep it that way. I'm almost done here, by the way."

After another moment the final bullet was yanked from its lodging. The man took large breaths that showed he was in less excruciation than before.

"Bandages, and water. And Neosporin… in the same drawer," the man said. His voice was getting weaker.

"Neosporin? Don't be a wuss," Chad chuckled. He got up and obtained the items. From inside the refrigerator, he picked up a bottled water, and the gauze with a particularly wrinkled bottle of Neosporin was in the same drawer as before. He grabbed paper towels and scissors for good measure and took the items to the floor.

Chad cut the clothing off the man's back poured the cold water all over. He used the paper towels to wipe the extra blood and finally squeezed a few drops of the ointment into and around the wound. While applying the ointment, Chad noticed something peculiar about it, enough so to make him pause for a few seconds in shock. But he held his tongue for the moment and resumed his work by promptly pressing gauze over the wounds on the patient's back. Only having enough wrap for a single wound, Chad searched for more in the surrounding drawers. Ultimately, masking tape would have to suffice, and Chad wrapped the tape all around the man's torso to ensure the gauze stayed in place for the remaining wounds.

"Yeah! All right, and I think we're done here," Chad said with a victorious voice. "Just don't sue me for malpractice or anything, deal?" The man only moaned, but at least he wasn't screaming. "You lost a crap ton of blood so you should probably eat something. Here, drink this water." He handed the weakened man an unopened bottle.

"Sandwich is in the fridge," he said in a weaker voice. Chad spotted the food and gave it to him. He grabbed the man by his bare shoulders and lifted him up until he sat upright with his back against the wall. The man feebly moved as he ate his sandwich, being careful not to ruin the bandages on his back. The nightlight brightly lit half of the man's body while throwing the other half in darkness.

Chad took a few steps back and observed the kitchen floor. There was blood all over his workstation, and he didn't feel like cleaning any of it at the moment. The more important task was making sure his guest, or host, or whatever this guy was, was feeling better. As the man took bite after bite, his pain seemingly subsided, and his breathing flowed more naturally. After a moment of silence, Chad picked the container of Neosporin off the floor.

"So, here's a question for ya," Chad said in a more serious tone. "What kind of Neosporin glows in the freaking dark?" He squeezed the bottle until a few drops spilled out onto the floor. The ooze had a dim luminance, but it was clearly there. The man chuckled weakly.

"I was hoping you wouldn't notice so soon. When did you figure it out?"

"As soon as I saw it." Chad walked over to the wall and flipped on a light switch. The light from the kitchen seemed to illuminate the entire cabin, small as it was. When Chad turned back around, he saw that the face of the man sitting against the wall was identical to the face of the lab-coated fellow who injected visium into his blood.

"Nice to meet you, officially," the man greeted awkwardly. "I think you know this already, but my name's Nathaniel."

**Chapter 14**

# Infiltration

The next morning Chad walked into the kitchen. He observed the blood that decorated the floor and tried to fill the shoes of a blood spatter analyst. He imagined what story a forensics team could piece together from an abstract painting such as this one. Dark pools of dried crust made a trail that led from the floor to the wall. But of course, any forensic scientist would assume the trail went in the opposite direction. Crime scene victims usually don't get shot on the floor and then climb up a wall as they bleed out.

In any case, this wasn't a crime scene. It was just the result of an unfortunate sunset outing. And as Chad pondered how long it would take to clean a mess like this, he wondered why white was such a popular color for kitchen tile floors. It didn't take very long before he stopped caring about the blood. It wasn't his mess to clean. Furthermore, it wasn't his cabin to clean, either.

Nathaniel Jones, who was fast asleep in the next room over, was the one responsible for this mess. In fact, Chad realized he was responsible for quite a bit. And as soon as he woke up, he would have plenty of explaining to do. Chad walked into the room where Jones slept. As with the rest of the cabin, there was very little furniture. Only a bookcase, a four-drawer filing cabinet, and futon were in the living room, and Jones was currently hogging the futon all to himself. Chad didn't mind since he hadn't felt tired all night, but he was bothered by the digital clock that hung on the wall above the futon. The clock read 8:54 p.m., but the sun had only just risen. Chad knew it wasn't uncommon for clocks to be wrong, but not knowing what day it was, or the correct time, or how long he was in that cave of death was starting to bug him endlessly. The only person who knew everything was lying unconscious. Fortunately, he was finally starting to wake up.

Jones slowly opened his eyes, struggling as he felt the weight of his eyelids like never before. He was sleeping on his stomach, and as he turned his head from one side to face the other, he felt a sharp pain in a few areas in his back. Remembering the events of the previous night, he stayed put for just a while longer. Chad cleared his throat to announce his presence.

"Finally," Chad spoke with clear impatience. "I was beginning to think you'd never wake up... Literally." Jones chuckled shyly. From his current position, he could see a bit of blood on the kitchen floor.

"We made quite a mess late night, didn't we?" Jones slowly rolled over on the futon until he was facing the ceiling, thus allowing him to see Chad better. "I didn't get to say this to you last night, but thank you for the help. I certainly would've died out there if you hadn't come."

"You can keep your thanks to yourself," Chad hissed. "Speakin' of dying..."

"That's right. I'm sure you probably have some questions for me, don't you?"

"I had all night to think up a pretty full list." Chad walked over to the wall right across from Jones' view and sat down. "Are you gonna help me out and answer them for me?"

"I'll do my best," Jones said, trying to find his normal gregariousness. His exhaustion made that difficult. "It's the least I can do for the help, after all." Chad took a moment to cycle through the questions in his mind.

"First thing's first," he began sternly, "are we safe here?"

Jones nodded. "No one knows I own this location. And neighbors are spaced far enough away that no one will notice us coming or going."

"All right, next question: Why were those NegaSentries gunning you down like you owed them money?"

"Good question," Jones said laughing slightly harder, "but that's sort of a long story. Would you mind if we came back to it?"

"Fine. Why the hell was that Neosporin glowing?"

"Also a very good question... and related to the last one. Are you sure you'd like to know everything now? Honestly, I thought you'd be more curious about your new 'prowess.'" Jones made air quotes with his fingers.

"Trust me, I was getting to that. And I really don't wanna hear any crap about a long story. Neither of us really have anyplace to go right now, so I wanna hear it all." Chad raised his voice slightly to display that his impatience was only growing. "In case you didn't know this, I used to share a cell with Jason Whatshisface, and it didn't take very long to figure out that you guys were doing shady crap behind closed doors. So give it to me straight, Doctor."

Jones yawned as he thought of a concise way to explain all the details. He rubbed his eyes in an attempt to wake himself up more. Once he was comfortable he began.

"So then, as you may know, I'm a scientist. To be specific, I'm a Biochemical Engineer, and my work in the field was quite well known amongst my peers in the community. If a young man such as yourself even knows who I am, I suppose my reputation preceded me."

"Don't flatter yourself," Chad retorted.

"Well, as it were, I was contracted—rather secretly I might add—to work on a *very* important project for a very wealthy group of individuals. I did not realize it at the time, but my cooperation with the project was not quite as optional as I would have preferred... Since they didn't want me focused on anything else at the time, and due to the rather unethical nature of the project, they faked my death so I could have all the time I would require to work on this new venture."

Chad followed Jones' story word for word. Had it been anyone else, Chad would have no way of fact-checking what he heard. But this was Doctor Nathaniel Jones. Chad was perfectly aware of this man's field of expertise, and despite how popular Jones fancied himself to be during his past life, Chad was one of few people in his generation that cared anything for Jones' research. Chad remembered reading news articles about Jones' supposed death, so as far as he could tell, Jones' story checked out.

"Okay, I'm with ya," Chad said, "but biochemical stuff wasn't the only thing you were into. I know because I was into that stuff, too. You tried to prove Psychokinesis was real."

"I made pretty good headway, if I do say so myself." Jones put his finger to his lips, signaling Chad to be quiet.

"What? Is someone here?" Chad asked alarmed.

"Nothing like that." Jones closed his eyes and scrunched his eyebrows. There was a moment of complete silence, but suddenly Chad heard a soft noise.

"You hear that? Someone else is here!" Chad exclaimed in a semi-panic. Jones said nothing, but continued to keep his eyes closed. Chad continued to hear the sound, which he likened to a mouse trying to free itself from a trap. After several seconds passed, the source of the sound was free. A loud crack came from the front of the room near the bookcase. Chad looked over and only saw a single marble rocking in place. Chad realized it must have fallen from one of the bookcase shelves. He turned his attention back to Jones, who was still lying with his eyes closed. *Did he know that was gonna happen?* Chad thought. He fixed his lips to say something when he heard the marble move again.

The sound of the glass ball rolling on the hardwood floor sent a chill up Chad's spine as he watched the marble move closer to him. Chad could not see any incline on the floor, and there was no air vent providing a current for the ball to ride on. The marble rolled in a very controlled path. And it was moving by itself. It was slow to move, but after an eerie eighteen seconds, the marble rolled to the space just between Jones and Chad, where it stopped completely.

"That's something I like to call: Headway. A *Marvel of the Mind*," Jones said as a large prideful smile dominated his face. Chad gawked at the ball, which sat completely motionless in the center of the room, seemingly awaiting commands. Jones was satisfied with Chad's reaction. "It looks like you're still processing that, so I'll just continue with my story."

Chad had never experienced such a combination of emotions at once. It was a vexing mixture of wonder and astonishment with utter disbelief. Most of all, he just witnessed something he only ever imagined was possible. It may have been on a minuscule scale, but it was the most amazing feat he had ever seen. Even though jumping a few stories high was cool, moving matter with one's mind was a whole new level. He tried his best to respond evenly, though. He did not want to seem too impressed by the man he was technically still upset with.

"That… That's what I mean," Chad said after clearing his throat again. "You were trying to show people this, so what kind of project would've needed you specifically?"

"Psychokinesis is more than just moving items with mental power; that's specifically called 'telekinesis.'" Jones made more air quotes. "I wanted to demonstrate to the world the complete potential of the human body, and as I was contracted by my employer, they promised to provide for me a platform and a facility which to accomplish it. I couldn't resist."

"And by facility, I'm guessing you mean the prison execution room?"

"Er, yes… And that very year, Sanctum was established." Jones observed Chad as he took in the information. He was not pleased by what he was hearing, but he did not appear so offended that he would not listen to the rest. "So, are there any other questions?" Chad took a minute to process before asking anything else.

"Why visium? How did that happen?"

"My employer insisted that would be the most effective ingredient in any life potion. He even insisted that visium be the only thing I use. The experiments were more about the humans than the visium. It was about figuring out what worked."

"And by life potion, you mean what exactly?"

"Sure you want to know?" Jones chuckled. Chad nodded apprehensively. "I was given the task to discover immortality." Chad's eyes narrowed, and he gave Jones a skeptical glance, but after all he had witnessed over the last 24 hours, he figured Jones deserved a little credit. "I have to admit, I thought of visium granting humans such gifts was dubious myself, but then I played around with that Neosporin you're so fond of…" Jones slowly raised himself and sat up. Before Chad knew what was happening, Jones ripped off the bandages that wrapped his torso. Chad saw dried blood where the gauze pads were, but Chad's surprise came when he saw a completely healed back. There were no signs of the three bullet holes anywhere. "Turns out, visium as a topical treatment isn't so bad. On top of that, look at your shoulder."

Chad checked his shoulders, and on his left side he noticed a dark red horizontal streak.

"Oh wow, I completely forgot about this," Chad said with widened eyes. "I got shot."

"And it's healed already. Unfortunately for me, I have a bit of internal healing to do, but at least my skin is all patched up."

"I don't get it. I don't get any of this." Chad ran his fingers across the red streak and left them there. "How is all this happening right now? Just because of visium?"

"You don't sound like a guy who just discovered he has superpowers," Jones jested. "More like a man whose life just ended. Whoops, too soon?"

"So you're saying I *did* die?!"

"I suppose so. I would know. I'm a doctor, after all."

"Then how am I alive now?"

"That's the million-dollar question, my friend." Jones yawned big and followed it with a stretch. "I'd love to discuss this further, but I'm still pretty drowsy from the blood loss. If you don't mind, I'm going to take another nap." Jones lay down again on the futon and pulled a blanket from underneath it.

"Fine, but one more thing, first."

"Yes?"

"Who is your employer? The person who contracted you to do all this…" *And the guy responsible for me being here…*

"His name is Vasya Negatov. We can talk again soon. I'll tell more, but in the meantime, please do not leave this cabin." And within minutes Jones was fast asleep. Chad looked into the marble that remained in the center of the room. He stared at his own tiny reflection as he thought about everything Jones said. Jones would likely be asleep for another few hours, and Chad would have to wait until then before he could receive more answers to his burning questions.

Ultimately, a few hours would be too long of a wait.

It took almost an hour for Chad to retrace his steps. After following the fairly conspicuous trail of blood that led to where Jones was shot, he found the path that led back to the stream he first heard the NegaSentry gunshots. From there, it wasn't long before Chad found his way back to the deceptively green hill he rose from the day before. There were no signs that someone had come around, but the hole he emerged from was still very visible halfway up the steep mound.

He walked closer to the hole and peered inside. Though the sun was high in the sky, the light could not deeply penetrate the darkness in the cave. Suspecting as much, Chad pulled from his pocket a flashlight he grabbed from Jones' kitchen drawer. *There's still something I need to know, and the answer is in here.* He gently thumbed the flashlight's on switch without activating it. *I really hope you're not in here...* He took a deep breath, flipped on the flashlight, and crawled through the hole.

There was a small drop inside the cave, and as Chad hit the ground he heard and felt the loudness of crunches beneath his feet. He pointed the flashlight forward and watched the trail of light quiver as he tried to remain calm. He took small steps, and he examined as much of the cave he could stomach. What he saw was just as he expected, to his dismay.

The inside of the cave was filled from one corner to the next with corpses. Some of them were more dried and decayed than others, but all of them were wearing orange jumpsuits. Chad had no doubt these were all the result of Jones' experiments, and the combination of anger and mortification came close to distracting him from his goal. He carefully stepped around the bodies as he continued to search the area. It wasn't long before he found a familiar face.

"Trey?" Chad stepped closer to a body that had not decayed very much yet, but still smelled like the others. Trey's face had the same look of pain Chad remembered on his face from the day he was electrocuted, but it was dramatically more peaceful than the expression on the other deceased faces. Chad couldn't tell if the natural decomposition of the older bodies was to blame for that or not. "I may have wanted you gone, but I didn't want you here..."

Chad slowly walked away and continued his search. Five minutes passed, and there was no sign of who he was looking for. After ten minutes, he was satisfied and relieved. He wanted to take a relaxing breath, but he figured it would be best to wait until he was around fresh air. He turned back to the hole, which gushed sunlight, and quickly walked towards it, no longer worried about what he stepped on. After a few steps, he stumbled on another corpse, but this one didn't crunch.

Chad pointed the flashlight directly on the figure beneath him. It was lying face down and wearing orange pants like the rest, but it was wearing a black top. Its body seemed fresher and healthier than the rest. He shined the light on the head of the corpse, but it was covered by the black hood that draped clumsily over its shoulder length, brown hair. Chad gulped as he slowly reached down grabbed its shoulder. *Three, two... one.* Chad flipped the body on its back and shined the light on its face. Chad covered his mouth as he uneasily coughed breaths of shock.

"Damn... I... I guess I found you, huh?" he said softly. Motionless beneath him was Andreas. Her eyes were open, but there had never been less life behind them. Chad clicked off the flashlight and put it away. He gently reached down and scooped Andreas' body up with his arms beneath her shoulders and her legs, and once he had a comfortable grip he walked towards the exit. Chad carefully shimmied her body through the hole, and after her feet fell through to the other side he left the cave himself.

Chad examined Andreas' body with an apprehensive fondness.

As the sun beat down on everything below it, the light illuminated Andreas auburn eyes. Her face was peaceful, and though her lips could not say anything about how her last moments might have been, her eyes showed no signs of distress. Her face was blank and calm, as if she died without pain, even though Chad knew with certainty that was not the case.

A deep distress wrung at Chad's heart. As he collapsed to his knees right above Andreas, he welcomed the flashback of his father's death. The image of a broken body leaking blood that was blackened by the night was mentally juxtaposed with the peaceful girl who lay before him. Andreas' corpse was infinitely more beautiful than his father's, but in this moment they were both equally lifeless. Chad was still as he watched tears drip from his face onto Andreas' body.

"I really don't know what to do with you," he said, wiping his tears with the back of his wrist. "I can't give you a funeral or anything fancy, but I guess I'm pretty good at digging now, right?" Chad picked up Andreas and carried her to the nearest patch of soft land. He didn't have to travel but a few trees away. He laid her down again and began scooping up as much land as he could with his hands. Before long he dug a small trench just over a foot deep, and he dragged Andreas' body right in the center. In what he thought to be an almost obligatory act, Chad closed her eyelids. He placed her hands, which appeared reddened and bloodied along the tips of her fingers, over her chest to simulate slumber. And with a reverent moment of silence, he finally said, "See ya, buddy."

Chad pushed the dirt back into place until Andreas was completely submerged. He made sure that dirt did not stick up above the ground so much that it would look to bypassers like a makeshift grave, but the spot stood just enough so that he would know where to find her. Chad walked to the closest tree and sat down, staring at Andreas' grave.

*His name is Vasya Negatov.*

Jones' words whispered through Chad's mind. *Vasya Negatov made him do it… That's what he said. The guy from the news… The guy from all those tech magazines. Is that why Catherine Negatov was at my trial that day?*

He jumped back to his feet with the distressful wringing in his heart slowly turning into a burn. *He's the reason why she's dead... why all of them are dead. That asshole! He's... he's the reason I'm here!* Chad looked all around for clues as to where he was in relation to the prison. He ran to the top of the mound full of bodies and used the elevation to study the area. Almost immediately, he found grass that was flattened in what looked like the tracks of a vehicle. His eyes followed the tracks, and the farther away they went, the more pronounced they became. Chad had found his trail of breadcrumbs.

"Vasya Negatov, we're gonna have a nice, long talk."

"Today is a very important day for me, maggot." Moriz spoke without his normal amount of aggression. His tone almost sounded like cheer, much to the bewilderment of the guards in the room. "And can you imagine why this is?" Jason heard Moriz's footsteps get louder as he approached his isolation cell.

"I could think of a reason," he said.

"Unfortunate recent events have led to me being solely responsible for electing the candidates for execution."

"You can stop calling it that. I thought it was clear to you by now that I'm aware of your whole operation."

"That is why I'm going to rectify that issue soon," Moriz said as his face came combatively close to the bars of the cell. "I believe tonight would be an appropriate time. It would be only a couple days after we terminated your friend."

"Friend?" Jason said with genuine curiosity. "You'll have to be more specific."

"Chad Galen, dumbass! The one you spent so much time with in a cell." Jason shot to his feet in shock. "Struck a chord, did I? So you do actually care about someone other than yourself. Well, you should know that Galen breathed his last a couple nights ago. If only you'd informed the fool of what happens when you try to escape, maybe you could have saved him."

"H-How did he not survive?" Jason blurted. His voice was shakier than Moriz had ever heard it, which pleased him intensely. "You chose him for a reason, didn't you? Wasn't he supposed to survive your damn project?"

"Guess there's no hiding it from you, after all. But yes, we thought he'd be different from the rest of you. I'll give the thug some credit, though. I didn't expect him to fight off the injection for as long as he did, even though he screamed like a bitch almost the whole time. In the end, he died just like the rest of them."

"What was the point?" Jason said, his volume rising noticeably. "I don't care about that clutz! He was supposed to survive it for you! To figure it out..."

"Looks like you had a lot riding on that guy, didn't you? Well, he's gone now, and you are here to figure it out all on your own." Moriz chuckled as he watched Jason's eyes waver. His voice was cracking, and as nervousness overwhelmed his body Jason tried to calm himself and think the situation through. "I almost forgot: You had another friend, didn't you?" Moriz teased. "Turned out Andreas Lazara was just as foolish as Galen, and she is dead now, too."

Jason stepped back as he felt his own weight seemingly shift to his head. In his disorientation, he sat on his bunk. "Screw you," he said after regathering his thoughts. "You think I need them to survive whatever crap you're going to put inside me? I don't need them!" Jason stood again and began pacing wildly around the room as he yelled, almost in a tantrum-fashion. "I don't care when you pump that crap into me, I'll be ready for you assholes anytime! You think this is just some game, don't you?!"

"It may not be a game, but I'll certainly enjoy playing Doctor with you later tonight." Moriz took a few steps back as he continued to watch Jason pace around in aggravation. "As much as I'm enjoying watching you piss on yourself, I have other things to do. I'll just let you get ready for tonight by yourself. It's much more maddening that way." Almost on cue, a siren started blaring through the hallways and could even be heard from down in the ISO chamber. "What the hell is it now?"

From the top of the stairwell, a guard came running down the steps and Moriz met him at the bottom.

"Warden, there's an emergency that needs your immediate attention," the guard said as urgently and authoritatively as he could.

"Why the hell is the fire alarm on and why aren't you handling it?" Moriz asked, returning to his signature angriness.

"Sir, we are under attack!"


Chad withdrew his fist, revealing a sizable hole in the front shell of a NegaSentry. He was slowly becoming more familiar with the internals of the robots as he pounded away one after another. He found that his most recent hypothesis regarding the location of the robot's main computer was correct, and he took pride in the fact that he only needed to break five NegaSentries on the way to Sanctum before he figured it out. A single blow to that location makes the drone go haywire. After knocking his most recent victim on its side, rendering it immobile, he urgently ran closer to the prison.

Chad noticed that the number of robots being sent his way increased dramatically after he hopped the outer fence of the campus, a feat he accomplished in a single bound. But as he approached the main facility, it was becoming clear that they knew he was coming. He didn't mind that at all.

Before long, he could see the large structure that housed the inmates. As he got closer, he saw a second fence that served as a barrier between himself and the yard where he spent so much of his time. The inmates themselves were being rushed back inside the prison as guards were being simultaneously dispatched. Among the men to enter the yard was Warden Moriz, who took a position on a raised platform that looked like it was built just for an occasion such as this. On either side of him, guards lined up in a formation that reminded Chad of something a platoon in the 1800s might have done. Each guard cradled what appeared to be a large, musket-shaped weapon with orange outlines or a small handgun. Moriz raised his arm, and all guards, regardless of their weapons, took aim.

"I'm ready when you are, old man," Chad said aloud, aware that Moriz likely couldn't hear him.

Moriz watched the incoming assailant intensely as he closed in. One hundred feet away. Eighty feet. Fifty-five feet. It didn't take long until he noticed that the man approaching them was running, not driving a vehicle as previously suspected. Moriz brushed off the false intelligence and waited for the proper time. Within seconds, the target was thirty feet away from the yard's fence. He was within range.

"Tranks, FIRE!" Moriz shouted as his arm came down. The guards with handguns fired their weapons, and small tranquilizing projectiles ripped through the air.

Chad flinched as he heard the projectiles whip by his ears, and he quickly altered his route away from the firing guards, while still heading toward the fence. When he was close enough he hopped the fence and landed expertly inside the yard.

"Nets, FIRE!" Moriz grumbled with a voice even more exasperated than before. The guards' disbelief of what they just witnessed delayed their response, but after a few seconds and a repeated growl from Moriz, they obeyed their command. One at a time, five-foot wide nets shot from the muskets. Chad bunglingly leaped out of the way of each net. More nets fired, and Chad knew he couldn't keep up his evasive maneuver for much longer. He spotted the platform Moriz was standing on and sprinted toward it, dodging everything that came his way. Moriz realized he was the target and braced himself for impact.

Chad charged straight through the wooden structure, causing pieces of its frame to fly everywhere. The guards stopped firing their weapons as they heard their warden growl ferociously as he fell ten feet onto the debris below.

"Hold your fire," Chad heard one of the guards say. Moriz shoved the debris that fell on top of him out of the way and tried to stand, though he had difficulty finding his footing.

"Sorry, Warden," Chad said, "but I've been wanting to knock you on your ass for a while now." Moriz followed the voice until he saw the man talking to him. He was standing only a few feet away, and when their eyes met, Moriz's jaw dropped. "I really wanted to use my fist instead, but this'll do, I guess."

"Galen?!" Moriz said. "What... How are?"

"Yeah, your boss is gonna help me figure all that out." Chad heard a deep *clank* sound to his right. As he looked up, he saw that several more guards were coming through the door. "And that's my cue," he said before sprinting toward the door. The guards cocked their weapons at Chad, flustered by the speed at which he was advancing.

"No! Do NOT let him inside!" The officers heard Moriz's command, but by the time they could react Chad had already charged through them and made his way inside the prison. Chad bulldozed his way through the hallway, punching the occasional guard and kicking over the NegaSentries. After a couple turns he ended up in the commons, where the prisoners were eating what Chad assumed was their second meal.

"Kyle! Where are you?" Chad's voice bounced off the walls, and everyone in the room heard him, but there was no answer. "Are you here? Kyle!"

"Freeze!"

"Don't move!"

Guards began flowing back inside from the courtyard and fired a couple warning shots at the ceiling. The cracks startled Chad and he slid across a cafeteria table to the side opposite the yard door. Once there he flipped the table on its side, creating a shield. The guard's response was to shoot at the table, thus prompting Chad to kick the bullet-ridden table toward the shooters. The inmates dropped to the floor to avoid the gunfire, and Chad flipped more tables to throw off his pursuers.

The shots continued. Chad resumed his earlier evasive actions. He noticed the path to the cell block was being strategically cut off, so there was no place else to go, except the balcony that overlooked the commons. Kicking one last table at the guards, Chad jumped and cleared the balcony's ledge with ease. The guards resumed fire, and Chad ducked so his head could not be seen over the ledge.

There were doors everywhere. *One of these has to be Vasya Negatov's office*, he thought as he crouched along the floor. He moved along the balcony until he arrived at the first door. Without a moment's notice, he rammed it down. There was nothing inside the room but a cleared out office space. He moved along.

Chad kept his head low as he made his way to the next door. He knocked it down, and after a brief analysis concluded his target was not present there either. On to the next one. The third door, unlike the previous ones, had text written across the translucent glass. It read "Catherine Negatov". This one was the easiest to break down.

Chad burst through the door and was immediately greeted with two needles attempting to permeate his chest. The needles simply bounced off, and Chad saw they were fired from Catherine Negatov herself. She was holding her trusty taser, though she was disappointed in its performance at the moment. Chad promptly slapped the taser out of her hand.

"Where the hell is your father?" he said.

"I don't know… what do you want?" she said as she stepped backward.

"Bullshit! You know exactly where he is! Was he here when I got executed?"

"I… Wha—Why would he be here? What makes you think—"

"Cut the shit, lady! Nate Jones told me everything." Chad turned his head as he heard footsteps behind him. The guards were on the balcony. Noticing Chad's distraction, Catherine ran to her desk and reached underneath the surface. In an instant, the wall beside Chad opened and a NegaSentry came rolling out, ramming him down.

Chad recovered and quickly disabled the machine the best way he knew how: with his fist. The guards were now at the door.

"This isn't over, woman," Chad said. As tranquilizer rounds shot past him again, he ducked behind the broken robot. He wrapped his arms around its frame and with a heave, lifted it off the ground. Chad heard the shots cease. "Coming through!" Chad ran through the door using the robot as a shield, and the guards jumped out of the way. Chad was on the balcony again. He noticed the blockade to the cell block was now gone, so he hopped from the balcony and sprinted through the corridor without a hassle.

The hallways were in disarray as the prison guards rushed to herd the inmates back into their cells. The inmates themselves appeared more amazed than anything to see Chad. The guards, however, were flustered as he passed them by. They didn't know what was the bigger priority: securing the prisoners or apprehending the intruder. That confusion gave Chad the edge he needed to find his destination. Before long, he reached Kyle's cell.

"Miss me?" Chad said as he grabbed the bars of Kyle's cell. Kyle, who was sitting upright in his well-made bed, gawked at the figure outside his cell. He grabbed the top of his head and stood, moving towards the bars. "Of course you did. Now stand back!" Still not managing to find words for the situation, Kyle did what he was told. Chad pulled the bars, trying to bend them outward, but a few tries made it clear that there were still some things he was not strong enough to do. "Okay, plan B."

Chad hopped down to the level just below and startled a guard. "Yo, give me your keys. I'm not gonna ask again." The guard fumbled with his belt, but as he struggled it was clear he was going for his gun. Chad sighed and punched the man in his face, knocking him out. Chad took the keys and climbed back up to Kyle's cell.

"Which key is it?" Chad said thumbing frantically through them.

"Third one," Kyle stuttered. Chad found the key, unlocked the door and walked into the cell. "All this commotion. It ain't about you, is it?"

"What do you think?" Chad turned his back to Kyle. "Just get on my back! No time to explain…"

"Why?"

"I'm bustin' you out! Just get on… No homo. It's quicker if I carry you." Voices from all over the cell block were almost too numerous to understand. Chad could tell the guards were close to figuring out which cell he was in. "Let's go, already!"

"No."

"What?"

"I ain't going anywhere. We've been over this, ya know."

"We really don't have time for this." Chad grabbed Kyle's arm to lead him to the cell door, but there was much resistance. "Quit screwing around. We have to leave now!"

"I said no!" Kyle snatched his arm from Chad's powerful grip. "I don't know what you're doin' here, or why you came back. But I told ya I'm not leavin' this place."

"I'm back because I'm trying to save your ass!"

"I don't need to be saved. I already told you. This is what life has for me now."

They both stood in silence for short a moment. Chad saw Kyle's eyes had the same sternness as his voice. Both of which were more aggressive and certain than he had ever seen them. The silence was broken by the sound of Chad's fist hitting Kyle's gut.

"Are you kidding me?" Chad yelled. "This is your ticket out! This is your chance to do something with yourself, and you're just gonna sit here and die?! You're choosing to do that?" Chad grabbed Kyle by the collar and lifted him with one arm.

"This is what I deserve." His voice was unrelenting. "Don't matter what you think I should do. I've made peace with it. Ima stay and face punishment."

"You're such a freaking wimp!" Chad shoved Kyle into the wall, and he fell onto his bed. "I'm so tired of your pity stories. It's like watching a soap opera. Life backs you into a corner, you just sit there and take it. Jason swings at you, you just sit there and take it. I throw you into a freaking wall, you just SIT THERE and TAKE IT!" Chad grabbed Kyle's collar once again. "For once in your life, would you just FIGHT BACK!?" Kyle locked eyes at Chad again, but they began to glisten as tears welled in his angry eyes. He did not speak.

"Hopeless," Chad said dropping Kyle back onto his bunk.

"Freeze!"

"Halt!"

Voices from outside the cells spoke in unison. Two NegaSentries and a human guard stood with their weapons pointed at Chad. In his anger, he did not hear them approach, and as he took a step away from the door, his back hit the wall.

"Trapped like a raccoon," said the guard. "Sentries, fire nets in: Three…"

*No, no. I can't get past them or through them*, Chad thought.

"Two."

"Okay, wait! Stop!" Chad said as he made the appropriate gesture to stop with his arms. He desperately held his hands up as if he could catch the net.

"Fire!"

Chad braced himself with closed eyes for impact.

But nothing happened.

Chad heard the guard, along with others who had joined him gasping. Kyle made a similar sound. Chad cautiously opened his eyes, as if something was waiting to scare him. When his eyes were opened, his gasp was the loudest.

The two electric nets fired by the robots were in the air, suspended without motion. The tranquilizer round was floating between them. Even though the nets and round were completely still, the air around them seemed to be vibrating. Chad looked back and forth between his awkwardly raised hands and the suspended objects. Instantly, he realized the connection.

Chad exaggerated the gesture of a push, and the round and nets immediately returned from where they came. The result was a group of guards being tased by their own robots. Careful to avoid getting shocked himself, he walked over and picked up the closer of the two NegaSentries, and as forcefully as he could, he threw it through the wall opposite the cell door. An instant exit to the outside.

Chad walked to the edge and gauged the long drop. It was doable. He then looked back at Kyle.

"Better start fighting for yourself," he said, "'cause from now on, I'm not gonna be around to fight for you." He leaped out of the hole.

Kyle heard furious shouts come from around the corner. Warden Moriz ungracefully stumbled over the group of guards who were still twitching from their previous tasering. Moriz was holding his elbow and covered in scratches and bruises, though none of them seemed significant. As he walked to the ledge, he noticed Chad as he ran into the forest, hidden from view by the canopy of trees.

"Miss Negatov, please. You can't," A guard said as Catherine tried to force her way through.

"Jael, are you there?"

"Let her through," Moriz demanded. Catherine walked into the room and she looked in horror at the hole in the wall. "What happened here?"

Moriz pointed to Kyle and looked at the closest guard. "Get the maggot out of here and into a new cell!" He screamed as if it were the obvious first response.

"That kid…" Catherine continued. "It was Galen. But how is that possible? How did this happen?" Moriz wiped the sweat from his forehead and calmed himself down. He stared at the damaged wall, and then finally turned toward Catherine.

"Contact your father. We need to meet with him. Immediately."

## Chapter 15

# Samaritan

"I asked you not to leave, and you went where? Back to the prison?!" Jones sat up in the futon as he buried his face in his palms. "This is not good. NOT good."

"Well, I sure as hell wasn't gonna wait for you to get back up and talk to me," Chad said.

"That's not the point! We were both safer when they thought we were dead. Now they are going to come looking for us. This is not good at all! You should have trusted me."

"Trust you? Why the hell would I do that? In case you didn't realize, I'm still pretty sore about that whole trying-to-kill-me thing."

Jones continued to squeeze his head as if to keep his sanity from escaping through his ears, but after sharp pains shot through his back he slowly calmed down again. "Okay, okay. They still don't know about this cabin. Unless… were you followed?"

"No. I was running too fast; there's no way they could've kept up," Chad said confidently. Jones' stress subsided further and he lay back down on the futon.

"What were you even trying to accomplish with that stunt?"

"I was going to look for Vasya Negatov and have a *friendly* conversation with him. Don't worry, he wasn't there. Or at least I didn't find him when I was trashing the place."

"I could have told you that much had you stayed put. He only comes around during special trials or emergencies."

"Emergencies, huh? Good to know." *I'm sure he'll be around pretty soon if that's the case.* "By the way, I've got something pretty interesting to show you." Chad searched the floor for the marble he saw earlier that day, and he found it right where Jones mentally left it. He squatted and outstretched his hand toward the ball. "Watch this." And with a deep breath, Chad imagined moving the ball. He stared at it with purpose, but as seconds passed, nothing happened.

"Are you trying to… You mean you can move objects without touching them now?" Jones' asked excitedly.

"Shut up, kinda need to focus here." Chad kept his mind on the marble but his hands off of it. With each passing second he imagined a mental heave lifting the glass sphere into the air. *Come on, come ON! Freakin' move already.*

Nothing.

"Use your head," Jones said. "Getting it to move is just like using a muscle. You've got to mean it." After another moment of struggling Chad eventually gave up. A wave of embarrassment washed over him after realizing how silly that attempt at a magic trick must have looked. "What's wrong?"

"I don't get it! It worked earlier. I was able to lift a couple of those taser nets and throw them back at those robots, and the same thing with a tranq dart. I don't know what the issue is now."

Jones stroked his chin. "Hmm. From what I understand, those nets are fairly heavy; much more so than this marble, obviously."

Chad picked the marble up and studied every side of it, making sure there was no glue holding it to the floor. It was definitely a normal little ball of glass. The only thing unique about it was a white graphic that was drawn on the blue glass. The graphic resembled an elaborate spiral with a line that split it down the center. He allowed the marble to sit in his palm as he gauged its weight.

"I know I did it once. I should be able to do it again, right? It's not like it's a one-and-done thing, is it?"

"Of course not," Jones said as he slowly raised himself from the futon again. As he got to his feet, his movements were careful as he tried to not agitate any internal wounds. "But this is why I strongly suggest you don't go anywhere until we figure out what you can do. You seem much more stable than Arbo was when he survived the trial. We need to take time to figure this out."

"Arbo? I'm pretty sure his name was Trey. See, this is exactly why I don't need you around me. You keep looking at me like I'm just another experiment of yours. I don't live to be your science project; I have my own life! Wait, oh yeah, I don't have it anymore, because you and your stupid employer took it away from me!"

"Chad…" Jones pointed, wide-eyed, at Chad's hand, which was previously still cradling the marble.

"What?!" Chad looked at his hand. The marble was no longer in his hand, but hovering noiselessly inches above his palm. Chad's jaw dropped, and as his focus broke the ball came crashing back down into his hand, which was shivering with excitement. "I told ya I did it," he said in a tone that could have been meant to convince himself.

"That's fantastic! And it only took you a few tries in your new state. Try it one more time."

"AND I told you I didn't need your help. Stop acting like you're my coach."

"Well, excuse me, but you'll have to understand that this is the first time I've seen anything like this. Arbo… I mean Trey… was the only success that came out of Sanctum, and he never displayed anything other than increased strength and resilience. But you're something more entirely." Jones' giddiness was beginning to make Chad slightly uncomfortable. And although he hadn't made up his mind about Jones' trustworthiness, it was difficult to pretend to not be excited about what was happening himself. "So please, can you try it one more time?"

Chad sighed heavily and held out the marble that rested in his hand. "Back at the prison, I was flinching because I was scared. Yeah, I reacted to the nets. And here I was—"

"You were upset, yes. So that must be it: Focus your emotion as well as your attention into making it float." Jones rested his hands on his knees as he leaned forward, being uncomfortably close to Chad's hand.

Chad did as he was told. He stared hard into the ball, again peering into his own reflection. This time, there was movement, but not from the ball itself. All around the marble, there was motion in the air, as if the fabric of the space itself was being agitated. The harder Chad tried, the more motion he saw. The disturbed air circled the ball viciously, and it was only when the entirety of the marble was enveloped that it began to float.

"Yes, yes, YES!" Jones pumped his fist in the air triumphantly, and he flinched from the following pain in his back. "Of course, I should have known."

"Would ya care to explain it to me?" Chad said, fighting off a smile of pride.

"Look closely at the area around the marble. I'm sure you see that strange anomaly, don't you?"

"Yeah. It kind of looks like those heat waves that rise up from the streets on hot days."

"Precisely. Well, it's not heat. It is vibrational energy. You are not moving the marble as much as you are manipulating the space around it." Testing the theory, Chad immediately began transferring the ball from hovering above one hand to the other. He was successful. And as he began laughing in a prideful hysteria he made the ball float all around the living room they both stood in, guiding its path with his finger. "Looks like you need me more than you think you do," Jones added.

The ball's path shifted from a smooth orbit around Chad to a straight line as it returned to his hand. As he caught the marble, he felt the vibrations subside in his palm. "No, I don't need you. And come to think of it, I'll be getting out of here now." Chad put the marble in the pocket of his vest and made his way to the door.

"No, you can't! It's not safe."

"Since you missed what happened earlier, I'll let you know that there's clearly nothing on the planet capable of stopping me. Plus, we just established that I have a new weapon in my arsenal." When he reached the door, he examined his wardrobe. His vest was dirty but still wearable, but he was still wearing the orange jumpsuit pants from the prison. "Umm, how about you give me some pants and we call it even for me saving your life?"

Jones pointed to the bottom shelf of the bookcase, where a duffle bag was stowed neatly. Chad searched its contents. "I suppose I can't stop you," Jones relented.

"No one can."

"But what are you even going to do? You can't live a normal life. Your death certificate was sent out the day following your execution, so you're technically a dead man."

"I've got a fix in the works for all of that, don't you worry." Chad changed into some dark colored, sweatpants that almost seemed to match his black vest. After a moment of fancying himself, he returned to the door. "Welp, it's been real, but you won't be seeing me again."

"Hold on," Jones called hesitantly. "Listen, I know you don't owe me anything."

"Not a *damn* thing."

"Can you at least do me a simple favor? Don't mention to anyone that I'm here… alive. Can you do that for me?"

"Whatever." And with that Chad walked out the door.

The sun burned brightly in the center of the sky, and for the first time in a while, Chad realized how beautiful the day really was. There was no sign of rain, no sign of authorities looking for prisoner escapees, and with Chad's fresh new disguise—which equated to nothing more than a pair of pants—there was no reason for anyone to think he wasn't a normal citizen. Even if he did raise any suspicion, he was confident his new set of skills would be enough to get him out of any conceivable mess. Chad walked down the gravel driveway and onto the freshly paved road. He took a whiff of the asphalt.

"Violet City," he said, "I'm coming home."

Vasya Negatov glanced at his watch without lifting his arm. He could see that the time was around nine in the evening, and the blood orange sky was losing its brightness as it shifted into night. The black car he rode in was not a limousine, but no matter how discreet he needed to be, riding in anything cheaper than a Cadillac was unacceptable. The driver pulled into a long driveway, showed his credentials to the security guard, and pulled through the back gate of Sanctum. He pulled up by the back loading docks of the prison and parked.

Negatov did not wait for his driver to open the door, and instead hastily exited the vehicle with a disgruntled look on his face. Within view of his position was the prisoners' recreational yard, which resembled more of a junkyard. A large pile of wooden planks and dust stood where the small lookout platform once did. Beside it, an even wider heap of metal occupied a larger area of the yard.

"Sir, please come in," Moriz said as he briskly walked toward Negatov.

"What is the meaning of this scene over here?" Negatov said gesturing to the adjacent yard.

"I'll explain inside. Now, please, sir." Moriz turned and walked back into the prison at a pace that made Negatov feel like he actually did not want to be followed. They walked through the discreet loading dock entrance and navigated through the corridors, some of which required very inconvenient detours due to untimely construction. They walked up to the balcony, and Negatov observed the trashed commons area below before walking into Catherine's office. Once everyone was in attendance, Moriz closed the newly installed and reinforced door. "Sir, has Catherine briefed you on the situation?"

"The only thing I was informed of was that there was an emergency that required my immediate attention. I'm hoping there wasn't another outbreak with the prisoners that you were incapable of properly handling."

"There was an outbreak, but it wasn't a riot," added Catherine. "Regular people can't do *that* to our NegaSentries." She pointed to the window behind her desk.

Negatov walked over to the window and looked outside. The yard was in view, and he had a better perspective of the guards dragging pieces of what he realized were NegaSentries into the trash heap. "Who is responsible for this mess?" he demanded with a sudden burst of urgency. "Has someone declared war on the prison?"

"Do you remember the inmates we executed a few nights ago?" Catherine said. "The ones who tried to escape."

"Of course I do."

"One of them is alive." She paused for a moment to let that fact sink in. "It was Chad Galen, and by the looks of things, the trial was actually a resounding success," she said, trying not to let her enthusiasm be mistaken for cheer.

"Where is he now?"

"The thug fled after blowing a large hole in the wall in cell block C," Moriz said. "He picked up one of the machines and threw it at the wall. That's one of the reasons we called you in tonight. We're dealing with something that's much bigger than that punk Arbo. This one is much stronger."

"I see," Negatov said. Moriz watched his eyes flicker back and forth as if he were considering options. The large scowl on his face slowly crept into what appeared to be a small smirk. "This project turned out well then, I suppose. What do we know about the girl?"

"There was no sign of her nor any mention of her from the boy."

"Mention, you say? Are you saying you had a conversation with the boy?"

"That's the second thing we needed to speak with you about," Catherine interrupted. "When the kid broke in here he was clearly looking for someone. He broke down my door, and when he saw me he asked for *you*... specifically."

Negatov felt his face go ever so slightly numb, but he was able to form his lips just enough to say, "What?"

Catherine continued. "He burst in here looking for you. He even seemed to know that you were present during his execution, and that's when he told me about Nathaniel. He's still out there, too."

Moriz stepped closer and lowered his voice. "We currently have no knowledge of how much Jones revealed to Galen. We can't figure out how either of them are alive, and when I sent some men on a hunt around the vicinity all they could find were more broken NegaSentries."

"Dad," Catherine said. "This guy Galen is pretty serious about finding you... And he probably knows about the projects if he has been hanging around Nathaniel. I'm worried he'll go to the authorities."

"We are the authority," Moriz said sternly, "and we just need to remind the punk of that."

"He will not go to the police," Negatov said calmly. "He is a convicted felon. More accurately, he is a deceased convicted felon. Going to the police would only help us find him, but this does pose a severe problem." He returned his gaze to the yard and the pile of debris. The guards were lined up along the fence more diligently and numerously than usual, and as the sun finished setting they were visibly more on edge than before. A night battle would put them at an even bigger disadvantage than they already felt they had.

"How would you like to continue, sir?" Moriz asked.

"We will forthwith proceed with the trials."

"Dad! You can't be serious. The prison and your reputation are on the line right now and we can't afford to focus on anything other than finding that kid!"

"I've already considered all of that, but knowing what we currently do I've concluded that the most appropriate response is to reassess our recent advancements in the project. Since you justly found it necessary to summon me here, we should start tonight." Negatov turned to Moriz, who stood expectantly at attention. "Warden, do you have an inmate in mind that would be a proper subject?"

"Why, yes," Moriz grinned. "I know just the one."

For a gorgeous night in the summer, Violet City was certainly peaceful. Being a modest suburb right outside of a small but growing metropolis, most businesses closed right around the 10 o'clock mark. Consequently, the nightlife would normally pick up around then too, but tonight was not party night for most, it seemed. Though there weren't many people out on the streets, Chad made sure he stayed out of sight as best he could. He successfully and discreetly delivered a special note to an old friend, and now the only thing left for him to do was wait patiently. And he knew just where to go.

Since a vast majority of the Violet City population were concerned with becoming homeowners, there weren't very many apartment complexes. This narrowed Chad's search down quite a bit as he looked for the possible location of his old friends, but it made sneaking around the city quite difficult. Instead of taking a walk through complexes where it would not be uncommon to see an unfamiliar face, he would have to run inconspicuously through private neighborhoods and avoid being seen. There was an upside, however. Violet City was a predominantly Caucasian area, and it was perceived to be so safe that the city decided putting up light poles in the neighborhoods would be a waste of taxpayers' dollars. This always made night walks through the town a pain, but on this night Chad found a reason to appreciate the lack of lighting.

Instead of using the sidewalk along the main roads, Chad took the side streets that required more turns due to their curves. The affluent residents of the city were keen on keeping much of nature intact as they built their homes around it. That meant there were plenty of trees and a fair amount of foliage for Chad to hide behind. As stealthily as he could, he ran from bush to tree, then stopping to check if he'd been seen. When there was no sign of onlookers he sprinted into the next yard and took cover again. The process took much longer than he wanted, but within an hour's time he finally arrived at his destination.

"It looks the same," Chad said softly and slightly surprised. He stepped out of his dark hiding spot and was drowned by the light from a pole. He first observed the pole, which was just as tall as he'd remembered, but slightly more ominous. And when he turned his gaze, he saw his old home. The two-story apartment where he had spent most of his life, except for the previous couple months.

His eyes went to the front door, and imagining himself with X-ray vision he followed the awkwardly placed staircase up to the second floor where the bedrooms were. He mentally walked into his room, then to the window, heard a familiar bang, and leaped from the window and onto the ground—something that, now, would not have been so difficult. Finishing his imaginary tour, he walked closer to *the spot*. He stepped to the place on the sidewalk where that dreadful moment happened.

The sidewalk itself was clear, seemingly scraped spotless of any red blemishes that weren't part of the original design. But one cannot clean memory. Chad welcomed the vision that left an uncleanable stain upon his consciousness as he looked at the ground. His father was there. Cranium leaking. Eyes open, almost intently so. Was he expecting Chad to speak?

"That stupid adage," Chad said. "Whatever doesn't kill you… makes you stronger." Chad clenched his fists, and he felt the other muscles in his body follow. "You didn't kill me. You couldn't do it, and we both know you sure as hell tried to… and look at me now: stronger than I ever thought I could be. I should love you for what you did for me, even though I know this wasn't your plan." He kneeled over the mental projection of his father, who continued to return his gaze. "So why do I still hate you. So. Freaking. Much?"

A car's headlights turned the corner and Chad looked up from his trance. The projection of his father disappeared. As the vehicle drove by, Chad walked to the rear of the apartment unit as casually as he could. The driver didn't seem to notice him.

Deciding he had spent enough time in the past, Chad continued into the wooded area behind the apartment. Even though he was urged to take his old hiking route for nostalgia's sake, he was no longer limited to taking predetermined paths thanks to his new abilities. He stepped to the edge of the steep cliff and peered down, and then he jumped off. He landed on his feet on a fallen tree trunk, then hopped another distance to the patch of grass just twelve feet or so away. He spent the following time experimenting with his dexterity, and pleasantly surprising himself with every leap and bound. Even his balance seemed to have improved. After a few moments longer, he arrived at the stream he was so familiar with. And just in front of that stream was the boulder he was fond of. His meditation zone.

Chad hopped on top of the boulder and crossed his legs. He filled his lungs with as much of the stream-humidified air as he could before slowly letting it escape through his lips. He relaxed his body as he softly looked at the reflection of the newly waxing moon. This moment was something to be treasured. It brought something almost forgotten:

Peace.

But it was only temporary.

Chad felt a lump in the chest pocket of his vest. Unable to ignore the discomfort, he removed the marble from his pocket and studied it. The blue of the glass almost appeared completely black in the night, but the white spiral on the side was still prominent. *Manipulating the space around it, huh? He opened his palm and let the ball sit in the center just as before. Attention and energy on the space around… okay, then.*

Chad stared at the ball. Immediately he saw the air around it begin to move. He tempered his excitement as much as he could, focusing harder on making the ball float. Without much more effort, the marble was airborne. "Gotta give Nate credit, I guess," he said. "I might not've figured that out by myself." He looked to the ground and saw a large rock, one he recognized from earlier days of being down by that stream. He gathered from previous attempts to pick it up that the dense and smooth slab was no less than thirty or so pounds. It was no challenge for him to physically lift now, of course, but there were new ways to lift objects. "Like a muscle, hmm? Alright, let's see how strong mine is."

He returned the marble to his pocket and turned his attention to the rock. He instantly saw motion in the space around it, but it did not budge. He then pointed to the rock, as if to guide it upward with his finger. Chad had no idea why he thought that would work, but a few seconds after he tried it the rock started moving. At first, it hovered in place, drifting clumsily to the left or the right, but soon Chad managed to lift it from the ground completely.

The slab floated at eye level, rolling in place like a bowling ball that could not find the floor. As Chad tried his best to hold it steady, he looked closely at the waves of energy around the rock. The air, which Chad still likened to heat waves rising from the desert highway, rippled uncontrollably from the object it enveloped. "I think he said it was vibrational energy. It's sure shakin' like crazy, I guess." Chad felt a sudden fatigue in his head, and as he brought his free hand to his forehead the rock could no longer stay afloat. It dropped as if falling from an invisible shelf and splashed into the stream below.

*Okay, I get the muscle analogy now*, he thought catching his breath, *but I've got one more thing to try before I call it a night.* Chad held his hands out in front of him as if holding a crystal ball. *What if I try to move empty space?* He imagined another marble floating between his palms and tried to move the space. There was an instant result. The air rippled rapidly within the small space between his hands. *How about some more?*

He focused on lifting something heavier and heavier, and the harder he pushed the stronger the vibrations became. The energy expanded wider and wider. Within seconds it filled the volume of a large beach ball. Chad slowly placed his hand inside the distorted space. His fingers felt like they were submerged in boiling water, but there was very little heat. He chuckled as the tingle tickled his hand, but he still was not done.

"Come on, get smaller for me," he whispered. The cloud of energy, which was previously amorphous, began to form a large sphere, and as Chad moved his hands closer together, the sphere shrunk in size. Consequently, it was becoming harder to maintain. Chad felt the fatigue again, but he fought it off as he continued to compress the cloud. He squeezed tighter and tighter until finally the cloud was compressed to the size of a basketball. "It even sounds like boiling water," he said, beaming with pride. "This is amazing! This thing… I think I'll call it—"

"Who are you?"

The lapse in concentration made Chad drop the sphere, and before he could recover it, the compressed ball of energy exploded. The force of the shockwave smacked Chad in his chest and face and knocked him backward and completely off the boulder.

"I said who ARE you?!"

"Relax," Chad said as he nonchalantly got back to his feet. "I'm the guy who sent you the message." He scanned the boulder for any salvageable bits of his experiment, but all the energy had dissipated. Chad moaned with annoyance as he turned back to the man behind him. "Is that a bat? What the hell for?"

"It's for the crazy person who invites me into a dark section of the woods at night for a meeting!"

"And you're crazy enough to accept the invite! I knew I could count on you, Ricky."

"This would go a lot smoother if you just tell me who you are," Ricky said, gripping his bat ever tighter.

Chad sighed. "I know it's dark out here, but I was hoping you would at least recognize my voice. That takes a bit of fun out of it. Oh well."

Ricky dropped the bat. "Chad?"

"Yep."

Ricky walked closer to the darkened figure in disbelief. It was true. "H-How?" he said, aggressively fighting back tears. The two embraced. "How… You're alive? But the certificate… It said—"

"Give me, like, 20 minutes, and I'll explain the best I can." Chad started his story from the moment he first arrived at Sanctum. He told Ricky about the visium mines, about Trey, about the execution, his apparent resurrection, the infiltration of Sanctum, but most importantly, about Vasya Negatov. "From what I can tell, that guy is the main person behind this whole thing. He apparently had some hand in getting me here, that's why I had an unpleasant run-in with Catherine Negatov outside the courtroom. You following this?"

"As best I can," Ricky said. "But you're back now, right? I mean, are you staying, uhh, here in the city?"

"That's the plan, but I need your help with something. Remember back at the trial, when Miss Vonda went missing? All we need to do is talk to her and get her to testify for me in an appeal! Everything seemed to rest on what she saw, so if we get her to talk, I'll be… What's with that look?"

"So, there's something I need to tell you. About Vonda." Ricky paused to figure out the best way to word his next statement. In the end, the best he could come up with was: "She's dead."

"What?! How the hell? Wha-—When?"

"Believe it or not, it was around the same time we got your death certificate in the mail. The cops found her body in the woods not too far from here. They said they suspect 'no foul play.'"

"No foul play?! Of course it's foul!" Chad whaled his arms in almost a full-on tantrum, and Ricky tried his best to shush him. "You're tellin' me they found her the exact day AFTER I died so-to-speak, and they saw NO connection!?"

"We tried to get Schone & Park on the case again, but they said there's nothing they could do."

Chad fell to his knees as his thoughts flew out of control. "This can't be possible, man. I mean, it's like I can't catch a break. I was so close to freedom. I made it out of prison; I'm BACK HOME! But I still can't escape this freakin' curse because my one hope to a fair trial died on me, and no one suspects a thing! This is bullshit!" Chad punched the ground repeatedly and Ricky was distracted by the small tremor he felt through the dirt. He heard Chad sniffle. "She was never there… no one was ever there when I needed them. All these so-called neighbors; they've always been freakin' shitty. Screw 'em all."

Ricky spoke softly as a subtle hint for Chad to calm down. "There's one silver lining, though." Chad looked up with patronizing disbelief. "Turned out, it was her that called the cops for you all along. The records even stated that she suspected your dad was the one starting stuff. Then come to find out she got killed. That's pretty shady."

Chad wiped his face. "That's the shittiest silver lining I've ever heard." Ricky helped Chad to his feet. They walked to the stream. Chad sat on the boulder again while he regained his poise.

"So?" Ricky said. "What now?"

"She was my last shot at getting out. I just don't know."

"Not like you to give up." They sat and listened to the sounds of crickets and water as the stream rushed by them. "I'd have to talk to Chris and Karli about it, but I'm sure they wouldn't mind housing a dead man for a while," he jested. Chad did not laugh.

"Don't tell them about me. I'm not going to be a wanted man for very long."

"Got a plan?"

"Something close to one."

"Wanna share?"

Chad stood and brushed off his pants. "The only person in the world who can get me out of this mess is the person who got me into it: that Negatov guy. Whether he was influencing crap from the background or not, the stuff he's doing is messed up. And I bet my life I'm not the only one he screwed over."

"Can't we help you out?"

"Hell no. I can't have you guys ending up like Miss Vonda. I gotta do this myself." Chad felt a sense of renewed urgency; one that made him want to go back to Sanctum right away and go find Negatov himself. But he knew there was much work to be done first. He hugged Ricky again. "Thanks for everything, bro. I'll see you again when I'm a free man." With that, he turned and ran, but only for a few paces. He halted abruptly. "On second thought, Hocking Hills is kinda far. Mind if I get one more ride?"

The hour-long trip to Hocking Hills was a great end to an otherwise horrible night. The nostalgia of riding in Ricky's car only served as a reminder of the life that was taken from him. It was a life he would fight to obtain.

Ricky pulled up to a small rest area just before the correct exit. "Right here is fine," Chad said. "I'll be better off walking from here." Chad got out the car, gave Ricky a final wave, and then rushed into the woods. He was far enough from Sanctum to not worry about security cameras hiding in the forest, but he was still careful to not be seen by any residents of the rural area. Eventually, he arrived at the cabin he was looking for. He straightened out his clothes and made himself look presentable, though he wasn't really sure why he cared so much about his appearance. He knocked on the back door.

Chad heard a small rattling in the house. The type of quiet footsteps one would hear from someone trying to pretend he or she isn't home. "Nate, I know you're in there," Chad called. "It's me." After another long minute, the lights inside the cabin turned on, and the door opened. Chad walked in and Jones swiftly closed the door behind him.

"You're back," he said suspiciously. "Why is this?"

"Yeah, well, listen carefully, because I'm only going to say this one time.

I need your help."

Jason glanced toward the hall by his cell as he heard very deliberate footsteps from someone coming down the stairs. He was familiar enough with the sound of Moriz's shoes to recognize it was him coming. This time, he wasn't alone.

Moriz approached Jason's cell with noticeably less satisfaction in his eye than he had earlier that morning. Without speaking, he unlocked Jason's cell, opened the gate, and stepped to the side. Hesitantly, Jason walked out of the cell and stood by Moriz, expecting to be handcuffed. Moriz did not oblige.

"What's this about?" Jason said. He glanced at the hallway that led to the stairs. "What's keeping me from running away?" Moriz did not respond, but the footfalls of a few more people echoed from the hallway. Catherine and Vasya Negatov stepped out from around the corner, and with an exaggerated clearing of Moriz's throat, the two guards who accompanied Moriz walked away and back up the stairs. When they heard the shutting sound of a door, they knew they were alone.

"If you have a moment, I'd like to make a proposal," Vasya Negatov said. "My name is—"

"I know exactly who you are," Jason interrupted.

"You know too much for your own good," Moriz snarled.

"However, that is why I want to speak with you personally," Negatov said.

Jason's eyes narrowed with suspicion. "What do you want?"

Negatov continued. "I've taken the liberty of reading through your personal profile, and I was quite surprised. Not many people who have killed as many as you have actively chosen to turn themselves in. Moreover, you are the only inmate in the prison's history who appears to want to be here. Would you mind telling us why?"

Jason paused before speaking. "I had a feeling I could get something I need here. You all do a horrible job of hiding your dirt. You, specifically, Negatov." Negatov raised an eyebrow. "Not many people can bounce back from a car accident as quickly as you can."

"That couldn't have been all you had to go on!" Catherine blurted.

"It wasn't. It was just the most obvious. Now, what is this proposal you have."

"One more thing first," Negatov said. "How much do you truly know about our operations?" Jason looked at Moriz, who seemed eagerly waiting for a reason to throw him back in his cell. "And do not worry about any punishment. After all, you are in this prison because you are supposed to be executed, and that is not set to change."

"Alright, then," Jason began. "To put things simply: Your daughter is your talent scout, your warden is your slave driver, and we prisoners are just guinea pigs for your visium experiments—Trey being the only success produced since I arrived. Did I miss anything?" Jason could feel Moriz's eyes burning a hole through his face. "Clearly, I'm on to something, otherwise the Warden wouldn't be so upset with me." He looked at Moriz. "Is there a reason you aren't giving me an earful? I'm sure you have an opinion on this, unless of course your boss here renders your opinion irrelevant."

"My mind has already been decided on the issue," Negatov said. "Since you've been kind enough to reveal what you know, allow me to return the favor.

Indeed, we've been experimenting on the prisoners here for quite a while. Though Arbo has passed away, he was our one true success, until now. Earlier today, Sanctum was attacked by a former cellmate of yours, Chad Galen."

"So I've heard," Jason said. He looked to Moriz as if he'd been deceived. "One of your guards felt the need to interrogate me not long after you left. You told me he and Andreas were executed."

"They were," Moriz responded. "We were all there and personally watched them take their last breaths. When Arbo was injected with the visium he never died, but his health took a beating."

"Vega is much stronger than Arbo," Negatov said. "The unprecedented amount of damage he dealt to this facility in the short time he was here is a testament to that."

"Well, aren't *you* proud?" Jason said.

"He is very powerful, and driven. He's a rambunctious fellow, and most importantly he is knowledgeable about our business here at Sanctum, which brings me to the reason I have come to see you tonight. I am willing to grant you freedom to walk away from the prison, without the fear of being pursued. I will give you this if you are willing to do one thing for us."

"Silence the kid," Jason presumed.

"Specifically, we would like you to capture him and bring him to us, alive."

Jason nodded. "Just him, and anyone else?"

"We have no reason to assume the girl is alive at the moment. However, Doctor Nathaniel Jones, who you've likely seen around the prison, is also alive and a danger to our well being. You're free to kill him, but bring the boy and you're free to go."

"Well, that seems reasonable, but how do you expect me to capture someone who single-handedly raided this place? Unless..."

Moriz laughed, "Now you're catching on! You can leave if you catch the thug and bring him to us, but you can only do that if you're strong enough, if you catch my meaning." He winked fiendishly. "This thing that you say you 'need', it wouldn't happen to be power, would it? If you survive this visium injection you'll have all the power you could want. That's if you survive, of course."

Jason peered at Moriz's grin. It only made sense for him to want Jason to take the injection due to the high probability of failure, but that same vibe was not coming from the other two in the room. Jason thought for a long moment, and everyone waited patiently for his response.

"What you said earlier wasn't entirely true," he finally said. "You'll grant me freedom if I do one thing for you, but I'm actually doing two things for you. I'm getting that fool out of your hair, and I'm also figuring out the secret to surviving your formula."

Negatov smiled, "Your profile said you were a smart one. You are absolutely right. Are you capable of meeting the challenge?"

"If you're asking me if I think I can survive the execution, then the answer is:" Jason paused. "Yes."

"Wonderful." Negatov stepped back and made a path to the hallway behind him. "Warden, would you please escort our volunteer to the execution chamber so we can have him prepped?"

"With pleasure," Moriz said. He bumped Jason's shoulder and then he led him up the stairwell to the main cell blocks of the prison.

As Jason entered the hallway he squinted as his eyes adjusted to the light. He became so accustomed to the darkness in the isolation chamber that he felt like his eyes were being reintroduced to the real world. Moriz walked through the halls, through the cell block, into the commons, and into the medical wing of the prison. During their journey, Jason noticed two things. The first was that he was oddly tired, but he attributed that to the fact that he hadn't walked this distance in quite a long time. The second was that certain sections of the prison were in shambles. And it was difficult to believe a single person caused this.

"My cellmate did this… are you sure?" Jason said calling to the man ahead of him.

"Without a doubt," Moriz responded. "Are you afraid?"

Jason did not respond. He actually was not afraid, but he felt something strange. It was excitement. This was a glimpse of the power he would soon possess, and it was more than he imagined was possible. They traveled further down the halls until Moriz stopped at a large, metal, and unmarked door on one of the lower levels.

"Wait in here," he said as he held the door open. Jason walked inside, and the door slammed shut behind him. He looked around. There looked like a battle had taken place inside that execution chamber. The tile floor was cracked in multiple spots, the one-way mirror was severely shattered, and there was a mess of trash and broken glass that was only halfway cleaned up. The air in the chamber was filled with the sound and weight of lifelessness. Jason had seen much death, but he had no doubt this room had seen much more. This room was the trap where hundreds of people had their souls snatched from their bodies. Unless, of course, they were the two anomalies that got away.

A few minutes later Moriz returned to the room with a syringe filled with glowing liquid.

"That must be the visium," Jason said. "Is that all that's in there?"

"Yes, it's all we ever used, just in varying dosages." Moriz sat the syringe on the counter in the back of the room, and then he walked over to a table with straps dangling from it. "As promised, I get to be the one to plunge the needle."

Jason again didn't reply, but he sat on the table. Moriz strapped him in, and in the meantime Jason noticed the one-way mirror transitioning to being completely transparent. On the other side, Catherine and Vasya Negatov were seated in the back row of seats.

"Can you hear me over there?" Jason said.

Negatov reached behind a desk and the sound of an intercom clicked on. "Yes, we hear you."

"Good. I have a request to make."

"Are you losing confidence in your ability to survive?"

"Not at all," Jason smirked. As Moriz finished restraining Jason, he reached under the table and pressed a button, raising the platform to be perpendicular to the floor. "I know I am going to survive, and I'm also aware of your project naming scheme. That's why I want to make a suggestion before you give me some ridiculous name like Arbo or Vega."

Negatov chuckled. "Very well, what is your suggestion?"

"You can call me, Project: Lynx."

Moriz went to pick up the syringe. "We're ready, sir," he said looking through the glass. Negatov nodded. Wasting no time, Moriz found Jason's vein and squeezed every drop of visium from the syringe into Jason's arm. He covered the entry point with a bandage and walked out of the room, joining the others in the witness room.

Jason felt the liquid travel up his vein and reach his heart. Within the next minute he felt a uniform surge of immense pain all over his body. He closed his eyes as he embraced the agony.

There was nothing on the face of the earth quite like this pain, but that's why it was so familiar.

## Chapter 16

# Purgatory

The hurt ran deep. But Jason felt much more than pain in that moment. It was the coalescence of multiple emotions:

Fear.

Anger.

Confusion.

Despair.

The combination of all of these things manifested itself as something that he could only compare to a heart that was on fire. The burn radiated through his chest until his entire body seemed under its paralysis. There was very little he could feel outside of his body. He couldn't feel the ground beneath him, nor could he smell the damp air around him. He could, however, taste the flavorlessness of his own saliva as it congregated in his mouth. He could hear the taunts of his offenders as they stood watch over their prey. But most clearly of all, he could clearly see the motionlessness of his parents. His father had collapsed backward onto his mother, and they both lay inert on the cement sidewalk, seemingly floating in a pond of their own blood.

The blood was darkened by night, and because of the rain, the wetness of the ground beneath them made it difficult to tell where the sidewalk ended and the blood began. The breeze in the air was very light, but it blew with just enough force to make the blood puddle appear to have its own current. And just downstream, a trembling child tried to keep himself from fainting from the horrific sight.

"Whatcha gon' do wit tha kid?" one of the offenders asked. Jason shifted his attention to the group of men surrounding him. The one who spoke was beside him and speaking to the one standing directly over the bodies, who was still brandishing his weapon. The man spoke again. "Yo, DT, whatchyou gon' do?"

The man known as DT pointed the gun at the bodies beneath him and stared viciously. He wiped his face, which had been bloodied by the previous confrontation, and then he fired several more times at the bodies. Jason squealed from the thunderous gunfire, which officially announced his presence to the gunman.

"I'll handle 'em," DT said. "Hold 'em down."

The man standing beside Jason stepped backward and kicked him in his back. Jason went from his knees to lying face-first in the diluted blood puddle beneath him. The man's foot pinned Jason to the ground as DT walked toward him.

"Hurry up, 5-0's comin'!" Another offender shouted from somewhere beyond Jason's limited field of vision. The only thing he could see was DT aggressively pointing his gun at Jason's face, but he could hear sirens approaching from the background. DT casually tilted the firearms sideways.

"Your folks' pick'd tha wrong day ta be heroes, kid," he said. He pulled the trigger. A loud click ripped through the air. He pulled the trigger a few more times. The gun was audibly empty. "Shyiit," he said as he searched himself for a new magazine. At that moment blue and red lights lit the whole area as they were reflected off the wet ground.

The gunman ejected the empty magazine, replaced it with a new one, and turned the gun on the incoming squad cars. He and all the other offenders took the opportunity to flee as the cars pulled in. As the police were finally able to return fire, DT ran, turning his back to Jason for the first time. He was wearing a jacket with black sleeves, a white torso, and most noticeably an emblem of a cat's head on its back. As he turned the corner of the large building he vanished from sight, prompting two police officers to follow them. Jason heard the other policemen calling for backup on their radios.

Jason lay just as motionless as his parents, but the officer came to his aid first. He was whimpering uncontrollably, and the officer tried his best to calm him down. He picked the young boy up and walked him to the squad car, sitting him on the trunk so he would not be able to see the crime scene. "Hang in there, buddy" and "We're gonna get you home soon" were among the phrases the officer kept repeating. But Jason had a hard time listening to the officer's comforting words. He was too focused on the fire in his chest, and the burn would leave a scar for a long time to come.

As years came and went, Jason became familiar with the story of an old forest fire. The blaze, which consumed hundreds of acres of vegetation in an Illinois state park, seemingly emerged overnight. No one quite knew who was responsible for starting the fire, but it was irrelevant at the time. The only thing that was important was containing the destructive force before it consumed the entire park and eventually the surrounding cities. The response of the people in that area was to drop everything they were doing, regardless of occupation or any prior plans, and assist in extinguishing the flame. In only a few days time the fire was completely contained, and the imminent destruction of the forest was averted.

The story of the forest fire was always meant to be one of morality. It emphasized the importance of many people coming together in order to achieve a common and more important goal. What was most astonishing to Jason was that the story was true. It was as well known as classic adages, and it inspired countless Ventustonians who lived only a couple hundred miles north of the state park to establish a sense of community. The renegade fire that consumed the park became known simply as *The Wildcat*.

Jason found that to be an appropriate name. After all, no one knew who started the fire, and within a short amount of time it roared through the hills of the Midwest. What was unfortunate was that the tale of The Wildcat Fire seemed to have influenced more than just law-abiding citizens. There were some rough folk who also found something to take from the story, but the destruction caused by the flame was apparently much more appealing.

Over the years the cat emblem on the back of that man's jacket did not fade from memory. It did not take more than a few hours of internet access to discover what the emblem signified. The cat symbol was representative of the newest gang to terrorize the streets of Ventuston. They called themselves Wildcats.

Their rise to influence, however, did not bring much inspiration to the people. A group that began with no more than five or so members grew to be about thirty strong within the span of a few months. And though they always felt the need to keep their numbers below forty, like their namesake they often went on lethal raids, leaving nothing but destruction in their wake. No one knew who their leader was. No one knew what they wanted. But everyone knew that the ten-block span between Garfield and Roosevelt was no place to be when the sun went down. Now, Ventuston was a large metropolis—one of the largest in the nation and just off of one of the Great Lakes—and having a relatively small span of area that hosted a lot of crime was not uncommon, but that did not stop the people in that city from avoiding that area completely. The Den, as it came to be known, was no place to trifle.

But even so, if there was any place the man known as DT might be found, it was more than likely in the Den, so that's where Jason decided to focus most of his investigation. There were not many people who wore the retro, black and white jacket of the Wildcats. The most obvious reason for that was because no one who was not a member wanted to be associated with them in any way, especially since that warranted frequent attention from the police. The other reason was that even among the gang themselves only select individuals wore that jacket. Jason came to learn that these individuals were faction leaders. There were four in total, and DT appeared to be the most influential among them.

What their roles were within the group was ultimately irrelevant, however. They were all involved with the group that was responsible for terrorizing an entire community. And more importantly, they were all responsible for killing Jason's mother and his father. For that, they had to face justice, but only in the way Jason saw appropriate.

Jason sat in front of a computer, scrolling between multiple internet tabs. On one tab there was a map, on another there was a diagram, and on others there were random bits of information—anything that may prove useful on the day Jason sought out his justice. That day would be today.

Three hard knocks rattled the door to Jason's bedroom. "You have a minute?" a voice called.

Jason minimized that window of his internet browser. "Come in." A large and fit man entered the room. He left the door open behind him as he apprehensively took a seat on Jason's bed, which was right next to the desk Jason currently sat behind.

"I want to talk to you about something. I've been meaning to for a while, but I never…"

"What is it?" Jason asked in a to-the-point, but relatively respectful voice.

The man scratched his forehead. "It's about today. You know what it is, right?" Jason nodded almost unnoticeably. "Well, it's the anniversary of that day… When your parents—"

"I know, Darren. What about it?"

The man cleared his throat and suddenly became slightly assertive. "Well, it's been nine years, I believe. I know we've talked about how you felt on the issue and whatnot, but there's something else I have to make sure I pound into your head." Jason curiously looked at the man. "You know that all of this training we've done over the years has strictly been for self-defense, right?"

"I remember you saying that," Jason said apathetically.

"Then you know that everything you know is to be used to protect yourself and others. Nothing more. Do not abuse this, Jason."

Darren's assertiveness grew.

"I remember you saying that, too," Jason said swiveling calmly in his office chair, "but I can't help but think that you know that's not really what you taught me these skills for. I just know far too many lethal moves, and I've learned how to use too many weapons for my ability to be used *just* on self-defense. Never once have you handed me mace or a shield, but those samurai swords over there, that's another story."

"I taught you because I had a feeling you may put yourself in a bad situation at one point in the future, and no one else who may have adopted you would have been able to teach you these things."

"I've done a fairly good job staying out of bad situations, haven't I?" Jason stopped swiveling and planted his feet firmly toward Darren. "I saw more blood at twelve than most have seen in their life. I'm twenty-one now, and I think I've had enough violence for one lifetime."

"I would love to believe that, Jason. But the older you get the more time you spend loitering around in the Den, and there is no one down there worth your time."

"DT is still out there. If nothing else I'd say he's worth my time."

"That's exactly the shit I'm talking about! I'm no fool. I thought you just said that you'd had enough violence for a lifetime."

"I did say that. But I have two other lifetimes to live for."

Darren spotted a lightly packed sling bag sitting next to the bedroom door. He could not tell what was inside of it, but something very recognizable protruded from the top. "What the hell are you going to do with this?" He walked over to the pack and pulled the object from the bag entirely. "The wakizashi? What in the hell do you need this for?"

"The katana was too long for the bag. Clearly."

Darren brought the bag over to the bed and unzipped it all the way. Though Jason suddenly felt compelled to stop him, Darren had already begun pouring out the bag's contents before anything could be done. Darren's chest churned as has he gawked at the weaponry that lay before him. Multiple sets of throwing knives, small lighters with refill packs, bandages, and a key picking set lay spread out on the bed.

"This is," Darren began, "it's exactly what…"

"What you thought?"

"It's what I feared." Darren dropped the empty pack on top of the items that once filled it. He turned to Jason with a voice that was oddly calm. "How long have you been planning this?"

"How long have you known me?"

"Long enough to know that you know better than this," Darren said with conviction. "But instead you are choosing to do worse. You're going to become just like them if you go through with this. Don't go down this path."

"Unfortunately, I didn't choose the path. They chose it for me." Jason rose from his chair and stepped over to his bed. He began reorganizing the items as he slowly repacked them in the bag. "My mind's made up, but I'm having trouble understanding something. Are you worried for me or for the Wildcats?"

"I know what you are capable of, and that's why I pity them, but that's also why I'm so disappointed in you." Darren sniffled and walked back over to the bedroom door. "I don't want to lose another son to the streets, but if I must then I want to be very clear about one thing."

Jason threw his newly packed bag over his shoulder. "What is that?"

"You're free to walk out of these doors, but a murderer will never be allowed back in." Jason paused, then opened his mouth as if to speak, but then decided against it. He simply slipped on his shoes and adjusted his belt. He looked around his room one more time, and after a breath he approached the doorway. They stood glaring at each other, exchanging mixtures of anger, regret, and acceptance simultaneously. The conversation was silent, but powerful. Darren stepped to the side. Jason passed him and headed for the front door. He put his hand on the knob.

"You are not my father," Jason said softly, "but you were damned close." He opened the door and the hydraulic mechanism on the hinge closed it behind him. As he walked out of the house, he wanted to take a final look at the place where he resided for the past nine years, but he made a point not to. That house served him well to get him where he was, but it was officially in the past. Furthermore, it was a distraction. There was only one thing that was important now. Only one person to focus on.

Jason walked to the nearest bus stop. As he waited, he took a mental inventory of the items he packed. His sling, which concealed very effectively all the smaller objects within it, failed to cover the handle of his sword. Fortunately, the blade was short enough that the handle didn't protrude very far, but in the Den, there wouldn't be enough people around to notice him anyway. The bus pulled up, he paid the fair and rode for about a half hour until he arrived at the Den.

The sun was setting right on time. As the darkness slowly began filling the sky Jason walked down the street looking for anyone who appeared suspicious. He stayed close to the sidewalk, but he remained on the road, as was custom for people in that area to do. The sidewalk was an easy area to be ambushed, but Jason's black cargo pants and tank top allowed him to effectively fade into the night, even despite his white complexion. Before long he approached a house with many people surrounding it. Instead of stopping there, he passed it until he found a good spot to watch its inhabitants from a distance.

The people were standing in the front yard. A few of them were sitting on the porch, but none of them appeared to be socializing. The yard-dwellers were standing in a circle and smoking, and the familiar scent of Black & Milds rode the wind all the way over to Jason's location.

Jason kneeled behind a car for a long time. He watched the house for any sign of illegal activity. There were no other visible residents in the area; all of them were either locked up safely in their homes, or the houses themselves were vacant and boarded up. Minutes slowly passed as he kept a tight watch. After what felt like an hour, his patience was rewarded. Three men emerged from an old SUV, all three of them wore black and white. However, only one of them wore *the jacket*. The man's face was hard to make out, but his silhouette was familiar, and as he walked through the yard it was clear that there was an emblem in the middle of his back. No one else was wearing anything remotely similar. There was no mistaking it.

As the man in the jacket entered the house, the people on the porch scanned the neighborhood for onlookers. As if being signaled, the rest of the yard-dwellers finished their smokes and entered the house as well. Once the vicinity was clear, the men on the porch were the last to enter the house. The front yard was now empty.

Jason quickly made his way over. He sneaked into the yard and over to the side of the house. There was loud conversation inside, which was fine since it allowed him to hear exactly where they were. As a shadow floated by the window Jason ducked his head and pressed his back against the wall. The shadows and voices were migrating downstairs. Now was the time to prepare the trap.

He reached into his sling pack and pulled the lighter fluid and bandages from it. He generously poured fluid on an Ace wrap that he previously cut to be a foot long. There was a small ground level window that led to the basement. He laid the soaked wrap right next to the glass and finally took the lighter fluid bottle and poured a stream that went from the basement window, up the wall, and all the way to the closest main level window. He observed his work. All was good. As stealthily as he could, he repeated the process for every remaining window he could find on the sides of the house until every corner was lined with a healthy layer of lighter fluid. It was time for phase two.

Jason walked to the front of the house, stepped onto the porch, and rang the doorbell. The strong voices that could be heard from the basement suddenly weakened as the ding-dong of the doorbell echoed through the thin walls. Jason waited calmly. Heavy footfalls of what sounded like only a single man approached the door. The figure paused at the door, and then the door opened. On the other side, a threateningly large, yet obese, man walked through the doorway. He lifted his shirt to show off the gun tucked in his belt.

"What you want, homie?" he said.

Jason lifted his hands in submission. "I'm just looking for someone," he said in his most wimpy voice. "Is someone named DT here?"

The man came within arm's reach of Jason, trying to make him feel smaller. "What you want wit' DT, white boy?"

A smile broke through Jason's fear facade. "To kill him." Jason reached for the man's head and twisted it all the way around before he could react. Jason used the grip he had on the man's head to ease the body down as softly as he could. Quickly, he moved the body to the side of the porch and walked in the house.

There were still no voices from the basement, so Jason knew he was being listened to, but it didn't matter. Within seconds he found what he was looking for. The empty kitchen was around the hallway corner, and he briskly went to the stove and turned on all the gas burners to full blast.

"Who was at tha doh'?" A voice called from the basement. The staircase was on the side of the room opposite the stove. Jason did not reply. He casually walked back to the front door, but he did not exit just yet. He stood in the threshold. Menacing stomps climbed the stairs, and Jason prepared by reaching into his bag. Several people, most male and a couple female, entered the kitchen and searched for the intruder. The man named DT was not among them. Jason cleared his voice. All turned toward him. They aimed their guns.

"Whatever you do," Jason said as he stepped backward out onto the porch, "don't shoot me. It's not a good idea."

One spoke up. "Where Lloyd at?" Jason raised his leg and planted it firmly on an object. It was Lloyd's inverted head. "Aah shit! You gon' die now!" the man screamed as he took aim again. Jason jumped and took cover on the floor of the porch. A shot fired.

A thunderous roar came from inside the house, and a

shockwave blew out all the windows on the first floor. Jason peaked his head into the house and saw the entire home engulfed in flames, the bullet from the gun igniting the gas-filled air. The stove was covered in a steady and hellish flame, and the people in the kitchen were screaming in pain and shock, some covering their faces. Those that could still see tried to escape to the front door. Jason reached behind him and gripped his sword.

The first man ran through the door, and in a single motion Jason drew his blade and lopped off the fiery figure's head. Its momentum allowed its body to tumble off of the porch. Jason readied himself for the next person. One by one, each flaming Wildcat charged mindlessly through the door and screamed until the moment Jason removed their heads. He counted each one as their bodies ragdolled at the base of the porch.

*One, two, three... ten.* He turned to the bodies lying in the kitchen. *Thirteen. None of them are wearing the jacket. There's still one of them missing. There's no way he escaped through the back, not with that fire blocking the way. Unless...* Jason hopped off the porch and carefully walked around the house, keeping his back close to the wall. He looked around the left side. There was nothing except flaming windows and bandage wraps. He proceeded. He eased around the corner and walked to the back of the house. No one was there either, but the back door was indeed open. Had DT escaped? *He couldn't have gotten far.*

Jason scanned the backyard. There was an SUV. He ran to it and tried to peer through the tinted windows to no avail. He circled the car a full time and then got on his knees to see if anyone was hiding underneath it. Suddenly, the back door swung open and the butt of a gun whacked Jason in his back. It was DT. Jason fell over but regained his footing. He rolled out of the way just as DT fired a round at him.

Jason moved out of the gun's firing path as more bullets whizzed by him. DT kept firing until the gun repeatedly clicked. It was empty. Jason swiftly reached into his sling bag and drew a throwing knife. He launched it. Bullseye, right in the man's trachea.

The man choked and gagged as he reached for the knife, which was lodged in his throat. Shock overwhelmed him as he dropped the gun and fell to his knees.

"There you are," Jason said, panting more from excitement than any real fatigue. He kicked DT in the chest causing him to fall back, the knife in his throat erect. "Do you remember me, DT? Please tell me you do." DT continued to choke, but he did not say a word. As Jason spoke, DT slowly turned his eyes to examine the man that won a gunfight with a knife. He stared blankly at the man. And then his eyes widened in horror. "There it is; the look of recognition. I've been waiting for a full nine years now just for that. It's too bad our time will be cut short." In the distance, sounds of police and fire engine sirens blared.

Jason circled DT, finding the perfect angle of access to his neck. He sufficed with a position right beside him, and then he yanked out the throwing knife from his throat. "Since I won't be able to savor this moment like I planned, I'll just have to take something from you as a souvenir. How does that sound?" DT coughed as blood spurted from his mouth and throat.

Jason drew his sword once more and raised it in the air with a single arm. He aligned the blade's path with DT's neck. "You picked the wrong day to be a thug." The blade came down.

The death of DT and the eastern faction of the Wildcats was a polarizing event for many Ventustonians. For some, they were relieved that one of the most notorious gangs in the city had finally taken a demoralizing blow that was nearly impossible to recover from. For others, the event signaled an unprecedented turn in the nature of gang violence. The idea that Wildcats (or whomever) were resorting to decapitation as a method of intimidation was absolutely terrifying.

The events were equally polarizing to Jason, but for different reasons. It had been three years since the day he exacted his revenge on the man who stole his family from him. Part of him felt a deep satisfaction. He was grateful. Not many people could achieve their life's ambition so early in life. But he was also plagued by the weight of hatred, and this was confusing. There was no one left to hate; the man who nearly eradicated the Lynx family was no more. Be that the case, why was it so difficult to move on?

The answer came in the years after DT's death. There were a couple gifts that Jason obtained when he acquired his souvenir: DT's jacket. The first of which was an ungodly amount of cash stowed in his pocket. That held Jason over long enough for him to get a new job. However, the second gift was significantly more rewarding, and it came in the form of a driver's license. DT was only a nickname, and a rather unclever one at that. But out of all the offenses he committed, adopting that lazy moniker was much more forgivable. After all, DT sounded much more threatening than David Tamores.

And that was when the revelation hit. Even in a metropolis as large as Ventuston, Tamores was not so common of a name. In fact, there was only one man in the world who Jason knew shared that last name, and it was the same man to lose his son to the streets. Darren Tamores, Jason's adoptive father, was the biological father of David Tamores, the most prominent figure in the Wildcats.

Once again, Jason was beside himself. He was first hit by a wave of intense anger, feeling betrayed by the man who raised him. But then there was a glimmer of hope. Suddenly, Jason knew why his rage had not subsided over the years after DT, and it was because the man responsible for creating the killer who murdered his parents was still alive, and he was still due for comeuppance.

But unlike the Wildcats, assassinating Darren would not be an easy task. Not in the least. Jason was well aware that everything he knew—every kick he threw, every sword he swung, and every knife he hurled—was taught to him by Darren. Be it far beyond a student to challenge his master head on, especially when that master has assumed the role of a father. But it was foolhardy to think that Darren was ignorant about the transgressions of his blood son after all this time. And if he had the power to stop him, why didn't he? As far as Jason could tell, there was no good answer to that question. Therefore, the sins of the son were the sins of the father.

That only left one question: How could he kill Darren? Enlisting help and bringing anyone else into the matter was out of the question, and using a firearm to kill was an irony that he would never allow. Jason had no problem admitting that Darren was too much for him to handle as he was. He needed to attain more combat experience. He needed to build his skills. What he needed was power. But where could he find that?

Fate had an uncanny way of answering questions.

Downtown Ventuston was a common location for social gatherings. Though Jason was not one for sociality, he had nothing against gatherings. And for any pop culture savvy young man, the VenTechStone Technology Convention was a must-go. This year, there was a very special guest said to give an uplifting speech to the local entrepreneurs. The man who was responsible for discovering the American-mined miracle mineral that launched the beginning of the Visium Renaissance; Vasya Negatov himself.

Jason attended the event with low expectations. He roamed around the convention center without many products or innovations peaking his interest. When Vasya Negatov arrived on the scene, however, there was finally something that warranted excitement. It was difficult to not be sucked into a celebrity that garnered so much attention, after all.

Negatov stepped onto the stage and the entire crowd erupted in applause. His speech was intriguing, as he announced his newest invention and gift to law enforcement around the country. Never missing the opportunity to extend the brand of NegaLabs, the product was known as The NegaSentry. The visium and electric powered machine looked impressive, but it was slightly out of place for an event that was focused more on consumer electronics. The average consumer had no use for such a thing. But Negatov emphasized that "This is just the beginning… The beginning of a new era in which the vast applications of visium in all aspects of life will be explored. Technology is only the first phase." *What is that supposed to mean?* Jason thought.

Out of the entire speech, those words held extra weight.

Before the speech was over, Jason had had enough of the event. He shuffled through the crowd and left the convention center. He hadn't quite decided where he'd go from there, so he relaxed outside of the main entrance and contemplated to himself. Time passed, and a sizable group of people began leaving the convention center as well. *Negatov's speech must have ended.*

As people continued to flood out of the area, Jason was urged to turn his head. He spotted a group of several people who seemed to be walking at a hastened pace. They were a good distance away, but just the colors of their wardrobe were visible enough to recognize. Tones of black and white. They were Wildcats. Jason patted his body, futilely searching for the weapons he already knew he did not bring. They would be allowed to live on this night, but why were they walking away so quickly? The Wildcats went to the closest bus stop that had a clear line of sight to the convention center. However, they were not loitering, chatting amongst themselves as they waited for the bus to arrive. No… they were waiting, but for something else.

After ten minutes or so passed, a small paparazzi pack migrated from the entrance to the center to the main drop off location for celebrities. Negatov was making his big exit. Jason watched Negatov as he gave a casual wave to the photographers and fans who clustered along the velvet rope that separated the driveway from the people. As he stepped inside his limousine, Jason noticed the Wildcats move from standing in front of the bus stop shelter to behind it. They peered through the glass shelter. Something was about to happen.

The limo pulled off and photographers snapped pictures of the black Cadillac as it left. The car came to the intersection and waited for a green light. The signal turned. The limo driver punched the gas, and immediately an explosion blew the car into the air. The blasts knocked the nearby photogs off their feet, and the limo itself rolled onto its side, engulfed in flame. Panic ensued. Police and firefighters were dispatched. And sometime during the outbreak, the Wildcats fled the scene.

Jason followed news reports closely over the following days. The police had no leads for suspects for the bombing, but they had not seen what Jason had. There was no mystery as far as he was concerned, not when it came to the bombs, anyway. But there was a deeper concern that the public seemed to ignore.

There were two bodies recovered from the burning limousine. One was the driver, who was burned almost beyond recognition while also being nearly bludgeoned by the overprotective airbags; and the second of Vasya Negatov, who was in critical condition after the accident. The doctors who were interviewed by the press kept saying that it was a miracle Negatov survived in the condition he was in. The crime scene investigators also said it was a miracle he survived, given that the explosives detonated right below the limo's main cabin. "On all accounts, he should be dead," spoke a representative from the police force.

"But he's not," Jason said staring at the television. He turned down the TV volume and walked over to the table beside it. On it, a new computer, filled with several open tabs again, and each tab loaded with information relevant to his new investigation. But it wasn't related to the Wildcats, that group of gangsters was so desperate for attention nowadays that they would turn up eventually. Instead, there was strangely no one more fascinating than Vasya Negatov. Surely, by all paths of logic he should be dead from this episode. The blasts that propelled his vehicle into the air was much stronger than the explosion that burned down DT's house, and there was a lot of gas involved in that one. So how could this old man survive such an attack?

Que Google. Jason searched for the background of the man called Vasya Negatov. There were plenty of virtual files to sift through, all of which dated back to the discovery of visium almost a decade prior. But surely, this man had a life before he came across this shiny new element, didn't he? Jason kept searching, even going as far as checking the seventh page of Google results for a relevant search. There were none.

*It's like this man came out of nowhere; like he just materialized during the introduction of visium into society.* The music jingle for breaking news alerted Jason and he turned his attention back to the TV. It was an announcement about Negatov. He was going to make a full recovery. That didn't particularly shock Jason. If he could survive a blow like that he could definitely come back from it. The surprising part was who made the announcement. It was Negatov himself.

Negatov spoke behind a podium, as if the press were waiting for him to walk out and give another inspirational speech. Whatever he said was practically inaudible to Jason, since he was not listening. Jason was staring at the face of the man who was a burn victim. Or at least, he should have been a burn victim. His face, his neck, his hands, his arms... all of it perfectly fine. Not a single burn anywhere to be found. The man kept attributing his full recovery to "the magnificent surgical work", but Jason had a good nose, and he knew bullshit when he smelled it.

Jason continued his tireless investigation into the scientist. There were no articles written nor official documents to be found that were more than ten or eleven years old. But there were common tags that appeared along with his name. "Visium." "Nega". "Labs". "Robot." "Sentry". "Electronics". "Revolution". "Renaissance". "Daughter". "Catherine". "Sanctum". *Sanctum? That's a new one...*

Jason dug deep into the bait. Fortunately, there was much written about this topic. There was definite controversy over a penitentiary that was brought into existence for the sole purpose of capital punishment. But there was something even more odd about it. The prisoners sent there mine almost the entirety of the United State's visium supply. That was quite an important task to demand of inmates who were going to die soon. But for some reason, the politically shady Catherine Negatov seemed to be rather supportive of the idea. Even assuming the role of a district attorney to make sure only the worst of criminals find their way to this unorthodox prison. If Negatov said technology was only the first phase, did Sanctum house the second?

A limited history.

A miraculous recovery.

A shady daughter.

A powerful element.

And a mysterious prison.

None of it added up, and ultimately, that is what made it so conclusive. This old scientist with a dead wife, a missing son, and an excessively zealous daughter are cashing in on a billion-dollar empire and getting prisoners to do the work for them. A solid enough business plan, but somehow Negatov managed to attain healing abilities that would make a superhero jealous. He managed to attain something Jason had been searching for:

Power.

But of course, it did not come without sacrifice. Jason switched back and forth between the filled internet tabs and Negatov on screen. "It looks like the only way I'm going to find out about your moonlight activities is by visiting your Ohio-bound playground. I have a feeling that's where your secrets are kept, but I'm sure getting in there isn't easy." Jason found Catherine in the background on TV. She was standing behind her father with a relieved look on her face. The look seemed rehearsed. "I'll need to do something horrible to be admitted into Sanctum, won't I? I'd need to kill a lot of people."

Jason laughed out loud. The answer was obvious. Darren Tamores would have to wait, but the rest of the Wildcats were a different story. "Problem solved," he said. He found DT's jacket, put it on, and grabbed his sling bag.

His plan worked. All of his plans worked a little too well, which landed him a spot within the execution chamber with limited time to think.

He thought back to the time he arrived at Sanctum. It was not very long before Trey Ashley, the loudmouthed fool who constantly initiated confrontations with other inmates, was finally taken into execution. It was a relieving day for the inmates. It looked like for the first time they would be able to live out the rest of their lives on death row in peace. Or at least, it was a peace relative to what was possible with Trey around.

That period of tranquility lasted what was perhaps a full twenty-four hours. But then, in an unprecedented turn of misfortune, Trey Ashley returned from the execution. All the prison's inhabitants, including the guards, had no idea how to process the situation, but while Trey's return was more of an annoyance to his fellow inmates, the guards were the ones who were truly in trouble. Feeling the need to show off his newfound ability, he continuously picked fights with the armed officers in the prison. Every time he chose to act out he was violently put back in his place. This became a normal occurrence, and everyone just learned to deal with it.

After witnessing Trey's new strength, most inmates chose to simply keep a distance from him at all times. No one knew what to make of it, but Jason had found something very important. It was the first clue to figuring out what the administration of Sanctum was up to, and Trey was clearly the fruit of their labor. Jason began to communicate with Trey and asked him everything he knew of the execution, which turned out to be very little. It was obvious to Jason—if not to Trey—that Trey became something of a favorite to the administration. His medical appointments were fairly numerous. Guards paid closer attention to his actions. And most importantly, he was allowed to live. Considering that the very reason Sanctum exists was to execute and house death row inmates, the idea that one was allowed to slip through the cracks just because the injection didn't work was unfathomable. In order to keep tabs on the man without raising suspicion, Jason commissioned Kyle, a young inmate who tended to slip under the radar, to be the middleman and messenger between parties.

Life was routine during the months after Trey's return. New inmates were brought into Sanctum and older ones were executed when the time came. However, none of them survive the execution. One by one they all were escorted to the medical wing, never to be seen again. But Trey remained. Jason remembered studying every new inmate that came in: the fit, the fat, the tall, the short. Each visibly different from one another. None any stronger than the next. One by one they came, and one by one they died.

Until one day, Jason received a cellmate.

This kid, seemingly fresh out of high school, was the most recent prospect chosen by the administration. Physically, he was more of a package than all the others. Athletic, tall, full head of hair, and skin only half as brown as his eyes. He seemed like a good candidate since he fit the trend of recent recruits. But if there was one way he stood out, it was with his insufferable obnoxiousness.

He was not aggressive like Trey, but he had nearly as much energy. It was unbearable spending every night with him. He seemed no smarter than anyone else, no matter how much he may have felt otherwise. Jason knew the depths of his stupidity when he revealed his big plan:

"We gotta get outta here," he said. Jason knew he couldn't blame the guy for wanting to escape from a prison, but his foolishness came from truly believing he could do it.

Jason couldn't wrap his mind around it. *How did those fools survive?... Out of all of the ones who came into this place, what made them cling to their pathetic lives so desperately...*

Jason's eyes widened as he stared off into the wall in front of him. The answer suddenly became clear. In that moment, Jason realized he discovered the factor that everyone in Sanctum's administration had somehow missed. The very thing that made Trey and that young kid unique among all the prisoners, and it had nothing to do with their physiology. It had nothing to do with the strange concoction of visium that was pumped into their blood. It was something so much simpler. Almost too simple to believe, but alas, there was evidence to the truth.

The factor that kept those two bombastic bozos alive was in their personality. It was the very fact that they clung to life as desperately as they did that they were able to survive. Trey, the alpha male who was so self-conscious that he needed to bully those around him to obtain validation; and the kid, a foolhardy teenager so desperate to escape from his fate that he would risk his life by running away. To the average man, those two would be nothing more than cowards, running from their own sad reality.

Jason, however, knew to look deeper. They were both fighting for something, and that fight must have kept them alive at the point where everyone else died. Whatever it was they were fighting for, it was hard to tell. For Trey, possibly validation; for the kid, maybe freedom. Ultimately, it wasn't important. What was important was the realization that no one else in the entire prison had the same amount of vigor that those two did. They were immune to the curse that swallowed every new inmate that arrived.

Skull and Bones were affected, and being Trey's yes-men was the only thing that made them feel better. Kyle was effected, and the only time he seemed to not be sulking was when his new friend—the kid— was around. And most importantly, Andreas was affected. Jason had never known her to be anything other than a quiet and self-alienating girl who only cared about finding her own quiet corner to isolate herself in. That being the case, how in the world did some kid who was new to Sanctum's culture convince this girl to run away? Something she knew, from Trey's attempt, was a suicide mission from the start. Was she affected by the energy or—dare he think—charisma of this teenager? It was the only explanation that made sense.

But as fate would have it, Andreas was not immune to the Sanctum Depression like Trey and the kid were. And that must have been why when the foolhardy teen returned to Sanctum to cause a stir, Andreas was not with him. She was not capable of fighting off death like he was. But if there was anyone Jason knew who was experienced at fighting off death, it was himself. The Depression never affected him during his tenure at the prison. Of course, he was the only person who truly wanted to be there, and after nearly a year and a half, he was on the cusp of obtaining the prize he so fiercely desired.

All he had to do now was endure this pain. This overwhelming agony that consumed every inch of his body like fire. There was almost nothing on earth that was comparable to the feeling that he experienced, the feeling of battling death. The only thing that may be worse would be the pain of watching your parents gunned down in front of you and then bathing in a bloodied sidewalk. Compared to that, this was doable. This was bearable. All he had to do was endure for just a while longer. The pain was almost over.

**Chapter 17**

# Profile

Nathaniel Jones squinted as sunlight began to fill his bedroom. As the sun shone brightly through the east window of the room, a beam of light struck his face, forcing him to close his eyes more tightly than they already were. Unable to resist the sun any longer, he rose up and swung his feet over the side of his bed. He massaged his temple and eyelids as if to rub the sleepiness out his eyes. Once he was comfortable enough to open them completely, he looked at the nearest clock.

8:10 a.m. Any other time this would've been considered sleeping in, but since he was forcibly terminated from his job just over a week ago he was still having trouble settling in. He reached for his glasses on the nightstand and put them on. He looked out the window from his bed. Outside, he could see varying colors of green from the grass, brown from the bushes, and blue from the sky, but the most dominant object in his view was a large tree. The tree had a wide trunk and far-reaching branches. Certainly, it was well-rooted within the ground. So why was it shaking?

Jones cocked his head slightly as he studied the tree. The shakes came in pulses, as if a large giant was approaching and causing an earthquake. Jones listened to the shake, and then he heard the sound.

Dooomf… Followed by a shake.

Dooomf… And then another shake.

Jones rose from the bed and slowly approached the window. The sound got progressively louder the closer he came. Even the shake became more pronounced. The glass of the window lightly rattled. The sound repeated. And repeated. And then… It stopped.

The sudden silence prompted Jones to raise his level of cautiousness as he approached the window. He stepped forward and there were still no tremors. He slowly unlocked his window, and with the utmost care he slid the framework upward. There was still silence, and nothing but the sounds of nature entered the room. Jones slowly poked his head out of the window and looked down.

DOOOMF!

A powerful force ripped through the air and knocked Jones' head back through the rattling window and he fell straight on his back. He quickly recovered and raised his guard as he stared at the window again.

"Hey!" Chad said as he popped his head through the window. A startled Jones fell back once more. "What are you doing?" Chad laughed as he gripped the window pane from outside the house, holding himself in place.

"What am I—What are YOU DOING?" Jones asked incredulously. He got to his feet and tried to recompose himself.

"I'm just putting the finishing touches on my new trick. You need to see this, come down!"

Jones walked over to the window again. "This is the second floor... How did you get up here?"

"I jumped, obviously. Hurry up and get down here." Chad released the window pane and kicked away from the cabin, landing on his feet on the ground below.

"Show off," Jones muttered, and he slipped on his shoes, threw on a robe, and made his way outside. When he arrived Chad was stretching his arms, making a windmill motion as if he was about to start an exercise. He had a broad grin on his face like a kid about to show off a new toy. Behind him was the tree visible from Jones' room.

"What in the world happened to that tree?" Jones asked, pointing to its trunk. The trunk looked completely shaved of bark on the side nearest Chad, and the naked wood underneath appeared incurved, as if it had been carefully pounded inward by a large mallet. "Please tell me you weren't tackling the thing all night..."

"Nope, much better." Chad turned to the tree. "I hope you're taking notes."

He opened his arms wide and squeezed the space in front of his chest. Immediately, the area between his hands began to ripple and spin. He shaped the energy cloud into a sphere, and then he shoved it forward, causing it to careen toward the tree. The rippling sphere impacted the tree and popped like a balloon, sending a shockwave that shook the tree and sent tremors through the air. Its sound echoed through the trees. "Add THAT to my list of new superpowers! HAHA!"

Jones picked up his jaw as he tried to form a sentence. "So… that's what made all that noise earlier."

"Oh yeah! Wanna see it again? I can do it again."

Jones walked closer to Chad. "Yes, but not so much this time, if you can."

"Of course, I can." Chad outstretched his arms and brought them together again in a squeezing motion. The cloud of rippling energy appeared again, and he formed it into a much smaller sphere. "See that? And I'm sure it looks familiar to you."

"That… that's incredible," Jones said adjusting his glasses. "This is the same vibrational energy that manifests when you lift objects telekinetically, and you are summoning it at will." He moved his face even closer to the sphere.

"Careful!" Chad said taking a step away from Jones. "This thing explodes, you know."

"It's a bomb?"

"I prefer the word: Buster. That sounds cooler." Another smile crept on Chad's face. "Whatever that viby stuff is, I can make it into a ball like this whenever I want. All I gotta do is compress the stuff, and boom; Instant Buster!"

Jones stepped back in wonder and placed one hand on his hip and the other on his forehead. "That's absolutely amazing. You've only been working at this for a week and you're already inventing new ways to use your psychokinesis. A vibrational concusser... that's wonderful."

"I don't know about all that, but I know I can definitely jump higher and run faster than before. I bet I can even beat a bear in an arm wrestling match if I wanted! If nothing else, I'm sure I could've beat Trey's ass one-on-one." Chad made a motion to stroke his chin and suddenly remembered he was still holding the energy. "Hmm, watch your head. I gotta do something." He then turned and shoved the buster into the tree again and another shockwave surged in all directions. An unprepared Jones stumbled and fell as the force knocked him over.

"Watch it, will you?" he said.

"I told you to watch your head. I can't really uncompress the thing once I make it. Oh well."

Jones once again stood up, and he walked back to the cabin. "I suppose you were right about one thing: I should have been taking notes after all." He walked inside and grabbed a clipboard and pen and returned outside. After jotting down a paragraph worth of words, he spoke again. "Strength, speed, stamina all have been increased steadily. Are you ready to keep the streak going on the obstacle course again?"

"You know it."

Jones pulled a stopwatch from his robe's pocket as Chad took his place behind an imaginary starting line. The entire obstacle course itself was imaginary, but Chad had no problem visualizing objects and obstructions for him to try to cross. All he had to do was remember the layout of the prison. After spending so much time in Sanctum, it would have been a sin to forget. Running through an imaginary replica would be the perfect simulation for the day he would be ready to go back.

He stared at the elevated field in front of him. The trees were nothing but pillars, the boulders were but stationary NegaSentries, and at the finish line stood one man. The one responsible for this whole mess. Vasya Negatov. Chad could clearly see the tall suited man at the end of the course. He dug his toe into the ground, planting himself. Jones raised his arm.

"Aaaaand. Go!"

"Why do you keep staring at me like that?" Jason asked. "Like you have never seen this work before."

"It's a rarity," Catherine said. "It isn't like it happens very often, but it's refreshing to see that some of the recruitments I made actually worked out." She stood watching Jason as he calmly paced around his cell. With her arms crossed, she shook her head. "After all this time, it's finally happening. Anyway, how do you feel?"

Jason was put off by her apparent friendliness but still responded normally as he closed his eyes and assessed himself. "I feel stronger. Like I'm more of myself than I ever was before. I'm focused… and I'm aware."

"Mhmm," Catherine acknowledged. Just then she received a message on her phone, and she pulled it from her pocket to check. After viewing the illuminated screen for a couple seconds she put the phone away again. "Well, I've got some good news. My dad will be down to see you momentarily… Did you hear me?" Catherine raised an eyebrow as she watched Jason seemingly stare off into space. He looked from one corner of the cell's ceiling, and then he slowly shifted his eyes to the other. "Ahem."

Jason turned back to Catherine. "He's coming down now? I see," he said trailing off. Ignoring his behavior, Catherine walked over to the wall and sat in a small folding chair as she fiddled around on her phone again. A few moments passed. Jason chuckled.

"What is it?" she said.

"He's at the steps now."

"Hmm? No, he's not." At that moment, the locks on the door at the top of the staircase clicked loudly, and the door to the isolation chamber opened. Catherine's headshot from the stairs to Jason. "Wha? How did you know that?" Jason only laughed softly. Two sets of footsteps made their way down the stairs, and Jason saw Warden Moriz and Vasya Negatov as they reached the bottom.

"All right, lock it back." Moriz shouted to the top of the stairs, and the sound of a closing door and more clicks echoed through the chamber. Negatov slowly stepped toward the bars of Jason's cells. There was more surprise in his eye than any of them had seen before, but he still remained calm.

"How long has he been awake?" Negatov asked.

"Several days, already," Moriz said. "I have to admit, it was a good idea to keep his body under surveillance, sir. He was only out for about a day's time before he woke back up again."

"How did you do it?" Negatov asked, signaling to Jason through eye contact that he was speaking to him.

Jason approached the bars. "Look at everyone who died, and then think of the only other two that ever survived this place. It turns out, the only thing one needs to do is fight through the pain as hard as they can. Of course, fighting death isn't the easiest thing for someone to do, especially when it comes to death row prisoners. Maybe if you looked for candidates among willing volunteers instead of demoralized inmates you'd have saved yourself a lot of time and resources."

"Noted," Negatov said as he walked backward and away from the cell. "Release him." Moriz grunted with hesitation, which Jason assumed was the warden's way of saying *Do I have to?* Negatov scowled, and receiving the message, Moriz did as he was told. He stepped back and Jason walked out of his cell. He stopped only a few feet away from Negatov, and he immediately broke out in laughter.

"What's the joke, maggot?" Moriz said.

"Do you know the feeling," Jason began, "the one you get when you finally have the confirmation that everything you thought you knew for so long was all true the whole time? The truth that only you knew, but no one else was smart enough to figure out. That's the feeling I have right now." He turned his head to see Moriz out the corner of his eyes. His laughter turned to sudden seriousness. "And also, you *will* call me Lynx from now on."

"In any case, there's the matter of business," Negatov said. "Evidently, you have held up the first part of your side of the deal, Lynx. Congratulations are in order. However, before there are any celebrations, I'll need you to fill the second part of the deal as well."

"The two runaways… I'll need at least a couple days before I can do that. I've only been able to see a fraction of the things I can do while in this cell. I'll need more time to build my competency with my new strengths before I execute my assignment."

"I suppose that's fair," Negatov made his way to the exit. "Warden, can you make sure our asset here is well accommodated? His development will be most ideal to our success. Make sure he remains in secrecy and his advancements are documented."

"He could try to escape, sir!" Moriz said. "You know he can do that easily."

Negatov halted and glanced at Jason with a smirk. "I don't think he will."

"Yeah, he's been very cooperative up until now," Catherine added.

Feeling abandoned in his opinion, Moriz relented. "Understood, I'll prepare a space for him." With that, Negatov nodded and continued up the staircase. Catherine followed him and briefly left Moriz and Jason alone.

"Back in the cell," Moriz said. "I'll come for you once a facility is prepared."

Jason smiled arrogantly at Moriz but did as he was told. "What's my name, Warden?"

"Shut up, Lynx."

"I'd say that's enough training for today," Jones said. He slipped the pen he was using underneath the clamp of the clipboard and turned for the cabin. "We've been out here all day. How about a breather?"

"I don't need one," Chad said. He observed the cabin's backyard where his training took place. There were sporadic patches of unearthed dirt, branches of varying sizes that had fallen from their respective trees, and tree trunks that had been explosively debarked. He was proud of the mess he made. "I bet I could keep going for another hour or two if I really wanted."

"Well, rest is pretty important to development as well, mind you. Plus you've been making good progress. Take it easy." Jones walked up the back porch steps and walked inside the cabin.

Chad gave the yard one more glance. *I guess I gave the landscapers enough work for one day.* "All right, then." He hopped the length of the stairs and walked in right behind Jones. They both took off their shoes by the back door and placed them right beside the remains of a partially cleaned blood stain. Chad walked into the living room and plopped onto the futon. "I guess rest is okay," he said as a yawn escaped him.

"Do you even sleep anymore?" Jones said searching the refrigerator.

"Not much. I can't seem to stay asleep for more than an hour and a half every night. I'm never exhausted when I wake up, though, so I guess that's cool."

"Trey Ashley was similar. He also saw a shift in his circadian rhythm, but he still slept for at least three hours every night." Jones pulled a water bottle and a bag of grapes from a shelf in the fridge. He stepped into the living room. "His appetite dropped as well, but we thought it was only because of his health. Speaking of food—THINK FAST!" He reached into the bag of grapes, grabbed a few, and hurled them into the air. Before they hit the ground, Chad held out his hand as if to catch them, and immediately the three airborne grapes halted in midair. They spun slowly as the vibrating space around them held them in place.

"HA! And I didn't even miss a beat," Chad said. He made a twirling motion with his finger, and the grapes orbited each other as they moved closer to him. He opened his mouth and the grapes floated inside one by one. "And just like that, I got nourishment for another day. Not needing to eat much isn't so bad, but it'd be even cooler if I could just eat whatever I freaking wanted and not get fat!"

"Who knows? Maybe you can." Jones walked across the room and placed the bag of grapes on the black filing cabinet. With clipboard still in hand, he unclamped the paper that Chad could tell had many scribbled notes on it and opened the filing cabinet drawer. "I've got a feeling we're only scratching the tip of the iceberg, here." He slipped the paper into a manila folder, one that he took the time to search for. Once the sheet was tucked away, he closed the drawer back. "I would appreciate it, however, if you did not do anything to jeopardize your life while we try to figure out what you can do."

"Trying to figure out what I'm worth to a military?" Chad said. His tone sharpened.

"What?"

"I've been doing some thinking. Why in the world would someone like Vasya Negatov—a bazillionaire who does robotics— want to make an immortality serum. And then it came to me... He wants to make super soldiers, doesn't he? That's why he's making those ridiculous lookin' robots."

Jones chuckled. "That's not it at all."

"How could it not be?"

"If he was amassing an army underneath Sanctum's deepest dungeons, I would know about it, or at least would have caught wind of it."

"So you think he honestly wants to make this immortality formula for the good of mankind? Puhleeeze! He probably wants to find a cure for cancer and then sell it for a fortune."

"Possibly," Jones' voice wavered slightly. "I suppose I never considered."

"What did you consider? You were doing this for a very long time to not think about what you were doing."

"I was thinking of it. Constantly. That's what made me continue even though lives were threatened." Jones walked over to the staircase but paused after the first step. "I may have been coerced into doing this, but I thought that the remuneration of discovering the potential of humanity with this new technology would be worth the possible retribution. I wanted to take the Visium Renaissance even further. That's why I kept that spiral to remind me."

"What spiral?" Chad suddenly remembered the marble in his pocket and pulled it out. "You don't mean this thing, do you?"

"Yes, that's the one." Jones watched as Chad fiddled with the marble and tried to decipher the marking on it. "The white swirl is called the Reiki Spiral."

"What's it mean?"

"Different things to different people, but to me, it represented the power of the universe that can be manifested through man. That's all I ever wanted to see in life."

Chad glanced up at Jones on the stairs. He was staring off and his eyes seemed to be glistening with moisture. "Guess you got your wish," Chad said.

"I did. Thank you for that."

There was a pause. "I'm not thanking you for killing me, if that's what you're waiting for."

Jones laughed. "Of course not. Anyway, get some rest. I know I will." He walked up the stairs and Chad heard a door close behind him. After about fifteen minutes, all motion upstairs halted. Jones was fast asleep.

But Chad was not.

He played with the marble, rolling it around in his palm. Then when he was bored of that, he made the marble float in the air. It orbited his hand at first, then Chad expanded its range so that it became a satellite for his entire body. It moved slowly, then quickly, then slowly again until finally, he became so disinterested that he let the marble drop where it was floating. Another hour passed and Jones was still asleep. And Chad was still downstairs. Awake. And alone.

There was something enlightening about the inability to sleep. Chad had pulled plenty of all-nighters before, but it had been over a week since he woke from the cave, and he hadn't slept more than two hours in a single night since. It was as close to insomnia as he had ever gotten. It wasn't so bad considering he had plenty to think about nowadays, but there are only so many things one can think about in a single night before thinking itself becomes tiresome.

And since that point had arrived, there was nothing else to do except sit and look. It didn't matter what he looked at. Whatever was closest. That was what he would entertain himself with in that moment. His eyes wandered around the room. Below the futon lay a folded blanket that had fallen. Chad picked it up and placed it back on the futon. Mission accomplished.

His eyes wandered up at the wall. A digital clock hung above him. He was already aware that the time and day were incorrect, but he was eternally grateful that the clock itself was digital and not mechanical. Hours and hours of the sound of a ticking second hand would certainly have eroded at Chad's sanity slowly and effectively. His eyes continued to search the room for anything that stood out as odd or new. Nothing of the sort. Bored of playing I-Spy with himself, Chad decided to look for the marble again. It didn't take long to locate it since it was in the very front of the room, directly in front of the large filing cabinet.

The cabinet itself was nothing new or special. Being as big as it was, it was hard not to notice. But seeing it and seeing what was inside of it were two different things. *I haven't been through that thing yet, but Nate goes through it all the time. Must be some pretty important stuff in there…* Chad wrung his hands together with a mischievous grin. Finally, something to do.

Chad got up and walked over to the cabinet. He picked up the marble below it and returned it to his pocket, then he softly grabbed the handle. With a gentle tug, he pulled the drawer until it could go no further. Manila folders filled the drawer from front to back. There were no empty spaces anywhere, and each folder was uniformly organized with a label on every flap. It didn't take long before he noticed that the labels had names on them. Chad reached in and grabbed the first folder his hand touched. The name read: Dionte Summers.

He opened the folder. Inside there was a picture of an inmate with several blocks of text written below it.

"Profiles?" Chad whispered. He looked back at the drawer full of folders. "These are probably all the people at Sanctum." He closed the folder and put it back in its spot. "I hope they don't mind if I do a little background check on 'em."

Conveniently, the entire top drawer was alphabetized from A to G. After a few seconds, Chad found his own profile and checked it out.

---

```
Name: Chad Galen, M

Project: Undesignated

Blood Type: A+

Birthplace: Violet City, OH

Ethnicity: African-American

Age: 18

Body Type: Athletic

Medical Conditions: Thigh Contusions

Criminal Background:

    Two counts of First Degree Murder/Plead Not guilty/
Convicted.

Misc. Notes:

    Killed parents, but no prior incidents. Likely
mentally unstable.
```

Chad tried not to take offense to the idea that Jones thought he was mentally unstable. This was before they got to know each other, after all. Surely he couldn't still feel that way. But he hadn't written any recent notes on this profile. *These must be old versions of the profiles. He's got to have updated ones somewhere around here.* Chad closed his folder and put it to the side in case he felt like coming back to it. There was more snooping to be done. He thumbed through the folders again. *Azal, Attwell, Atnis... Ashley!*

---

Name: Trey Ashley, M

Project: Arbo

Blood Type: B+

Birthplace: Xenopool, TX

Ethnicity: African-American

Age: 29

Body Type: Thin

Medical Conditions: N/A

Criminal Background:

Assault with deadly weapon/Plead Not guilty/ Convicted

Battery/plead not guilty/convicted

First degree murder/plead not guilty/convicted

Misc. Notes:

Survived the trial! Will keep subject under surveillance.

Increased physical strength obtained.

Increased speed obtained.

Health of subject deteriorating. Health worsening with no sign of improvement; brought subject in for testing.

        Subject killed through accidental electrocution. His
blood demonstrates apparent vulnerability to electricity.


        With his curiosity satisfied, he decided to move on to the next
section: The 'L's...

---

Name: Kyle Lyons, M

Project: Undesignated

Blood Type: O

Birthplace: Golden Gate, CA

Ethnicity: Caucasian

Age: 19

Body Type: Average-Athletic

Medical Conditions: N/A

Criminal Background:

    First degree murder/plead guilty/convicted

Misc. Notes: N/A

---


Name: Jason Lynx, M

Project: Undesignated

Blood Type: AB+

Birthplace: Ventuston, IL

Ethnicity: Caucasian

Age: 25

Body Type: Athletic

Medical Conditions: N/A

Criminal Background:

    Arson/plead guilty/convicted

    First degree murder - 24 counts/plead guilty/
convicted

Misc. Notes:

    Killed 24 people! Decapitation and arson.

    Martial arts practitioner and reported 159 IQ. Very
dangerous.

---

Name: Andreas Lazara, F

Project: Undesignated

Blood Type: A+

Birthplace: Cape Sol, FL

Ethnicity: Cuban-American

Age: 23

Body Type: Average

Medical Conditions: Schizophrenia

Criminal Background:

    Three counts of murder/plead guilty/convicted

Misc. Notes:

    Displays highly unsociable behavior

    Severe mental instability

"What are you doing?" Jones said, his head leading his body down the stairs. "Why in the world are you looking through those?"

"Your super secret documents aren't all that secret if you just kind of leave them here, out in the open." Chad put Andreas' file back in the drawer.

"They were not out in the open. They were hidden within the filing cabinet, you Nosey Nancy!" As he got to the bottom of the stairs, he walked over and took all the profiles and stacked them neatly and frantically.

"Hidden? They were sitting right here in this unlocked cabinet in the front of the room, in the front of the house. This is literally the worst way to hide things. You're just lucky I know what these profiles are for. It would be so hilarious if the cops saw all this crap and you had to explain how you're not actually a super stalker! They'd *throw* you in Sanctum!"

"Is one of your powers not being funny? Because you're doing a great job of that right now. I hope you can tell I'm not laughing."

"Lighten up, Nate. Why do you even have this thing? Never heard of the Cloud?"

"The Cloud can get hacked. There's nothing more secure right now than paper and pen. This is best for me."

"If you're willing to put up with the wild inconvenience, then sure it is."

"Inconvenient for me means inconvenient for others as well," Jones sighed. "This was supposed to be for my eyes only, but I'm guessing you probably have some questions for me now?"

"Just a few on my list, but you should've seen this coming."

Jones finished closing up the cabinet, sighed again, and took a seat at the bottom of the steps. "I'm listening."

"First up: What made you choose certain people the way you did? Like, why us? And what took you so long to get anyone to survive?"

"There are quite a few questions there," Jones chuckled, "but I think I have an acceptable answer for you.

Years ago, when Doctor Negatov approached me, he insisted that the way to achieve results was through the appropriate dosage and implementation of a visium formula. I took him at his word, and from that point, I tried to find just the right dosage to administer to subjects. All inmates that came to Sanctum were recruited based on criteria that I deduced would produce survival in a trial run. As is often the case with science, my early hypotheses were wrong, so over the years I tweaked the criteria as the trials lasted longer and longer. Ultimately, Trey Ashley was the only true success."

"Criteria? So stuff like...?"

"Physical fitness, ethnic background, mental stability—which can be shaky at times. It took a few years, but eventually Sanctum became a bit of a melting pot."

"I guess that makes sense," Chad said.

"Anything else you'd like to know?"

Chad paused. "Yeah, what about Andreas?"

"What about her?

"What made you pick her? She seems fit like the rest of us, but there aren't that many girls at Sanctum. So what in the world made you choose her?"

"Yes, well, your friend was a bit of a puzzlement. To be completely honest with you, she is one of the few people who Doctor Negatov appointed to the prison himself."

"Why?" Chad asked emphatically. "Does it have something to do with her crime?"

"Likely, but he never shared his reasoning with me. She seemed to fit all of my requirements, so I never questioned it." Jones stared blankly at the floor for a second longer than Chad thought was comfortable, but before he could ask him something, Jones shivered. "Phew—chills," he said. "Let's talk about something else. I'll take one more question from you, but then I need to get back to bed. Curious about anything else?"

"Hmm… yeah! Just one more thing!"

"Yes?"

"What the hell did my profile mean by 'mentally unstable'?!"

## Chapter 18

# Lynx

Several days later, Chad woke to the sound of footsteps on the floor above him. Jones had clearly just woken up, and the sound of him fumbling through his closet while looking for his robe and slippers was something Chad became familiar with. Chad remained on the futon as Jones came down the stairs.

"Morning!" Jones said. Chad looked over and gave him a halfhearted wave as he yawned. "Looks like you actually got some sleep last night," he continued, strolling through the living room and into the kitchen.

"A couple hours, I think," Chad said.

"Oh, good. Then I suppose you are ready for another day of training?"

Chad yawned again, "Whenever you are. Just let me know when you're done eating. I'll be out back warming up." He sat up on the futon and swung his legs over the edge and onto the floor. "You hear me?"

"Uhm, yes… One moment." Chad tried to peer around the corner and into the kitchen. Though he couldn't see Jones, he could clearly hear the cabinets opening and closing one after another. Jones' breaths were becoming heavier as he searched the kitchen, and Chad was certain whatever he was searching for was nowhere to be found.

"What are you looking for?" Chad asked as he stepped into the kitchen.

"We have a small issue," Jones insisted as he rummaged through the refrigerator. "We don't have any food left. I thought I had plenty in the cabinets but I can't find any of it!"

Chad sighed incredulously. "Okay, I'm sure that's not nearly as big a problem as you just made it out to be." He peered in the empty fridge and saw the blank shelves staring back at him. He then opened the freezer above to be greeted with more of the same. After taking a few more seconds to ponder, he turned his focus to the cabinets above the oven, and with an emphatic wave of his arm he opened all the cabinets and drawers in the kitchen all at once. After a few more seconds, he finally conceded. "Okay, this is a bit of a problem."

Jones ran his fingers through his hairs and began rambling to himself. "This is not good; I should have prepared for this sooner! I need to find some way to make do."

"Would you knock it off with the panic attack? On the bright side, this is the perfect time to get you back into the world."

"What?!"

"You haven't left this place since you got here! How long's it been, like, two weeks? Clearly, you're healed, so stop being a hermit and go to the store already."

"I have a bounty on my head now! I can't be seen out in public."

"Ugh... drama king. There're no bounty hunters out looking for you. Everyone thinks you're dead."

"No, no. It's not people I'm worried about, it's the NegaSentries. They have facial recognition, and they patrol the public establishments in town since we are so close to the prison. When they see me they may either kill me on site or take me back to the prison, and they will just terminate me there."

"Well, then we're screwed," Chad exasperated. "I don't know what you expect me to do here. In case you forgot, I'm technically an escaped convict... and the robots know *for sure* that I'm not dead. They'll hunt my ass down."

Jones paused as he stared off past Chad. Then his face lit up as if he just concocted a plan. "You know, that is not such a bad idea!"

"Getting hunted?!"

"No, no, no. Hunting! I can cook whatever you find out in the wild. Preferably deer."

Chad took a moment to think up an excuse not to go, but after failing to find any, he eventually relented. "I guess it's not such a bad idea," he groaned.

"Marvelous, we're in agreement!" Jones closed the cabinets that Chad left open and began pulling out random cookware from a drawer just below the oven. "I'll go ahead and get the grill ready," he said excitedly. "You get going. I'm sure that you're strong enough to carry whatever you find back here without too much hassle. Just remember to stay out of sight. You can consider this a new type of training."

Unable to find any more reasons to object, Chad walked back into the living room. He put on his hiking boots and vest, and after a few minutes he was off.

There was nothing like a hike. Even though walking through the hills reminded Chad of his previous couple outings, which were both wildly unpleasant, he managed to find just a hint of enjoyment from taking a stroll through the rural neighborhood. Other homes were few and far between, and avoiding being seen by the neighbors was an easy enough task.

But the task of finding edible wildlife and returning to the cabin with it was somewhat daunting. It wasn't that carrying the unlucky beast was going to be difficult. Instead, Chad became increasingly aware of the fact that he didn't know the first thing about hunting. He had never been interested in those kinds of outdoor activities, which he found slightly embarrassing considering his own outdoor-prone nature. But all he knew about it was that there were usually guns involved, perhaps an early morning departure, and, at the very least, some camouflage apparel. Chad inspected his own outfit, his dark cargo pants, black hiking vest, and hiking boots and figured what he was wearing would have been more appropriate for a night raid. But he'd been walking for almost twenty minutes already, and turning back was out of the question.

Before long Chad found a stream that ran between multiple hills. Though some of the grass along the hills looked brown and dried out, the plant life just around the stream was green and lush. *This looks like a good enough spot for deer to hang out. I'll post up here until something comes along.* He went to lean his back against a tree trunk and slowly slid down until he was sitting on the tree's bulging root.

All was calm. Chad took a deep breath as he felt the bark of the tree gently scratch the back of his head. The only noise he could hear was the light breeze caressing the leaves and grass and the sound of miniature waves crashing over small rocks in the stream. It was the most he was reminded of his special meditation spot since he left Violet City. The memory was comforting, and he welcomed the distraction as he closed his eyes.

*Ploop.*

Chad opened his eyes again as what sounded like a loud bubble interrupted the steady stream of water. He searched the stream for the source but found nothing. The sound repeated, only this time it was louder and more exaggerated. With a light chuckle, Chad stood to his feet. "Of course, I should've thought of this before," he said. He spotted a large rock in the middle of the stream that was a short eight-foot hop away. He jumped and gracefully landed on the rock and turned his attention to the stream. After a few seconds, he found one of the culprits.

He outstretched one of his hands above the water, halfway balled his fist as if squeezing a bottle, and finally elevated his hand. The gestures produced a corresponding reaction in the water, and emerging from the surface of the stream came a fish that violently flapped in the air. Bound by the air that surrounded it, the fish continued to struggle as it floated closer to Chad.

"Who needs to hunt when you can fish like a magician? You don't look much bigger than a sardine, but beggars can't be choosers." Using his free hand, he lifted more unsuspecting fish from the water and inspected them. They were satisfactory. "Sorry, little buddies, but you're all coming with me."

He casually counted how many fishes he pulled into the air,

but before he counted the last one, he felt a strong jerk in his chest. Alarmed, Chad squeezed his chest with both hands, and his loss of focus caused the almost-dozen fishes he levitated to all crash back into the water. He released a few panicked breaths and leaped from the rock back onto land, taking account of himself. "What was that? Am I dying? No, no. Pleeease, I can't die now!" he said, checking his heartbeat.

The pounding stopped. In fact, there was only ever a single heartbeat that seemed out of place, or at least more intense than it should have been. There was no pain, no excessive sweating, and no intense discomfort; all things that were more consistent with Chad's last experience with death. He calmed himself, relieved that he would not need to worry about waking up in another mound of dirt. But this feeling in his body didn't subside. He was not dying—that was clear. But what was surprising was how he felt instead: More alive.

Chad paid attention to the sensation that gently flowed through his body. It was similar to when the visium first made its way through his veins. But instead of the agonizing chill that overtook him last time, this feeling was subtly electrifying. It tingled. The sensation created goosebumps, and for the first time Chad felt like the visium in his body was trying to communicate with him. It was trying to speak to him.

Chad closed his eyes and listened to the feeling. *It tickles a bit. What's going on? Why does it tickle less here...* Chad stepped over to face the stream... *than it does over here?* He turned back toward the direction of the Cabin. *It feels like there's something over here that's makin' me feel funny, but...* He opened his eyes and scanned the area... *there's nothing but grass and dirt over here.* He walked up the hill, further away from the stream but closer to the source of the sensation.

"This is stupid," he said aloud. "There's nothing around here that should be makin' this happen. There're no power lines and no electricity gettin' shot at me. What in the hell makes visium react like this?"

He took a moment to think, then a smile struck his face as a thought came to mind. He recalled the day he followed Jason around Sanctum's mine. It was the same day Jason was able to pick up a stone— one that was clearly an ore of visium—simply hold onto it for a few seconds, and was suddenly able to detect where more visium was. It was one of the more bizarre things Chad witnessed Jason do, but it was also one of the most educational. It was that day that Chad realized there was a bit of finesse involved in the visium-scouting process, and after spending the next few days testing the method for himself, he became somewhat good at finding visium ores. That nugget of information along with the old mishap from his science class in high school taught him two important lessons:

"Visium doesn't just amplify other types of energy, it also reacts to other sources of visium in its environment. I must be sensing the presence of some visium in the area!"

*But then why am I only just feeling it right now?* He looked in the direction he came from, but turned his head slightly to the left. *A second ago it felt like the source was coming from over there by the prison, but now it's moving closer to me. That doesn't make any sense! Visium sources are just freakin' rocks; they can't move around unless they're getting hauled by something.*

*Or someone.*

"Oh, shit."

Chad started sprinting as fast as he could back to the cabin. He wove between the trees and paid closer attention to his tingling blood. The sensation was getting stronger. Even though he was far from where he first felt the tingling, the source still seemed to be moving closer to Chad. The faster he ran, the faster it approached. It couldn't be a coincidence. There was no way a random source of visium would stray off its course and continually adjust its speed.

Something was following him. Someone was following him.

Chad kept running, incautious of whether neighbors or anyone else noticed his speed. Being noticed was the least of his problems. Potentially being found was the biggest. He kept going, searching his surroundings for anything that could cause the feeling, but finding nothing each time. He felt like he was running from a ghost in broad daylight. He halted at the base of the hill where Jones' cabin stood, looking for pursuers once more. When he saw there was no one to be seen he ran to the cabin's back door.

"Nate! NATE!" Chad banged on the door while checking over his shoulder. "It's me! Hurry and open up!" Jones peered out the backdoor window before opening it. As he fixed his lips to say something Chad cut him off. "We have to get out of here, now!"

"What happened? Were you seen by a Sentry?"

"No, worse. I'll explain later, just hurry and get your stuff." Chad tried to poise himself as he checked his body's state. The sensation was intensifying. "Ugh, nevermind, there's no time. Let's go!"

Jones squatted to tie his shoes. "You have to tell me what's going on. If one of the NegaSentries saw you then there are certain places we can hide for a while. Just tell me."

"I don't think it's a robot, okay? I didn't see anyone behind me. You'll just have to trust me on this. I think we're being followed by a person!"

"Like a police officer?" Jones said putting on his jacket.

"Naw, it's not a cop or guard or anything like that! I—I think it's another person from the prison… someone like me."

A loud STOMP came from outside the cabin. Chad felt his heart thud one more time, but he wasn't sure if it was from the visium in his blood or from fear. Outside, something calmly climbed the staircase one gentle step at a time. The sound of the creaking wood echoed in the quiet cabin. Jones stood in place by the front door, and Chad stepped between him and the open back door. Neither of them bothered to run. They only mentally prepared themselves for whatever they were about to see.

The figure reached the top of the stairs and stepped into the threshold of the back door. The bright sunlight behind it created a silhouette that kept Chad from discerning the person's face, but it was definitely a man's frame. As the man entered the kitchen, Chad's eyes readjusted to notice the black and white colors of his jacket and the natural spikes of his blonde hair.

"Jason?" Chad hesitated.

The man responded. "Just call me Lynx."

"I have to admit I was wrong about you," Jason said calmly. "I suppose you weren't like every other fool in that prison after all."

"It's nice to see you, too," Chad said, nervously forcing out a joke.

"Out of all the idiots who came and went," Jason continued, "I never expected you to be the one to allow me to figure out the big secret to surviving." Chad almost thought he heard appreciation in Jason's voice, but it was buried somewhere underneath a thick layer of menace.

"Jason... Lynx," Jones interrupted. "Is that your project name?"

Ignoring the question, Jason exhaled sharply and took a few steps in Jones' direction. "Let's just get this over with."

"Whoa, now," Chad said stepping in front of Jones. "What's all this about?"

"I've only got two things to do here," Jason said keeping his eyes on Jones. "The first is to kill Nathaniel Jones, and the second," he shifted his gaze to Chad, "is to bring in Project Vega. If I do this I get to go free. So step aside." He continued his approach but Chad did not budge.

"You can't kill him!" Chad said. "He's a victim just like I am... I mean, like we are. He's on the run, too. If we keep him alive, he can help us testify against the prison. Listen, if you want to stop these experiments Nate is not the guy you need. You'll never guess who's responsible for this whole thing! "

"Vasya Negatov is the one who sent me. I'm not going to tell you again. Move." Jason was only an arm's reach away from Chad, but he still did not move. Chad planted a foot firmly on the ground and met

Jason's eyes with his own. Jason sighed. "Fine."

Jason's foot greeted the side of Chad's face in the form of a kick, and the force sent Chad flying headfirst into the cabin wall. Jones stared blankly at the cratered drywall, and before he could run he felt Jason's grip around his neck, lifting him off of his feet. Jones gasped short breaths as he struggled to break free. He could hear the blood rush through the side of his neck as Jason's fingers caused a forced spike in pressure.

"I really don't care for you," Jason said evenly, "but considering all the people you killed, I'm sure you deserve this." He tightened his grip and felt his fingers press into the bone of Jones' neck. "Goodbye." Jason squeezed, but he lost his grip when the loaded filing cabinet came barreling into him, smashing him against the wall. Jones dropped to the ground and hacked for air with his own hands around his neck.

"Come on," Chad called, and Jones attempted to get to his feet. The process was interrupted by a loud grunt, and the agitated Jason freed himself from the wall. He kicked the filing cabinet back at Chad, but Chad managed to catch it with telekinesis. Before he could hurl it back again, Jason came charging from around the floating cabinet and tackled Chad with enough force to send both of them completely through the side of the cabin. Chad felt another strike to the chest before landing on the ground outside. The hit stunned him.

He tried to get back to his feet but Jason was already up and making his way back inside the cabin. "No, wait, Jason!" Chad called out. "Don't do—"

Chad was silenced by two very distinct sounds. The first was a muffled pop, similar to the cracking of knuckles. The second was a heavy thud, similar to the sound an unconscious person makes when he hits the ground. In that moment, Chad wished his hearing had never improved.

Chad stood frozen as Jason slowly emerged from the hole in the cabin wall. The shade uncovered him as he stepped outside and onto the ground, and in his left hand was Jones' hair, which was being used as a handle for the rest of his body. At first, Jones only appeared unconscious, since his skin was still flushed from excitement, but his eyes—though open—were not looking at anything. They were blank. And that was an expression Chad recognized. Chad's lips quivered as he took in the sight.

"You act like you haven't seen death before," Jason said. "You're not fooling anyone." Jason looked up into the canopy of the trees, and it was then that Chad noticed a quiet buzzing noise. A small, black quadcopter drone hovered just above the scene. The small camera just below its frame swiveled and zoomed into Jason, and in response Jason held up Jones by the scalp like a prized fish. "One down," he yelled, dropping the body onto the ground. "The next will be in soon." The drone appeared to buzz in acknowledgment, and without adieu it turned and flew away toward the prison.

Chad watched the drone fly away as he grit his teeth, rage welling up. "You. Freaking. PRICK!" he managed to articulate.

"Here's how this is going to go down. I'm not here to kill you, and I don't really need to hurt you unless you decide to be a pain in my ass as usual. All you need to do is come with me and this will be over. But since I know how you like to run away, I told the warden to do something for me to make sure you don't run again." Chad's teeth loosened, and it was clear that he was listening, albeit grudgingly. "Kyle is on his way to the execution table."

Chad's jaw and heart dropped together. "Wha—no… wha-when?" he stuttered.

Jason stroked his chin. "They went to get him as soon as I left, almost 10 minutes ago. I think you and I both know he doesn't have what it takes. He and Andreas will both be buried in a ditch soon."

Images flooded Chad's mind. First of Andreas. Then of his father. His mother. Jones. Pictures of their corpses flowed through his head like a montage, recycling over and over. He would not allow another person to get added to that list. He would not allow Kyle to die. Kyle could not die. *Kyle will not die.*

Chad opened a tight fist and directed his hand toward Jason. "Kyle WILL NOT DIE!" he closed his hand into a fist again, and Jason—who was in the middle of stepping forward—froze in place.

"Why can't I move?" Jason asked in a demeanor that was no longer calm. He felt the pressure covering his entire body as he floated just above the ground, completely immobilized. Chad elevated his arm and launched Jason into the air. With an angry shout, he swung his arm downward, and the airborne Jason came plummeting down, crashing like a meteor into the roof of the cabin. Dust and broken wood discharged through the windows and openings of the former home.

Fighting the tear in his eye, Chad took a final look at Jones, who was lying face down in the dirt, and then he ran after the drone and toward the prison. Only a few seconds later, Chad heard another crash from the cabin behind him, and the tingle in his blood told him something was coming again. He looked back to see how much ground he had gained, but the only thing he could see was the fist that hit his face. The punch sent Chad tumbling as he lost his footing.

"I'm so glad you picked the hard route!" Jason grinned. "Now, we can see what we both can do with this new power!" Chad recovered and charged Jason, throwing a punch but missing entirely. Jason countered with multiple punches of his own, all of them hitting their target. Chad threw a kick at Jason's side, but Jason simply jumped just high enough to evade it, and he kicked Chad in the chest as he landed again. "I sure hope you can do better than that," he said.

Chad responded with a shout and quickly made a shoving gesture, resulting in Jason falling back a few tens of feet. Chad took the opportunity to start for the prison again, but Jason wasn't far behind.

*How the hell is he so fast?* Chad thought. *I can barely get a hit on the guy and he keeps sneaking in hits!*

Jason whizzed by Chad as he left a blurring trail in his wake. He sharply changed directions and came straight for Chad, sideswiping him and then gaining distance again. Before Chad could recover, Jason came again, landing several consecutive punches and kicks before speeding off.

"I heard about your ability to throw things from a distance," Jason yelled, taking cover behind a tree. "It's a neat trick, but it doesn't do you any good if you can't see where I am." He left his cover and came for Chad again, this time only landing a few punches while getting a couple others blocked. But it was good enough. He sped off again.

Chad panted and wiped what felt like blood from his lips. *I don't have time for this. I need to keep moving and get the hell outta dodge.* He took off again, this time leaping onto the branch of a tree and bouncing from the top of each branch to stay away from the ground.

"Not gonna help," Jason yelled as he did the same. He matched every step Chad took until he finally came up right behind him. As Jason took a swing, Chad dropped back down to the ground, narrowly avoiding the strike. As Jason followed, jumping back to the floor, Chad raised his arms again and caught Jason in midair. He was immobilized again.

"Phew," Chad said, "looks like your game plan didn't account for this, huh?" Jason squirmed and kicked but was unable to break free. Chad twirled his finger, and Jason likewise spun in the air. When Chad was satisfied he stopped the spinning. Seeing that Jason was clearly too dizzy to be a threat, he spoke again. "You like this new trick of mine, and you knew about it long enough to prepare for it before you came here. How come you just don't do the same thing to me?"

Jason gathered himself before replying. "Looks like your gifts are a little different from mine."

"And that's why you're so freaking fast. Oh well. Now that I got you danglingly so helplessly, the better question is what should I do with you?"

"You're not going to kill me?"

"Kill you? I'm not a freakin' murderer like you are. I read your profile, and there's no way I should be lumped in the same group as a headhunter like you! That's why I never belonged in prison to begin with."

"I've seen enough people die in that prison to know when people come along who belong there. Most of them did. I could also see the ones that were stronger." Jason had nearly regained all his equilibrium. "People like you and Trey, dumb as you are, are still much stronger than every other punk who thought they were worth a damn.

Andreas didn't have what it takes, and Kyle sure as hell doesn't, but we do. That's why we earned this power, Vega."

Chad swung his arm down, casually throwing Jason headfirst into the dirt and lifting him back up again. "Stop calling me that. 'Vega' is not my name."

Jason spit some dirt from his mouth and then began to chuckle. "You know, I just figured out why you piss me off so much," he began. "It's been months since you came to Sanctum, and you still hold on to this hope that you'll be able to escape all of this someday."

"I did, didn't I?"

"You call this escaping? You're only goal right now is to get back to Sanctum to help your friend not get killed. And even if you manage to do that, even if you escape that place one more time, you're never going to be free. You'll always be a fugitive because the past you keep denying will keep coming back to haunt you." As Chad began to snarl, Jason felt the pressure around his body tightening, almost in direct correlation. "You might as well embrace this new name of yours, because there's no going back to your old life."

"Shut up!" Chad threw Jason into the air and slammed him against the ground repeatedly. "I'm tired of your shit! Just shut up already!" Jason tried using his hands to soften the impact, but he only managed to grab onto a few rocks. That was good enough.

Chad elevated Jason one more time and glared at him. It took only a second before he noticed Jason's fist full of dirt. "What's in your hand?" he asked suspiciously.

"See for yourself." Jason threw the rocks, and they hit Chad directly in the face. The pain caused him the lose focus, and Jason returned to the ground.

As soon as his feet hit the dirt, he darted toward Chad and unleashed a barrage of punches and kicks. They came too quickly for Chad to dodge. All he could do was block. *There's only one more thing I can try, but I need to get some distance on him for it to work. If I can just...* Chad took a few wild swings, none meant to actually hit a target, but at least it got the attacks to stop for the moment. He hopped back to gain some space while bringing his hands together in front of him.

"Okay, Lynx, I got one more trick to show you," he said generating the energy cloud as fast as he could. Ignoring him, Jason moved in his sideswiping attack pattern again, making it difficult for Chad to concentrate as blows were dealt from all angles. "This one's even got a name!" He compressed the energy into a dense and whirling sphere. It was ready.

Hiding the sphere close to his chest, Chad broke into a dash, throwing off Jason's pattern. He wove through the trees again, with Jason not far behind.

"Quit running," Jason scorned. Chad kept moving, doing a much better job of avoiding getting hit.

"Ya wanna know what it's called?" He found the perfect tree. He hopped on one of the branches once more. He turned to face Jason. "It's called…" Jason vaulted full force at the branch Chad stood on. In the middle of his leap, he realized he made a grave mistake. "…The Buster!"

Chad fired the sphere at the mid-flight and defenseless Jason. The buster hit Jason directly in the chest, stopped his momentum in the air, and sent him plummeting back toward the earth. As he impacted the ground the buster detonated, sending shockwaves that could be felt from the top of the tree and blowing a cloud of dust into the air. Jason screamed something that resembled a man getting the wind knocked out of him and then getting painfully knocked unconscious. Chad took that as a good sign.

Chad hopped out of the tree and waited for the dust to clear. When it did, he saw Jason, weak and coughing and seemingly in a daze. Chad stepped closer so Jason knew he was there. He gave the weakened man a once-over and disappointingly shook his head.

"You've been wanting this power for a while now," Chad said. "Now you finally have it, so go do whatever it is you wanted to do with it." He turned toward Sanctum. "As for me, I have to go save my friend."

**Chapter 19**

# Invasion

Chad surprised himself at how quickly he learned to use the tingling in his blood effectively. As he ran farther from Jason the tingling subsided accordingly, but as he approached what he knew was the prison, the sensation grew again. He supposed it made sense, since there were all kinds of visium in and around the prison. Since Sanctum and its mines were not far from each other and covered a wide area, Chad figured the sensation would grow uniformly throughout his body, which it did.

As he ran, Chad took a quick account of his condition. His quarrel with Jason may not have been his first experience with combat with his new abilities, but it was certainly the first time he took so much damage. He observed the gashes in his skin, no doubt from one of Jason's many hit-and-run attacks. But he noticed something else that was quite shocking to him: he wasn't very tired.

Chad ran longer distances before on his trip to Violet City, but he figured that taking a barrage of punches and kicks would have at least tuckered him out a bit. There was the occasional pant here and there during the battle, but stamina did not seem to be an issue.

And on that note, the gashes didn't hurt very much either. He took another look at the red lines in his arms. They were still there, but they looked smaller than they did just a few moments ago. Chad laughed in relief. *Ah, yeah. Rapid healing. Totally forgot about that. That'll probably come in handy pretty soon.*

Before long, Chad approached a deep cavern. Its size almost made it appear like more of a shallow valley than anything else. He stepped to the ledge of the cliff and looked over the edge. To the left was a five-story waterfall that poured into a large pond that had its own beach, one that was seemingly man-made. He didn't remember passing a cavern any time before now, but he was positive he was going in the right direction. He had his handy new body radar to confirm that, but there was something else that gave it away. From the ledge he stood from, he could see the top of a large structure just a short distance away. It was Sanctum.

"There's no other way around this cavern," he said to himself. "I'm just gonna have to jump right over it." He took a few steps back, just enough for a run start. But before he took off he heard a rumbling in the bushes. "Oh, no."

Chad turned around and tried to brace himself as he saw Jason rushing toward him. Most of Jason's momentum was stopped by Chad, but there was still enough to push them both just over the ledge. The two tumbled down the cliff, trading blows as effectively as they could until they both reached the ground. Jason landed gracefully on his feet, and Chad flopped on his back.

"I changed my mind," Jason said as he swiftly approached Chad. "You don't have the option of going in alive anymore." Knowing he couldn't defend in time, Chad telekinetically flung the nearest rock he could find toward Jason. Jason ducked the near-chair-sized obstacle, but he could not avoid the second wave of Chad's attack. A small buster hit Jason in the chest, stunning him and allowing Chad to get to his feet. With the free second he earned himself, Chad lifted Jason into the air once more and hurled him as far as he could into the waterfall behind him.

That was when the fatigued kicked in. Chad kneeled as he tried to recompose himself. His body was still fine and ready to fight, but his mind was nearing exhaustion. *Okay, I'm gonna need a new plan. I doubt Jason's gonna fall for another trick and get hit by a buster, so I'm gonna have to fight him the old-fashioned way. But I'll still need a minute to chill...*

Chad kept his eyes on the back of the pond. Jason emerged from the waterfall within seconds, pushing his way through the pounding force of the water above. When he got to the other side he stood still and gathered himself. The floor Jason stood on seemed to have its own buoyancy, and when Chad noticed why, he groaned emphatically.

"Ahh, come on, man!" Chad whined. The floor Jason stood

on was the surface of the water, and as each wave passed beneath his feet it caused the rest of his body to rise and fall accordingly. "You can even walk on water, too?!" Jason didn't appear particularly good at standing on the water, as he struggled to keep balance. However, that only slightly waned on Chad's discouragement. Stalling for more time, Chad continued. "I should've figured you'd be able to heal quickly like I do, but this has gotta be cheating, amiright?" *He's fast enough to hit me from every angle.* "Well, if you can do it, I probably can too, I guess." *I can only hit him head on, but he always sees my attacks coming.* "Looks like you're pretty angry. Still think you got something left in the tank?"

Jason leaned forward and pushed off against the water, kicking large waves behind him like a motorboat. *I've already hit him from every angle I could... except—that's it!* Jason approached and Chad stood his ground. This time Chad threw the first punch.

There were three things Chad noticed while he was fighting Jason in hand-to-hand combat. The first was that Jason was much slower than he had been previously. Since he didn't appear to be the type that got tired easily, Chad assumed Jason hadn't completely healed from the buster attacks he received earlier. That only made the fight they were currently having much more viable, which Chad appreciated.

The second thing he noticed was that Jason was clearly a much better fighter than he was. Though Jason's speed was hindered, he was still moving at a pace Chad had trouble keeping up with. He used kicks that Chad had difficulty countering, and even though his punches weren't particularly dangerous individually, they collectively were annoyingly damaging. The third thing Chad noticed was that Jason wasn't just fighting to win the bout, he was truly fighting to kill, which gave his attacks a lethal level of intensity Chad had never seen before.

As Jason's attacks came, Chad kept getting pushed back. Within moments Chad's back was only a few feet from the wall of the cavern. A spinning kick from Jason forced him to flop against the wall. Before Chad could recover, Jason followed his attack by seizing him by the throat. Chad was pinned, and they both knew it.

"When Moriz told me the crime you committed to get into the prison," Jason said, "I didn't believe someone like you was capable of doing the worst thing imaginable."

Chad wanted to defend his honor, but focusing on setting his trap was of more importance. "I didn't. Kill." He managed to say. Chad kept his eyes on the top of the dirt wall behind him as the grip tightened around his neck.

"Why should I believe you?"

Chad gasped for air. "Why. Would I lie?"

"Because I have you trapped," Jason confirmed.

"Naw," Chad grinned. "I got...You!" Chad pointed to the ground, and the gesture was accompanied by a rattling sound, causing Jason to realize something was moving. He jerked his neck behind him but saw nothing. He only saw the shadow of what appeared to be a small cloud falling. He turned back to a smiling Chad, which was the last thing he saw before a large pile of coalesced rocks fell on his head.

The rocks narrowly missed Chad but fell directly on top of Jason, burying nearly his entire body in a pile of dirt and stone. Chad fell over the rock pile and rolled down the side of it as he caught his breath. He got to his feet and leaned over his knees in exhaustion. This time it was his mind and body that was tired.

"STAY DOWN!" he shouted, feeling that it was necessary to formally end the battle. He observed the mound. The only part of Jason that was visible was the arm that was holding Chad. The arm wasn't moving, but Chad was not worried. The trap did exactly what it was meant to do: knock Jason out. "How's *that* for multitasking? Ya never saw it coming." He took a few steps back and his eyes narrowed as he spoke softer.

"If I was a murderer, I'd take you out now... But I won't, because I'm not." He wasn't sure if he was speaking to himself or to Jason, but he said what he felt he needed to say. He gathered himself with a deep breath and resumed his trip to the prison.

Before Chad got to Sanctum's southernmost gate, the one that provided the shortest distance from the facility itself, he was torn between two options. Instead of considering which of several possible strategies would be the most effective for invading, he was more concerned with whether he should bother formulating a strategy at all. The first time he infiltrated the prison there was nothing to truly challenge him. Then again, that was essentially a surprise attack. And if they figured Chad ever had a reason to come back—which Jason made sure he did—then surely Moriz would have fortified the prison as well as he could just in case.

Of course, Chad wasn't quite as familiar with his powers back then. But even though he thought himself to be a much more capable fighter now, the idea of taking on a prison that was ready for him this time was slightly daunting. It wasn't that Chad felt he couldn't handle a bunch of armed guards, but he couldn't help but second-guess his ability to dismantle an army of robots with no weapon more threatening than a repertoire of basic kicks and punches and an explosion of vibrating airwaves. It just didn't sound like the best arsenal for the job.

Furthermore, his ability to produce busters was waning due to mental fatigue, which he was trying to recover from by not thinking too extensively about how to best invade the prison. But, clearly, he was failing at *not* thinking. So the only true option he saw was to break into the prison as quickly as possible, find Kyle, and then bust them both out.

"Get in. Kick ass. Get out." He repeated the simple game plan aloud, making sure he wouldn't overcomplicate things when the time came. Chad stopped as he reached the south gate. Even though he knew it was not the same fence he climbed on the day he escaped with Andreas, it was oddly similar in appearance. Reckoning that was a silly thing to notice, he shifted his focus to the sounds of nature.

There was a light breeze, rustling leaves, chirping birds, but no feet trampling on dirt. There were also no sounds of rolling tires and electric motors. Apparently, the NegaSentries were not around and doing their normal surveillance circuit. Chad took that as a good sign at first, but a second thought made it seem fairly odd. Without wasting any more time, he bounded over the gate and continued for the prison.

Moments later he arrived at the prison, and he realized why the path there was so obstacle free. The yard was filled with people—none of them inmates. Guards, wearing what looked like full SWAT gear, complete with a Sanctum-branded shield, as well as what was about two dozen NegaSentries, were all crowded behind the fence of the yard. With their shields facing the fence, they created a wall at the base of the gate. Behind them, more guards were standing with some sort of long firearm. And behind them were the NegaSentries, seemingly inactive since they had nothing to immediately do.

Chad maintained a safe distance from the building so he wouldn't be spotted. As he hid behind a tree, he peered over again to get another look. The elevated command station that he remembered leveling last time had been reassembled, but lazily so. There was plenty of reinforcement at the foundation, but the section that was holding the makeshift command center at the top had random wooden planks strewn about all over in an attempt to make it sturdy. It did its job well enough, Chad supposed.

"Ugh, there're way too many people in the way," he whispered to himself. "I could probably take 'em if I really wanted to, but I don't have time for all that. There's gotta be another way in." Chad gained a safer distance so he wouldn't be seen, then he circumnavigated the prison. There were very few doors, and the ones that were there were heavily guarded. That even included the giant hole from Kyle's previous cell.

The only entrance that was guarded even more diligently than the yard door was the front and main entrance. The formation that the guards and NegaSentries assumed even seemed more elaborate. As in the yard, fully armored guards formed a wall with shield, but behind them were several alternating rows of armed guards and NegaSentries.

"Apparently, they think I'm just gonna barge right in the front door," he whispered again. "I'd hate to disappoint them." He smiled and leaned forward as if to charge right through the array of obstacles. Before he moved, the mechanical sound of an electric motor made him pause. He hid behind another tree as he looked for the source. The sound of turning gears caught his ear once more, and he found the culprit. It was right above him.

A small security camera was hanging from the branch right above him. Its lens was facing the direction opposite the prison, but was slowly moving from left to right as it searched the area. The telescoping lens made more exaggerated noises as it zoomed in and out, and the fact that it was still searching made it clear that it hadn't seen Chad. He leaned against the tree and exhaled in relief, and that was promptly followed by a wide, sly grin.

He peered up at the camera and then over to the guards. "Well, it's worth a shot."

Warden Moriz stepped out of the prison from the front entrance and approached a man near the rear of the formation. "Robertson," he called, and the man stood at attention. "Have you seen any sign of him yet?"

"No, sir," the man responded, "but all personnel are prepared and have been assigned to their respective stations. We will be ready when he shows."

"Good," Moriz said, nodding. "Inform me immediately when… INCOMING! Above us!"

An object launched itself into the sky and cast a large shadow over the land in front of the prison. Multiple guards, guns at-the-ready, aimed their firearms at the object as well as they could. As the object began its descent, the shielded guards lifted their shields above their heads while the others fired indiscriminately. The object impacted the ground, just missing one of the robots. Every guard and NegaSentry aimed their weapon at the object, which was smashed into so many pieces it was difficult to discern its identity. Moriz pushed through the crowd and inspected the object up close. It was a security camera.

"He thinks we're stupid!" Moriz growled viciously. "Get in position!" There was a uniform affirmative response as everyone's attention was redirected back to the forest where the camera was thrown from. Moriz clicked on a radio. "All available hands report to Station AA. Repeat: All hands get your asses to Station AA!"

"Just what I wanted to hear," Chad said. As guards returned to their threatening formation, Chad faded back into the foliage once more and made his way to the yard. By the time he arrived there were far fewer guards at their posts. Half of the NegaSentries were gone as well, but there were still too many for a direct confrontation.

Chad ducked behind a nearby bush as he tried to maintain a clear visual on the remaining guards. They all had their eyes locked on the outside gate. The drones were equally as attentive, but that was about to change. Chad took a deep breath, outstretching his arms as far as he could without being spotted. His hands shook from either strain or exhaustion—he couldn't tell which—but it only took a few seconds before the NegaSentries began to clumsily float in the air. The ones that were able to process that they were no longer on the ground let out several solid tones that resembled more of an active smoke detector than any real notice of a threat. The tones went largely ignored until one sufficiently annoyed guard turned around to address the noise, but at that point, the drones were all floating two stories in the air.

Finally, Chad released the robots from his control, and they crashed against the concrete ground, severely damaging their weaponized arms. The dumbfounded guards gawked at the robots in confusion, and after regaining his slipping equilibrium Chad emerged from his hiding spot and leaped over the fence. He landed just behind two of the guards, and Chad rewarded their inattentiveness with a forceful knock to the back of the neck, knocking them out. The closest two guards to the right fumbled for their weapons, but Chad rushed them before they could appropriately respond. One punch to the solar plexus for each of them was enough to disable them.

The remaining three guards were not as unlucky or unprepared. The two with shields stood right beside each other to form an even larger shield. The wide barrier was separated only by a long-barreled gun that fired as soon as it poked its nozzle from its hiding place. The bullet whizzed by Chad as he jumped out of its path. *I guess not everyone got the memo about bringing me in alive.*

The three men rotated in their formation like a smooth turret and took another shot, this one grazing Chad on the torso as he leaped behind a pile of dead robot. The guards came closer as Chad lay behind cover. "Come on, come on, just one more," he said, trying his best to muster one more buster. After a few long seconds, he finally had a satisfactory bomb. The gun was the first thing Chad saw as the guards coasted around the rubble. The shooter took aim, but Chad fired his buster first. The blast knocked the shields out of the hands of both men as they all flew back. Since Chad saw the shield-men were either knocked out or injured, he made a move for the gunman, who was taking aim from his fallen position.

Chad rushed over and reached for the barrel. The gunman fired one more shot. This one hit its target; directly in Chad's chest. Chad dropped to the ground with a painful groan and rolled over to his back. The guard jumped to his feet and walked around to get a better position on Chad, who remained still on the concrete doing, his best impression of a dead man. The guard reached for the radio on his shoulder.

"Immediate backup requested in Station SY," he shouted. "Target is down in the south yard. Repeat: Target is down!" A response crackled through the speaker. Using the long barrel as a stick, the man prodded Chad's arm, gauging his responsiveness. "I think the target is dead."

With as much force as he could, Chad swiftly grabbed the gun and flipped it upward, causing it to fire at the sky. "Dead's a strong word," he said. The off-guard and unbalanced man tried to regain his footing, but Chad hopped up and punched him in the face. He dropped to the ground, unconscious. "I don't like being shot at, douchebag," Chad taunted as he inspected his chest. A small bullet was lodged in his skin, and he grimaced as he slowly pulled it out. The sound of a used bullet hitting the ground was joined by the noise of a live round echoing off the prison walls. Backup had arrived.

The second wave of men came from around the corner and the outside of the fence. Realizing the only other option, Chad ran to the yard's door that led inside the commons. Fortunately, it was propped open, and he burst through the metal door, closing it behind him. As a myriad of lethal sounding objects impacted the door, Chad locked the door using his own method. He telekinetically deformed the door frame, forcibly clamping the ingress in place.

"There," he panted, "much better than... deadbolt—" With nausea taking over, he collapsed to his knees and leaned against the door. "Head hurts. So... tired."

*Fight back.*

A voice whispered in the back of Chad's head. It was audible enough to be heard over muffled echoes of men stomping down the corridors. He tried to lessen the dizziness as he paid attention to the call. The voice sounded familiar. It sounded like his own.

*For once in your life.*

*Fight back.*

"I can't just stop," he said sliding one foot after another underneath him. "I have to keep going." His vision was returning, shifting from a blur to a more cohesive picture. The image in front of him was of several NegaSentries aiming their weapons. Chad created one more energy sphere. "I have to—" An orange net deployed. "fight back!"

Chad's buster sent the net back to the robot, which was also caught in the sphere's path. The NegaSentry went flying backward into several others and went offline. The last one that escaped the blast received a fist through its chest-plate, thus deactivating it. With a clear path, Chad ran down the corridor toward the commons area.

*Once I get to the commons I'll be able to get to all the wings of the building. Kyle's got to be in the medical wing… That's got to be where they'd take him, right? Is that where they took me?* Chad arrived at the end of the hall without any resistance. When he got to the commons he halted completely.

*Oh, no.*

A chain of NegaSentries and guards completely surrounded Chad. Robots were blocking every corner and door on the first floor, and the overhanging balcony was filled with guards whose orange-tipped muskets were aimed and at-the-ready. Chad slowly raised his arms in submission, and that was when an electric net deployed.

The net covered Chad with perfect accuracy. The electric current began running through the net and Chad screamed as he fell over. The current pulsed through his body with an intensity he had never felt before. The pain was excruciating, and his screams were deafening to everyone in the room. The shock lasted for what felt like an eternity.

The current finally stopped. As Chad jerked and spasmed on the ground he faintly heard the footsteps of a man come closer. The man kicked Chad repeatedly before even uttering a word. The pain of the kick did not bother Chad as much as the residual pain from the previous shock. In any case, he was fairly confident he knew who was kicking him.

"Welcome back, thug," Moriz said. He took a few steps back, and the tasering resumed. It only took several more seconds before Chad passed out.

Several poundings on Chad's chest woke him up, and he coughed and fought to catch his breath. He was able to see nothing but the floor beneath him, until what looked like the head of a baseball bat came into view. The bat gently lifted Chad's head by the chin until his view changed from the floor to the man standing in front of him.

"He's finally awake again," Moriz said with a grin. His grin changed to something more resentful as he withdrew the bat and cocked it in preparation of a swing. As Chad tried to brace himself for the hit, he noticed that his arms were tightly bound to some type of platform that was perpendicular to the ground. He struggled to break free, but he was unable to defend himself while Moriz took multiple swings at his head, taunting all the while. "You think you can—make a joke out of—me in my own—prison?!" The attacks hurt more than Chad wanted to admit to himself, but the pain was bearable.

"That's enough, Jael!" Catherine's voice called. "Knock it off. Did you get the sample like you were supposed you to?" Moriz took one final swing as the grin returned to his face. He dropped the bat.

"I got more than enough," he said, panting as he reached into the inside pocket of his jacket. He pulled out two vials, both containing a red, glowing liquid. Chad looked at the vials and immediately recognized their contents. He scanned each of his arms as best he could but wasn't able to find any marks from a needle. "Yeah, you figured it out," Moriz said. "This is from you, all right. It took a big ass needle to break that skin of yours, too. Looks like it even healed up already." He walked over to Catherine and handed her the vials. "Get this over to NegaLabs now."

"And what about the boy?" she asked, nodding in Chad's direction.

"Your father and I will take things from here. Just get going." Catherine nodded and gave Chad one final look. Chad couldn't tell if it was pity or acknowledgment in her expression, but whatever it was not very reassuring. She turned to the door and was escorted out of the room.

"Now that I think about it," Moriz continued, "you've figured out quite a bit, haven't you?" He took a step closer to Chad. "You're one of the only shits in this place who's survived a dose from the doctor. And from what I remember, you know about the big man himself, don't you?"

"That last part I didn't have to figure out," Chad interrupted. "Good ol' Nate told me that one."

"Then it's a good thing Lynx put his ass down." A look of confusion possessed Moriz's face. "What in the world happened to that maggot?"

"He's currently buried under a pile of rocks," Chad said matter-of-factly.

"You killed him?"

"Uh, no. I just knocked him the hell out."

Moriz chuckled. "I hope he screamed like a baby. It sounds like you've had a few stories since the last time you were on this table." It was then that Chad realized where he was. The platform he was strapped to was the table he was executed on, but almost everything else in the room had changed.

There were broken syringes and other various types of medical equipment on the cracked tile floor, the second table to his right looked forcibly disassembled, and there were signs of a bloody struggle all over the chamber. The one-way mirror was still in place and the glass had not completely broken, but the adjacent room didn't look like the safest haven from whatever took place. *No wonder I didn't recognize this place. Someone after me must've given them hell. Was it Jason, or…*

"Kyle!" Chad shouted. "Where is he? What did you do with him?"

Moriz raised an eyebrow. "That pussy, Lyons? What about him?"

"Jason told me you were going to execute him today! Don't you freakin' touch him or I'll kick your ass myself!" Chad pulled forward but the chains jerked him back to the platform.

An expression of amusement took over Moriz's face. "Interesting. Well, let me show you something." He snapped his fingers and pointed to something behind Chad. Guards, who were apparently behind Chad the whole time, stepped into view. They were dragging a large bag. Chad's blood went cold.

"What the hell is this?" Chad stuttered.

"I'll give Lynx credit. He did say you were sure to come back if your little buddy was in danger of getting tabled, but the truth is I wasn't waiting around for you to show up." One of the guards yanked down on a zipper, revealing what was inside. "But I still kept him around in case you wanted to say goodbye."

Chad's eyes widened as far as they could as he choked on his own saliva. As his gritted teeth bit his bottom lip, a drop of blood rolled down his chin. His lip started to quiver and a tear welled in his eye, but suddenly he found a reason to hold the tear back. And as Chad found a reason to smile, his teeth released his lip.

Kyle's face was all that was uncovered, and that was all Chad needed to see. The look on his face was not peaceful, nor was it one of utter submission. There was a hint of pain in Kyle's expression. One that told the story of a fight. From the wrinkles on his forehead to the frown that reached far below his mouth, Kyle had been in a battle. Chad couldn't tell if it was before the prison guards came to get him, if it was before the needle breached his skin, or if it was during what was likely the most painful experience of the end of his life. But one thing was certain about the young man who lay breathless in that bag:

"You went out swingin', didn't you?" Chad said through a sniffle. "You finally did it. You fought back."

"All right, that's enough," Moriz said waving his arm. "Get the kid out of here and stick him with the rest." The guards did as they were told and re-zipped the bag. The two men picked up Kyle and carried him out of the room through the same door Catherine used earlier. The only people in the room were Moriz and Chad, and a lone guard in the corner of the room. His electric net musket was aimed at Chad the entire time. After Moriz took a few seconds to retrieve his bat, which had rolled across the floor, he spoke again. "Listen to me closely. Until we get the results back from the blood samples, I've been encouraged to keep you alive, but the matter is completely up to my discretion. How does that make you feel?"

Chad kept his eyes on the floor, quiet and seemingly focused on something Moriz couldn't figure out. Since there was no response he spoke again.

"You look upset. Well, so am I. And do you know why I'm upset?" Still no response. "It's because I truly hate people like you. When Jones and Catherine told me about the opportunity to get a family killer like you behind bars, I almost pissed myself. Let's be honest, the judicial system often gets things wrong when it comes to thugs like you. That's why I didn't want to leave it up to chance..." Chad's head raised almost imperceptibly, but Moriz noticed. "...so we had that bitch killed."

Chad snarled as his twitching fingers formed fists, and the chains that restrained him tightened as he tried to pull himself free.

"I'm surprised you didn't see her in that hole you woke up in," Moriz mocked. "Did you actually give a crap about her, or are you just mad that you didn't get a 'fair trial'?" He loosened his shoulders and cocked the bat again. "Well, rest easy, Galen, because you're back in my prison, now. And when Warden Moriz is the Judge, Jury, and

Executioner, all is fair!" He brought the bat back as far as he could and swung it with all of his force, but right before it impacted Chad's head, it stopped completely.

Chad finally lifted his head as the frozen bat levitated right beside him. As Moriz tried to pull the bat from Chad's mental grip, he noticed the lights in the room flicker as Chad spoke. "You aren't gonna execute anyone else…" The chains holding him to the platform began to rattle wildly, and Moriz finally released the bat.

He stepped back. "Shoot his ass," he grunted at the guard. The man in the corner took aim and fired the orange net. As it flew through the air, it was also caught by Chad, and he sent the net back toward to the unsuspecting guard. The man shouted in pain until the taser deactivated and he went unconscious. Chad then turned his attention to Moriz, and with a sharp grunt he sent the bat flying. Moriz' attempt to evade was wildly unsuccessful, and the bat crashed straight into his chest. The old man clasped his chest and collapsed onto the ground.

Chad allowed rage to well up inside of him as he tried to pull away from the table with all of his might. He jerked and struggled, and the lights continued to flicker in response. With a final shout, he yanked out the bars on the table that the chains were anchored to, and the tensionless links slid off of his arms as he stepped away from the platform.

Chad walked over to Moriz, who was still clutching his chest and wincing in pain. "You've got no right to be the judge of anyone, and that's why I'm gonna drag your ass to the court myself."

Moriz coughed as he tried to chuckle. "If you've got a problem with me, you should take it up with my boss."

"And where can I find him?" Moriz released his chest so he could feebly point to the door, and as he did a slow but powerful clap echoed off the walls of the chamber. Chad jerked his head toward the source of the sound, and standing just under the threshold of the doorway was the man he was looking for. "You're Vasya Negatov?"

"That's correct, Mister Galen. Or, Vega, I should say." Negatov said calmly, "I have to admit, I truly feel the need to congratulate you for making it this far. I'm sure you don't understand the significance of what your survival means to me."

"Your Russian accent doesn't sound nearly as thick in person. Is it just for show? Is your freaking company for show, too?" Chad spread his arms wide. "Was all this prison crap just a show so you can hide the messed up things you were doing down here?"

"You're only partially correct, this time," he said walking further into the chamber. "I would prefer this to remain well hidden, but everything else you know about me is not a facade."

"Even the part about you being a disgusting mass murderer who pulled a scientist away from his life just to experiment on people who probably did nothing to deserve getting killed? How's that sound to ya?"

"That's not true either. All of you deserve it."

"Shut up!" Chad rapidly formed a buster and fired it at the ground in front of Negatov. The explosion blew Moriz even closer to the door, and it caused Negatov to fly back through the remaining glass of the one-way mirror. A group of men with their weapons drawn pulled Moriz out of the chamber and into the hallway, but with a dismissive wave Chad flung the bothersome guards out into the hall. Chad then kicked the heavy execution table as hard as he could, and the broken platform slid across the floor until it barricaded Chad and Negatov inside the chamber.

"Look at that," Negatov said rising back to his feet. He casually brushed the dirt and shattered glass off of his suit. "You're even capable of using telekinesis. It's no wonder you were able to do so much damage all over Sanctum's campus."

*Damage.* "You know what, you just gave me a great idea," Chad exclaimed. He scanned the chamber until he found a bright red rectangle on the wall. He pointed to it. "Ya see that? Looks like even in a place like this, you can't get away from a fire alarm." Chad walked over to the alarm.

"What are you doing?"

"Well, I figured that you can't possibly have bought off every cop in Hocking Hills; just the ones in this prison. So what if I call some other cops over here? I've wrecked this place up well enough over the last couple weeks that there's no way you'll be able to clean up and hide this mess before they get here in about... say, ten minutes?"

Negatov climbed through the opening in the wall and back into the chamber. "If you sound that alarm, you will regret the outcome." He reached into his pocket and pulled out a phone.

"Whatever, dude." Chad yanked the white lever down, and the fire alarm blared a high pitched squeal throughout the entire prison. Chad heard the commotion on the other side of the barricade as the guards began to panic. He took that as a good sign and yanked even harder on the fire alarm until he pulled it right off the wall. He threw the broken lever on the floor in front of Negatov. "There ya go. No regrets."

Chad watched confidently as Negatov kept tapping the screen on his phone. After several seconds, he smiled and stopped interacting with the device. After a few seconds more, the fire alarm's signature squeal changed into a low pitched woman's voice, one that Chad thought he recognized from an elevator recording. It was much more convincing than the synthetic voice of a NegaSentry.

"Override complete," it announced. "Countdown initiated. Five minutes."

"Countdown to what?" Chad asked.

Negatov crushed the phone in his hand like an empty soda can and tossed it to Chad's feet. "That is the self-destruct protocol. In five minutes, every man and woman in this facility will die."

## Chapter 20

# Vega

"I'm sure you understand why a fail-safe was a must-have," Negatov explained. "I never thought I would need to use it under a circumstance quite like this, but it's certainly a good thing I had it prepared."

Chad laughed incredulously. "You really expect me to believe you filled this place with bombs just for something like this? Seriously, how stupid—" A loud explosion went off just above Chad's head, and he hopped out of the way as large pieces of debris came crashing down. Immediately disregarding his last statement, he continued, "What the hell? I thought the lady said five minutes!"

"The facility will be demolished by that point, yes."

Chad turned his head from one corner of the room to another, following the faint sounds of screams that were penetrating the walls. "The people… All these people—you've got to stop it! They're all dying!"

"They have you to thank for that," Negatov peered through the hole in the wall, which was formerly the one-way mirror, and searched the witness room. The door was still there and perfectly intact. "Thanks to you, I have extracted all I need from this place; it only makes sense that I put this old dog down. So as this dog digs her own grave, I'll be taking my leave."

"No the hell you don't! What in the world makes you think I'm just going to let you walk away from all of this, huh?" Negatov did not respond, but he took a couple steps closer to the exit. "You're killing everyone here, you tried to kill me, and God only knows who else is dead because of you! If you leave this place, it's because I'm taking you to the cops myself."

"How noble of you. I'm assuming you have a stake in the

matter?"

"I'm here because of you, so damn right I do." More explosions
blared in the distance and more debris fell from the ceiling. Out of
the dust, Chad reached down and pulled out a large metal pole. It was
about as long as he was tall, and one of its ends had a very sharp point.
He almost wondered what part of the building's architecture the bar
came from, but it wasn't important. "Here's the deal: I'm going to take
you with me, but I don't want you squirming while I drag your ass to
the police. So how about I drive this pike through your freaking leg?
It'll keep you from trying to run from me. And, honestly, I just really
wanna hurt you right now."

Chad gently tossed the bar into the air and caught it
telekinetically, shifting its pointed edge so that it was facing Negatov. If
Negatov was at all dismayed at the fact he was about to get stabbed, he
did not show any signs of it, which only annoyed Chad further. Chad
raised his arm as he took aim, and as the sound of another faint scream
entered his ear, he flung his arm down and launched the bar.

The bar cut through the air like a javelin for the full fifteen-foot
distance between the two, but just before it reached its target, it froze.
Its sharp point was only inches away from Negatov's thigh when it
stopped and simply hovered in place.

"The hell?" Chad blurted out. He began making smaller gestures
in expectation that the bar would react, but as his gestures became
wilder and exaggerated the bar appeared increasingly unresponsive.
Chad tried to fight off his embarrassment as he inspected the piece of
metal from a distance.

The waves and vibrations that usually accompanied Chad's
possession of an object were still present, however, they looked far
different than they ever had before. The waves, usually radiating several
inches off the surface of an object, were much smaller on the pole.
Despite being smaller, the waves appeared much denser, stronger, and
more refined than usual as well. Chad made a pulling gesture in an
attempted to tug the bar back in his direction, but the object disobeyed.
Finally, it moved.

The bar slowly gained elevation until it was eye level with

Negatov, and it gracefully twirled itself around so that its pointed edge was now facing Chad.

Chad swallowed deep. "I'm… I'm not doing that," he stuttered.

"No," Negatov said raising his index finger and, in a separate motion, pointing to Chad. "I am."

The bar rocketed toward a flustered Chad, whistling as it careened through the air, and impaled him directly in his gut. Its momentum knocked its target off his feet, and Chad screamed as he stumbled to the ground.

Chad wailed as he stared at the bar that was sticking out of his body like a giant kabob stick. He grasped for the bar, but the pain stopped him from being able to remove it from his stomach. As he tried to sit up, he realized that something behind him was keeping him from getting good position. He glanced behind him and saw that at least two feet of the bar was protruding from his back.

Negatov slowly approached as he observed Chad's injury. Bright and luminant blood leaked from the hole in his abdomen. "Such a shame to see visium go to waste like this. If you weren't such an insurgent then perhaps you could have joined the next renaissance, but we can make more of you, I suppose." He stepped beside Chad, who was still squirming in pain, and grabbed part of the bar. He lifted one end up, which slowly caused Chad to slide down the pole until his body was on the ground again, but Negatov did not pull the bar out.

"Three minutes," the announcement said.

Negatov looked at the pile of debris beside them and pulled out another, similarly sized pole. Its ends weren't nearly as sharp, but that did not seem to faze him. He raised the bar and let telekinesis elevate it even further. The bar became perpendicular to the floor as it aligned itself with Chad's head. Negatov smiled. "Dasvidaniya, Vega," he said.

Just then, several pounding sounds came from the door. Negatov looked over, and the table that was barricading the door began to shake as someone forced his way in. Negatov stepped away from Chad and kept his eyes on the door. With one more bang, the barricade came crashing down, and Jason came barreling through the doorway.

"Ah, now this is a sight to see," Negatov said, opening his arms in a welcoming fashion. "Projects Lynx and Vega in the same room. I was beginning to think this day would never come."

Jason walked over to Chad and glanced at him. Chad feebly reached in Jason's direction and responded with a gurgling cough that resembled the word "help". Seeing the pole emerging from Chad's gut, Jason wasted no time grabbing the end of the pole, and he carefully scooped up Chad from the ground like a farmer lifting hay with a pitchfork. He ran toward the closest wall and plunged the bar deep into the drywall and concrete. Chad screamed again as he held on to the bar, and as he kicked his feet from the pain, he realized he was suspended above the ground. The bar was the only thing holding him in place.

Jason took a step back and groaned with satisfaction as he watched Chad struggle. "That's two down," he shouted. "I kept my end of the deal. You know what you have to do." As Jason fixed his lips to speak again, he heard a whistling sound behind him. Out the corner of his eye, he saw what looked like a javelin coming his way. With a single motion, he turned, stepping out of the object's path, grabbed the bar with both hands, and twisted to redirect its momentum back at Negatov. The whole act happened in about a second's time, but Negatov was ready for the returning bar. He raised his hand in a motion to stop, and the bar obeyed, floating still in front of Negatov's chest and then falling to the floor before him.

"*That* was not the deal," Jason said.

"Impressive reflexes," Negatov said, disappointed. "I imagined you would at least look surprised by that."

"Too bad. Clearly, I can't trust you, so I'm going to have to kill you."

Negatov smiled again, and brought a hand up so Jason could see it. "You're welcome to try." He slowly balled a fist. Jason gagged as he gripped his chest. After another quick spurt of coughing, he dropped to his knees and keeled over in pain. He felt his heartbeat thud slowly but erratically, as if someone was controlling it. It was clearly not beating of its own accord, and that was unacceptable.

Jason tried to control his breathing. He focused on the beat of his heart and tried his best to control his pacemaker, imagining each and every beat his heart should be making. He wasn't sure if it was actually working or not, but after struggling for another moment he felt his heartbeat return to normal.

"Damn, that usually ends a man instantly," Negatov said, disapproval written all over him. "You two are much more resilient than I thought." Jason looked around the chamber and tried to follow the voice. During his momentary cardiac arrest, he had lost track of where Negatov had gone.

"There!" Chad choked, pointing with one hand while the other one gripped the bar in hopes of keeping his full weight off of his wound. He pointed to the far side of the adjacent witness room, where Negatov had already stepped halfway through the emergency exit door.

"Your first deaths were not in vain," Negatov shouted at the two, "but your second deaths will be." He walked through the door, and a metal wall slid over, sealing the exit. Chad and Jason both gazed through the falling dust that was beginning to cover Negatov's escape route, and one thing was clear to them both.

Negatov was gone.

"Two minutes," the announcement said.

Jason stumbled as he rose to his feet, patting his chest to ensure his heart was working properly. All was in order. He turned to see Chad, who was staring back at him with helpless eyes.

Chad opened his mouth to speak, but his words were drowned out by the volume of Jason's glare. His eyes burned a hole into Chad's consciousness. The message Jason communicated was one Chad had become more familiar with over the last several months, though subtly. But never was it any louder or even more believable than it was in this moment, through Jason's silent words.

*This is what you deserve.*

When Jason finally took his eyes off Chad, he burst into a sprint. As he dashed out of the door he came from, it was clear that he had regained at least some of his speed back. In any case, he was more than fast enough to escape the dilapidating building, which was far more than what Chad could say for himself. Fortunately, with the time he had spent pinned to the wall, he was able to come up with an idea that afforded at the very least a small chance of survival.

Trying to pull the bar out of the wall was futile, as he found out the hard way after minutes of trying to pry himself free. But if it was lodged too deeply to remove, then the only solution was to leave the bar in place and somehow wiggle his way off of it, and Chad could only think of one way to do that. With all the concentration he could muster, Chad focused his power on bending the metal bar. The pain of his impalement was slightly less excruciating now, due to a numbness that Chad hoped was a rush of adrenaline and not a loss of blood, but he welcomed it if it meant being able to focus more on the goal.

A vibrating cloud of energy swirled around the thick piece of metal. As Chad grunted and winced every iota of concentration he could get out of his brain, the metal pole finally relented. It steadily bent downward under the weight of Chad's influence, and when it was almost completely pointing to the ground, Chad kicked off the wall, pushing himself forward and onto the steep decline. From there, gravity took over, and Chad slipped right off of the pole and flopped onto the bloody floor beneath him.

"One minute remaining. Please complete emergency evacuation."

Chad cupped the wound on his stomach and back simultaneously as he armlessly tried to work his legs underneath. He was surprised to learn how painful standing could be with a damaged core and back, but since the pain was becoming more bearable, he considered himself in luck, despite the highly undesired position he was in. He finally managed to get to his feet.

"Forty-five, forty-four." The announcement began counting by the second, which encouraged Chad to start moving toward the exit. He stepped through the chamber door and into the hallway. Nearly a dozen armed guards lay on the ground, dead. Since the explosions hadn't effected that hallway extensively, Chad figured Jason was responsible for this particular scene. Moriz was noticeably not among them. A ray of sunlight flooded the end of the hallway, and the array of corpses no longer bothered him as much as he stumbled through the hallway.

"Thirty, twenty-nine." Chad winced as he walked to the end of the hall. He couldn't help but think that walking with the pain from a limp for all those weeks somehow prepared him for this moment, though he still felt woefully unprepared. He gazed up through the hole in the ceiling and took a deep breath. With a strong blow, he jumped as high as he could, and despite only being able to jump half as high as normal, he still managed to reach the top. He was on the ceiling.

"Ten, nine..." Chad echoed the countdown in his head as he made his way to the closest ledge.

"Eight." He breathed deep to offset the nausea that was overtaking him. His hands continued to seal the holes on his body as best as they could. He tried not to think of how much blood he'd likely lost.

"Five." He reached the ledge. He was right above the front entrance to the building, and all guards, NegaSentries, and anyone else were long gone. There was only Chad, Sanctum, a twenty-foot drop, and the explosions.

"One." As more explosions started going off like a fireworks finale, Chad took a couple steps away from the ledge and prepared to jump. He started for the edge, and just as he kicked away from the building the largest explosion of all discharged heat and debris in all directions. The discharge added an extra bit of propulsion to Chad's jump, which was both unwelcomed and something that could not be braced for. Consequently, Chad's body spun in the air as the force pushed him and pieces of the collapsing prison into the distance.

Chad crashed against the asphalt as fire and ash erupted from throughout the building. Unable to keep the holes on his body covered, he dropped his arms in exhaustion. Coughing soot and spitting up the like, he panted as he watched what was left of Sanctum crumble to the ground. His vision was fading, as well as the rest of his consciousness, but he managed to stay awake long enough to watch as streams of white water flew into the fiery building. He looked to see where the water came from, but gave up after his head failed to move.

A second and third stream followed the first as large red trucks finally came into view. Chad allowed his eyes to close as a dark, man-shaped figure stepped into his line of sight. The figure approached him and said something that prompted a response. Chad could only cough again, and without saying a word he allowed himself to fade.

Chad woke up to what felt like airplane turbulence, but as his eyes opened he saw that he was in the back of an ambulance. He looked around at his body, which had a naked top half after his vest was apparently removed. His belly had a large and heavily folded piece of gauze taped just to the left of his navel, and an IV of transparent liquid was being fed straight into his left arm through the largest needle he had ever seen.

"How ya feelin' there, bud?" A man asked as he stood up and leaned against the bed. He was wearing firefighter's clothing but had removed his jacket. He had noticeably fewer dirt markings on him than the other two men that were sitting on the side opposite him. Chad looked at the man and took an oxygen mask off of his face.

"Tired... but all right," he said wearily.

The man laughed. "All right? You were awfully beat up to be feeling that way so soon. It's okay to feel shitty." Chad yawned and stretched his neck. He dropped the oxygen mask and reached behind his back to feel the second hole. There was gauze there as well. "We patched you all up, but you lost a bit of blood."

"I bet," Chad murmured. He tapped the gauze on his belly. There was still pain, but not nearly as much as earlier. He sighed in relief.

"Take a break, bud, you've earned it. You're a survivor. My name is Joey if you need anything." Chad knew there was irony there—

somewhere—but he couldn't figure out exactly where. Joey patted Chad on the lap and stepped over to view the pouch of fluid that hung by the head of the bed.

"Don't get too comfortable," the second firefighter said, trying to keep an equally light tone. He was holding an armored laptop that looked like it went into the fire with him. "We've got a little bit of info to get through; basic insurance and such." Chad nodded. "Okay, first name?"

"Chad."

"And last?"

"Galen."

The second man typed away onto the keyboard as he entered the information. "Okay, and how old are you?"

"Um, eighteen." Chad suddenly felt awkward about telling the man this information, as if he was supposed to keep it secret.

"Got it. Looks like you are already in the system," he said assuringly. He stared at the screen and was silent for several seconds before he made another sound. "Hmm…"

And in that moment Chad realized his folly.

The second firefighter nudged the third man to his right and they both looked at the screen quizzically. Joey was the next to speak.

"So what happened over there?" he asked.

"Huh?" Chad said.

"At Sanctum. The hazard that started the fire; do you know what that was?"

"It was…" there was a long answer and a short one, both of them were likely not the answer he was looking for, so Chad gave him another one. "I don't know. I think it was in the kitchen."

"And it created all that raucous? Can't be."

Chad glanced at the two men sitting at the foot of his bed. They were both in a much less talkative tone all of a sudden. And the third man quickly developed a habit of looking back and forth between the laptop and Chad.

"Where are we going?" Chad asked.

"Well, Hocking Hills is a bit far from any major hospital," Joey said. "We're headed to the closest one in Risington, and we're about a half hour away."

"And that's not far from Violet City, right?"

"Not at all," the laptop man said. "What were you doing out by Sanctum, by the way?"

"Hiking," Chad replied.

The two sitting men looked at each other and nodded. The third man stood up and reached into the chest pocket of his jacket, right above the badge shaped symbol and a name that read "Danson." He pulled a pair of old handcuffs from his pocket and walked over to the bed.

"What the hell's that for?" Chad asked.

"Sorry, kid, but you're not fooling anyone," Danson said. "Let me cuff you without a struggle and we won't have a problem."

Chad gritted his teeth but eventually gave a relenting sigh. "Fine," he said, and he held out his arm. As Danson grabbed Chad's arm, Chad yanked him within head-butting distance, and followed through with a solid noggin-bump. A knocked out Danson fell over.

The second man reached into his jacket, but Chad telekinetically grabbed the metal laptop and bashed it over the man's head until he joined Danson on the floor. Joey backed away from Chad as much as he could, but since the ambulance was only so wide, Chad was able to sit up and punch him in the solar plexus. Joey keeled over and brought his face closer, and one more uppercut finished the job.

"Crisis averted," Chad said, "for now anyway." He removed the IV from his arm and put pressure on the needle hole until it clotted, which only took about ten seconds. He reached for his vest, which was hanging on the bedside and carefully put it on, trying not to aggravate his injury. Fortunately, the driver didn't notice any quarrel, so Chad was able to travel in peace for the remainder of the ride.

Just as Joey said, they arrived in Risington about a half hour later, and the three firefighters only needed to be reminded once that they were supposed to be unconscious. As the ambulance started making more frequent turns, Chad knew they were close to the hospital. He gauged his condition. Mentally, he was strong. Physically, he was strong enough. The damage done by the bar had healed to the point where it only felt like a severe cramp. That was a welcome improvement. The vehicle made a few more slow turns and finally stopped. Chad got into position.

The driver turned off the siren as he stepped out of the vehicle. He walked to the back of the ambulance and fiddled with the door handle before opening it.

He opened the door and a small buster exploded in his face, knocking him over. Chad leaped out of the ambulance carrying the laptop, and before the driver could realize what happened Chad dashed out of the emergency room driveway and down the street. While he ran through the small town, he found a fountain in the middle of a courtyard. He decided to take a detour and ran beside it, dropping the laptop into the water.

Chad dusted his hands and laughed as he ran down the road, paying little attention to who saw him. He followed signs that led him to a small state route. Before long, he was back on a familiar path.

"Hold on, Violet City," he said. "I'm almost home again."

Nightfall in Violet City was much more peaceful than Chad remembered it to be. The leaves were officially beginning their transition to the red and orange colors that Ohio trees wore so proudly, but the humid days showed no signs of going away anytime soon. Though he hated the humidity, the wet air reminded him that there were still a few weeks left in the summer. And as the full moon's light bounced off the waters of the ponds and softly tinted the leaves in white, Chad was grateful he could enjoy one more day in something that at least resembled freedom.

He sat on his favorite boulder while overlooking the stream. The sounds of the waters seemed even crisper, the boulder slightly softer, and the stars just a little brighter than they were before. His wound had completely healed, and though he was hungry and dehydrated—something he attributed to the blood loss—he found plenty of reasons to smile as the breeze flowed gently over his body. It was a good night for a grand surprise.

"I'm pretty sure it's dangerous to be out here this late," Chad heard a female voice say. The sound of frustrated hikers walking through foliage was familiar.

"We'll be fine, Karli," Ricky said. "Just keep going."

"Don't get bossy with me," she snapped. "You act like you're doing us a favor."

"When are you going to tell us why we're down here?" Chris asked, swatting a tiny branch out of his way.

"Remember what this place is?" Ricky quizzed. "Chad used to meditate and stuff down here."

"Yeah, I remember," Chris said, softening his tone.

"Okay, and?" Karli said. "I'm really not in the mood for a memorial service right now. I hope that's not why we're doing this."

Ricky smiled big as they approached the last bit of brush before the stream. "It's not a memorial service. A friend said to meet him here."

"More like a reunion!" Chad shouted. Karli and Chris paused. They looked at each other and then to Ricky, who returned their look with an uncontrollable grin. Without a word, they pushed through the last bush and stepped out into the open shore by the stream. Chad slid off the boulder and waved shyly. "Guess who!"

Karli and Chris bolted for Chad, running into his open arms. Ricky was not far behind, but he waited patiently for his turn. Tears welled and fell as they all embraced. Chris tried to utter what sounded like a question, but it was unintelligible beneath his heavy sobs. Karli did something similar.

"I think they want to know what happened," Ricky said wiping the water from his face. "I could use an update, too."

"Don't worry," Chad assured, "I promise to fill you in on the whole thing. But can we just go home first? I hope it's not too late to take you up on that roommate offer."

Chad's night was filled with an impromptu pizza party, a tour of the group's new apartment, and long tales of the everyday monotony of prison life. Chad did his best to keep the stories interesting, which wasn't difficult to do after the conversation shifted to visium. He mentioned the friends he made, the enemies he made, and the friends he lost. He even gave a short demonstration of his new skills, which were applauded like magic tricks. After a long night of catching up on socialization, Chris and Karli finally went to bed. The time was about four in the morning, and they both had to go to work the next day.

"Shouldn't you be getting to sleep, too?" Chad asked.

Ricky shook his head, "I'm off tomorrow, and I doubt I'd be able to get to sleep now anyway."

"Suit yourself." Chad grabbed one more slice of the pizza and stuffed it in his mouth. It was a delicacy he missed like none other. He walked from the kitchen table and sat on the futon that was in the family room. He bounced playfully on it. "I guess this is gonna be my new bed for a while, huh?"

"Mi futon es su futon." Ricky walked over and sat on the couch that was across from the futon and watched as Chad spread himself out as far as he could on it. "So, I'd hate to get serious on you so soon, but…"

Chad yawned. "Yeah?"

"Well… what's your plan now? I mean, you have one, right?"

Chad laughed, realizing it was a fair question. "I kinda wanna take a break from plans, since they tend to always get me in trouble." He stared at the cream-colored ceiling as he gathered his thoughts. "I don't want to be a fugitive for the rest of my life. I know who's to blame for getting me thrown in Sanctum to begin with, and now I have even more dirt on him."

"Vasya Negatov? It's gonna be pretty hard to get him. Don't you think he'll just be going into hiding now? Especially since his prison blew up."

"But his business didn't. I'm sure he'll be finding new ways to get visium so he can keep getting piz'zaid." Chad sharpened his tone. "I don't really care what it takes. All I know is that too many people died because of him, and I don't think he's gonna stop those experiments any time soon."

*…we can make more of you.* Chad reflected on Negatov's words. They were more haunting than he wanted to admit. They didn't seem important, but he couldn't get them out of his head.

"He mentioned the 'next renaissance,'" he continued. "I've got a feeling that has something to do with…" *Immortality.* Jones' words filled in the blank, and suddenly a bigger—though not necessarily clearer—picture was drawn. "He's gonna inject more people with visium in the future. I can't let that happen."

"Well, I'm down for the cause," Ricky said. "Just let me know what help you'll need and I'll do my best."

"Thanks, man, but I'm not sure how much you'll be able to help." Chad raised his arm and created a small whirl of vibrating waves around his hand. "We're dealing with people of superhuman persuasion, here."

"Good luck trying to get anything done by yourself," Ricky laughed. "You can't even go out without a disguise, anymore. How do you expect to get around? Only leaving at night?"

"There's an idea… but I guess you have a point." Even though he didn't want to admit it, Chad knew he got lucky with the firefighters. He was able to destroy their only evidence that he was alive, but he may not get that opportunity again he if gets caught in the open. And then there was the larger issue.

Chad Galen was a name that became far too familiar for Chad's liking. The firefighter trio may have had a computer to remind them of who he was, but citizens of Violet City who were around from before and after the trial would likely be able to make an immediate connection. Even fellow former classmates would recognize him from a distance if given the chance. For the first time in his life, Chad regretted being popular.

"Just throwing it out there," Ricky added, holding back another laugh, "but you already got the superpowers. I think it's pretty obvious what you need to do. Shoot, just get a mask and call it a day!"

Chad waved him off. "I don't have time to put in superhero hours. Besides, masks are stupid. And overrated."

"Still, I can't just call you by your name in public. Just think of a new nickname or something."

"Okay, then. That should be a fun project." Chad sat up on the futon and felt something roll around in his chest pocket. He reached inside and pulled out the marble with the reiki spiral on it. He laughed as the answer popped into his head. Nothing had ever been so obvious. "Come to think of it, I think I've got the perfect one."

# Acknowledgements

This book is not just the product of my own accomplishments. This is a celebration of the village that fought to bring me to this point in life.

Thank you to my vast, blended family, who stretch across multiple states and have invested in me so that I may succeed.

Thank you to my insane friends, who give me all the inspiration I need to create crazy characters.

And thank you to the God who has blessed me with more favor and love than I deserve... and for giving me more imagination than I know what to do with.

# About the Author

Channing Chea is a proud alumnus of The Ohio State University and is an avid fan of superhero films. He has been writing poetry since junior high, and he jumped into fiction in college when a year of journalism helped him realize creative writing was a lot less stressful. When he isn't dreaming up stories to enthusiastically tell at night, he works as a web developer during the daytime.

Channing lives in his hometown of Columbus, Ohio and is currently working on the second installment of the Vega series: Vega the Psyki.